I0769662

Also by the Author

The Erin O'Reilly Mysteries

Black Velvet
Irish Car Bomb
White Russian
Double Scotch
Manhattan
Black Magic
Death By Chocolate
Massacre
Flashback
First Love
High Stakes
Aquarium
The Devil You Know
Hair of the Dog
Punch Drunk

Bossa Nova
Blackout
Angel Face
Italian Stallion
White Lightning
Kamikaze
Jackhammer
Frostbite
Brain Damage
Celtic Twilight
Headshot
Vino Blanco
White Lady
Blackjack
Last Round

Tequila Sunrise: A James Corcoran Story

The Coventry Adams Mysteries
Night Flower (coming soon)

Fathers
A Modern Christmas Story

The Clarion Chronicles
Ember of Dreams

Last Round

The Erin O'Reilly Mysteries
Book Thirty

Steven Henry

Clickworks Press • Baltimore, MD

First publication: Clickworks Press, 2025
Release: CWP-EOR30-INT-P.IS-1.0

Sign up for updates, deals, and exclusive sneak peeks at clickworkspress.com/join.

Ebook ISBN: 979-8-88900-038-9
Paperback ISBN: 979-8-88900-039-5
Hardcover ISBN: 979-8-88900-040-2

For all my readers
who have joined me on this journey
and stuck with it to its conclusion.

Special Preview

Keep reading after Last Round to
enjoy a first look at the new series
coming soon from Clickworks Press

The Coventry Adams Mysteries
by Steven Henry

Want a reminder when the new series is out?

Join Steven's list at
clickworkspress.com/join/steven

Last Round

1. *The final call before closing time at a bar, telling patrons to place any remaining drink orders before they have to leave.*
2. *The final bullet loaded in a gun's magazine or cylinder.*
3. *The final turn in a game before determining the winner.*

Chapter 1

"You know why they call it a stakeout, right?"

Vic Neshenko was grinning. Erin O'Reilly didn't need to look at him to know; she could hear it in his voice.

"I'm sure you're about to tell me," she said.

"Back in the old days, when a wolf was eating their sheep, farmers would lay an ambush," he said. "They'd get all their pitchforks and sickles, and they'd take a goat and tie it to a stake on the edge of the woods. Then they'd hide just over the hill and wait. When the wolf came after the goat, they'd jump him and stab the shit out of him."

"Thanks for that charming piece of agricultural history," she said. "So who's the goat in this scenario?"

"You could be," he said. "We could tie you out, alone and unarmed. When that punk came out to kill you, I'd bust his ass."

"That's a great plan, Vic."

"Really?"

"No. It's crap."

"I guess from the goat's point of view, that's true," he said, still grinning. "It beats sitting in this car all night."

He stretched as much as the passenger seat in Erin's

Charger allowed. Vic was a big guy, six-foot-three and broad-shouldered, and some of his space was taken up by Erin's onboard computer. He also had a regular buffet of snacks and drinks at his feet, none of them healthy.

"You know the other way shepherds got rid of wolves?" Erin asked from the driver's seat.

"How's that?"

"They bred great big dogs to rip the wolves to shreds."

Rolf, as if recognizing his cue, chose that moment to stick his furry head through the opening between the seats. The German Shepherd's tongue was hanging out in a doggy smile.

Vic handed the K-9 a pork rind and was lucky enough to keep all his fingers. "I can see the value of that," he admitted. "I remember that hitman a couple months ago, Black Jack McGraw. Rolf practically bit his friggin' head off. That's why we're out here babysitting the O'Malley brat. If he hadn't tried to have you whacked, I'd be getting a decent night's sleep, sharing a bed with a girl who's a lot prettier than either of you two. No offense."

"None taken," Erin said. "The only way I'd share a bed with you is if I got so drunk I passed out and tripped over something."

"I'm just saying, this would work better if we had some decent bait," Vic said. "The little jerk's out drinking with his buddies, having a good time, and we're sitting in this car like a couple of assholes. We're not even pulling overtime, since this isn't a sanctioned operation."

"You don't have to be here," she reminded him.

"Like I'm gonna let you follow Richie O'Malley around on your own," he retorted. "You'd screw it up and I'd have to ride in like the goddamn cavalry to rescue you. And I don't even know how to ride a horse."

"I appreciate it, Vic," Erin said, and she meant it. Cops

risked their lives every time they went out on the street. That was the Job and they all accepted it. But when the shit went down, they could count on thirty-five thousand other officers having their backs. Here and now, Erin and Vic were disobeying orders. They were putting their jobs and reputations, as well as their lives, on the line.

Erin's instructions were to leave Richard O'Malley alone. According to Captain Holliday, Richie was one suspect in a sprawling Narcotics investigation. He was helping move fentanyl for the Russian Mob. But Erin believed Richie was also behind two attempts on her own life. Richie was pissed because Erin had betrayed his dad's trust, thrown Evan O'Malley and all his associates in jail, and stripped Richie's inheritance away. Less desperate men had killed for less. Erin wasn't about to stand back and let the wheels of justice roll over Richie, however slowly.

"Yeah, whatever," Vic muttered. "Eight weeks we've been doing this. And what've we got to show for it? This guy's the lamest criminal in the history of lame criminals. We don't have a single thing we can use that Narcotics doesn't already have. We can't see anything the Narco boys aren't seeing, because we have to hide or we'll get made by our own damn people! The guy drives a friggin' Volvo, for God's sake! Just because it's red doesn't make it a Ferrari."

"What's your point, Vic?"

"My point is we're wasting our time. I get it, I don't want this asshole popping off rounds at you either. But the *bratva* are nasty SOBs. Did it occur to you that hanging around the Russian Mafia might be putting you in *more* danger, not less? These guys tried to kill me once."

"I remember."

He sighed. "Don't you think it might be better if we actually did what we were supposed to for a change?"

"Who are you?" she demanded. "And what've you done with Vic?"

He snickered. "Okay, okay. Sorry. I haven't been getting any damn sleep and it's making me grumpy. I have a day job, you know."

"So do I," Erin said. She sat back and rubbed her face. "I'm sorry too. We're all tired. I thought this would be easier."

"Because Richie's a moron?"

"Something like that, yeah."

"But he's clever enough that we can't get him on anything," he said. "So what's that make us?"

"Chumps," she said. "Maybe Holliday was right. This cowboy crap isn't doing anyone any good. Richie hasn't made a move on me since that thing in the parking garage. Maybe he's given up. We should concentrate on our normal cases. It isn't like I don't have other things on my mind, too."

"Yeah," Vic said. "Like the wedding. How's the final planning going?"

"Like you care."

"I don't. But Zofia keeps asking about it. She's got a calendar. A real paper one, like people used to use a hundred years ago. She's actually putting Xs in the days, counting them down. Three weeks now, and I can't believe I know that. I gotta be careful. Weddings are like the flu."

"Miserable and exhausting?" Erin guessed.

"Contagious," he said. "Between Ian Thompson and that rehab nurse, Cassie what's-her-name, getting hitched, and you and Carlyle, next thing you know, Zofia's gonna want me to put a ring on her."

"And you don't want to?"

"I don't want to do it just because everybody else is doing it. If I ever do get married, it's gonna be for the right reasons."

"Which are?"

"Tax breaks and regular sex."

"You're a real romantic, Vic."

"I know. I'm a softy. So what do you want to do?"

Erin shook her head and turned the key in the ignition. The Charger's engine rumbled to life. "Let's call it a night," she said.

"Are we giving up on Little Richard?"

"For now. We'll see."

* * *

Erin's fiancé was waiting up for her, even though it was after midnight. That wasn't surprising; Morton Carlyle had been, at various points in his life, a bombmaker for the IRA, a gangster, and a pub owner. All these occupations lent themselves to a nocturnal existence. The Barley Corner, Carlyle's pride and joy, was still open when Erin got there, and Carlyle was sitting in his usual spot at the bar. He was having a drink with James Corcoran.

"Evening, darling," Carlyle said, standing up to greet her.

"And a grand night it is," Corky added, bouncing to his feet. "It's scarcely begun. Have a pint with us, love!"

"How many has he already had?" Erin asked Carlyle in an undertone as she slid onto the barstool on the other side from Corky.

"Six," Carlyle said. "Unless he started drinking before he got here."

"I'm offended," Corky said with a display of wounded innocence that fooled nobody. "Everyone knows the Corner's the place to get the finest Guinness and whiskey this side of the pond. I'd never pollute myself with cheap rotgut before passing your doors, Cars. Have I really had six?"

"Aye," Carlyle said. "Three shots of Glen D and three pints."

"I could've sworn it was only five," Corky said. "But then, I never was much good at maths, and the more I drink, the worse I count. How's about you, Erin?"

"I'm good," she said.

"Grand," Corky said. "We were just talking about you, if you'll believe it."

"Only good things, I hope."

"What else is there to tell?" he replied. "In point of fact, we're discussing the wedding. Just round the corner, so it is."

Erin sighed. "I'm getting enough of that from my mom," she said. "And even Vic, if you believe it. You'd think Mom hadn't gone through this whole thing twice before, with my big brothers."

"It's different with a daughter," Carlyle said. "For fathers and mothers both."

"Aye," Corky agreed cheerfully. "There's likely to be more female guests, so there's better chances for the unattached lads."

"I'm a cop, Corky," Erin said. "That means half the guests on my side are going to be male police officers. Some of them will be armed. And you'll be attending with your girlfriend, unless I'm very much mistaken. That doesn't sound like good odds to me."

"Force of habit, love," he said, winking. "No fear. Terry's more than enough woman for me. Speaking of which, I've a responsibility to discharge."

"And that is?" Erin asked, feeling a twinge of dread.

"As best man, the stag party's mine to organize," he said. Seeing the look on Erin's face, he held up a hand. "Now, before you say anything, remember I've known Cars my whole life. I know what sort of lad he is, and the sort of revelry he'll enjoy. I'd not go planning anything of which he'd disapprove, nor yourself, come to that."

"I'm surprised at you," Erin said. "I'm starting to think Teresa really has reformed you."

His bright green eyes twinkled. "So I've a list of possibilities here, for your approval. The first thing I'd like to do is—"

"No," Erin said flatly.

Corky blinked. "But Erin, love, you've not even heard what it is."

"It's strippers, isn't it," Erin replied. It wasn't a question.

"Well, aye, but that's not the point."

"What is the point?"

"You didn't trust me enough to hear me out."

"But I was right. That means I trusted you exactly the right amount. Trust doesn't mean giving people the chance to screw you over, Corky. It means I trust you to be Corky."

"Well, by that measure, everyone ought to trust me," Corky said. "I'm an open book. But I can't deny I'm a bit hurt. I had it all planned out. It would've been very tasteful. A religious experience, you might say."

Erin put her face in her palm. "Oh God," she said. "They were going to be dressed as nuns?! What the matter with you, Corky?"

"I can see why they made you a detective," Corky said with undisguised admiration. "It's a wonder any crimes go unsolved in this great city of ours."

"And on that subject," Carlyle interjected. "What's our mutual friend been up to?"

"Nothing," Erin said. "I mean, Richie's meeting with bad guys. He's making phone calls. He's going to skeezy bars and hanging out with lowlifes."

"None of those are crimes," Corky observed. "Else you'd have to arrest yourself, love."

"What, exactly, are you saying about my pub?" Carlyle demanded.

"Only one of you is a lowlife, anyway," Erin said.

"Which one?" Corky asked. The twinkle was back in his

eye. "I'll have you know, those stripper nuns come highly recommended. I talked to a couple of lads who said seeing them was like seeing the face of God Himself."

"No strippers," Erin said. "Also no whores, drugs, gunfights, or explosives."

"A fine stag party this'll be," Corky muttered. "There go the next four things on my list. I might as well start over from scratch."

Carlyle smiled. "Nothing incriminating?" he asked Erin.

"Not outside of what the Narco boys have," she said. "He's involved with the Russians, all right. Vic says it's part of the same *bratva* we tangled with a couple years ago. You remember Peter Vlasov?"

"Quite an unpleasant lad," Carlyle said. "But he wasn't a drug smuggler. His traffic was young women. As I recall, he's a guest of the state now."

"Yeah," she said. "He lost a chunk of his guts when I shot him at the airport, but he's still alive. He'll be about ninety years old when he finally gets out of prison, assuming he gets time off for good behavior, which he probably won't."

"With Vlasov out of the picture, who's running their business these days?" Carlyle asked. "My contacts on the street aren't what they used to be, I fear, since you threw most of them behind bars."

"One of his cousins," Erin said. "Gennady Vlasov. According to the Narcotics file, he's branched out into hard drugs in a big way lately, filling the hole in the market we made when we took apart the O'Malley and Lucarelli narcotics operations."

"The more things change, the more they stay the same," Carlyle said quietly. "What do you know about this Gennady?"

Erin shrugged. "He's a nasty piece of work too," she said. "What do you expect? We don't think he's even in the country, though. He has lieutenants doing his legwork over here. He's in

Russia, as far as anyone knows."

"Too bad," Corky said. "Extradition's near impossible from that godforsaken place."

"Narcotics is trying to set up a sting," Erin said. "They're hoping to lure Gennady over here, so they can grab him on American soil. He's the big fish. Nobody gives a damn about Richie O'Malley but me."

"I assume Mr. Vlasov has quite the host of hardened killers about him," Carlyle said. "Which leads me to wonder why Richard might employ outside talent. One would think he could task a few Russian thugs to waylay you."

"I've been thinking about that," Erin said. "And my guess is the Narcs are right when they say Richie's just not that important to them. They're getting their fentanyl business established and they don't want extra police attention. If their people start offing cops, the NYPD's going to come down on them like the wrath of God and they know it. I think Richie probably asked to use some of their people and they refused."

"That's some consolation," Carlyle said. "Those Russian lads are nothing to sneeze at. They're cold, violent, and as tough as they come. At least the Irish have *some* rules. The Russians have none."

"So what are we doing about Richie?" Corky asked.

Erin spread her hands. "What can we do?" she replied. "I've been cranking out unpaid overtime for weeks now. Vic's been helping out when he can, but we don't want to get Lieutenant Webb or the rest of the squad involved. We're lucky this hasn't gotten back to Captain Holliday as it stands. I'd hoped to get this taken care of before the wedding, but it doesn't look likely."

"It'll all come right," Carlyle said. "There's no percentage in spending lives and resources on you, darling. Sooner or later Richie's going to give up. And perhaps in the meantime we'll get lucky and someone else will solve the problem for us. He's chosen a particularly dangerous line of work, and if he doesn't watch himself, his wife's going to be widowed and his lad will grow up fatherless."

"Yeah," Erin said. "I'm going to skip the drink."

"Why?" Corky asked. "Don't you want one?"

"I want three," she said. "But I don't think I should have them. I'm tired. I'm going up to bed."

"I'll be up shortly," Carlyle said. He kissed her cheek.

Erin said goodnight to Corky, for which she received another kiss on her opposite cheek. Then she went upstairs. She stripped off her work clothes and pulled on the old T-shirt she slept in. She brushed her teeth, but skipped the shower. She hadn't gotten too dirty, and she'd be taking Rolf for a run in the morning and getting sweaty, so she'd shower then. She climbed into bed, taking a moment to check her e-mail one last time for any urgent messages.

She froze, staring at the screen. "What the hell?" she murmured.

Rolf, hearing the strange tone in her voice, clambered up on the mattress next to her and thrust his muzzle in close, trying to see what was going on. He'd never understood the fixation those little black boxes had for humans. Strange sounds came out of them sometimes, but they didn't smell interesting, you couldn't eat them, and they didn't make good chew-toys. There was no accounting for human behavior.

Erin hesitated. But the message still sat in her inbox. It wasn't going anywhere. Finally, she jabbed it with a finger, opening it.

The e-mail was short, clipped, and formal. It was an official notification from Riker's Island Prison, informing her that an inmate, one Kyle Finnegan, had filed a request for her to visit him at her earliest convenience.

"Finnegan," she said softly. "That crazy son of a bitch. What on Earth does he want to talk to me for?"

She had no answer. Neither did Rolf. It shouldn't have bothered her. Finnegan was crazy, all right; Vic liked to recall how he'd once eaten a piece of a man's face, raw, with hot sauce. He was also clever and completely ruthless. But he was caged now, safely behind bars. He couldn't do anything to her.

That was what she kept telling herself as she tried to go to sleep. But she couldn't quite make herself believe it.

Chapter 2

"Kyle Finnegan?" Lieutenant Webb said. "He contacted you?"

"Yes, sir," Erin said. "Through official channels."

"And you reported it, which was definitely the right thing to do." Webb leaned back in his chair and rubbed his thumb and two fingers together, wishing for a cigarette. "Any idea what he wanted?"

"That's obvious," Vic said, getting up from his desk and coming over. Zofia Piekarski was also drifting toward the conversation.

"I must be getting slow in my old age," Webb said. "By all means, Neshenko, reveal the obvious to us."

"He wants to screw with you," Vic said to Erin. "That guy loved his friggin' mind games even when he was on the outside. Now he's in prison, he's got nothing to do but think up crazy shit. You ever see pictures of that snake eating its own tail?"

"The *ouroboros*?" Webb asked.

"The which?" Vic clearly had no idea what Webb was talking about.

"It's sometimes spelled *uroboros*," Webb said, which didn't clarify things. "It's an old Egyptian and Greek symbol for the cycle of birth, life, death, and rebirth."

"Whatever," Vic said. "My point is, Finnegan's the sort of guy who'll start eating himself if he doesn't have anyone else to snack on. Forget the *aurora borealis*. I got a better example. Ray Liotta in *Hannibal*, when Hannibal Lecter cuts open his skull and feeds him his own brain."

Zofia made a face. "Yuck," she said. "I should never have watched that with you."

"Now that's something I've never seen on the street," Webb said. "I don't think it's worth the trouble. There's easier and more painful ways to torture someone. We're discussing Finnegan. In what way do you think he wants to screw with O'Reilly?"

Vic shrugged. "What difference does it make?"

"He's a con artist," Erin said. "Playing three-card monte. If you sit down at the table with him and play the game, you've already lost. The only way to win is not to play."

"*War Games*," Vic said, grinning. "Great movie."

Zofia and Webb gave him a blank look. Erin just rolled her eyes.

"My concern isn't any psychological damage he'd do to you," Webb said to her. "I'm more worried about ways he might damage the case against the O'Malleys."

"What can he do?" Zofia asked. "That case is airtight."

"She's right," Vic said. "We have account books, witnesses, God only knows how many hours of recordings, and hard evidence up the yin-yang."

"Most of it thanks to O'Reilly," Webb pointed out. "He may be intending to threaten you, or bribe you to change or recant your testimony."

"I'm not scared of him," Erin snapped. "And there isn't a damn thing he can offer me. I'm not for sale, especially not to him."

"Of course not," Webb said. "But suppose he talks to you and makes you an offer, which you very correctly refuse. Then suppose fifty thousand dollars show up in your bank account. Even if you report it to IAB, it could still raise questions about your integrity."

"That's just the sort of thing I mean," Erin said. "Which is why I'm not going to Riker's."

"Good," Webb said.

"Remember last time we went to Riker's," Vic interjected. "We got jumped by a whole bunch of inmates. We got stabbed, and I mean a *lot*. Wanna see the scars?"

"Later, honey," Zofia said.

"Note Finnegan's request in his file," Webb said. "And forward the e-mail to the District Attorney, just to be on the safe side. Then, as you native New Yorkers are so fond of saying, forget about it."

*   *   *

That was good advice and Erin knew it. She did her best to follow it over the next few days. She still felt curious about Finnegan, but dwelling on him wouldn't serve any purpose. Maybe that was Finnegan's goal, she thought; to climb inside her head. He might not even have anything to say. The man talked and thought in riddles. His brain was a crazy maze that even he probably didn't fully understand. He'd been weird before his traumatic brain injury, and the tire iron that had left a permanent dent in his skull had only made him stranger.

He didn't have a damn thing to tell her that she wanted or needed to hear, Erin thought. So she shoved him to the back of her mind and ignored the request, not even sending a refusal. It wasn't like she didn't have plenty to keep her busy. New

Yorkers kept killing one another with depressing regularity, so her work hours were filled with garden-variety homicides with a few armed robberies for good measure.

Her downtime was really getting eaten up by wedding planning. She'd thought everything was sorted out: venue, reception site, guest list, dress. But a hundred little details kept springing up. Her mom and sister-in-law were calling her constantly with questions and suggestions.

"I don't know why anybody ever gets divorced and remarries," she told Carlyle the following Friday evening. "I only want to go through this hassle once."

"This is my second wedding, darling," he replied mildly.

"Yeah? How big was your first one?"

"Quite a modest affair," he admitted. "We took our vows in Rose's church in Banbridge, in County Down. We didn't advertise it widely, on account of the Royal Ulster Constabulary taking a keen interest in my whereabouts. Corky was best man at that one as well, I'm sure you're not surprised to hear."

"Wait a second," she said. "Are you telling me you were a wanted fugitive when you got married?"

"Of course," he said, smiling. "That's what I was doing at Banbridge in the first place. Corky and I were on our way south to the border, to lie low after we'd done a wee bit of fundraising for the Cause."

"By fundraising, you mean...?"

"A bank robbery," he said calmly. "Corky and three other lads went in. I'd built the charges they used to blow the vault. Nobody was hurt, you ken."

"Jesus," Erin said, shaking her head.

"I'll not bore you with the details," he said. "If you're curious, ask Corky sometime; he tells the tale better than I. Suffice to say, the RUC tumbled to our identities and we thought it best to step away from Belfast until the fuss died down. We'd taken lodging at the home of an IRA sympathizer near Banbridge while transport across the border was being arranged. After three days lying low, I risked stepping outside to take the air. As luck would have it, a fine brunette colleen happened to be walking along the green not twenty yards from where I was standing."

"And that was Rose?"

"Rosie McCann," he said, nodding. "I didn't love her at first sight, not precisely. But I was fascinated. During the Troubles, folk in Belfast developed a particular look. We all had a certain paleness in our faces, a drawn quality, shadows under our eyes. We'd learned to expect sudden violence, and what with the paramilitary groups, the RUC, and the British Army on every bloody corner, we were always looking out for trouble. Rose was as fresh as the country air, and as innocent. She lived on a farm and hadn't been much affected by the Troubles. She'd a spring in her step and a light in her eye that fair captured me."

"Good thing Corky didn't see her first," Erin said.

Carlyle laughed. "Aye, that's the truth," he said. "Once he knew I was interested, of course, he backed off. He'd never poach a mate's girl. In fact, he was cheering for me. He said Rose was just what I needed."

"So what happened?" Erin asked.

He shrugged. "I never crossed the border. I stayed on in Banbridge, in hiding, and the Brits never copped to my presence. The very foolishness of it protected me, I believe. Corky stayed, too, out of a misguided combination of loyalty and recklessness. I courted Rose, she was foolish enough to be won over, and we married. By that time I could go back to Belfast, and when I returned to duty with the Brigades, she went with me. You know the rest."

Carlyle wasn't laughing anymore. He didn't like to talk about his brief marriage, which had ended with his pregnant wife being murdered by a Northern Irish paramilitary terror group. He'd never known for certain whether it had been a botched hit on him or a random act of violence..

"This time it'll be different," Erin promised, squeezing his hand.

He nodded and smiled again, but it wasn't entirely convincing. "Every Irishman's a wee bit superstitious," he said.

"So is every cop," she said. "But luck isn't always bad. Haven't you ever heard of the luck of the Irish?"

"Would that be the luck that gave us the British occupation, the potato blight, and rampant alcoholism, darling?"

Erin was spared the need to reply by the buzz of her phone. She saw an unfamiliar number.

"Hold on a sec," she said to Carlyle. "Probably a robocall, since I'm not undercover anymore."

She swiped the screen and brought the phone to her ear. "O'Reilly," she said.

"Detective O'Reilly?" a man asked. She couldn't immediately place him.

"That's right," she said. "Please identify yourself, sir."

"This is Warden Vaughn," he said. "Calling from Riker's Island."

Do you have any idea what time it is? That was the question most people would have asked. It was going on eight on a Friday night and no rational person would make a business call at a time like that. But Erin was a cop and Vaughn was a Corrections Officer. Neither qualified as an entirely rational person.

"What's happened?" was what Erin said out loud.

"An inmate recently sent you a request for an interview," Vaughn said.

"That's right," she said cautiously. Little alarm bells were jingling in the back of her brain, the part of it where paranoia lurked.

"The inmate in question, Kyle Finnegan, has repeated his request."

"That's nice," Erin said. "I know he wants to talk to me. The problem is, I don't want to talk to him."

"The situation has changed, ma'am," Vaughn said.

The bells were getting louder. "In what way?" she asked.

"Inmate Finnegan is in the infirmary," Vaughn said. "He was stabbed in the cafeteria while eating supper."

"With what?"

"A fork."

"What's his status?"

"He's stable. After receiving stitches, he asked to speak with you. He was insistent."

"And this rates a personal call from the prison warden after hours?" Erin asked.

"The situation is complicated," Vaughn said.

"Is he going to die overnight?"

"The doctor is confident his condition is not life-threatening."

Erin closed her eyes. "I'll come first thing in the morning," she said.

Chapter 3

"First thing in the morning" was a figure of speech. Erin started her day with a long run in Central Park. It helped take the edge off her nerves and put her and Rolf in a calmer headspace. Then came the obligatory shower, coffee, and breakfast. She opted for cornflakes and an orange, knowing anything greasy or heavy wouldn't sit right in her jumpy stomach. Carlyle always had a box of cornflakes in the apartment. For reasons she'd never understood, the Irish absolutely loved the cereal.

After breakfast, Erin geared up like a knight arming for battle. She started with the bottommost layer. She still had the special bra from her undercover days; the one with a recording device sewn into the underwire. Over that she put on a dark blue silk button-down blouse Carlyle had given her. She'd read somewhere that silk was resistant to stabbing and cutting. It was also an attractive but non-sexual garment, not too tight-fitting and with a modest neckline, which made it suitable to wear into a prison. She wore comfortable slacks which she'd be able to run or fight in if necessary. She capped off the ensemble with a pair of black, rubber-soled shoes she'd liked to wear in her Patrol days. No stiletto heels for Sean O'Reilly's daughter; you never knew when you'd need to be on your feet for eight or ten hours or run like hell.

Rolf came with her, of course, as did her phone, her gold shield, her Glock nine-millimeter and her snub-nosed .38 backup revolver. Vic would be meeting her at the jail. Webb had offered to bring the whole Major Crimes squad, but Erin had refused. Finnegan wasn't exactly shy, but she didn't want too much of an audience. It would only encourage his bizarre behavior. Seeing Finnegan alone would probably have been best, but it would also have been dangerous. She couldn't deny it was comforting having Vic's bulk to back her up, and he wouldn't have taken "no" for an answer.

Carlyle was still asleep when she set out. That was typical. He was a lot of things, but a morning person he was not. He'd be up around nine or ten. She left the bedroom door closed and walked out as lightly as she could. Rolf padded beside her, looking up at her for instructions. She thought the K-9 looked a little anxious.

"Everything's fine, kiddo," she told him, speaking as much to herself as to him.

He wagged his tail.

*   *   *

"Remind me again why we're doing this," Vic said. He was standing in the visitor's lot at Riker's Island, looking unhappy.

"Someone tried to kill Finnegan last night," Erin said.

"There's a protocol for that," he said. "You don't have to show up in person. Just send flowers, or maybe one of those edible arrangement things. You know, the chocolate-covered fruit baskets?"

"I'm not sending Finnegan a fruit basket," she said, starting toward the prison.

"I didn't mean for *him*," Vic said. "I meant for the guy who shanked his ass."

"He asked to see me," she reminded him. "Then someone attacked him. I think we should find out what he knows. It might be something that can bring Richie down."

"You can't trust him," Vic argued.

"I don't. If we only interviewed people we trusted, we'd never use our interrogation rooms. Anyway, that's why I brought you and Rolf."

They checked in with the guard at the entrance to the cell block. Erin turned over her Glock and her .38. Vic handed in his Sig-Sauer and his little .32 semi-auto backup gun. Then, as Erin was turning away, he hauled out a massive nickel-plated hand cannon and slid it across the counter to join its buddies.

"Jesus Christ, Vic," she said. "Where did that come from? Did Russia declare war on us or something?"

"What?" he said. "It's just my Delta Elite. You've used it yourself. It's no big deal."

"Yeah," she said. "It nearly broke my wrist. That's three guns, Vic."

"So?"

"You've only got two hands."

"Look, Erin, we don't know what's going down on the street," he said, moving away from the guard. "Besides the O'Malley punk, now we've got the *bratva* involved, and I don't need to remind you what those guys are like. There's prisoners stabbing each other in here. Next thing you know, we're gonna be playing shootout at the OK Corral in the middle of downtown. If things go seriously sideways, I don't want to be running out of ammo at a critical moment, okay? The last thing any of us want is for me to have to beat some poor perp to death with my dick."

"No," Erin agreed, trying not to picture it. "We definitely don't want that."

"I could, you know," he added.

Erin decided not to say anything to that. It would only encourage him.

"Okay, Detectives," the guard said. "I'm buzzing you in now. The Warden sent a guy to take care of you."

"That's nice," Vic said. "Does he have a plate of cookies and a glass of warm milk?"

"Huh?" the guard said.

"Forget about it," Erin said.

The Corrections Officer waiting for them was a veteran: tough, scarred, and taciturn. He introduced himself as Bolton and didn't offer to shake hands. Erin respected that; experienced cops were careful about coming in contact with strangers.

"Where's Finnegan?" Erin asked as he led them down the cold concrete prison hallway.

"Infirmary," Bolton said. "Have you been to see him before?"

"We're acquainted," Erin said.

"Recently?"

"No. Why would I?"

Bolton shrugged. "I just thought... never mind. None of my business."

"Where'd he get stabbed?"

"Neck."

"Who did it?"

"Inmate Barsov."

"Russian?" Vic asked.

"Yeah," Bolton grunted.

"What's his affiliation?" Vic asked.

"*Vory v zakone*," Bolton said. "He's got the stars."

"The which?" Erin said.

"Tattoos," Vic explained. "Stars on the knees and shoulders. They mean he's a made guy in the Russian Mob."

"What happened to Barsov?" Erin asked.

"Solitary," Bolton said. "Thirty days. Warden's orders."

"He's not in the hospital?" Vic was surprised. "That doesn't sound like the Finnegan we know."

"He wasn't hurt," Bolton said. "It wasn't a fight. I was on duty in the cafeteria when it happened. Just one stab and done."

"You saw it?" Erin asked.

"No. By the time I knew anything was up, it was over. Finnegan was walking by Barsov's table. Next thing I know, he screams and he's down with Barsov's fork sticking out of him. Another CO was closer than I was. By the time I got there, the other CO had Barsov down and cuffed. Wasn't much, really. I've seen plenty worse around here."

"How bad was Finnegan hurt?" Erin asked.

Bolton shrugged. "Not as bad as you'd think. Fork missed his carotid, jugular, windpipe, all the important stuff. He needed stitches, that's all. They could've released him last night, you ask me, but they're playing it safe so they kept him overnight. For observation."

That reminded Erin of another question that had been on her mind. "Officer, the Warden called me personally," she said. "That's unusual. Any idea why?"

"Not my business," Bolton said.

"Let me guess," Vic said. "You guys at Riker's have been under investigation. There's this whole commission talking about shutting you down. After that mess a little while back, with guys getting killed in here, and the two of us getting jumped by that squad of losers, the Warden figured he was lucky to hang onto his job. So he's trying to show he's a team player and getting ahead of the next problem. Am I warm?"

"Could be," Bolton allowed.

"What're your orders?" Erin asked.

"Full cooperation."

"That sure sounds like an organization covering its ass to me," Vic said.

"Why did Barsov stab Finnegan?" Erin asked.

"Don't know," Bolton said.

"Didn't anyone ask him?"

"Yeah."

"What'd he say?"

Bolton rolled his eyes. "Says he didn't do it."

"Same thing he said at his trial, I'll bet," Vic said. "Eighty, ninety percent of the guys in here swear they didn't do what they're in here for doing."

"Something like," Bolton said. "Anyway, Barsov doesn't speak much English, and doesn't talk to cops if he can help it."

"What's he in for?" Vic asked.

"Human trafficking and murder."

"Yeah, that sounds about right," Vic said. "Guys like that make me ashamed to be Russian."

They arrived at the infirmary, which wasn't particularly crowded at the moment. Erin took a second to activate the recording wire hidden under her shirt. She exchanged glances with Vic, who nodded grimly. Then they followed Bolton in.

Finnegan's bed was in the far corner. Bolton led the way, then stood back and did a credible impression of a stone statue, standing against the wall and staring into space.

Kyle Finnegan was an odd-looking man. His face was off-kilter thanks to his partly caved-in skull, which made Erin want to keep trying to find an angle from which he'd look normal. His eyes were unfocused and vacant. His hair stuck out at odd angles. The wound in his neck was hidden by a surgical pad which had been taped over the stitches.

"Morning, Kyle," Erin said. "How are you feeling?"

"Good morrow, Catesby," Finnegan said. "You are early stirring. What news, what news, in this our tottering state?"

"Christ," Vic muttered under his breath. "Here we go again."

"You tell me," Erin said. "You wanted to talk to me; here I am. I'm listening."

"It is a reeling world, indeed, my lord," Finnegan said. "And I believe will never stand upright till Richard wear the garland of the realm."

"Richard O'Malley?" Erin guessed. "You're talking like he's some sort of prince."

"Aye, every inch a king," Finnegan said.

"So he's running things now," Erin said. "Or he thinks he is. But it looks like the Russians have other ideas. Want to tell me about them?"

"Are you afraid of them?" he asked.

"Why would I be?" she replied. "You're the one who got stabbed."

"O happy dagger," Finnegan said. "This is thy sheath. There rust, and let me die."

"You're not dying, dumbass," Vic growled. "All you're doing right now is wasting our time."

"Time is all I have," Finnegan said. "Deprived of meaningful work, men and women lose their reason for existence; they go stark, raving mad."

"Too late," Vic said in an undertone.

"Why do the Russians want you dead?" Erin pressed. "Can't you give me a straight answer to save your own damn life? What do you have on them? What do you know?"

"Look," Finnegan said, and his eyes focused on hers. "What is done cannot be now amended. Men shall deal unadvisedly sometimes, which after-hours gives leisure to repent. Richard loves Richard; that is, I am I. Is there a murderer here? No. Yes, I am. Perjury, perjury, in the highest degree, murder, stern murder, in the direst degree, all several sins, all used in each degree, throng to the bar, crying all, 'Guilty! Guilty!' Methought the souls of all that I had murdered came to my tent, and every one did threat tomorrow's vengeance on the head of Richard."

"Are you talking about yourself or Richie?" Erin asked, utterly baffled. "You say he's a murderer?"

"Yes," Finnegan said.

"Who did he kill?"

"You."

Erin blinked. "Come again?"

"He kills you, or you kill him," Finnegan said. "It doesn't really matter in the end. But he will kill you, unless you kill him first."

"Why? How do you know? I need *proof*, damn it!"

"What do you need proof for? You've killed without it, plenty of times. And you will again."

Erin fought down the urge to grab him and shake some sense into him. "You really did just call me up here to play games," she said. "Screw you, Kyle. I'll see you in court. Don't you dare die in here. You still need to answer for everything you've done."

His hand came up with surprising speed. She'd leaned in a little too close and was taken by surprise. His fingers wrapped tightly around her wrist. Erin gave a startled cry and tried to pull away, but he held on. Vic and Bolton both sprang toward them. Rolf growled and bristled.

"I'm trying to warn you," Finnegan hissed, as alert and urgent as she'd ever seen him.

Erin wrenched herself loose and backed away. *"Platz!"* she snapped at Rolf, who sank sullenly to the floor.

Bolton had a can of pepper spray in his hand and was looking for an excuse to use it. Vic's hands were curled into fists and he was even readier for action than Bolton.

"Guys, it's okay," Erin said. "I'm fine."

"My head," Finnegan said, sinking back onto his pillow. "It gets cloudy. Hard to say what I mean. Sometimes the sun shines through, just for a minute. Getting worse. Richard... he'll come after you. After your family. You need to stop him now. Before it's too late. Look what I have said, I will avouch it in presence of the King. I dare adventure to be sent to the Tower. Tis time to speak; my pains are quite forgot..."

His voice slurred and his eyes slipped shut.

"Shit," Vic said.

"Nurse!" Erin shouted. "Nurse!"

A tired and harried-looking attendant hurried over from the other side of the room. "What?" he demanded.

Erin pointed down. Finnegan was shuddering, eyes still shut. A rope of saliva trickled from one corner of his mouth.

"I'll call the doctor," the nurse said. "Everyone else out. Now!"

A moment later Erin, Vic, Bolton, and Rolf found themselves in the hallway outside the infirmary. They looked at one another.

"I believe that man is insane," Bolton said.

"You think?" Vic replied. "That guy's as crazy as an attic full of cats."

"I hope he's okay," Erin said.

"Good God, why?" Vic asked. "This world's bad enough. It'd be a little better if he wasn't in it."

"You're not wrong," she said. "But I think maybe he's on our side this time."

"No way," Vic said. "That man isn't your friend."

"Of course not," she said. "But we have a common enemy."

"Oh, good," he said. "Like us with Stalin in World War Two. Remember what happened after we got rid of the common enemy? The friggin' Cold War, that's what. Can we get out of this nuthouse now and maybe do some actual police work?"

"Yeah," Erin sighed. "We might as well go. I don't think he'll tell us anything else. And if he really had a seizure, or some other cognitive event, what he said won't stand up in court. Which I'll bet he knows perfectly well. What a waste of time."

"Follow me," Bolton said. They set off for the exit, Bolton locking the access door behind them.

"Let's see," the guy behind the counter said. "Three handguns for you, sir: one Colt Delta Elite, .45 caliber, two full magazines; one Walther PPK/s, .32 caliber, one full mag; one Sig-Sauer nine-millimeter, three full mags."

"That's right," Vic said, stowing his artillery in various places on his person.

"And for you, ma'am, one Glock nine-millimeter, three mags; and one Colt .38 revolver, fully loaded."

"Thanks." Erin took the guns and holstered the Glock at her hip and the .38 on its ankle clip.

"Have a nice day," the guard said with a bland smile.

"Getting nicer," Vic said. "As we get the hell out of here."

In the parking lot, both Detectives flexed their shoulders and took a deep breath. Even the air tasted better outside the prison walls. Riker's Island smelled like disinfectant, old body fluids, BO, anger, and despair. Erin felt like she was coming awake and alive again. Rolf planted his front paws, stretched, and yawned gloriously.

"Was that worth a single damn thing?" Vic demanded.

"I don't know," Erin said, turning off her recording wire. "But try to think like a detective, Vic. Finnegan doesn't have any interest in helping us. If he's the least bit sane, he's out for himself, just like everyone else in that place. So what we need to ask ourselves is what he stands to gain."

"Easy," Vic said. "He wants you to get rid of Richie O'Malley."

"But why? Richie's no threat to him."

"He's having trouble with the Russians in there," Vic guessed. "He's looking for a way to hit back. Maybe he figures if we lean on Dickie-boy, it'll lead us up the chain and we'll roll up the whole damn Russian Mob."

"He didn't tell me to arrest Richie," Erin said thoughtfully. "He told me to kill him."

"Well, we're not doing that," Vic said. "Obviously."

"Of course not," she said. But she was thinking about what Finnegan had said at the end, when he'd been lucid, about her family being in danger. She was remembering a broken front door and an empty house, remembering running through it, screaming the names of her niece and nephew.

Never again, she promised herself. *Never.*

Chapter 4

"Thank God for the Internet," Erin said.

"I still can't believe we're doing this," Vic grumbled. "It's like being back in high-school English class."

"O'Reilly has the right idea," Webb said. "Finnegan isn't as crazy as you think."

"He's exactly as crazy as I think," Vic said. "There's two kinds of psychos, you know."

"I'm well aware," Webb said. "I studied psychology in college, as I've told you and you've probably forgotten. There are disorganized psychopaths and organized ones."

"Finnegan's unusual," Erin said. "He pretends to be disorganized, but he isn't."

"Exactly," Webb said. "What he says sounds random on the surface, but he has patterns in his thoughts and his words. O'Reilly's been good enough to procure a recording of his recent conversation. She thinks those patterns might be useful for us and I agree."

"I don't give a damn how his mind works," Vic said.

"You should," Webb replied. "Because cracking his wacky little internal code might keep your partner alive. What's the first quote?"

Erin played back the recording for the second time. Finnegan's voice emanated from her computer speakers, sounding even weirder than in person, if that was possible.

"Good morrow, Catesby. You are early stirring. What news, what news, in this our tottering state?"

"What does your magic search engine tell you?" Webb asked.

"Catesby is a character in *Richard III*," Erin said. "This is from Act Three, Scene Two. Looks like a conversation between two guys, Catesby and Hastings, whoever they are."

"Hastings?" Zofia said. "Isn't that the battle where the French took over England?"

"The Battle of Hastings was in 1066," Webb said absently. "Harold of Wessex died with an arrow in the eye."

"What does that have to do with anything?" Vic asked.

"We don't know," Erin said.

"Finnegan talks in free associations," Webb said. "It's very stream-of-consciousness, probably a result of his brain trauma. Lots of people think that way, but they don't say it out loud. He could be referencing the play, or the battle, or poor King Harold the archery target. Or none of the above. You mentioned high-school English, Neshenko. Did you study *Richard III*?"

"Nope," Vic said. "I mostly studied the cheerleaders, especially on the days we had home football games. Then they wore those short little skirts all day. Those were good days, and—ouch!"

"Sorry," Zofia said unconvincingly, retracting her elbow. "I slipped."

"We did *Romeo and Juliet*," Erin said. "I never read any other Shakespeare."

"I've read *Richard*," Webb said. "But it was a long time ago. Play the next line."

"It is a reeling world, indeed, my lord," Finnegan's voice recited. "And I believe will never stand upright till Richard wear the garland of the realm."

"That's from the same play," Erin said. "Same scene, the very next line."

"The characters are talking about political instability," Webb said. "They're sounding each other out to see who they'll support as the next King of England."

"I think Finnegan's talking about the drug trade in Manhattan," Erin said.

"That's unstable, all right," Vic agreed. "The Lucarellis and the O'Malleys were two of the big players. They're both out of the picture, which leaves a vacuum."

"And Finnegan says Richard will stabilize things," Webb said. "I wonder why."

"He won't," Erin said. "Richie O'Malley doesn't have the stones to play with the big boys. If he tries, they'll eat him alive."

"Not if he has the Russian Mob at his back," Vic said.

"But then he won't be the one running the business," Erin said. "He'll just be a puppet at best."

"Go on with the recording," Webb said, tapping his chin thoughtfully.

"Aye, every inch a king," Finnegan said.

"That sounds like Shakespeare again," Webb said. "The man does have his favorites."

"That's right," Erin said, staring at her computer. "But it's a different play. *King Lear.* I don't know it. Act Four, Scene Six."

"Let's have a look," Webb said. "Here's a site that has the play. Just a minute."

There was a pause while the others clustered around his computer, reading over his shoulder.

"I don't get it," Vic finally said. "Except the part he says about letting copulation thrive. I can get behind that."

"Lear is talking about adultery and procreation," Webb said. "He's feeling down on women, since he's been betrayed by two of his daughters. He's talking about how the female reproductive system belongs to the Devil."

"Sheesh," Zofia said. "I didn't know Shakespeare was one of *those* guys."

"Finnegan could mean four things," Webb said. "As far as I can figure it. Either he's getting in a dig at women in general, and probably O'Reilly in particular; or he's referring to some other woman in a really oblique way; or he's feeling sexually frustrated; or he's referring to King Lear's most famous trait."

"What's that?" Vic asked. "I'm just a dumb community-college meathead, sir."

"Lear goes insane," Webb said. "And Finnegan is sane enough to know he himself is insane. So maybe he's talking about himself. What else have we got?"

Erin set the recording running again.

"O happy dagger," Finnegan said. "This is thy sheath. There rust, and let me die."

"I know that one," she said. "That's Juliet, the last thing she says before she stabs herself to death."

"And Finnegan just got stabbed," Vic said. "That isn't exactly rocket science. Too bad that Russian punk didn't aim a little better. I'm getting a headache just trying to wrap my brain around this guy."

"Then he says that if you take meaningful work away from people, we all go crazy," Erin said. "Or something like."

"Be specific," Webb said.

The recording said, "Deprived of meaningful work, men and women lose their reason for existence; they go stark, raving mad."

"It's attributed to Dostoevsky," Erin said after a few moments' search. "But I can't find the exact source. It may be a mistranslation."

"Dostoevsky," Vic said. "Awesome! I was just thinking we needed some depressing Russian literature to balance things out."

Webb sighed. "If there's a pattern here, I'm not seeing it. He goes back to the Shakespeare then, right?"

"Yeah," Erin said. "The last couple of quotes are *Richard III* again. Looks like the first one is when Richard's feeling guilty about all the crap he's done. The second one is actually earlier in the play, when he gets in a fight with some other characters and asks them to throw him in the Tower. I guess that means the Tower of London."

"Both lines are about guilt," Webb said. "That may be the closest thing to a confession we ever get from someone like him."

"Where's that leave us?" Vic asked.

"Finnegan's telling me the street's in transition," Erin said. "The old gangs are out and a new one is in. He thinks Richard is in position to benefit. He also thinks Richard's going to try to kill me. Finnegan is wounded and crazy so he can't take care of Richard himself, but he told me to do it. Then he talked about feeling helpless and going nuts, and feeling guilty."

"Your conclusion?" Webb asked.

"He wants me to take Richie out," Erin said. "I think he tried to put a contract on him through me."

"But they're on the same side," Vic said.

"Not anymore," Erin said. "Richie isn't working for the O'Malleys now. He's looking out for number one."

"Why does Finnegan care?" Zofia asked. "He's in jail no matter what."

"He's an agent of chaos who lives for disorder," Webb said. "He doesn't have any muscle on the street, so he's using what he has, which is his connection with O'Reilly."

"That's a pretty weak play, if you ask me," Vic said.

"Richie already tried to kill me," Erin said. "Twice."

"Unproven," Webb said.

"There're no lawyers here," Vic said. "Don't give us that 'allegedly' bullshit, sir. We all know what happened. You ask me, we should've already thrown his ass in jail."

"Unless I'm mistaken, Richard O'Malley isn't our case," Webb said. "But hypothetically speaking, what do we know about him?"

"He's married," Zofia said. "Six years now. To Kim O'Malley. One kid, a three-year-old son, Richard Junior."

"Of course he named his kid after himself," Vic said, rolling his eyes. "Guys with little dicks and big egos do that."

"My oldest brother is Sean Junior," Erin reminded him. "Are you saying something about my dad?"

"Guys also do it if they want to establish an honorable and lasting legacy," Vic said, not missing a beat.

"They live in Brooklyn," Zofia went on. "Brick house, single-family dwelling, pretty nice neighborhood. Right on the edge of Brighton Beach."

"Which is where the Russian Mafia hang out," Vic added.

"The house wasn't confiscated when we froze the O'Malley assets," Webb said. "Why not?"

"We couldn't prove it was bought with dirty money," Zofia said. "But the mortgage is fully paid off."

"He's been having regular meetings with members of Gennady Vlasov's gang," Erin said. "They're moving into the fentanyl trade in a big way. And Richard's flush with cash all of a sudden."

"You're very well-informed," Webb said dryly. "Considering it isn't your case."

"Narcotics has a file," Erin said. "I've read it."

"I see," Webb said. "And you wouldn't be doing any sort of extracurricular investigation, would you?"

"That would be against Departmental policy, sir," Erin said.

"That's right," Webb said. "And on the subject of the Department, we're still the Precinct Eight Major Crimes squad, so I think it would be a good use of taxpayer dollars to investigate some major crimes. Where are we with Arlen Ulrich?"

"We've got him right where we want him," Zofia said. "The Feds gave us their file on him. His computer's full of kiddie porn and the DNA match came back on that hair sample Rolf found. It's a match for Ulrich's niece."

"Good Lord," Webb said. "I suppose I should be glad, but I mostly just feel dirty."

"I got the warrants filled out and ready to go," Zofia said. "We're ready."

"Look at you," Vic said, smiling. "Our rookie detective, all grown up."

"I'll get the warrants to the Judge," Webb said. "Then we'll go nail this dirtbag. Excellent work, Piekarski."

*   *   *

Not having much to do while waiting for the warrants, Erin decided to go down to the firing range in the basement. Vic eagerly accompanied her. They set the targets to twenty yards. Long-range sharpshooting was for showoffs and snipers; in the NYPD, the average range in a gunfight was ten yards. The most important skills were rapid target acquisition and hitting with the first couple of rounds, which could be harder than it sounded, especially if you were taking fire yourself.

On the range, Erin and Vic both regularly scored in the high nineties. Vic in particular prided himself on his accuracy. But they knew that didn't transfer to the street. When the targets were shooting back, all that fine-motor control went straight out the window. You'd be lucky to hit with one out of six shots. That was why muscle memory and training were so vital; when the brain was panicking, the body would still remember.

They practiced the so-called Mozambique Drill, a pistol technique designed to quickly drop a target who might or might not be wearing body armor or cruising on hard drugs. The drill was to put two quick shots into the target's center of mass, then follow up with an aimed shot to the head.

Erin was good; Vic was better. Every time she lined up her third shot, Erin heard the bark of Vic's Sig-Sauer just a half-beat ahead of her. It was infuriating. She knew she had better reflexes than Vic. He was strong but slow. But without apparent effort, he kept putting rounds downrange both faster and more accurately than she did.

"You've been practicing off the clock," she finally said after they'd both fired off fifty rounds.

"Well, yeah," Vic said, looking at his well-perforated target with satisfaction. "You train Rolf in your downtime. I don't have a dog and I can't be having sex all the time, so I gotta do something to make the time pass."

"There's more to life than sex and violence," she said, ejecting the Glock's magazine and walking over to the gun-cleaning booth.

"I know," he said. "There's fried food."

"You're a disgrace to men and humanity," she said.

"So they keep telling me," he said. He joined her, broke down his pistol, and started cleaning it. "You going after Dickie-boy again tonight?"

"I don't know," she said. "But I want to know what he's up to. The way Finnegan was talking about him..."

"I can't go with you," he said. "Zofia's uncle is in town and he's been itching to meet Mina."

"I'll bet," Erin said. Mina, Vic and Zofia's daughter, was Vic's pride and joy; a bouncy, cheerful baby. Even Rolf found it hard to look at anything else when the little girl was around.

"We're going out to dinner, then spending the evening with Zofia's mom," Vic said. "So if you want my advice, don't get into anything heavy. You won't have backup."

"I've got the whole NYPD," she reminded him.

"I'm sure that's a great comfort in your little off-the-books surveillance op," he retorted. "Besides, you shoot for shit."

"I shot ninety-eight percent just now," she said indignantly.

"Amateur. I did a hundred."

"Showoff."

"You ought to see what I can do with a rifle."

"And the man is obsessed with size," Erin said, grinning. "Typical."

Vic started to say something else, but was distracted by an incoming text on his phone. "That's Zofia," he said. "The warrants for Ulrich just came through. Let's go drag his ass in."

"And hope we don't have to put all this shooting practice to use," Erin said.

Chapter 5

The raid on Arlen Ulrich's apartment was anticlimactic. Ulrich would have had to be crazy to try to fight off an ESU tactical team, reinforced by the Major Crimes squad. ESU Officer Parker smashed the door open, the unit flooded in, and Ulrich meekly surrendered without so much as a word of protest.

The end result was Erin closing out her shift with a lot of untapped adrenaline burning in her veins. The others had their ways of coping with it. Webb stepped outside and chain-smoked a full pack of Camels, reeking like an ashtray when he rejoined them in in the office for the post-arrest paperwork. Rolf chased a tennis ball that Erin obligingly bounced off the wall for him. Zofia dragged Vic into a supply closet. They didn't say what they did in there, and Erin didn't ask, but both were disheveled and glowing when they came out fifteen minutes later.

Erin was restless. After the obligatory DD-5 forms and arrest reports, the evidence cataloguing, and the filing of the interview transcript—a single-page document consisting of Webb asking Ulrich a question, only to be interrupted by the man asking for his lawyer—she jumped up and left the office in a hurry.

She was edgy and nervous, feeling like she did before a bad thunderstorm. Her skin was tingly and she could sense an ominous heaviness in the air. But the sky was blue and clear, the weather warm. She went down to the garage, loaded Rolf into the Charger, and drove out of the Eightball onto the Manhattan streets.

She kept thinking about Finnegan. Had he been telling the truth? Was Richie determined to kill her and her family? He'd never been a very dangerous guy. Compared to a hardened killer like Mickey Connor he was a pushover, a loser. Even with his new Russian friends, she didn't think he rated very high.

"Why is Finnegan so fixated on him?" she asked Rolf.

The K-9 poked his head through the hatch and nuzzled her ear.

"We should go home," she said. "It's been a long day. Get a drink, have something to eat."

But she didn't. Instead, she called Carlyle.

"I want to check on something," she said. "Down in Brooklyn."

"Would this something be pertaining to a certain Irish-American of dubious character?" he asked.

"Yeah."

"Darling, I'm thinking this is becoming something of an obsession for you."

"Finnegan told me to kill him," she said bluntly.

There was a short pause.

"I'm assuming that's not your intention," he said.

"Of course not! But I need to know why."

"Who's with you?"

"Rolf."

"That's all?"

"Yeah. Don't worry, I'm not looking for trouble."

"But it does have a way of finding you," he said. "No fear, darling. I'll be here when you're done. Only…"

"What?" she asked after a moment.

"I'm not worried about what Richard will do," Carlyle said. "It's Finnegan I don't trust."

"Then it's a good thing he's locked up at Riker's," she said. "I doubt I'll run into him. I'll call you again when I'm on my way home."

"As you wish, darling."

Erin hung up, but her nerves kept jangling. She couldn't shake the feeling that someone was watching her, or that something was about to happen. She kept checking her rearview mirror. A beat-up sedan in the next lane appeared to be following her, but so did a pickup two cars behind her, a minivan on her right, a black Charger a lot like her own, and fifteen other cars. After all, she was driving from Manhattan to Brooklyn during rush hour. Traffic was absolutely awful.

"I must be out of my mind," she told Rolf.

The dog's usual policy was to agree with his partner, so he cocked his head and didn't contradict her.

Erin put on some music, which helped a little. She drummed her fingers on the steering wheel and tried to think. Richard O'Malley had gone out of his way to antagonize her. Finnegan had asked her to kill him. She felt like she was being manipulated into doing something she'd regret, but didn't see how that could happen.

"Damn it, I'm not going to kill him," she said. "And nobody's going to force me to do it. He's nothing. He's a damn insect. Whatever Finnegan's up to, I'm not playing his game."

Once more, Rolf didn't disagree.

Finally, after a subjective year or two, Erin made it across the East River into Brooklyn and traffic eased up a little. She turned off onto a side street as quickly as possible, noting the pickup that had been behind her and the black Charger doing the same. She read the truck's license plate in her mirror and punched it into her onboard computer while she drove, just in case. The plate came back clean. But she kept an eye on it anyway. The truck's passenger seat was unoccupied, which was good. Anyone trying to do a hit from a moving car would be a two-man team: one driver, one shooter. The Charger was too far back to try anything.

As she got close to Richard's house, she abruptly made a hard right, just to see what the cars would do. Both sailed on by without slowing.

"I'm getting paranoid," Erin sighed. "That's just some civilian on his way home after work, which is where I should've gone too. Jesus. We'll just do a quick pass and then get out of here."

She circled the block and looped back onto her original route. As she came up on Richard's house, on 26th Avenue, she kept her head on a swivel. She turned the radio to the police band out of old habit, hearing nothing but the usual chatter. There was no sign of Richard.

"What a damn waste of time," she muttered. The neighborhood was peaceful. A couple of kids were playing in their yard a few doors down. A middle-aged lady was working in her garden. Nothing set off Erin's Patrol instincts.

Finnegan had gotten in her head. That was the only explanation. She'd walked into meetings with lethally dangerous gangsters more calmly than she was now driving down a quiet Brooklyn street. Nobody was gunning for her. Finnegan's whole spiel was probably just bullshit designed to make her scared of her own shadow.

"That'd be just like him," she growled. "He'd think it was hilarious to get me looking over my shoulder all the time for no damn reason. I bet he made the whole thing up."

"Dispatch, this is Six-Two Adam Seven," an excited voice suddenly crackled over the radio. "Shots fired, Scarangella Park! I don't have eyes on the shooter, but I've got at least two civilians down. People running every which-way. I need backup, all available units!"

"Cool it, Rookie," an older, calmer voice broke in. "This is Six-Two Baker Twelve. This is a 10-10S, possible active shooter, Scarangella Park, near the jungle gym."

"Copy that," Dispatch said. "Routing all available units. Is the area cleared for EMS?"

"Negative," the older guy said. "Keep the buses out. We don't want medics taking fire."

"Shit," Erin muttered. Scarangella Park was only a couple of blocks away. She shoved Richard O'Malley to the back of her mind, stepped on the gas, and grabbed her radio handset.

"Dispatch, this is Detective O'Reilly, Shield four-six-four-oh, responding to Scarangella Park. I'm in an unmarked black Charger, off duty. I have a K-9 unit."

"Copy that, O'Reilly," Dispatch said.

Erin flicked on her lights and siren. Rolf's ears perked up. He thrust his muzzle through the hatch again, pointed his snout upward, and howled in harmony with the mechanical wail. His tail was wagging. Sirens meant bad guys to chase.

The Charger covered the intervening distance in less than a minute. Erin hit the tight turn from Benson Avenue onto Stillwell doing at least forty-five. She laid rubber as she slewed the car around, coming to a halt less than ten yards from a Patrol blue-and-white. A pair of uniformed officers was advancing cautiously, one of them carrying the squad car's rifle, the other gripping his sidearm. They swung the weapons toward Erin as she dismounted.

"NYPD!" she shouted, holding up her gold shield. "What's going on?"

"We heard the shots from a block away," the younger officer said. Freckles stood out on his pale face. He looked about sixteen years old and scared out of his wits. "At least two people are down. Jesus, one of them's a little kid!"

"Where's the shooter?" Erin demanded.

"No idea," the older cop said grimly. He nodded in the direction of the park, where panicky people were running in all directions, individually or in little groups. "Could be any of these idiots, or none of them."

"Put up a perimeter around the park," Erin ordered, drawing her own gun. "I'll see if I can pick up the shooter's trail. Rolf, *fuss!*"

She jogged toward the playground, Rolf sticking close beside her. People were screaming, but she heard no gunfire. As she approached the jungle gym, she saw two bodies lying still and a third kneeling next to one of them. One of the bodies was very small.

The kneeling figure was a man, his back toward her. He gathered the little body into his arms. His head was bowed so Erin couldn't see his face. His shoulders were shaking as if he was having a seizure, but she knew it was shock and grief. A terrible sound, half sob and half scream, came out of him in broken fragments.

"Sir!" Erin shouted. "Are you injured?"

He took no notice of her whatsoever. The shoulder of his shirt was torn and blood was streaming down his arm, but he didn't seem aware of that, either. He just kept holding the kid in his arms and making that noise.

Erin holstered her Glock. "*Sitz!*" she told Rolf, who sank immediately to his haunches. Then she took in the bodies.

Caucasian female, she thought in the clinical, detached part of her brain that took charge in situations like this. *Age approximately thirty. Brown hair, brown eyes. Multiple gunshot wounds to chest and abdomen. Pupils wide and fixed, nonresponsive. Probably deceased, but get EMTs on scene ASAP to verify. Victim two: Caucasian male, age approximately six years. Black hair, brown eyes. GSW just above left eye. Obviously deceased.*

When she saw what the bullet had done to the little boy's head, Erin's detachment dissolved. She thought she might faint or throw up, just like a rookie. The kid was about the same age as her nephew Patrick.

The man holding the boy turned toward her, becoming aware of her for the first time. Tears streamed down his face. He looked like a man who'd gazed straight into the heart of Hell. His red-rimmed eyes were as dark and empty as an unlit subway tunnel. But that wasn't what made Erin take a stumbling step back, feeling as if she'd been smacked in the stomach by a baseball bat.

"Look what you did," Richard O'Malley said in a cracked, hopeless voice. "Look what you did!"

Chapter 6

"Get that bus here right now!" Erin shouted at the Patrol cops. Then she turned back to Richard. "Help's on the way. Try to stay calm. How bad are you hit?"

He didn't answer. She figured he was in shock. The shot to his shoulder didn't look too serious. The bullet wounds on him and the other two victims looked like they'd come from a handgun, not a rifle. That was good news. For one thing, it meant she probably wasn't about to get her own head blown off by an unseen sniper.

She knelt next to the fallen woman and felt for a pulse.

"You bitch," Richard whispered. "You fucking *bitch!* Don't you touch her!"

Erin ignored him, still searching for any sign of life. She found nothing. Either the woman's blood pressure had dropped so low that her pulse was imperceptible, or she was already gone.

"I said, don't touch her!" Richard screamed. He lurched toward Erin and grabbed at her.

Erin was astonished. She'd momentarily blocked out her ongoing feud with Richard O'Malley, recognizing the more urgent situation in front of her. She wasn't prepared for him to physically attack her. She went over backwards, grotesquely stumbling over the woman's body and falling to the bloodstained playground gravel. Richard was clawing at her, trying to get his hands around her throat.

"I'll kill you!" he choked. "I'll kill you!"

Rolf barked sharply. It was his one and only warning. He followed it up with his teeth.

Suddenly Richard was tumbling off Erin, bowled over by ninety pounds of fiercely protective K-9. Rolf's jaws were clamped around his right forearm. Richard's cry of surprise turned into a scream of pain.

"Rolf! *Pust!*" Erin gasped out, rolling onto her feet. She could have, should have drawn her gun, but she didn't. Now that she was up and ready, Richard was no realistic threat to her. Not when he was wounded, unarmed, and now sporting tooth-marks from her dog.

Rolf instantly released his target and sprang back, tail wagging, tongue hanging out, ready to be told what a good boy he'd been. Richard curled into a ball, sobbing and cradling his arm. Erin looked down at him with a mix of disgust and pity.

"What the hell is going on?" one of the Patrol cops demanded. He and his partner had just arrived on scene. The rookie was pointing his gun vaguely in Richard's direction, but wasn't sure whether O'Malley was a perp, a victim, or both.

"Give this guy some help," Erin said, pointing to Richard. "He won't let me do it. He's been shot in the upper arm and he's got a dog bite. And keep him under control. Don't let him do anything."

Sirens were converging on the park from all directions. Erin could see four squad cars already parked and more inbound. Some of the bystanders had dropped to the ground and were hugging the grass for cover. Others were milling around like a startled flock of pigeons. Several, predictably, had pulled out their phones and were making calls and taking pictures.

The older Patrolman got down on Richard's level and started checking him over. The rookie, staring at the body of the little boy, was abruptly and noisily sick. At least he was standing far enough back that he probably hadn't contaminated the scene.

"Who're you, ma'am?" the older cop asked.

"Detective O'Reilly," she said. "Major Crimes, out of Manhattan."

"You got here fast," he observed.

"I was already in the area," she said. "Who's in command here?"

"You are, ma'am. For the moment, anyway. You think Major Crimes is gonna take this one, or you kicking it back to the Six-Two's Homicide squad?"

"We'll take it," Erin said. She saw half a dozen uniforms on their way in, guns drawn, and raised her voice to talk to them. "I need witnesses, guys. Get someone who saw what happened. I want the shooter. If anyone got a picture on their phone, that'd be perfect, but a description's better than nothing. Don't let any civilians touch anything. We'll be looking for shell casings, footprints, you name it, so everyone keep back."

She wasn't used to being on the scene so fast. Usually by the time Major Crimes got involved, the area had been cordoned off and the uniforms had secured it. She called up memories of her Patrol days and the traffic accidents and violent confrontations she'd responded to. The Brooklyn cops were well trained and efficient. They fanned out and began talking to bystanders, directing people away from the bloodstained playground.

The ambulance showed up a couple minutes later, disgorging two EMTs. They hustled over and quickly checked the boy and the woman. After a moment they both stood back, shaking their heads.

"No good," one of them said. "DOA."

Richard, sitting on a platform of the jungle gym at the direction of the Patrolman, shuddered. He buried his face in his hands, shoulders trembling. The paramedics examined him in turn. He didn't seem to notice them, even when they probed his wounded arm.

"Let's get him to the hospital," one said.

"You want someone to ride along with him?" the Patrolman asked Erin.

"Yeah," she said. "We'll want a statement from him as soon as he's able to talk. He's our best chance at IDing the shooter. Don't let him wander off."

"Copy that," the Patrolman said. "Hey, Cooper!"

"Sarge?" the freckle-faced kid said weakly. His complexion had gone so pale it was a little green.

"I gotta take a ride on the bus with our victim here, so that means you gotta operate without adult supervision. We're shorthanded, kid, so I need you to dig in. You do whatever Detective O'Reilly here tells you. Copy?"

"Copy that, Sarge," Officer Cooper said.

By the time the EMTs had loaded Richard into the back of the ambulance, Erin was on the phone to her own commanding officer.

"This had better be good, O'Reilly," Webb said. "I'm on my way to the airport."

"Airport?" she echoed. "Where are you going, sir?"

"Nowhere. I'm picking up Danielle and Erica. They're flying in from LA this evening."

"You didn't tell us your kids were coming," she said, startled out of what she'd been about to say.

"It was none of your business," he replied. "And it still isn't. What is your business is major crimes, which I assume are what you're calling about."

"Yes, sir. Someone just tried to kill Richard O'Malley."

"What?! When?"

"A few minutes ago. He got grazed, but we have two GSW fatalities. I don't have positive ID on them, but I think it's his wife and son."

"Dear Lord," Webb murmured. "Okay, where did it happen?"

"Scarangella Park, Brooklyn. I'm there now."

"What in God's name are you doing in Brooklyn? Never mind, I don't need to know. I'm close to JFK right now, so I'm not that far away. I'll pick up the girls and still get there ahead of the others."

"Vic and Zofia are doing a family visit tonight," Erin said.

"So am I," Webb replied. "Your point?"

"Vic's going to be unhappy."

"As opposed to his usual state? Where are they?"

"Either at dinner or with Zofia's mom."

"Good. Mrs. Piekarski lives in Queens. That means they're already on the right side of the River. Do you know anything about the shooter?"

"Not yet. I've got unis canvassing for witnesses. O'Malley may know something, but he's pretty out of it. When I went to talk to him, he tried to strangle me. He's on the way to the hospital with one of our guys riding along."

"Copy that. See you soon." Webb hung up.

"Hey, Detective!"

It was Cooper, the rookie. He was all excitement now, actually jumping up and down like a hyperactive puppy, nausea forgotten. Erin shook her head and smiled to herself, remembering that she'd been like that once upon a time, back when the uniform still felt new and she wasn't used to the shield on her chest or the gun on her hip.

"What is it, Cooper?" she asked.

"It's the weapon!" he exclaimed, pointing into the grass near the playground.

Erin felt some of the kid's excitement. Finding the murder weapon right away was a huge break. Even if it didn't have fingerprints, a gun could be traced through its serial number. Ballistics might match it to other crimes. At the very least, they'd be spared an exhaustive search of all the storm drains and garbage cans in the area.

She followed his finger and saw a black, boxy shape in the grass. "Looks like it," she said. "That's a gun all right. Good eye, kiddo."

Cooper visibly swelled with pride. "Looks like a Glock 17," he said. "Nine-millimeter, seventeen-shot capacity, semi-automatic. You can get the thirty-three round extended magazines, but—"

"I know a Glock's specs," Erin interrupted, patting the identical weapon on her hip. "I've carried one just like it for twelve years."

She knelt and examined the gun without touching it. It looked innocuous enough: black polymer frame, squared-off slide, textured grip. It was as familiar to her as her toothbrush. She could disassemble it and put it back together blindfolded. It was simple, reliable, and had probably just ended two lives less than thirty yards from where it now lay.

"Leave it there," she said. "You don't move from this spot until CSU takes over. Don't touch it. Don't even breathe on it."

"Copy that, Detective," Cooper said. His eyes were shining. Erin felt a perverse urge to offer him Rolf's rubber Kong ball, just to see what he'd do. Maybe he'd try to catch it in his mouth.

Erin pointed to the discarded pistol. "Rolf, *such!*" she ordered.

Rolf sprang forward and sniffed at the Glock. He paused, looking up at Erin and wagging uncertainly. One paw was poised in midair. He cocked his head.

"Go on, Rolf," she said. "*Such!*"

Rolf sniffed it again. Then he went in a circle around Erin, snuffling. His tail was still wagging, but it was drooping low, like it did when he was apologizing for something. He circled her a second time and whined.

Erin was baffled. Assuming this was the murder weapon, it hadn't been lying there more than a few minutes. The shooter's scent should be fresh, all over the gun and the ground. The K-9 ought to be making a beeline after the gunman. Instead he was milling around her, acting like an untrained puppy.

"What's the matter, kiddo?" she asked. "Are you okay?"

Rolf whined again. But his nostrils flared. He hesitated a second. Then he began trotting south, slowly at first, but gradually picking up the pace.

Erin felt the old thrill of the chase rising in her. The shooter had a head start, but unless the killer had a car waiting, they'd run him to ground. She drew her gun as she jogged after her dog. Just because the murderer had dropped a gun didn't mean he wasn't carrying a backup weapon.

They left the park and crossed the sidewalk. Rolf came to the curb and pulled up short. He looked back at Erin and whined once more, unhappily. His tail drooped until it was pointing straight down.

She understood. "The bad guy got in a car," she sighed. "Forget about it, kiddo. Good boy."

She tossed him his rubber ball. He'd earned it by tackling Richard off her in any case. Rolf perked up immediately. His tail was up and wagging again even before he'd snatched the ball in midair. He made a perfect leaping grab, landed lightly, trotted off the sidewalk onto the grass, and dropped to his belly, holding the ball between his front paws for optimal gnawing.

"Damn," Erin murmured. She turned back toward the park and saw a uniformed officer talking to a gray-haired woman. The cop waved Erin over. She flicked the leash and started moving. Rolf followed, carrying his ball in his mouth and working it around with his jaws, making the occasional squeak.

"What've we got?" Erin asked the uniform.

"This lady says she saw the whole thing," the cop said, gesturing to the woman.

"That's right," the woman said. She looked to be about sixty. She was dressed in an old sweatshirt and jeans, her silver hair pulled back in a ponytail. She was holding a brown paper bag in one hand. Erin hoped it didn't contain a bottle of cheap liquor, but thought it might.

"What's your name, ma'am?" she asked.

"Linda Driscoll," the woman said.

"And your occupation?"

"I'm retired. Before that I was in dental insurance, and the Marine Corps before that." Linda's eyes flashed with sudden pride. "*Semper fi.*"

"Thanks for your service, ma'am," Erin said automatically. "Where were you when the shooting happened?"

"On that bench over there," Linda said, pointing. Her hands were the tough, callused hands of a woman who liked to do things for herself. "I was feeding the squirrels."

"Excuse me?" Erin said.

"The squirrels," Linda repeated, shaking the paper bag. It rattled. "Dried corn. I like the fluffy little guys. I come down here every couple days and give them a little something. They're getting nice and plump."

"I'll bet," Erin said. "What did you see?"

"Well, it's a funny thing," Linda said, giving Erin an odd, sidelong look. "I was just sitting there, and I had six or seven of my little buddies around me. One of them, I call him Barney, actually lets me pet him if he's in a good mood. He was right there on the bench beside me when I saw a woman get out of black car on the street, just about where you were standing a minute ago."

"It was a woman?" Erin asked.

"That's right." Linda gave her that funny look again. "She didn't run. She just walked straight across the grass, over to the playground. That family was there, the mom and dad and kid. The kid was playing on the monkey bars and his mom and dad were watching him. The lady went right up to them and pulled out a pistol. She shot the other woman four times. No warning, nothing. Just bang, bang, bang, bang."

"She shot the woman first?"

"She sure did." Linda sounded sure of herself. "Then she aimed at the kid. The man jumped between them right as she fired, so he got hit in the arm and went down, wounded but not dead. Then she shot the kid, bang in the face. Then she turned around and ran back to her car. I didn't see her get in, but I heard the engine start up and it drove off in a hurry."

"Why didn't you see her leave?" Erin asked.

"Because I was taking cover," Linda said. "The way they taught us in the Corps. When there's incoming coming, you get low and put something thick between you and the bullets. I was behind the bench, calling 911."

"What kind of car was it?" Erin asked.

"Black sedan," Linda said. "Dodge, I think. It had a squarish look and those outline taillights. Yeah, I'd say it was a Dodge Charger. The four-door model, not the coupe."

"Did you get a good look at the shooter?"

Linda nodded slowly. "Pretty good," she said. "I wasn't paying much attention to her, you understand. I was feeding my little buddies. But they all ran off once the shooting started. Smart little guys, you ask me."

"What did she look like?"

"There's the funny thing," Linda said. "I'd say she looked one hell of a lot like you."

Chapter 7

"That's what she said," Erin said.

"Damn," Vic said. "Maybe you've got a long-lost evil twin. I saw this one movie where—"

"Not helping, Neshenko," Webb said.

The rest of the Major Crimes squad had gotten there as fast as they could. Even though they'd all been on the Brooklyn side of the East River, this had still taken a while. JFK Airport was forty-five minutes away from Scarangella Park. Webb had driven it in forty flat, which had been very exciting for Danielle and Erica Webb.

Erin had never met Webb's daughters. They looked young, pretty, and full of life; in other words, pretty much the opposite of their dad. Erin would never have guessed they were related. The girls stood a short distance away, watching the detectives with interest.

"This is weird," Zofia said. She and Vic had come straight from dinner. She was wearing a dress and heels, which Erin found extremely odd. Zofia was a slacks-and-sneakers street cop. Seeing her dolled up for an evening out was sort of like picturing Rolf wearing a tuxedo.

"I still like the evil twin angle," Vic said. He was dressed up too, which in his case meant a shirt with buttons on it that was actually buttoned all the way up, a pair of pants that wasn't worn through at the cuffs, and a clean-shaven chin.

"I don't have an evil twin," Erin said. "Ms. Driscoll insists the killer was a black-haired woman about my height and build. But that could be any number of people. They wouldn't have to be my double, or whatever you want to call it."

"*Doppelgänger,*" Webb said. "It's German. It means a twin or double."

"No wonder O'Malley got mad at you," Zofia said. "If he didn't get a good look at the shooter, he might've thought it was you coming back to finish the job."

"What I don't get is why she shot the chick and the kid first," Vic said. "That's messed up. And it doesn't make sense. Even if she didn't know who O'Malley was, the dad's the biggest physical threat. I'd shoot him first. If I was the kind of guy who'd mow down a whole family, I mean. Which I'm not, obviously."

"I'm thinking jealous girlfriend," Zofia said. "Maybe O'Malley had a side piece and got her pregnant. Then he cut her off and she decided she wasn't going to let him push her out of his life. Like Glenn Close in *Fatal Attraction.* You know. 'I'm not going to be *ignored,* Dan.'"

Zofia did her best Alex Forrest impression. It was scarily accurate. Vic shivered appreciatively.

"That's possible," Webb said. "It would definitely explain why she'd target the woman and child. CSU's checking the gun now. If we're lucky, it'll be registered to a black-haired woman with a history of mental instability and a black Charger. Then we can close the case and get back to our family time."

"Sorry about this," Erin said, glancing at Webb's girls.

"Don't be," he said. "They said they were looking forward to seeing me work. Here's their big chance. You might as well come get to know them a little. We don't have a lot to do here until CSU finishes up."

"Hey, I know a black-haired woman who's mentally unstable and drives a black Charger," Vic said.

"Shut up," Erin said.

"And she owns a Glock," he added.

"You're funny like a heart attack," Erin told him.

Webb stepped toward the girls. "Erica, Dani, this is my squad," he said. "Erin O'Reilly, Zofia Piekarski, and Vic Neshenko."

Danielle had a charming smile that showed slightly crooked front teeth. "Hi," she said. "I read an article about you, Ms. O'Reilly."

Erin's own smile felt forced and artificial. "Is that so?" she said.

"Yeah," Danielle said. "In *Time* magazine. Did you really do all that stuff?"

"And then some," Vic said, grinning. "You should hear some of the crap they don't dare put in the news."

"Really?" Erica said. "That's interesting. I'd like to hear your opinion on the NYPD's record *vis-à-vis* civil rights violations, Detective O'Reilly."

"You're pre-law at UCLA, aren't you?" Erin asked with a sinking feeling.

"That's right," Erica said. "I'm going to be a public defender, to help disadvantaged members of the community defend themselves against unjust and unlawful persecution by law enforcement."

"I think you mean *prosecution*," Zofia said.

"I meant what I said," Erica replied through her own artificial smile.

There was a brief, awkward pause.

Vic whistled. "I can see you've got your work cut out for you with this one, sir," he said to Webb.

"You're right," Erin said to Erica. "There've been a lot of abuses by police officers through history. I'm not an Internal Affairs cop, so I'm not qualified to comment on the current situation in the NYPD. But your dad or I can put you in touch with our very own IAB commander, Lieutenant McDowell. I'm sure you and she would find a lot to talk about."

"I'd like that," Erica said. "And I'm just screwing with you, Ms. O'Reilly. Profiling works both ways. I know there's good cops out there. After all, my dad's one of them."

Webb's face broke into a surprised, delighted smile. He clearly wasn't used to receiving compliments of that sort from his family.

"Have you ever been to New York before?" Zofia asked.

Both girls shook their heads.

"I've been bugging Mom about it for months," Erica said. "But she kept putting me off until Dad set it up. He said we'd better get it in before school starts up again. We have a whole week. I have a list of all the things I want to see."

"It's a spreadsheet," Webb said, still smiling. "Color-coded."

"Wow," Vic said. "I don't even write down my grocery list."

"And he forgets the milk all the time," Zofia said.

"Who wants to drink milk?" Vic retorted. "If we were supposed to drink milk, we'd all be cows."

"But fermented potatoes are so much better?" Zofia asked.

"*So* much better," Vic said, licking his lips. "When milk goes bad, you have to throw it out. Vodka just gets better."

"Is he really like this all the time, Dad?" Erica asked.

"No," Webb said. "Right now he's on his best behavior."

"So tell us about the case," Danielle said brightly, doing her best to change the subject.

"The NYPD doesn't comment regarding ongoing investigations," Vic said.

"That's what we teach them to say," Webb said. "Look, Dani, you really don't want the details on this one."

"Dad, we do have the Internet in California," Danielle said. "I guarantee you I've seen worse."

Webb made a face. "Right. Okay, here's the short version. We're after a gunwoman who just killed two people and wounded a third. We don't know who she is yet, or why she did it. But we hope we will soon. We have at least one good eyewitness who can probably pick her out of a lineup, we have what's most likely the murder weapon, and we have a description of the getaway vehicle. That's usually plenty for us to make an arrest. Off the record, I think we'll close this one pretty fast."

"A gunwoman?" Erica repeated. "Isn't that a little unusual?"

"Evil is equal-opportunity," Vic said. "Not all bad guys look like me."

"Just most of them," Zofia said. "I think it's the nose."

"What's wrong with my nose?" Vic demanded indignantly.

"How many times has it been broken?" Zofia asked.

"Two, I think," Vic said. "It might've been more."

"And you never got it set?"

"Why bother? It'd just get broken again. I can still smell just fine. I thought you liked it. You said it makes me look tough!"

"That's the point," Zofia said. "That scares some people. I think it's cute."

"Do you get in a lot of fights?" Erica asked.

"Only on duty," Vic said. "And only with guys who want to fight."

"Have you ever killed anyone?"

"Erica!" Webb snapped.

"Why do you want to know?" Vic asked.

"I read an article on police brutality last month," Erica said, meeting his gaze squarely. "I was curious how accurate it was. You seem like a good source."

"How's this for police brutality?" Vic replied. He pulled up the leg of his trousers, revealing a pair of puckered scars on either side of his calf muscle. "See that? It's from a bullet. Seven point six two millimeter, from a Kalashnikov assault rifle. An inch or two in and it would've taken out my shinbone and blown my leg clean off. If you ask Erin nicely, and she's in a good mood, she's got an even better one to show you. It's on the side of her skull. A bad guy shot her in the friggin' head, not knowing she's got the thickest skull on the East Coast. Your dad took a twelve-gauge shell to the back, point-blank. The only reason he doesn't have scars from that is he was wearing his vest, which is also the reason you've still *got* a dad instead of a folded flag from the Commissioner. Have I been in gunfights? Yeah. Have people died in those fights? Yeah. But I've never shot a guy who wasn't shooting back. Does that match what you read in your friggin' magazine?"

Erica took a step back. "Sorry," she said quietly. "I didn't mean—"

"Police brutality," Vic snorted.

"Neshenko, that's enough," Webb said. "Erica, didn't they teach you anything in school about making assumptions?"

"He burned you good," Danielle said to her sister.

They were interrupted by the CSU Lieutenant. "Excuse me," he said. "Lieutenant Webb?"

"Give me good news," Webb said. "Did you run the serial number on that Glock yet?"

"Can I talk to you for a moment?" the evidence tech asked. "Alone?"

"I suppose so," Webb said, perplexed. "Excuse me a moment, please." He followed the CSU guy back toward the crime scene, leaving the others behind.

"What the hell?" Vic said. "That's never happened before."

"Something's wrong," Erin said. "Can't you feel it? Something's really off about this whole thing."

"You're just saying that because your evil twin did it," Vic said.

"For the last time, I don't have an evil twin!"

"So you're saying you're the evil one and your twin is the good one?"

"No! I'm saying this case stinks. There's too many coincidences."

"You think someone did this to make it look like you did it," Zofia said.

"Yeah," Erin said.

"Who?"

Erin shrugged helplessly. "I don't know! But it's all tied up with Kyle Finnegan and the O'Malleys and the Russians."

"Well, we know it wasn't Finnegan," Vic said. "Unless he busted out of jail and got a sex change sometime in the last six or seven hours."

"The Lieutenant's coming back," Zofia said.

"And he looks *pissed*," Vic added.

Webb extended his arms and waved his hands. "Everyone get back!" he ordered. "All the way across the street. *Now!*"

Mystified, they obeyed. Rolf gave Erin a curious look, but she had no explanation to offer him. They gathered on the far sidewalk.

"Dad?" Danielle said. "Are you okay?"

"Did any of you touch anything?" Webb asked. "I want specifics. This is not the time to lie or tell me what you think I want to hear."

"Nope," Vic said. "But what does it matter? We're wearing gloves. This isn't our first crime scene."

"I didn't," Zofia said. "You've been with us since we got here. I don't understand, sir."

"O'Reilly?" Webb asked.

"I checked the woman's pulse," Erin said. "Then Richie—Richard O'Malley, that is—grabbed me and knocked me over. I tripped on the woman's leg and landed in the gravel next to the body. Other than that, no. I didn't touch a thing."

"Good," Webb said. "Now I need all of you to stop talking about the case right now. Don't say another word about it to anyone, for any reason. Don't even discuss it with each other. I need to make a call. We'll have another team coming to take over. Until they arrive, you stay right here on this spot. You don't move, you don't even go to the bathroom without an escort."

"Sir?" Erin said. Confusion was rapidly giving way to alarm. "I'm telling you, I didn't mess with anything."

Webb held up an open evidence bag. "I need you to place your sidearm in this bag," he said. "Now."

"I didn't fire a shot!" she said.

"Good," Webb said. "The gun."

Erin slowly took out the Glock and dropped it into the bag, which Webb immediately sealed.

"Is someone going to explain what the hell is going on?" Vic asked.

"CSU got a match on the serial number of the Glock in the park," Webb said, staring at Erin. "It's yours."

Chapter 8

"That's impossible," Erin said.

"Damn right," Vic said. He pointed to the evidence bag. "That's her gun, right there."

"What's the serial number of your service weapon?" Zofia asked.

Erin had to stop and think for a moment. "DB... seven six three four US," she said.

"We really need to stop talking about this right now," Webb said.

"Why?" Vic wanted to know.

"Because any one of us may be asked to testify about it under oath," Webb said. "Also, civilians are present."

Erica and Danielle were listening intently, eyes wide. "He's talking about us," Erica murmured to her sister.

"We're family," Danielle objected.

"That doesn't matter," Erica said. "When something like this happens, there's cops, there's everybody else, and there's a wall between us. That's what they call the blue wall."

"I have to be here," Webb said to the girls. "Otherwise I'd be taking you somewhere safe myself."

"It's not safe here?" Dani asked. Her eyes went a little wider.

"That's not what I meant," Webb said. "But things are going to get complicated and messy, and I'd rather not put you through it. Nobody wants to see how the sausages are made. Piekarski!"

"Sir?" Zofia replied.

"Here's my keys. Take my car and drive my kids to my apartment. You know the address?"

"Yes, sir."

"Let them in. This is the key to the front door. Their luggage is in the trunk. Then get back here. No stops, no detours, no matter what they say."

"Copy that, sir. Come on, ladies."

As Zofia led the protesting girls away, Webb took out his phone and stepped around the corner to call for reinforcements. Erin and Vic looked at one another. Rolf sat back on his haunches and scratched an ear with his hind leg.

"You didn't do it, right?" Vic said.

"We're not supposed to talk about it," Erin said.

"I know," he said. "But you didn't blow away Dickie-boy's family."

"Of course not!" Erin said angrily.

"I know," he repeated. "You'd never wax a little kid. And if it was you, you'd have wasted Little Richard first."

"First and last," she replied. "I wouldn't have shot his wife and kid at all."

"Exactly. I'm saying this because I know you. But the jackasses who're gonna be prying into this aren't gonna be me. It'll be Internal Affairs, and that means the Cast-Iron Bitch herself."

"She knows me," Erin retorted.

"You think that makes a damn bit of difference? That piece of work would turn herself in if she so much as put one toe over the line. You gotta be careful here, Erin. You better get your story lined up before she gets here."

"I don't have a story!" Erin snapped. "All I have is the truth!"

"Is that gonna be enough?"

"Of course it is! Because I didn't kill anyone!"

"Shut up!" Webb shouted. He'd come back around the corner and he looked about as angry as Erin had ever seen him. "I give you one simple order, just one, and the second I turn my back you're jabbering away like a couple of chatty old ladies. Do you think this is a game? O'Reilly, your service sidearm was just used to commit a multiple murder. Even if someone else pulled the trigger, do you have any idea how much trouble you're in?"

"Yes, sir," Erin said stiffly.

"I doubt it. Because if you did, you'd be paying a little closer attention. I'm trying to help you, damn it! Neshenko, I want you to put at least twenty yards between you and O'Reilly, and keep your big mouth closed. You don't get any closer to her unless I'm present. Start walking."

"Did you just slap me with a restraining order, sir?" Vic asked in disbelief.

"I gave you an order," Webb said. "If you'd like me to slap or restrain you, I'd be happy to oblige. Or you could break the habit of a lifetime and do what you're told."

"Sir! Yes, sir! Right away, sir!"

Vic snapped an exaggerated salute, clicking his heels together like a German officer in some old war movie. Then he walked away. He even managed to make his retreating footsteps sarcastic.

Webb took out a pack of cigarettes, shook one loose, stuck it between his lips, and flicked his lighter. He took a long, slow drag and blew the smoke out his nose.

"What a mess," he sighed.

"Sir," Erin said. "I didn't shoot anyone. I wasn't even here!"

He plucked the cigarette from his mouth and pointed its glowing end at her. "You, too?" he said. "How long have you been a detective?"

Erin opened her mouth.

"Don't answer, it's rhetorical," he said. "And that's my point. You insist on talking, as if that's going to get you off the hook. Put yourself on the other side of the interrogation table, because that's where you're going to be sitting this time around. You've interviewed dozens of suspects. Some of them were guilty, some of them weren't, but every single one of them who didn't ask for their lawyer had one thing in common: they talked too much. You're not under arrest, O'Reilly, not yet, but you still have the right to remain silent and you had damned well better start exercising it. There isn't a thing you can say to me right now that will make things better, and about two hundred that will make things worse. Nod if you understand."

Erin nodded.

"Good." Webb took another drag at his cigarette. "And I thought things were bad back when you had two bodies bleeding out in your living room. I guess those were the good old days. Captain Holliday is on his way down. So is Captain Horner from the Six-Two, and our very own Lieutenant McDowell. I'm going to move you somewhere off the street until they arrive."

"Why?" Erin asked, disregarding Webb's earlier order to shut up.

"Because reporters are going to be here any minute," Webb said. "And we don't want you visible when the cameras show up. Take out your phone. You're going to place exactly one telephone call, to your fiancé, letting him know where you are and that you're okay. I'm going to listen. Then you're going to turn off your phone."

"Are you sure I'm not under arrest, sir?" Erin asked, unable to keep the petulance out of her voice.

"That can be arranged," Webb replied.

Fuming quietly, Erin called up Carlyle's number on her phone.

"Evening, darling," he said.

"Hey there," she said. "I ran into a little problem in Brooklyn, so I'm going to be late getting home."

He caught the wrong note in her voice immediately. When he replied, his own voice was slightly more guarded. It was subtle and not many listeners would have caught the difference, but Erin did.

"Is everything all right, sweetheart?"

He was using their codeword. If she used that term of endearment in reply, it meant she was in danger and couldn't speak freely.

"It's just a misunderstanding," she said, choosing her own words carefully. "But it's sweet of you to ask. You'll hear about it pretty soon if you haven't already. Richard O'Malley had some trouble tonight and I have to help sort it out. I'll call you again once I'm on my way home."

"I understand," he said, and she hoped he did. She'd used only half the codeword, thinking he might take it to mean she was in trouble but not deadly danger.

"I love you," she said.

"And I love you," he answered. "I'll wait up for you, darling."

*   *   *

Nobody knew who had coined Fiona McDowell's nickname. It was unkind, but accurate, and so had stuck to the Internal Affairs Lieutenant for her entire career. Very few cops dared use it in her presence; nobody wanted to piss off the Cast-Iron Bitch.

McDowell brought her whole team with her: four men and two women, unsmiling, clad in dark suits. McDowell herself was wearing her dress blues. The Major Crimes detectives watched them from the lobby of a small brick apartment building across from the park.

"Jesus," Vic muttered. "They look like a damn Secret Service detail."

The Internal Affairs squad fanned out to secure the scene. CSU had rigged floodlights to drive back the encroaching dusk. The evidence guys were still hard at work. Sarah Levine, the Medical Examiner, was making her initial observations of the bodies. Levine completely ignored the IAB suits. The men who drove the Coroner's van, Hank and Ernie, loitered a short distance away.

McDowell made straight for the apartment. Webb nodded to Vic, who grudgingly held the door for her. McDowell's face was cold, grim, and unyielding. She gave the squad a quick once-over and focused her attention on Erin.

"Detective O'Reilly," McDowell said.

"Lieutenant," Erin replied. She stood stiffly, not quite at attention but very far from at ease.

"I've been informed that a semi-automatic pistol registered to you as your service sidearm was used this evening to commit a double homicide. Is that correct?"

"Is this an official inquiry, sir?" Erin asked.

"Yes," McDowell said.

"Then I'd like to assert my right to a Union lawyer at this time," Erin said, hating the way it sounded. She sounded guilty. But she knew it was the right answer, the only answer to give.

"That won't be necessary," McDowell said. "I won't question you further at this time. However, I will expect you to present yourself in the third floor conference room at Precinct Eight at 0900 hours tomorrow morning, regardless of extenuating circumstances. Is that understood?"

"Understood, sir," Erin said.

"In the meantime, you are suspended from duty, effective immediately. Your shield and weapon, Detective."

"Now just a damn minute," Vic growled.

"Neshenko..." Webb said in dangerous tones.

"No, hold on!" Vic said. "Erin's a highly-decorated member of the Department. You can't treat her like some goddamn trigger-happy rookie!"

"Not only can I, it is my sworn duty to do so," McDowell replied calmly.

"It's okay, Vic," Erin said.

"Like hell it's okay!" he retorted. "She didn't even fire a shot!"

"Did you witness the shooting?" McDowell asked.

"I didn't need to," Vic said.

"Thank you, Detective Neshenko, for demonstrating the necessity of an outside investigator," McDowell said. She still didn't sound angry, which only made her scarier. "You are understandably but irretrievably compromised with respect to your partner. Your blind loyalty is personally admirable but has no place in a homicide investigation. Detective O'Reilly, your gun and shield."

"I have the sidearm she was carrying when I encountered her," Webb said, holding up the evidence bag.

"I believe you carry a backup weapon as well," McDowell said.

"It's my personal property, sir," Erin said.

"What is it?"

".38 caliber revolver, snub-nosed."

"May I examine it?" McDowell pulled on a pair of disposable gloves.

Erin knelt and drew the .38 from its ankle clip. She reversed the gun and handed it to McDowell butt-first. McDowell flipped open the cylinder and checked the loads. Then she sniffed the barrel.

"It hasn't been fired recently," Erin said.

McDowell nodded. She emptied the cylinder into her other palm and handed weapon and bullets back to Erin. "You may retain it for the present," she said.

Erin unclipped her gold shield. She tried not to flinch when she handed it over, and almost succeeded.

"You may also retain custody of your K-9," McDowell continued.

Until you pry his leash out of my cold, dead fingers, you bitch, Erin thought. "Thank you," she said.

"And we'll need a swab of your hands," McDowell added.

"What for?"

"GSR."

Erin did wince then. "That won't be necessary," she said.

"It's extremely necessary," McDowell replied.

"And it's bullshit," Vic said. "Because Erin and I were on the firing range earlier today. It'll be on the station security cams, which I know you're gonna check. So if you're looking for gunshot residue on her hands, you're gonna find it, but it doesn't mean a damn thing because it's on mine too!"

"I see," McDowell said. "That's convenient."

"Not from where I'm standing," Erin said bitterly.

"I believe you were suspended on one prior occasion," McDowell said. "So I assume you understand your position?"

"Yes, sir."

"Good. Do not leave the city limits. Remember, 0900 hours tomorrow. Dismissed."

Erin and Rolf walked out of the building. Erin paused at the corner, looking back toward the floodlit crime scene. Levine was there, listening to the whispers of the dead, analyzing the patterns in the blood and bodies. CSU bustled everywhere, labeling, bagging, photographing. Uniformed officers stood on the perimeter, shooing away rubberneckers.

She ought to be there, in the middle of it; collecting clues, talking to witnesses, doing her job. Instead, she was on her way home. That almost hurt worse than handing over her shield.

Rolf was staring up at her with his thoughtful brown eyes, head cocked slightly to one side. He didn't understand and she had no answers to give him.

"Come on, kiddo," she said heavily. "Let's go home."

Chapter 9

"And she threw me out!" Erin said angrily. "Like a teacher sending a naughty kid to the principal's office!"

Carlyle listened to her with the patience of a veteran pub owner. She'd punctuated the story with gulps of Guinness, which cooled her temper a little. A late supper sent up from the Barley Corner's kitchen had also helped a bit, but it wasn't nearly enough.

"She treated me like a suspect!" she finished.

"Are you?" Carlyle asked quietly.

"Everyone knows I didn't do it!"

Carlyle said nothing.

"I'm innocent!" she insisted.

"Is it me you're trying to convince, darling?" he asked. "Because I'm already on your side."

Erin deflated. "No," she sighed. "I just felt so damn helpless! For a second there I thought McDowell was going to slap the cuffs on me, right in front of my squad! You're right. I *am* a suspect."

"How strong is the evidence against you?"

"What difference does that make?"

He reached out and squeezed her hand. "You may find it makes a great deal of difference, darling."

"I'm not going to jail for this!"

"You'll find you're not the first innocent lass in danger of prison," he said gently.

"But it's a setup!" Erin was blustering and she knew it, but she couldn't seem to stop. If she eased up, the fear bubbling under the surface might boil into full panic.

"Aye," he said. "So we'd best be considering how skillful it is, and how we can go about defeating it."

She took a deep, shuddering breath and forced herself to think slowly and carefully. "Okay," she said. "The big piece of evidence is my gun. And it really is mine. The piece I was carrying around has a different serial number."

"How did your pistol end up in the hands of an assassin?"

"I don't know!"

"When did you last check the serial number on your weapon?"

She shrugged. "I don't know. It's not like I'm in the habit. I just assumed the gun in my holster in the morning was the same one that was there the night before."

"I'd stake my life nobody broke into our bedroom overnight," he said. "We've good locks, a strong door, and your fiercely-protective dog, not to mention Ken Mason and his lads during business hours. But surely there's other times your pistol's not on your person."

"Well, yeah," she said. "Sometimes I shower at the Eightball. They say Glocks are waterproof, but I don't take mine into the stall with me. And..."

"What?" Carlyle asked.

"Son of a bitch," she said. "Son of a bitch!"

Rolf perked up his ears at the sudden change in her tone. He sat up and looked at her.

"Riker's Island," she said. "When I went to see Finnegan. I turned in my guns. So did Vic. They gave them back when we left, but I didn't check the numbers. Why would I?"

"It wouldn't be the first time a prison guard was corrupt," Carlyle observed.

"That must be it!" Erin said, feeling energized. Then she sagged again. "Only one problem."

"It's a grand theory, but you can't prove it?"

"Yeah."

"What else will Lieutenant McDowell have against you?"

"There's the eyewitness, the squirrel lady," Erin said. "If they put me in a lineup and she picks me, it's a problem. And she might do that anyway, damn it. She saw my face this evening and associates it with the scene. Even if the shooter didn't look that much like me, she still might put the finger on me in a lineup. And Richie definitely thinks it was me. He tried to strangle me on the spot."

"Two witnesses," Carlyle said thoughtfully. "That's a wee bit of a problem, aye."

"My fingerprints are on the gun," Erin went on. "Of course they are; it's my goddamn gun! And the witness said the getaway car was a black Charger, four-door, just like mine. Then there's the fact that I was only a couple blocks away when Dispatch got the call. I have gunpowder on my hands. And... shit."

"What else?" he asked.

"There's a recording," she said miserably. "Of Finnegan warning me Richie was after my family, and encouraging me to kill him before he killed them."

"Who else knows about that recording?" Carlyle asked.

Erin gave him a sharp look. "What are you suggesting? You want me to destroy evidence?"

"If it's false evidence pointing your lads in the wrong direction, what's the harm?" he replied.

She shook her head. "It wouldn't matter even if I wanted to get rid of it. I already played it for Webb, Vic, and Zofia. It's saved on the Department's database."

"How incriminating is it?"

"With all that other crap?" She spread her hands. "It's the sort of thing that sounds pretty bad to a jury. Put it all together and we've got a nice little package of motive, means, and opportunity. Hell, if I was investigating this, I'd think I was a pretty attractive suspect."

"I'll call Mr. Walsh," Carlyle said, standing up. "It's a bit late, but he'll take my call at any hour."

"Walsh the Mob lawyer?" Erin was appalled. "He's Evan O'Malley's attorney!"

"He's an expert defense attorney with many years' experience," Carlyle countered. "You don't want to be trusting your fate to some time-serving clerk who rides a desk at your precious Union. This is a criminal frame-job, so we're needing a criminal attorney."

"A criminal *attorney* or a *criminal* attorney?" Erin retorted.

"He's never been charged with a crime," Carlyle said with a thin smile. "He's a member in good standing with the New York State Bar Association. And he really is very good. I'll ask him to meet you at your station at quarter of nine tomorrow."

"Goody," Erin muttered. "I can hardly wait. He's expensive, too."

"I've plenty of money," Carlyle reminded her. "And I'm more than willing to spend a bit of it to get my sweet colleen out of trouble."

"I don't think this is a good idea," she said.

"I know your feelings about lawyers," he said. "Particularly ones who defend criminals. But you have to consider your own position."

"I am considering it," she said. "Everyone knows who Walsh is. If I show up with him, I'll look guilty."

"Begging your pardon, darling, but you already look guilty. You've said so."

"Aren't you the one who's always saying the truth doesn't matter as much as the perception? Walsh defends murderers and gangsters. He's going to be representing Evan O'Malley, for God's sake! I'll take my chances with the Union, thanks just the same."

"Erin, I don't want to see you putting yourself in more danger than necessary," he said. "That's why I really think—"

"That's the last word," she interrupted. "The decision's made. No Walsh. Now I'm going to bed. I'm going to need some rest before tomorrow's big interview."

Carlyle, looking at her face, decided not to argue.

*   *   *

Erin would rather have walked into a warehouse full of armed drug dealers than the conference room on the third floor of Precinct 8. At least the pushers didn't wear the same uniform she did.

Her belt felt strangely light as she and Rolf climbed the stairs from the basement garage. She missed the weight of the gun at her hip and, less heavy but more meaningful, the gold shield next to her belt buckle. Without that scrap of metal, she felt oddly naked and helpless.

The climb seemed to take forever. Four flights was a lot, but Ian Thompson had instilled a wariness of elevators she'd never managed to shake, even in a secure police station. The phrase "ready-made killbox" was hard to forget. But nobody was waiting to ambush her at the top of the stairs. The ambush, she thought grimly, would be in the interview room. The only man in the stairwell was the lawyer from the Police Union.

His suit was tasteful, not too expensive. He wore a pair of wire-rimmed glasses and carried a briefcase. He looked to be in his mid-forties. He extended a hand.

"Detective O'Reilly? I'm Emmett Donohue. I'll be representing you in this meeting. So that we're clear, this doesn't obligate either of us with respect to the future. If this matter goes beyond an internal inquiry, and civil or criminal charges are filed, you're at full liberty to retain other representation."

"You sound like a lawyer, all right," Erin said.

Donohue laughed. It sounded natural, not forced. Erin liked the look of him. He was no wet-behind-the-ears rookie, fresh out of law school, but he didn't seem too worn out or cynical either.

"That's why they pay me the big bucks," he said. "Do you have any questions before we go in?"

"Not really," she said.

"Remember, you aren't obligated to answer any questions. This meeting will be recorded and every word of it is admissible as evidence. If you're in any doubt, or if you feel uncomfortable, refer the question to me. It's my job to see that your rights are fully respected, and that you receive every protection afforded you by the law."

Erin squirmed internally. This felt way too much like being a defendant. "Copy that," she said.

"Your Captain's in there," Donohue continued. "You're a police officer and you're used to your commander having your back. But don't assume he'll have it today. The one person guaranteed to have your best interests at heart is you. I'll do what I can for you, but I can't protect you if you don't let me. Are we clear?"

"Yes," she said. "Let's do this."

Lieutenant McDowell sat on one side of the conference table with a notepad and a recording microphone in front of her. Captain Holliday was at the far end, entrenched behind his mustache. Both officers stood up when Erin, Donohue, and Rolf entered.

"Thank you for coming, Detective," McDowell said, giving brisk handshakes to her and Donohue. "Do you have anything to say before we begin?"

"No, sir," Erin said.

"Would you like some coffee or a glass of water?"

"Water would be nice," Erin said.

Holliday was closest to the water cooler in the corner. He filled a paper Dixie cup and handed it to her. His eyes were unreadable above his mustache, but his head moved in a fractional nod of acknowledgment.

"Then let's get started," McDowell said, gesturing Erin to the spot opposite herself. Donohue took a seat next to Erin. Rolf settled on the other side, but didn't lie down. The Shepherd could feel the tension in the room. He sat bolt upright, watching Erin carefully in case she told him to bite the lady across the table. McDowell pushed a button on her recorder.

"Voluntary interview with Detective First Grade Erin O'Reilly," she said. "First interview subsequent to homicides of Kimberly O'Malley and Richard O'Malley, Junior, Wednesday, August Seventeenth. The time is 0900 hours on Thursday, August Eighteenth. In attendance are Captain Fenton Holliday, Precinct Eight commanding officer; Lieutenant Fiona McDowell, Precinct Eight Internal Affairs; and Emmett Donohue, attorney representing Ms. O'Reilly through the Police Union."

She didn't mention Rolf, Erin thought. But then, it wasn't like Rolf would be saying anything.

"Detective O'Reilly, what is your relationship with Richard O'Malley, Senior?"

"I have none," Erin said.

"What contact have you had with Mr. O'Malley in the past six months?"

"He showed up at my engagement party at the Barley Corner uninvited earlier this year," she said. "He also approached me, along with several other NYPD officers, at a bar called the Final Countdown about two months ago."

"What was the nature of your meetings?"

"Richard was upset," Erin said. "He made veiled threats and was disruptive. He was asked to leave on both occasions and did so, without violence."

"Why did he threaten you?"

"He holds me personally responsible for his father's arrest and the loss of his family's fortune."

"Did you feel threatened by Mr. O'Malley?"

Erin almost said "no." Then she almost said "yes." She glanced at Donohue, feeling herself hesitate, knowing McDowell was noticing and cataloguing it.

"I'm an active-duty police officer," she finally said. "I get insulted and threatened on a near-daily basis by lots of guys. Many of them are more physically dangerous than Richard O'Malley. I knew he was angry at me, but I didn't find his threats particularly convincing."

"You narrowly escaped injury or death in a hit-and-run automobile accident two months ago," McDowell said. "According to your report, an unknown man, who may or may not have been Mr. O'Malley, attempted to run you down with a stolen sedan. A short while later, you were attacked and wounded by a professional criminal, John McGraw, alias Black

Jack McGraw. Your K-9 killed this man, which prevented him from testifying whether he was acting on his own behalf or under orders from another party."

McDowell hadn't asked a question, so Erin saw no need to reply.

"Who do you believe was behind these attacks?" McDowell asked.

"I have no conclusive evidence," Erin said stonily.

"I didn't ask for conclusive evidence," McDowell said. "I asked your opinion."

"I have no opinion, sir," Erin said, thinking of what Ian Thompson would have said in this situation.

"I see," McDowell said. "Why did you visit Kyle Finnegan at Riker's Island yesterday morning?"

"Mr. Finnegan had been stabbed in the throat," Erin said. "He had requested a meeting. I thought he might have valuable information to impart, and had been stabbed to stop him talking. I had refused a previous request, but after the stabbing I thought it would be a good idea to see what he had to say."

"What did he say?"

"I recorded the entire conversation. I'm sure you have access to this recording."

"I do," McDowell said. "In it, Mr. Finnegan tells you that Mr. O'Malley is a threat to you and your family and advises you to preemptively kill Mr. O'Malley. What is your relationship with Mr. Finnegan?"

"He's an enemy, sir," Erin said promptly. "I neither like nor trust him, and would be very suspicious of any advice I received from him."

"What were you doing in Brooklyn last night?"

That was one question Erin didn't want to answer, and she very nearly didn't. But she thought again about perception. Refusing to answer was just as suspicious as the truth.

"I was checking into Richard," she said, meeting McDowell's eye. "I wanted to follow up on the tip from Finnegan and see if he was up to anything."

"Were you aware that Mr. O'Malley was already under surveillance by the NYPD's Narcotics squad?"

"Yes, sir."

"Were you ordered not to interfere with that investigation?"

Erin's eyes flicked toward Holliday, who had indeed given her that order. "Yes, sir."

"But you still felt it necessary to mount a private investigation?"

"Yes, sir."

"Why?"

"Because I felt the Narcotics Squad wasn't paying enough attention to Richard," Erin said. "They didn't consider him an important player in Gennady Vlasov's organization. I think what happened proves I was right."

"How so?" McDowell asked.

"If he'd been under tight surveillance, a Narcotics unit would have witnessed the shooting, wouldn't they?"

The ends of Holliday's mustache twitched, usually a sign he was smiling behind it. McDowell gave no reaction whatsoever.

"Yesterday evening, your sidearm was recovered from the scene of the shooting," she said. "Why did you not report it missing?"

"I didn't know it was," Erin said. "I believe my Glock was switched with the one I gave to Lieutenant Webb last night."

"Deliberately or accidentally?"

That's a stupid question, Erin thought. *It's part of the setup; of course it was deliberate!* "I have no way of knowing that," she said.

"Do you know where the alleged switch took place?"

"Not definitively," Erin said. "I suspect it happened at Riker's Island, when I turned in my guns at the start of my visit yesterday."

"Are you in the habit of blindly accepting weapons?" McDowell asked.

"I verified the weapon I was given was loaded and functional," Erin retorted. "I practiced with it on the range the same day."

"But you didn't confirm it was the same gun you had turned in?" McDowell pressed.

"I'd like to ask Captain Holliday a question," Erin said.

A flicker of surprise flashed across McDowell's eyes. "All right," she said.

"Captain, what sidearm do you carry?"

"Smith and Wesson .38 revolver," Holliday said. "Just like my father before me."

"Where's the serial number on your gun?"

"It's engraved on the metal tang on the butt," Holliday said.

"When's the last time you looked at it?"

Holliday's mustache shifted in a thoughtful frown. "The last time I polished it, I suppose," he said. "That would be... Saturday before last."

"So you can't confirm that's your gun?" Erin asked.

"My .38 has a wooden grip," Holliday said. "I've carried it my whole career, so it's pretty well-worn. I know the feel of it. If it had been switched out, I'd know. But—"

"Does that answer your question?" McDowell interjected.

"Please don't interrupt an answer to a legitimate question, Lieutenant," Donohue said. "I'm interested in what Captain Holliday was about to say."

"Proceed," McDowell said, her expression unchanged.

"A Glock doesn't have a wooden grip," Holliday continued. "Its frame is molded polymer. Detective O'Reilly's is identical to thousands of others. It would feel exactly the same in her hand as any of its fellows. She is correct. She'd have no reason to check the serial number on her sidearm after leaving it in the care of a qualified Corrections Officer. If I had been in the same position as her, I would have behaved identically."

"Thank you, sir," Erin said. "That's what I wanted to know."

"Are you accusing another officer of complicity in this homicide?" McDowell asked.

"I don't have enough evidence to make an accusation," Erin said. "It could have been an accident. Or I could be mistaken about—"

"She's answered your question," Donohue cut in. "Detective O'Reilly is making no accusations at this time. She is declining to speculate."

Erin shut her mouth. She decided she liked lawyers a little better than she'd thought. Donohue was right to have cut her off. She was talking too damned much.

"Understood," McDowell said. "Why did Richard O'Malley attack you at the park?"

Because he thinks I killed his wife and kid, Erin thought. But she stopped herself. That was speculation, and as Donohue had just said, this was no place for it. "He has previously expressed his hatred for me," she said. "He was emotionally distraught due to witnessing the deaths of his family and receiving a wound to his own arm. He said, quote, 'I'll fucking kill you!' and tried to choke me. I didn't draw my weapon or otherwise threaten him. My K-9 subdued him with a non-lethal bite to the arm, as Rolf's trained to do when I'm attacked."

"Did he identify you as the person who had just shot his family?" McDowell asked.

"Not in so many words," Erin said. "If I'd been trying to kill him, why wouldn't I take that opportunity to put him down? He was lunging at me. That's a legitimate self-defense situation for a police officer. I could have legally shot him."

"I'm declining to speculate," McDowell said. "Do you have anything else to add to your testimony?"

"Who's in charge of the investigation?" Erin asked.

"I am," McDowell replied. "I am liaising with Captain Horner in the Six-Two, since the homicides occurred in his Area of Service. His Homicide unit is providing assistance."

"What is my current status?"

"You are on suspension, without pay," McDowell said. "This is a disciplinary action resulting from loss of your registered sidearm. At the current time, you are not being charged with any further infractions. However, you are a person of interest in a multiple homicide. You are expressly forbidden from leaving New York City without permission from my office. You are not to speak with any representative of the media regarding this case, or any other ongoing investigation. You are not to have any contact whatsoever with Richard O'Malley or any member of his family. You are not to discuss any aspect of this case in any online forum, nor with any investigating officer unless that officer initiates contact. These guidelines are not to be broken, upon penalty of immediate termination from the Department, confiscation of all Department-issued equipment including your K-9, and possible criminal charges. Have I made myself clear?"

Erin's jaw was so tight she could hear the squeak of her molars as her teeth gritted. "Crystal clear, sir," she grated out.

"Thank you for your cooperation, Detective O'Reilly," McDowell said. "This concludes our interview." She turned off the recorder and stood up, offering her hand.

Accepting McDowell's cool, firm handshake without wrenching the woman's arm out of its socket was one of the hardest things Erin had ever made herself do.

Chapter 10

Donohue led the way to the elevator. Erin was too distracted to notice or protest. He pushed the button for the basement and the doors slid shut. Then he smiled at her.

"That went well," he said.

"Really," Erin said flatly. "How do you figure?"

"You didn't lose your temper," he said. "You gave calm, reasonable answers. I only had to step in a couple of times. You presented yourself as innocent."

"Yeah," she said. "Maybe because I *am* innocent. How, exactly, could that have gone worse?"

"You could be leaving this station for good," he said. "Possibly in handcuffs, prison-bound."

"That wasn't on the cards," she said.

"Are you sure of that?" he replied. "Because McDowell's done it before. There's something you need to understand, Ms. O'Reilly. You are not untouchable. I've seen officers lose their pensions over less, and with less evidence. You do know Mr. O'Malley identified you as the shooter, don't you?"

"Of course he did," she growled. "And the DA knows the history between his family and me. Nobody's going to take his word for it."

The elevator slid to a halt on the garage level of the basement. Donohue stepped in front of the door and planted a foot to hold it open.

"If his word was the only one, I'd agree with you," he said. "But there's more than one eyewitness. This looks pretty bad, Ms. O'Reilly."

"Do you think I'm guilty?" she challenged.

"It doesn't matter what I think," he said. "I'm a professional. I'd defend a guilty client just as vigorously as an innocent one."

"How do you live with yourself?" she asked.

"How do you go twelve years as a cop without a better understanding of the legal system?" he countered. "I can't believe a veteran like you is this naïve. Do you really think the system is perfect? That it only funnels guilty people to prison? A defense attorney's job is important. Lawyers protect everyone's rights, guilty and innocent. If we make the distinction before the trial, there's no way of getting a fair trial. Then I'm just a vigilante in a nice suit. The law assumes you're innocent until proven guilty. But I guarantee there's plenty of people out there who will assume no such thing. Lieutenant McDowell is fair, but she's also relentless. Do you know how many cops she's thrown off the Force?"

"Too many," Erin muttered.

"Sixty-five. You should be counting your lucky stars that she isn't convinced of your guilt yet."

"How do you know?"

"This isn't the first time I've tangled with her. If she was sure you were guilty, you'd already be fired, arrested, and charged. She isn't your friend, but she also isn't your enemy. It's best to think of her like a blizzard, or maybe a tornado. A force of nature. She doesn't hate you, but it's better not to be in her way."

"What's your advice?" she asked. "As my lawyer?"

"Keep your head down," Donohue said. "Do as you're told. Be as honest as you can. And let things play out. You have a good chance of getting through this okay."

"Define a good chance. Give me odds."

He considered. "At the moment? Sixty-forty odds you won't be fired or charged with any crimes."

"Those are shitty odds," she said.

"They could be a lot worse," he replied.

*   *   *

"Freeze, lady."

The rough, brutal male voice came from behind Erin as she and Rolf stepped into the parking garage. Adrenaline poured into her system in a full fight-or-flight reaction. Rolf barked sharply and raised his hackles.

Vic stepped around a concrete support column and guffawed. "You should've seen your face," he said.

"You should know better," Erin said, waiting for her heartbeat to steady. "Keep doing that and you're liable to get shot."

"With what?" he retorted. "Those bastards took your gun away."

"They left me my backup piece, dumbass," she said.

"You would've known it was me before you had time to fish that little squirt gun out of your pants," he said, falling in step beside her.

"You'd know all about hiding a little squirt gun in your pants," she said.

Vic snorted. "Good one."

"It's not funny, Vic. A guy tried to murder me in a parking garage a couple months ago, remember?"

"Oh, yeah," he said, the smile slipping off his face. "Sorry. I didn't think."

"Do you ever?"

He chose not to answer that. "So how'd it go with the Wicked Witch of the Third Floor?" he asked.

"I'm not supposed to talk about it," she said.

"Not even with me?"

"Not with anybody, I think. If I talk to the media, I get fired."

"Who'd want to talk to those sons of bitches anyway?" he said. "That's why I'm being clandestine, meeting you in the basement. Just like Deep Throat in that Redford movie. Except I'm not taking a nickname from a porn star."

"That movie's based on a true story. That was a real guy."

"Yeah, I know. That's the guy who brought down Nixon, back when people cared if a politician was a liar and a crook. So I guess if they only threatened to fire you, that means you still have a job?"

"For the moment," she said. "But I'm still on suspension and under suspicion."

"Sheesh," he growled. "Okay, I'm in."

"In what?"

"Whatever you're doing, I'm in. How do you want to play this?"

Erin shook her head. "Vic, this is a big deal. I'm the prime suspect in a double homicide. What do you think I'm going to do? Conduct some bullshit private investigation under the table to clear my name?"

"Well... yeah." His grin was back. "Of course you are. Remember when Zofia's teammate Janovich got shot? That's exactly what we did then."

"That's true," she admitted. "But—"

"And then again when that bastard Keane killed Kira," he went on.

"Yeah, but—"

"Not to mention *faking a murder* to trick the NYPD and the Mafia. Jesus Christ, Erin, don't you go taking the high road now. We gotta save you!"

"That's sweet of you, Vic," she said. "Really. But this is dangerous."

"More dangerous than swapping bullets with crooked cops and gangsters, and building bombs?"

"It's a different kind of dangerous. McDowell's something else, Vic. She'll nail me if she thinks I've stepped out of line, and if she even suspects you're involved, it'll be your ass, too."

"She's gonna nail you anyway," he replied. "What've you got to lose?"

"We're talking about you, not me. You need this job. You have a kid, for God's sake! Think about Mina!"

"I am," he said. He was no longer smiling. "Maybe you'll get this once you have one of your own. When Mina looks at me, I feel like she sees the best guy in the whole world. And I gotta live up to that, you know? I gotta do my best to be the man she thinks I am, and that means I gotta do the right thing. So don't you dare lecture me about doing right by my little girl."

"Okay, okay," Erin said. "Sorry."

"Forget about it. So what's the plan?"

"I don't have a plan! I just got suspended, remember? The only reason I was in the building was so Internal Affairs could ream me out. I haven't figured my next move."

He nodded. "The way I figure it is, first we want to suss out who'd want to kill Richie and his family."

"No," she said. "They didn't want to kill Richie. He only got tagged because he got in the way. His wife and son were the targets."

"Unless the shooter screwed up," Vic said. "You and I know it's not as easy to kill someone with a handgun as they make it look in the movies. Maybe it was a botched hit."

Erin shook her head. "I don't think so. This was set up by professionals. If Richie was a target, he was a target for a message they were sending."

"Gotcha," Vic said. "You think maybe it's his new business associates? The Russians?"

"Or his competitors," she said. "It's worth looking into. But this isn't your case, Vic."

"You think I give a crap? I know some stuff about the Russian Mob. I think I should check into Gennady Vlasov and his bunch of goons. I can't do it on the clock, but after work I can drive down to Little Odessa and poke around."

"That's a good idea," Erin said. "And find out who else is trying to muscle in on the fentanyl trade. But what I can't figure is why they'd want me to take the fall for it."

"The only thing I can think of is that they're trying for two birds with one stone," he said. "Hurt the O'Malley brat and take you out of the picture. Who do you know who wants you gone?"

"Take your pick," she said. "I know Kyle Finnegan's involved somehow. I'm still trying to figure out why he tried to warn me. I think he knows something more, but they won't let me into Riker's to talk to him. Not while I'm on suspension. And there's the crooked Riker's guard to think about."

"Yeah," Vic said. "Did you catch his name?"

"I never asked. But it shouldn't be too hard to find out who was working the checkpoint."

"I'll see what I can dig up," he said. "Do you think IAB has your phone tapped?"

That was an unpleasant thought. Erin swallowed. "I don't think so," she said. "But they might. Jesus, maybe that's why McDowell didn't arrest me. She wants to see where I'll go and what I'll do. She thinks I'll lead her to the other conspirators, whoever the hell they are. Shit, they're probably watching us right now!"

"Relax, Erin," he said. "IAB aren't a bunch of superspy James Bond assholes. Sheesh, calm down. Didn't you just do all that undercover bullshit? You've got this. Just keep your eyes open. But you're right, we can't trust your phone. You can get a burner, right?"

"Of course," she said. "Carlyle probably has a couple, just in case."

"Good. I'll pick one up, too. Tell you what; I'll drop by the Corner around midnight tonight. Then we can exchange numbers and figure out what to do next."

"Copy that," Erin said. "Vic?"

"What?"

"Thanks."

"For what?" He seemed genuinely confused.

"For having my back. And believing me."

"Forget about it," he said. "See you tonight. Just try not to get in any gunfights before then."

"You're the one who's going to be poking around a bunch of Russian Mafia. Be careful."

"Don't worry about me," he said. "Worry about them."

*   *   *

The Barley Corner did a brisk brunch trade, so the pub was bustling when Erin and Rolf arrived a little before ten. Erin scanned the room and was pleasantly surprised to see what she'd been hoping for: a shock of flaming red hair in the middle of a crowd under the big-screen television. She slipped across the room and into the circle of people in time to hear the punchline of a story.

"...So I said to the lad, I don't know what you're planning," James Corcoran was saying. "But you've only the one bullet in that revolver, you're standing in a pool of petrol, and I'm holding a cigarette lighter. If you pull that trigger, you'd best make certain that last round puts me down, or you'll be lit up like it's Guy Fawkes Day."

Some of the listeners laughed. Others looked confused. "Like which day?" someone asked.

"It's like the Fourth of July, but in England," someone else explained.

"And Occupied Ireland," Corky added.

"What's he talking about?" a third person asked.

Erin saved Corky having to explain the history of Ireland and the Troubles by drawing him away from his audience. He gave them a smile and a wave, leaving with a promise to come back and "sort the whole tangle out for you" on a later date.

"New friends?" she asked, maneuvering him into a quieter corner.

"There's only four types of folk in this world," he replied, winking. "Friends, lovers, mortal enemies, and those I've yet to meet. How's about you, love?"

"Out of those options, I guess I'm your friend," she said, smiling in spite of herself. Even in her dark mood, Corky's good spirits were infectious.

"I'm glad you stopped in," he said. "I've a question for you."

"Oh?"

"How much clothing, precisely, must a lass keep on for her to be a dancing performer instead of a stripper? Would a wee pair of pasties and a thong be sufficient, or is something more required?"

Erin's smile turned into a grimace. "Corky, for the last time, we are not having strippers at Carlyle's bachelor party."

"But that's just my point," he said. "What's your definition?"

"It's like pornography," she retorted. "I'll know it if I see it. And if I see it, you'll be sorry."

"If you see it, you've an even stranger definition of a stag party than you do of a stripper," he shot back. "Very well, have it your way. But if his stag party falls flat, you'll have to work all the harder on your wedding night to cheer him up."

"What we do on our wedding night is none of your damn business," she said.

"Cars tells me you're in a wee spot of trouble," he said, recognizing a change of subject was called for. "Something I can do for you?"

"I don't know," she said. "Who do you know at Riker's Island?"

"A great many folk, thanks to you," he replied.

"I meant the guards."

"Ah. Not so many of those. What is it you're needing?"

"Two things. First, someone set me up."

Corky was still smiling, but his eyes had gone serious. "What did they do?" he asked.

"A guard swapped out my gun for another one," she explained. "Then he passed my piece on to the woman who shot Richie O'Malley and his family."

"Which guard?"

"I don't know the name, but it's the one who was handling the weapons check-in yesterday at nine in the morning."

"Your lot should be able to find him," Corky said.

"They won't be able to prove anything," she said grimly.

"How do you know?"

"Because this is a professional frame-up. I need to know who got to this guy and how. Is he just on the take, or was he blackmailed, or what?"

"And the other thing?"

"An inmate named Barsov."

"What about him?"

"He stabbed Finnegan in the neck."

A mischievous sparkle kindled in Corky's eyes. "Grand! He's done us a favor, then."

"Maybe," Erin said. "Except Finnegan's still alive. I need to know what Barsov's deal is. The problem is, I can't do it officially. I'm on suspension."

Corky nodded thoughtfully. "You need someone on the inside," he said. "A lad who knows the ins and outs of the prison, particularly the trade in favors and black-market items."

"Yeah," she said.

"And you thought I'd know such a lad? Why?"

"Because you're Corky Corcoran."

His smile widened. "Of course I am, love," he said. "Wayne McClernand's the lad you want."

"Wayne the truck driver?" Erin felt her eyebrows try to climb clean off her forehead. "Is he going to be willing to talk to me?"

"Why wouldn't he?"

"Oh, I don't know. Maybe because I'm the reason he's warming a cell right now instead of driving his rig down the highway?"

Corky waved a hand dismissively. "That's all water under the bridge," he said. "Wayne's always liked you. More to the point, he's a good lad. If you hurry, you can make visiting hours."

"I can't just flash my shield at Riker's," she said. "Didn't you hear me? I'm on suspension."

He shrugged. "You're visiting an inmate," he said. "There's nothing official about that. Anyone can do it. Anyone without outstanding warrants, that is."

"He won't be expecting me," she said.

"Of course he will. A bit of faith will take you far in this world, love. Well, that and taking care to know a few of the right people."

"Thanks, Corky," she said. "I owe you one."

"Then perhaps we could revisit the matter of my best mate's stag party?"

"No strippers, Corky."

Chapter 11

Erin left Rolf at the Corner, to the dog's deep disgust. Not wanting to use her official vehicle, she borrowed Carlyle's Mercedes. For most people it would have been a step up, but she missed the Charger's deep, muscular rumble. The Mercedes was a little too smooth, a little too fancy for her blue-collar Queens taste. But she couldn't deny it gave a nice ride.

She found herself thinking, as she rolled across the bridge that would take her to the prison, that this might be the shape of her future. Even if she beat a murder rap, if she was arrested and formally charged it would mean the end of her career. No more gold shield, no more sidearm, no more NYPD-issued car—and no more Rolf.

The Shepherd was nearing the end of his career in any case. He was only seven, and K-9s often worked until they turned nine or ten, but he had a lot of mileage. He'd been shot more than once, Tased, lit on fire, concussed, broken ribs, and suffered any number of lesser injuries. He'd never admit it, but his working days were running out fast. Erin quietly dreaded the day she'd see him, game as ever, trying to haul his unresponsive body out to the car to go to work one time too many.

But to have him taken away from her would be more than she could bear. Maybe, if she got fired, Webb could talk them into retiring Rolf and giving or selling him to her. That was always assuming she wasn't spending her own enforced retirement as a guest of the state in a women's penitentiary, trying not to get shivved in the showers.

It was funny, she mused. Her entire future was at stake, maybe her life, and what she was most concerned with was what would happen to her dog.

"Damn it," she muttered. "Damn it, damn it, *damn it!*"

What the hell was she doing? Wasting time going to see an inmate who, if she was lucky, wouldn't want to bash her head in for getting him busted. She wished she had Corky's optimism. Maybe she'd been too hard on him about the bachelor party.

"Carlyle doesn't even like strippers," she said, falling into the habit of talking to Rolf, even though he wasn't there. "He's got class. I'm all the woman he wants."

Corky knew that, of course. He was just messing with her. Why was everybody yanking her around? Corky, Finnegan... even Vic did it, and Vic *liked* her. So did Corky, come to that. But cops got tired of people screwing with them. It was nice to get a straight answer every now and then, just for the sake of variety.

"The bachelor party is just going to end up being a bunch of guys getting drunk in a pub," she said. "Singing Irish drinking songs and talking about the old country. Then the groomsmen are going to show up to the wedding hung over and smelling like beer. It'll be just a typical weekend for the boys."

Maybe she should have brought Wayne a case of Guinness. Now *that* would put him in a good mood. Not that they'd ever let her give something like that to an inmate. Maybe she could smuggle it in. Corky probably knew a guy.

"Corky *definitely* knows a guy," she decided. "Jesus. Now I'm encouraging criminals. What's the matter with me?"

Rolf wouldn't have had an answer even if he'd been there. As far as Rolf was concerned, his partner could do no wrong.

*   *   *

It was weird checking into the Riker's Island visiting area like a private citizen. She'd left her snub-nosed .38 in the car, under the seat, so she didn't have any weapon to hand in. The guy behind the bulletproof glass wasn't the same one she'd given her Glock to, but she was taking no chances this time. She signed a form that said she'd read and understood the rules of conduct. She wasn't to give him anything, wasn't to provide any sexual favors, and wasn't to plan or encourage criminal activity. Then the guard buzzed her through into the visiting area.

It was a sterile concrete-block room, chopped up into booths by concrete and Plexiglass dividers. She sat down on an uncomfortable chair and waited. On her left was a stringy-haired, tired-looking woman who was obviously struggling with a meth habit. On her right sat a skinny, dark-skinned young man who kept fidgeting.

A gaunt, graying guy came in and sat opposite the kid. He smiled, which made the kid burst into unexpected tears. Erin guessed they must be father and son. She looked away, embarrassed at intruding on their private moment.

The door on the other side of the Plexiglass opened again and Wayne McClernand squeezed through. Wayne was a big guy, big-boned and big-bellied. He had a surprisingly pleasant smile and gentle manner given his record and his tattoos, but Erin recalled that the last time she'd seen him he'd been fighting off three NYPD officers with his hands literally cuffed behind his back—and *winning*. She had no idea what to expect from him.

He managed somehow to fit his bulk into the chair facing her. He nodded politely and touched his fingers to his forehead in a gentlemanly way. Then he picked up the phone receiver next to him. Erin did the same with her own.

"Good morning, Wayne," she said.

"Morning, ma'am," he said. "Nice of you to come see me."

"Forget about it," she said. "How'd you know I was coming?"

Wayne winked and smiled, showing a couple of missing teeth. "Word gets around," he said. "Could be I know a guy who's got something he shouldn't technically have."

Translation: black-market cell phone, Erin thought. "Thanks for meeting me," she said.

"Of course," he said. "I owe you."

Erin knew the surprise was showing on her face. "You're not mad at me?" she managed to say through her confusion.

"Mad? Why'd I be mad?"

"Well... I mean, I'm out here and you're in there," she faltered. "I thought you'd be pissed about the whole O'Malley thing."

"Oh, that," Wayne said, as if a RICO indictment naming almost two hundred people was some sort of afterthought. "That ain't nothing. When it rains, everyone gets wet. You were just doing your job. I never blamed you for that. It's the game, isn't it?"

"Yeah," she said, fighting a whiplash feeling of guilt. "I guess so." It would have been easier if he'd been angry.

"Nah," Wayne said. "I always knew you were a cop, and I figured you were a good one, so it's not like you were pretending or nothing. No, I'm talking about the Beast."

"Your truck?" Erin said. The Beast had been Wayne's pride and joy, a massive semi tractor. The way he talked about it was similar to the way Erin thought about Rolf; more partner than possession.

"Yeah," he said. "See, the way I figure it is, you could've done me for that thing on the highway. Remember when I gave you and that other cop that lift to Connecticut? I was carrying... I mean, I *might've* been carrying some stuff over the line without paying taxes on it. Which would've been smuggling. Technically. And if that had been in my indictment, since it was across state lines, it would've been Federal and I'd be looking at Fed time along with the State time I'm gonna do. And the Beast would've been used in this crime—in this *alleged* crime, you understand—which means the goddamn FBI would've taken her. But this way I know she'll be waiting for me when I get out in a couple years. She'll be good as new. Corky's got a guy taking good care of her."

Erin realized she was wrong. Wayne didn't think of the Beast as a partner. She was more like a girlfriend or lover.

"Glad to help with that," she said, feeling another stab of guilt. She hadn't thought about Wayne's truck. But Corky apparently had it handled. Somehow, in the course of an utterly insane series of events that had left Corky himself in a hospital bed, the little Irishman had spared enough attention to take care of a friend's beloved truck. No wonder Corky had friends everywhere.

"So what can I do for you?" Wayne asked. "Sorry I can't do anything outside. My lawyer tells me I'll probably do about thirty months, best case. But that ain't so bad. It'll be medium-security, since it's all non-violent crap, and if I plead out I can do my time in a pretty good joint."

"Corky tells me you know how stuff gets in and out of here," she said.

Wayne nodded, but his smile faded a little. "Yeah, I might know some guys," he said. "But I ain't no rat, Miss O'Reilly. You know that. I ain't gonna squeal on my buddies."

"Of course not," she said. "I'm talking about a guard."

His grin resurfaced. "Oh, that's different," he said. "Which one?"

"It's a guy who handles the weapons desk," she said quietly. "I think he's involved with smuggling guns."

"There's no guns in here," Wayne said, sounding shocked. "There ain't nobody crooked enough to sneak a piece in."

"That's not what I mean," she said. "I just need to know if he's on the take, and to whom. The weapons stuff is happening on the outside. He got his hands on my sidearm and slipped it to someone else."

"That's a lot of trouble to go to for a handgun," Wayne said. "Jeez, there's pistols *everywhere*. This is America, you know?"

"Can you find out about him?" Erin asked.

"I can check around," he said. "But I can't make promises. You gotta be careful, asking questions in a place like this. I don't want to get in any trouble I don't have to. I'd rather do my time quiet and get out early for good behavior."

"I understand," she said. "One more thing: Barsov."

"I know who he is," Wayne said. "That's the guy who stuck Finnegan night before last. What about him?"

"I need to know what his deal is. Was it a private beef, or did he have orders? Is he Russian Mafia or what?"

"Those Russians aren't anyone you want to mess with," Wayne said.

Erin nodded. "I understand. If you don't want to get involved, I get it."

"I ain't scared of them," he said. "But maybe I oughta be. Those guys are *crazy*. Why's this so important, anyway?"

She quickly considered what to tell him and surprised herself with the truth. "I'm being set up," she said. "For murder. And I didn't do it. Barsov might be involved, and so is this guard. I don't want you getting in trouble. More trouble, I mean. And I don't want you getting hurt. I can't offer you anything right now, but—"

He nodded. "Okay," he said. "I'll find out everything I can about the Russkies. I'll find the right guys and lean on them."

"Thanks, Wayne," she said, meaning it. "You're a better friend than I think I deserve."

"Hey, forget about it," he said. "Maybe you can pay me back one of these days. At least you can drop in now and then to say hi. It gets pretty dull in here."

"I'll do that," she promised. "When I can."

*   *   *

It would have been good police work to follow up with Finnegan, as long as Erin was at Riker's, but she didn't. She couldn't. The mad Irishman could probably have shed some light on what had happened to Richard's family, assuming she could sort out the useful information from his sly hints and asinine quotations, but she was under explicit instructions not to investigate the O'Malleys. If she asked to see Finnegan, it would be recorded in the prison's visitor log, where McDowell would certainly see it. Then, best-case, she'd be looking at witness tampering and obstruction of justice. Obstruction cases were almost impossible to prosecute; cops threatened them a lot, but practically never followed through. But in this case she had a feeling McDowell might make an exception. Erin further felt the exception might take the form of getting her thrown off the Force at minimum.

So she took her leave of Wayne McClernand and put the prison in her rearview. That left her with the problem of what to do next. She considered it while she drove across the bridge over the East River.

The obvious thing was to look into the Russian Mob connection, but she'd already talked to Vic about that, and he wouldn't be available until the end of his shift. She should probably stay away from him anyway, in case McDowell had eyes on him.

"Shit," she said. "I'm thinking like a goddamn perp! I'm innocent, damn it!"

But nobody, not even Rolf, was there to agree with her.

"Follow the evidence," she muttered. "What've we got that *doesn't* point to me?"

It was a depressingly short list. She tapped the steering wheel as she reeled the items off.

"The gun," she said. "The Glock I was carrying is different, probably stolen. Why would I use my service weapon when I had access to a completely different gun? It's circumstantial, but I guess that'll help my defense. A little. Where'd the second gun come from? Can we trace it through the guard at Riker's?"

The Internal Affairs detectives would be trying to do just that. McDowell was a bitch, but a competent one. She'd want to know all about Erin's other gun.

"My alibi," she went on. "I wasn't at the park when they were shot. But I was pretty close by. I was one of the first couple of responding officers. But that was luck for the bad guys. They couldn't know I'd be there."

She paused. She'd just made an assumption, and in police work, assumptions could be dangerous. "Of course they could," she said, snapping her fingers. "All they'd need would be a trace on my phone. Or somebody tailing me. Damn it, I *thought* that guy was following me! I shook him off, but so what? He'd know I was close by, and that's all they'd need!"

Her mind reeled. If that was true, it meant this had been a very well-coordinated hit. The perps had been watching her and waiting for their moment; for a time she'd been alone, near

Richard's family, when the O'Malley kid had been exposed and vulnerable. The assassin had been lying in wait for God only knew how long. And she'd handed them the opportunity on a goddamn platter.

She checked her mirrors. She didn't think she was being followed now, but how could she be sure? Even the ubiquitous yellow taxis in New York seemed sinister. The bad guys had been ahead of her every step of the way. They'd known she'd visit Finnegan. Maybe the stabbing had been designed to get her to do just that.

"Of course it was," she said. "That's how they got my gun. Barsov has to be in on it. Maybe Wayne can get something on him. But Barsov's Russian Mafia and those bastards are tough. It's not like he'll just spill his guts. Wayne's a good guy, but he's just a big dude who drives a truck. He's not a detective and he's not an undercover cop. Jesus, maybe he'll get stabbed next."

She hoped not. She was already feeling guilty about Wayne.

Erin was starting to realize the implications of what was happening. She was being attacked by a conspiracy: organized, methodical, and deadly. And the very worst of it was, she was dancing to their tune. That meant whoever was behind it knew her very well, and was at least as smart as she was.

"Probably smarter," she said under her breath.

Chapter 12

The buzz of a phone startled her out of her thoughts, just as she reached the far end of the bridge in Queens. Contrary to what Webb had told her, she'd turned her phone back on. She just had to be careful what she said on the line, in case unfriendly ears were listening.

It was an incoming text from an unfamiliar number. She flicked the screen on with one hand and glanced down. The text consisted entirely of a telephone number that wasn't listed in her contacts. No identifying information, no hint of who had sent it.

Unable to think of any way a phone call could make her situation worse than it already was, she pulled into a gas station that still had a pay phone, in defiance of all modern technological trends. She dug out some spare change and made the call.

"Top of the morning, love," a familiar Irish voice chirped in her ear. "It's grand to speak to a lovely lass on such a fine day."

"How'd you know it was me, Corky?" Erin asked.

"I always answer the phone that way, love," he replied. "In seriousness, though, I made an educated guess. This is a brand-new burner you're calling, and you're the only one I've given the number, so it seemed a fair chance it'd be yourself on the line. If not, I'm quite prepared to flirt with telemarketers. I'm rather fond of all this cloak-and-dagger business. Just like old times, aye?"

"Yeah," she said. "Of course, if they subpoena my phone, they'll get this number."

"By which time my phone will be at the bottom of the river," he said, unperturbed. "They're welcome to discuss matters with the fishes. I assume you're on a clean telephone yourself?"

"Pay phone," she said.

"Grand. Was Wayne any help to you?"

"He'll try."

"I knew we could count on the lad. Now, I've made a few wee inquiries of my own, and I've a name for you."

"What is it?"

"Desmond Chaney," Corky said. "Des to his mates. He's the guard you're wanting. An old-timer at Rikers and as dirty as they come. He was working the past two days, but he called in sick this morning. Did the lad have a cough when you saw him?"

"No," Erin said, gripping the phone tightly. "He seemed perfectly healthy."

"That's what I thought," Corky said. "Where are you now?"

"Queens. Around 19th Avenue."

"Lovely. If you're wanting to pay a call on dear Des, you'll find him at 19-25 76th Street, just off Hazen. Scarce a hop and a jump from where you're standing."

"Thanks," she said. "You didn't make too many waves asking about this, did you?"

"I'm the soul of discretion," he said. "I can be circumspect when the situation requires it, believe it or not. Ta, love."

He hung up, leaving Erin with another dilemma. 19th Avenue was only two blocks from the gas station. She was itching to charge in and get some answers out of Chaney. But what would he tell her? It would tip her hand, and probably for nothing.

She settled for making a drive-by of his apartment. That ought to be safe enough; she wasn't even driving her own car. She got back in the Mercedes and looped around onto 76th.

The neighborhood was a lot like the one she'd grown up in. Minivans and sedans lined the street, parked outside red-brick row houses. It was a blue-collar area where ivy scrabbled at the brick and stubborn clumps of grass thrust up between concrete sidewalk slabs. Some of the ground-floor windows had bars on them, but it was a quiet part of town. Carlyle's Mercedes was by far the most expensive car on the street.

Chaney's unit looked just the same as the ones on either side. His car appeared to be an olive-green Honda CRV. The car in its space outside his door suggested he was home. Maybe he really was sick. Erin slowed down as she passed.

The door was ajar. Only a little; maybe an inch and a half. But even in quiet parts of New York, *nobody* left an exterior door standing open, least of all a professional Corrections Officer. The hairs on the back of Erin's neck tingled and she braked to a stop, staring at the door.

The protocol for what to do next was so obvious, so ingrained, that Erin had her phone in her hand before she'd even thought about it. Call it in, tell Dispatch about a probable break-in. Wait for at least one backup unit, then knock and make entry.

But what would she tell Dispatch? *"This is Detective O'Reilly, currently on suspension, investigating a crime for which she's the prime suspect. Send some more cops, because I've uncovered evidence of yet another crime."*

"Yeah," Erin muttered. "That'd go over real well."

What was the alternative? Place an anonymous 911 call? Those things were recorded. McDowell would match her voice to the call. That would only make her look worse. Her options were simple, neither of them appealing: ignore the open door and drive away, or go in alone without backup or permission. She didn't even have Rolf with her.

In twelve years wearing a shield, Erin O'Reilly had never felt so alone.

Seconds ticked by. She wasn't doing a damn bit of good here. The Mercedes was a distinctive car; someone was bound to notice if she loitered. She made her choice and shifted into Park. She took a second to retrieve her backup pistol from its hiding place under the seat and palmed the revolver. Then she got out of the car and walked up to the door.

She made no effort to hide her approach or to sneak. The best way to avoid notice was to act like you belonged wherever you were. So she stepped briskly and obviously, walking with a purpose. She came up to the door and nudged it with her shoulder, uncomfortably aware that she hadn't brought her usual crime-scene gear. She didn't have a pair of disposable gloves, and the very last thing she wanted to do was leave fingerprints.

The door swung open onto a narrow staircase. Unit 19-25 was on the second floor, so Erin ignored the closed door on her right and climbed the stairs, keeping to one side to minimize creaking floorboards. She shifted the .38 into a two-handed grip and kept it pointed upward. The door on the second-floor landing was Chaney's. Like the ground-floor entrance, it was standing open.

Every instinct Erin possessed told her not to go through that doorway. If she'd been in a horror movie, there would have been ominous background music and everyone in the theater would have been yelling at her to stay out and not be an idiot. Maybe she should call Vic or Zofia. But they were in Manhattan, half an hour away. What could they do?

She stepped over the threshold, pistol leveled. "Mr. Chaney?" she called quietly, expecting no answer and getting none.

Chaney's living room was sparsely furnished. This was obviously a bachelor pad where he lived alone. He didn't even have a couch, just a pair of old armchairs facing a very nice flat-screen TV and speaker set. An AC unit poked out of the wall under the picture window. The air conditioner was on a little too high, its icy breath raising goosebumps on Erin's arms and neck.

She checked the corners to make sure nobody was waiting to ambush her. The room was deserted. She sniffed the air and caught the distinctive scent of coffee, but under it was the faintest undertone of copper.

"Shit," she whispered. She angled toward the kitchen. A coffee machine was bubbling merrily away. The kitchen was otherwise deserted. She walked through it toward the dining room. A plain wooden table stood there, two coffee cups on the tabletop. One cup sat full and apparently untouched. The other lay on its side, a pool of coffee drenching the wood and dripping down to the floor. The chair next to that cup had tipped over and also lay on its side.

Erin went around the table with slow, careful strides, making sure to avoid the spilled coffee on the floor. Gradually, the figure of a man came into view. He lay in a strangely twisted posture, hips turned to the left, back flat against the floorboards. His face was turned toward her. Erin recognized it at once, even in its frozen grimace of surprise and pain.

Desmond Chaney had seen the attack coming, but not in time to stop it. His throat had been cut. One hand was tight against the gaping wound, as if he could hold the torn edges together. His blood mingled with the coffee in a dark puddle. The knife that had probably killed him lay a few feet away, the blade shining redly. Chaney's other hand was clenched in a fist. A few dark strands of hair trailed out from between his fingers.

Erin bent over him. She saw at once that there was no point in taking a pulse. The blood was still wet, she thought distractedly. He hadn't been dead long. She held a hand over the full coffee cup and felt warmth rising to her palm.

Chaney had been entertaining a guest who had repaid him by slashing his throat. It wasn't much of a stretch to conclude the guest had been a woman with shoulder-length black hair; a woman who looked a whole lot like Erin.

Her eyes went to the hair in the dead man's hand. Had Chaney grabbed his assailant's hair in his final struggle? When the Crime Scene Unit technicians ran a DNA test on the fibers, what would they show? Synthetic hairs from a wig? Black-dyed hair belonging to some career criminal? Or would they be a match to a certain Irish-American detective, already under suspicion for two murders?

The rules of investigating a crime scene were ironclad. Don't touch anything. Don't contaminate the scene. And don't remove evidence. It was time to break at least two of those rules.

Erin went back into the kitchen and used the barrel of her revolver to pull open drawers until she found the one she wanted: a drawer containing a package of Ziploc plastic baggies. Very carefully, not touching any surface with her bare skin, she managed to wiggle a baggie out of its box. She opened it and turned it inside out. Using it as a makeshift glove, she quickly plucked the black hairs out of the corpse's hand. Then she reversed the bag and pressed it closed. It wasn't proper procedure; it broke chain of custody and would make the hair utterly inadmissible in a courtroom. She might have just destroyed the only piece of evidence that would tie the real killer to Chaney's death.

Or she might have saved herself.

She hesitated, looking at the knife. Was it important evidence, or just one more link in the chain of conspiracy being welded around her? To take it or leave it? And then what? Walk away or call the crime in?

Erin decided to make one more quick circuit of the apartment, looking for obvious evidence that might have been planted to implicate her. Then she'd make up her mind about the knife. She quickly cleared the rest of the unit; something she should have done before poking around the corpse. Bedroom and bathroom were empty, showing no signs of robbery or ransacking. She went back into the living room and orbited the room, trying to take in everything.

Movement caught the corner of her eye, through the front window. Movement, and flashing blue and red lights. All her life she'd been taught to be glad of the sight. It meant help had arrived. The cavalry had ridden over the hilltop to the rescue. New York's Finest were on the scene.

Here and now, that was no comfort at all. Erin finally understood how a guy like Wayne McClernand felt when he saw those flashers coming up behind his big rig on the highway. She finally knew, deep in her guts, how it felt to be a criminal. How it felt to be hunted.

*   *   *

When Erin had graduated the NYPD Academy, her dad had given her some advice. Sean O'Reilly, career Patrolman, had known what his only daughter was getting herself into.

"Kiddo, when you're a rookie, you think things are simple. You think you're going to do everything by the book, and as long as you follow the Patrol Guide, everything's going to be fine. But I guarantee, there'll be a time when you screw up. It'll happen. A situation is going to go sideways and it'll be your fault."

"Dad, that's a hell of a thing to tell me," a young and foolish Erin had said. "A real confidence booster."

"No, listen to me. You aren't going to do everything right. It's possible somebody's going to get hurt because of something you did. You'll be in the shit—don't tell your mom I said that—and you're going to feel like crap. You'll want to beat yourself up and throw a nice, fancy pity party. That's when you'll need to really dig in, kiddo. Because you won't be out of it yet. Self-pity is a luxury on the Job. You'll need to set that aside and do what needs doing. That's how you'll get through it. Work the problem. Feel bad later."

Thanks, Dad, Erin thought. This probably wasn't the situation he'd had in mind, but that wasn't the point. He'd been right on the most important count: she had no time to beat herself up for being stupid. But it was never too late to start being smart.

Only one squad car was outside. Lights, but no siren, parked directly under the front window, right next to Chaney's CRV. The Patrol guys didn't know they had a corpse on their hands. Either someone had reported the open door, or the real killer had tipped off the cops. They would have been vague; probably "sounds of a struggle." A pair of Patrolmen would be plenty to respond to a minor domestic disturbance. And the important thing was that they'd both come up the stairs, covering one another, which meant that for a precious few seconds the street would be empty of officers. They were on their way up at that very moment.

Erin swung her heel back against the door, shoving it shut. The door slammed with a bang. She heard a startled shout from the stairwell. She'd just told them Chaney's apartment was occupied, but she'd also bought a few more seconds. Cops always hesitated to barge through a sealed door. She took a quick look at the front window. It was plate glass, a single large sheet. It didn't open.

Footsteps rumbled up the stairs. A fist hammered on the door. "NYPD!" a man shouted. "Open up!"

Erin ignored him. She could break the glass, but a broken window made a very distinctive sound. Jumping through plate glass was also a great way to rip herself to shreds. You could open an artery that way and bleed out. Even if she didn't, she'd leave clothing fibers and possibly blood and tissue behind, and she'd carry glass shards away in her hair and clothes. If she was going to do that, she might as well stay right where she was and save them the trouble of chasing her.

So instead she planted a foot on the air conditioner, under the window, and kicked it out of the apartment. Metal squealed in protest, but it was a cheap AC unit and it gave under the pressure. It tumbled out and dropped ten feet, landing square on the squad car's windshield. It sounded like a car crash. The windshield shattered under the impact, the air conditioner coming to rest on the dashboard.

"Holy shit!" one of the cops yelled from the hallway. "What the hell was that?"

The other cop, less excitable, was already on his radio, doing the correct thing. "This is 60 Charlie," he said. "Requesting backup to 19-25 76th Avenue. Possible home invasion. You in there! You've got ten seconds to stop what you're doing! We're coming in! Keep your hands where we can see them!"

Erin didn't wait for him to finish. When a guy was talking, he usually wasn't acting. The outside wall was brick, which wouldn't take fingerprints. She shoved the plastic baggie with the hair sample into her left pocket, her pistol into her right, and made a jumping foot-first slide through the hole left by the AC unit. She grabbed the edge of the hole and swung herself out into space, saying a quick silent prayer.

Her momentum was just enough to carry her over the Patrol car. The concrete came up on her way too fast. She tried to turn her fall into a forward roll and almost succeeded. Her legs buckled as her feet hit the sidewalk and she tumbled, curling her shoulder in. She bounced into an awkward half-somersault, banged her knee, and somehow ended up on her feet in a stumbling run.

She didn't look back. On the way down she'd seen enough of the squad car to know it was wrecked, and its dashboard camera was probably disabled into the bargain. There'd be no hot pursuit. She went over the hood of Carlyle's Mercedes, sliding on her ass, fumbled the key fob out of her hip pocket, got the door open, and was behind the wheel with the engine purring before she'd fully processed what she was doing. She stepped on the accelerator but didn't stomp it flat. Better to pull out smoothly than to lay rubber. Squealing the tires would attract attention and leave evidence.

Erin forced herself to drive calmly in a straight line. She glanced in the rearview mirror as she reached the intersection at 76th and Hazen. A man in a Patrolman's cap was sticking his head through the hole left by the AC, goggling down at what was left of his car. He wasn't paying the slightest attention to the expensive German automobile half a block away.

Erin turned onto Hazen and out of line of sight of Chaney's apartment. Another Patrol car whipped past her and made a wrong-way turn onto 76th. This one was using both lights and siren. The alarm had been sounded. The cops didn't even notice the Mercedes. Erin disappeared into the everyday traffic of Queens.

It wasn't until she was half a mile away that she finally let herself breathe and lean back into the leather embrace of the driver's seat.

*   *   *

"Did you talk to him?" Corky asked by way of greeting.

"No!" Erin snapped, squeezing the pay phone so tightly she was surprised it was holding together. "Who gave you the tip on Chaney?"

"A lad I know who does business at Riker's," Corky replied, sounding bewildered. "A small-time smuggler, name of Fenwick. You don't sound yourself, Erin. Is everything all right?"

"No, damn it!" she said, trying to keep her voice low. The convenience store where she'd parked was sparsely populated, but she didn't want to attract attention. "Everything is pretty goddamn far from all right! He's dead!"

"Chaney?"

"No, the goddamn Easter Bunny! Who do you think?!"

"You didn't happen to slay him, did you?" Corky asked.

"Someone wants people to think I did," she said. "You got played. Jesus, they nearly got me!"

"The killer?" Corky's voice grew more serious. "Did you get a look at the scunner's face?"

"No, my people! The dead guy had hair in his hand that's probably mine. If I hadn't grabbed it, IAB would tie me to another murder. I took evidence from a crime scene and I trashed a squad car on the way out!"

She took the opportunity to toss the baggie with the hair into a nearby trash can. It couldn't help her and would only be dangerous.

"Congratulations, love," Corky chuckled. "You're finally one of us. Isn't it grand to feel wanted?"

"Fuck you," she growled. "This isn't funny."

"If you say so," he said, but she could feel him grinning even over the phone. "Did you really disable a police car?"

"Yeah. I'm committing actual crimes now. Maybe you're right. I'm better than half a gangster."

"You'd be surprised how many folk just fall into the Life," he said. "It's easier than you think. And you really oughtn't to be telling me this sort of thing."

"Why not?" she demanded. "Are you saying I can't trust you?"

"Nay, love. You can trust me with your life. They can put the bloody thumbscrews to me and I'll never breathe a word. But it's careless, even over a burner phone. You've been a copper long enough to know that. Are they onto you?"

"No, I got away clean."

"That's the main thing. I'll get in touch with Cars. Anything you're needing right now?"

"Who is this Fenwick mope? How's he connected?"

"He used to work with the O'Malleys," Corky said. "These days he's a freelancer, for obvious reasons. As I said, he's a smuggler, specializing in high-value items for the lads on the inside. You know the sorts of things: cigarettes, girlie magazines, cellular phones."

"Is he linked to the Russians?"

"Not that I know of, but it's possible he's made contact with them lately."

"I'd like to talk to him. Can you arrange that?"

"I'd be delighted. I'll set it up. Erin, hand to God, I'd no idea this would play out like it did. I'm sorry."

"Forget about it," she said. "I asked for your help. But I think we need to be more careful with our questions. Some of these guys are playing for the other team and we don't know which ones."

"That's what I'm thinking, too," Corky said. "I'll get on Fenwick, no fear. He'll sing like a canary for you. That's a promise."

Erin hung up, shaking her head. Corky might be reformed, but he was still Corky. She had no doubt he'd do what he said. She only hoped it wouldn't cause more problems. The worst of it was, he'd been giving her good advice.

"How screwed up do things have to get before Corky starts being smarter than I am?" she asked the world once she was behind the wheel of the Mercedes again.

Once more there was an empty space where Rolf's head should have been.

"I need to start being smarter," she told herself. And the first step was to stop making things worse. She'd been running around like a drunken idiot, reacting to her enemy. Only dumb luck and quick reflexes had kept her out of even more trouble than she was already in. The only good she'd done at Chaney's apartment was recovering the hair samples, and it was only a guess that they were hers. What if the forensics team had discovered the hairs? Would the planted evidence have fooled them?

"Levine is smarter than that," Erin said. She really wanted to believe it.

No; she *needed* to believe it. If she was going to get through this, she had to accept she was in over her head. She felt alone but she wasn't. Whether she was allowed to talk to her team or not, they were still her team. The NYPD wasn't her enemy; not even McDowell. If she let the bad guys isolate her, she'd be vulnerable. She had to trust her people to do their job.

Another piece of her dad's advice came to her. "Sometimes, kiddo, the hardest thing to do is nothing. But it can still be the best thing to do."

She needed to regroup, to figure out her next move. She needed more pieces of the puzzle. She needed Rolf by her side. She needed Vic, Webb, Zofia, Levine, and Holliday to help her. She needed to know why Chaney had been murdered, what Fenwick knew, and who was killing people all over New York. Most of all, she needed to be patient.

"I hate being patient," she growled.

But that was part of the Job, so she turned the Mercedes toward Manhattan and the Barley Corner. Erin O'Reilly would be back in the game soon, but for the moment she was going to sit on the bench. Just like McDowell had told her to.

Chapter 13

SARAH LEVINE

Social cues were difficult. They were a kind of emotional muscle memory. Children internalized them at a very early age, both at home and with peers. Most people learned them almost by accident through trial-and-error, discovering both how to correctly interpret incoming signals and how to transmit signals with a reasonable degree of accuracy: within, say, one standard deviation of the transmitter's intentions.

"Normal" people found Sarah Levine socially awkward. She missed important cues, both verbal and nonverbal. Levine answered rhetorical questions and didn't laugh at jokes. She generally came across as either disinterested or mildly irritated. People thought she was odd at best, creepy or unpleasant at worst.

All of this was true. Where the typical outside observer was in error, however, was in assuming Levine was so antisocial that she didn't even know it. This was an incorrect hypothesis. Levine was perfectly aware of herself and her eccentricities. Her worldview was far too analytical and scientific not to have turned the lens of her intellect inward.

Ever since her first difficult interactions with other girls and boys in preschool, Levine had known she was different. It wasn't until medical school that she'd been able to put a label on it. The simple act of labeling, which some people apparently found offensive or reductionist, was comforting to her. Concrete diagnosis was always preferable to ambiguity. "Asperger syndrome" sounded like a disease to the uninitiated, but to Levine it was an explanation and a justification; the most accurate one she'd yet found.

She was quite capable of detecting social cues. Most of the time, however, she didn't. This was for two main reasons: she preferred to concentrate on more important subjects, and she just didn't care what most living people were communicating most of the time. Living humans were noisy, chaotic, unpredictable, and annoying to be around. They were so worried about being overlooked or ignored that they shouted and screamed over one another, drowning the ambient noise out in their desperate desire to be heard.

Levine's calling was to listen to the quieter voices, the ones few others could hear. She attended to the whispers of the dead and translated their last words for the living. These whispers were so soft, it didn't really surprise her when others couldn't make them out. In her experience, other people were just too *loud.*

Before entering her current crime scene, therefore, Levine took a moment to put on her birthday present from Jasper. His thoughtfulness in coming up with such a perfect gift gave her a warm feeling. Her fiancé understood her better than anyone else. They communicated well, they enjoyed talking and spending time with each other, and simply looking at him gave her system a mild dopamine spike. She supposed that was what people meant by being in love.

The gift was a pair of cordless noise-cancelling headphones. They worked quite well; so well, in fact, that Levine didn't realize the woman in the NYPD uniform was arguing with the pair of Homicide detectives for several moments. Levine was too busy looking at the corpse, listening for its voice.

Male, Caucasian, age between forty and fifty years, Levine thought, already filling out paperwork in her head. *Black hair turned mostly gray. Gray mustache. Blue eyes, pupils wide and fixed. Height approximately 180 centimeters. Weight approximately 100 kilograms.*

It really wasn't difficult to estimate a corpse's weight. There was a simple equation based on height and build, so easy that carnival sideshow performers could do it quite reliably. Interestingly, many people were poor judges of their own weight, probably due to subconscious bias leading them to consistently over- or underestimate. Levine had read articles on the subject, but still didn't fully understand why such perception bias existed.

The basic description of the body was probably superfluous. The identity of this particular victim was not in question. He was a civil servant, a Corrections Officer. His photograph and fingerprints were on file in the NYPD database. But Levine believed in being thorough. She made as few assumptions as possible.

Having catalogued her observation of the body's ethnic and demographic characteristics, Levine moved on to the obvious injuries suffered by the victim. It was helpful in such observations that the human body bled in bright, distinctive colors. Blood was tremendously valuable to a Medical Examiner. Its color told whether it was arterial or venous; its wetness and temperature gave an indication of how recently it had been shed; spatter patterns told whether the body had been moved, and whether the wounds had been inflicted pre- or post-mortem.

Preliminary cause of death was very easy in this case. Any first-year medical student would be able to make the determination. *Single laceration transecting windpipe, left carotid artery, and jugular vein,* Levine thought. *Depth of cut indicates a very sharp blade, lacerating through to vertebrae. Spinal column nicked.*

Levine became aware of raised voices, loud enough to pierce the wonderful cocoon of silence which encased her ears. She paused a moment and listened, on the off-chance it was pertinent to her examination.

"No, we don't have a suspect!" one of the detectives said loudly. "And I know you do, Lieutenant, because otherwise you wouldn't be here. I don't know how IAB does things, but in Homicide, we look at the evidence before we decide who did it!"

"I'm not suggesting otherwise, Detective," the Lieutenant replied. Levine appreciated her calmer, quieter tone. "In fact, I'm not suggesting anything. At present, this is a normal Homicide investigation. I suggest you carry on just as you would if I wasn't here."

The detective's snort in reply to this was loud enough to cause Levine to briefly wonder whether he suffered from an undiagnosed respiratory ailment. But since nobody had asked her a question, she decided the conversation was irrelevant and returned to her analysis.

Likely cause of death: rapid exsanguination from bisected carotid artery. Bloodstained knife less than two meters away is likely the murder weapon, but cannot assume it before comparing kerf marks on victim's neck to blade and matching blood types and, if necessary, DNA. Absence of extraneous blood spatter or other visible wounds on victim strongly supports hypothesis of single lateral slash with knife, probably taking victim by surprise, especially considering absence of defensive wounds on hands or forearms.

"Doctor? Doctor!"

One of the detectives was standing in front of her, a little closer to the body than Levine liked. He knew better than to touch or step on it, but he might shed hair or clothing fibers and contaminate the scene. Levine didn't know his name and didn't particularly care. But he was looking at her face and clearly wanted to discuss something.

Levine suppressed a sigh of exasperation. Jasper had explained how annoying her sighs could be, for which she was grateful. If more people were willing to be open about their feelings on such subjects, social interactions would be much less prone to miscommunication. She reluctantly removed the headphones, letting them rest around her neck, and stood up. Not wanting to guess what he wanted, she waited for him to say something else.

"I'm Detective Simpson," he said. "From the One-Fifteen. I introduced myself when you got here, but I don't think you heard me."

"That is a correct assumption," Levine said. She hadn't even noticed him. Her attention had been focused on the body.

"That guy over there is my partner, Detective Wrigley," Simpson continued. "But we all call him Spearmint."

"Why?" Levine asked.

Simpson stared at her. "Because his name is Wrigley."

Levine waited for further clarification. The only reason long pauses in conversation bothered her was because they were inefficient.

"As in... spearmint chewing gum?" Simpson said. "Wrigley's? The brand name...?"

Levine realized he was making a joke. She thought about smiling and laughing politely, but Jasper had told her that her artificial laugh tended to make people uncomfortable, so she didn't.

Simpson cleared his throat, reinforcing Levine's hypothesis of an upper respiratory infection. "Anyway," he said. "We haven't worked together before, so I just wanted to say how glad I am that you're on this body. From what they say about you downtown, you're some sort of wizard."

"I'm a Medical Examiner," Levine corrected him.

Simpson blinked. "Right, of course," he said. "But here's the thing. This looks like your standard home invasion and murder, except it isn't, right?"

"What do you mean by standard home invasion?" Levine replied.

"Some asshole kicks in the door or breaks a window, finds the guy at home, knifes the poor bastard, and takes off," Simpson said. "But that doesn't fit the MO here."

"No forced entry," Wrigley said, entering the conversation. Levine wished he hadn't. It was hard enough paying attention to one person's words and gestures. Two at a time was extremely distracting.

"Right," Simpson said. "The air conditioner was knocked out of the wall, but that was done from the inside, meaning the killer was already here. In fact, he was here when our first unit arrived on scene."

"Who called it in?" the Lieutenant asked. Levine finally recognized her. The woman's name was McDowell. She was the Internal Affairs commander at Precinct 8. Levine had no idea what she was doing in Precinct 115.

"Anonymous 911 call," Simpson said. "Somebody heard a disturbance."

"What was the response time?" McDowell asked.

"I don't know," Simpson said. He raised his voice. "Hey, Oakley!"

"What is it?" a Patrolman asked, sticking his head in through the doorway. He'd been guarding the entrance to the apartment.

"How long did it take you guys to get here after you got the call?"

"Five minutes, give or take."

"More like ten," another Patrolman interjected.

Now there were five people talking. Levine resisted the urge to put her headphones back on. She was working on being more approachable. Jasper seemed to think it was an important growth area.

"Yeah, ten I guess," Oakley said. "We were on this other call, and this one wasn't a high priority, so—"

"Ten minutes," McDowell said. "Copy that. And the perp was still inside?"

"Yeah," Oakley said. "The son of a bitch dropped the goddamn air conditioner on our car! That's why we couldn't give chase."

"Was the perp on foot?" McDowell asked.

"No," Oakley said. "He booked it in a dark-colored sedan. Didn't catch the plate or the model. It was too far away by the time we spotted it."

"Dash cam?" Wrigley suggested.

"No good," Oakley said. "It's pointed the right way, but the AC landed right on top of it. We haven't even pried it out yet, so I don't know its condition, but even if it wasn't trashed, the AC is blocking the lens."

"Nice shot," McDowell observed. "You think they did it on purpose?"

"Does it matter?" Simpson asked.

"It might," McDowell said. "Doctor?"

Levine had returned to her examination of the body. She straightened again. This time she sighed audibly, forgetting to mask her exasperation.

If McDowell noticed, she didn't say anything about it. "Have you determined time of death?" she asked.

"Not yet," Levine said. "I am being continually interrupted."

"The Dispatch call came through at eleven-fifteen," Oakley said. "It's safe to assume Chaney here was dead by then."

"Not necessarily," McDowell said. "May I borrow a thermometer, Doctor?"

"Yes," Levine said. She opened her kit and handed one to the other woman.

McDowell went to the table and stuck the thermometer in the cup of coffee that hadn't spilled. It beeped. She took it out and looked at it.

"Thirty-three point five Celsius," she reported. Then she walked into the kitchen, took the coffee pot out of the machine, and compared it. "This is eighty degrees even."

"I've read an article about coffee cooling," Levine said, impressed. McDowell had a more scientific mind than most police officers she'd encountered. "Given the current ambient temperature, I would estimate that cup was poured approximately thirty-six minutes ago."

Simpson checked his watch. "Just before the 911 call," he said.

McDowell rinsed the thermometer off in the sink and handed it back to Levine. "I think you'll find the body temperature consistent with a time of death matching that," she said. "Oh. Was the 911 caller male or female?"

"I'll check," Oakley said and stepped away to call Dispatch.

"What're you thinking, Lieutenant?" Simpson asked.

"I thought you didn't like having IAB looking over your shoulder," Wrigley said in an undertone.

"I'm not proud," Simpson said. "I'll take my leads wherever I find them. Anyway, my conscience is clean. IAB hasn't got a thing on me."

"I'm glad to hear it," McDowell said.

Levine stopped listening. She was busying herself checking the body's temperature. A corpse cooled about one degree per hour at normal room temperature, so body temp was one of the best ways to check recent time of death. "You are correct," she reported. "Temperature puts time of death at thirty-five minutes ago."

"Chaney knew his killer," Simpson said thoughtfully. "Or at least he was expecting him. He brewed up the coffee and poured two cups. What I don't get is why he'd hang around afterward. It would've been a lot safer to run right away, especially if there was enough noise to trigger a neighbor calling the cops."

"You're making a couple of assumptions," McDowell said. "Doctor Levine, has this body been moved or disturbed?"

"Yes," Levine said promptly. "The right hand was moved postmortem."

"How can you tell?" Simpson asked.

"The fingers are saturated with blood," Levine said. "And the left hand is still at the neck. The staining is consistent with attempting to stem the bleeding with both hands. Given that one hand is still at the throat, it is highly unlikely he would have used the other hand for any other activity. Survival is generally of paramount importance. Additionally, note the smearing between the fingers. Someone manipulated this limb."

"Why would they do that?" Simpson wondered.

Levine didn't even hear him. She'd just noticed something else in the hand. She bent closer, taking a magnifying glass out of her kit and gazing through it.

"What is it?" McDowell asked.

"I see a pattern of fine lines in the partially-dried blood on the palm," Levine said. "They are consistent with strands of hair. However, I see no hairs remaining in the hand."

"Hold on," Wrigley said. "You mean he grabbed his attacker by the hair before he got cut? That's great! We need to find those hairs!"

"That's not what happened, Spearmint," Simpson said patiently. "If it was before his throat was cut, he wouldn't have had the blood on his hand. He grabbed the hair afterward."

"While he was bleeding out?" Wrigley asked. "You think he had the strength to do that?"

"No," Levine said. "I postulate hair was placed in the hand and the fingers curled around it. Note the smeared blood on the outside of the knuckles. Then the hand was opened again and the hairs removed after the blood had partially dried."

"That doesn't make a damn bit of sense," Wrigley said. "Why would anybody do that?"

"No one person would," McDowell agreed.

"So it's bullshit," Wrigley said. "Begging your pardon, Doctor."

"It is not bullshit," Levine said calmly. "The pattern is much more consistent with human hairs, as I said. I am providing no mental justification for what happened. I am merely attempting to reconstruct events on the basis of available evidence."

"Available evidence," McDowell repeated. "And I said no one person would. But two people might."

Simpson's mouth dropped open. "You mean the killer left something in his hand," he said. "But then someone else came and took it away?"

McDowell nodded. "That would also explain the lag time during which the responding officers found someone in the apartment. I think two intruders have been here, about ten minutes apart. The first one was expected by the victim, who probably didn't expect to be murdered by them. The murderer left the knife and a few hairs behind, on purpose. Then the second subject arrived, examined the scene, and took the hairs."

"Why would he do that?" Simpson asked.

"He or she," McDowell corrected him.

"Yes, he or she," Simpson said impatiently. "Why? And why not wait for the cops?"

"The same reason they took the hairs, I expect," McDowell said. "They didn't want to be associated with the crime."

Oakley came back into the room. "Dispatch says it was a female caller," he said. "They played the voice for me. It was definitely a lady."

"I'll need a copy of that call forwarded to me," McDowell said.

"You think the killer and the caller are the same person," Simpson said. "The killer *wanted* the body found right away. With incriminating evidence in its hand."

McDowell nodded.

"You think this was a frame job," Simpson concluded. "Who's the target of the frame? Is it the same person who cleaned up the scene? Is that why you're here? Is it a goddamn cop?!"

"Now you're asking the right questions," McDowell said. "Doctor Levine, I'll expect a copy of your report as soon as you complete it."

"I will complete my examination much more quickly in the absence of additional interruptions," Levine said. Not waiting for a reply, she pulled the headphones back over her ears and went to work in wonderful peace and quiet.

Chapter 14

VIC NESHENKO

The quiet was getting to Vic. It wasn't that he was a violent guy. Well, maybe he was, a little. He didn't like killing, but he did get a kick out of beating down a perp who had it coming, if the bastard was fighting back. But mostly he was restless. He got easily bored in the absence of action. If he'd wanted to sit at a desk all day, he could've gone to friggin' business school. Then he'd be making twice the salary, he'd wear a suit and tie every day, he'd have a wife and two-point-five kids, and it'd be a good thing he wouldn't own a gun because otherwise he'd shove it in his own mouth and take a nine-millimeter early-retirement plan. Instead he had a gold shield, too many guns, a job he loved, and a girlfriend and daughter he loved even more. Life was pretty goddamn good.

So why was he so pissed?

He didn't even realize it until Zofia hauled him into the break room during their lunch hour. He thought maybe she was planning on a noontime quickie. Webb disapproved, but that was part of the point. Zofia liked action as much as Vic did, maybe more; it was what had drawn them together in the first place. If she couldn't get jazzed off busting perps, she could at least get a little thrill out of going behind their commanding officer's back. But Vic was doomed to disappointment.

"Okay, buddy," Zofia said, planting her hands on her hips. "What's the deal?"

Startled, Vic fell back on his usual neutral response. "Huh?"

"Sheesh," she said. "I'm sleeping with a caveman. You're hunching around the office, dragging your knuckles on the floor and muttering, and when I ask you what's up, you just grunt. It's eating you, isn't it."

"What is?"

"He speaks! It's a miracle! Erin, of course. Ever since she got suspended, you've been mooning around like a teenager who got stood up by his prom date."

"I have not!" he snapped. "Erin's just my friend and partner. There's never been anything else between us. You know that!"

"Of course I do!" Zofia retorted. "It was a goddamn metaphor! She's my friend too. What are we doing about it?"

"Nothing," he said. "That's the problem."

"No! You're pretending to do nothing. But you have a plan. Spill."

He shook his head. "It's better if you don't know," he said. "This could blow up on us. If it does, at least one of us ought to be in a position to collect a pension."

Zofia planted a fingertip in the middle of his chest and pushed. She was strong for her size, but she was five-foot-three and weighed a hundred ten dripping wet. Vic had a foot of height advantage and weighed two of her. She actually slid backward a couple of inches, and he didn't budge, but it didn't bother her.

"We're two adults," she said. "In an adult relationship. A *family.* Or at least I thought we were. Which means when there's a big decision, we discuss it and come to a goddamn consensus! I'm not just talking about my career. I'm talking about yours. If you're going to do something that puts our future in jeopardy, you'd better consult me."

Vic put up his hands. "Okay, okay. I told Erin I'd go down to Brighton Beach after work and poke around a little."

"Jesus," Zofia said. "You're going after the *bratva* again? Why?"

"Because they're working with Richard Dipshit O'Malley," Vic said. "And one of their guys tried to clip that loony Irish punk Finnegan in prison. There's Russian fingerprints all over this and I'm gonna figure out what Gennady Vlasov knows."

"Isn't that the cousin of the guy whose people tried to kill you a couple years ago?"

He shrugged. "What's that got to do with anything?"

"The ones who shot you? *Twice?*"

"Yeah, that's them."

"Don't you think they might shoot you again?"

"Not the same guys," Vic said. "The ones who shot me are all dead or locked up."

"So what? You're planning on picking a fight with buddies of theirs."

"I'm going down there for information," he protested. "Not for a fight."

"Bullshit. I've been watching you clench your fists and growl for the last hour. I know you, Vic, and right now you want to hit somebody."

"Hell yes I do," he said. "These guys are coming after us, Zofia. The NYPD. Major Crimes. I'm gonna take the bastards down. Are you telling me I shouldn't?"

"No!" she exclaimed. "I'm telling you I want in!"

"No!"

A dangerous spark kindled in her eyes. "No?" she repeated quietly.

"I mean, I don't think it's a good idea," he said, trying to think how he could backpedal, hopefully all the way out of the conversation. "It could be dangerous—"

"Too dangerous for me but not for you?"

"You have a kid!"

"*We* have a kid! I want our daughter growing up with a living, breathing dad. Not a dead hero. So either I'm going with you to keep you safe, or you're going to *promise* you'll come back alive. You copy that?"

"I've survived everything the Job can throw at me," he said. "I'm a tough guy to kill."

"Promise," she said stonily.

"Okay," he said. "I promise I'm not gonna get killed in some back alley by Russian punks."

"And if things look too dangerous, you'll call for backup or you'll get the hell out of there."

"Copy that," he sighed, resisting the urge to call her "Mom." That would probably have gotten him punched in the face.

Zofia nodded. "All right then," she said. "You'd better get going."

"Now? I'm on the clock until five."

"And you're not doing a damn bit of good here. You're not paying any attention to the Ulrich case and you're distracting the rest of us. Tell Webb you're not feeling good and you're going home early. Take a half day."

"You want me to lie to the Lieutenant? He'll see right through it."

"Of course he will," Zofia said. "He's not a moron. It's called deniability, honey. You lie to him so he won't get in trouble with the Captain if shit goes down. I can't believe I have to explain this to you."

"You're smarter than I am," Vic said, smiling at her.

She smiled back, her anger finally fading a little. "Better looking, too."

"No argument there."

* * *

The warm fuzzy feeling Vic had gotten from Zofia lasted until he got to the edge of Brighton Beach. But driving through his old neighborhood, barely recovered from Hurricane Sandy, and thinking about what he was doing there made his hands clench tight on the Taurus's steering wheel. He didn't need his GPS; he knew exactly where he was going. Coming home was a bitch sometimes.

They had a running joke at the Eightball about Vic: he hated everything and everyone. It wasn't entirely true. Vic was grumpy, sure, but he wasn't a hater. It was easier to hate something than it was to fully engage with it, especially some of the shit he ran into on the Job. He was a lot smarter than most people realized, but he was intellectually lazy. Those were the exact words his twelfth-grade math teacher had written on the parent-teacher form:

"Viktor is a very bright young man if you can convince him to apply himself, but he is intellectually lazy. He prefers simple solutions."

That was the most accurate thing anyone had ever said about him. Harsh, but accurate. He liked straightforward situations where he didn't have to think too hard. His shorthand for that was claiming to hate things that made him think.

Right now, however, he was thinking how much he genuinely hated the Russian Mafia, the *bratva*. And it wasn't because he didn't want to make the effort to understand them. He understood them perfectly. He knew exactly what they were and he hated them with every piece of himself that was worth a damn.

The Russian Mob came from a place that didn't believe in freedom and they imported slavery to New York. Sometimes it was literal slavery, like the teenage girls they lured or kidnapped into prostitution. Other times it was the chemical slavery of drug addiction. Or both. They were evil bastards who deserved everything the law could do to them and plenty of things it couldn't or wouldn't.

Vic had tangled with them twice in recent years. The first time, they'd used a pretty girl to catch his eye, then lured him into an ambush. The bullet scar in his calf still itched at the thought of it. The second time, they'd nearly killed Erin and Webb. The *bratva* were more than criminals; they were personal enemies.

He'd told Zofia the truth, but he'd left a few things out. He didn't want her with him because he knew what these punks did to attractive women, and he'd burn in Hell before he let that happen to her. But in the deep, dark parts of his brain, the parts that neither knew nor cared that he was a cop, he'd told her to stay away because she acted as a restraint on him. With Zofia watching him, Vic was a better man than he was the rest of the time, and right now that wasn't the man he needed to be.

Vic Neshenko really, really wanted to hurt some people right now.

Matrushka's Restaurant looked the same as it had the last time he'd seen it: plain brick, heavy curtains, quiet and ordinary. It had belonged to Peter Vlasov, before Erin had punched a medium-caliber hole in his guts and left him leaking shit out of his innards in a prison hospital. Unfortunately, the restaurant itself hadn't been implicated in any of Vlasov's crimes, and couldn't be seized, so its management had devolved onto his cousin. Gennady, from what Vic had been able to find out, was at least as bad as Cousin Peter. He was one of the main targets of the Narcotics investigation that considered Richard O'Malley to be small fry.

Fentanyl was Gennady's main product. Vic didn't see any being handed off in dime bags as he walked up to the restaurant, but he hadn't expected to. Matrushka's was a hangout for Russian gangsters, nothing more. They didn't do illegal things here. The actual drug dealing went on elsewhere.

A tattooed guy with a scraggly beard was loitering just outside the door, smoking a godawful Russian cigarette. The tattoos told Vic he was a low-ranking member of the *bratva* who'd done time in both Russian and American prisons, but hadn't done anything truly spectacular.

The punk tossed his glowing cigarette to the concrete at Vic's feet and took a single step to the side, blocking Vic's path. The two men stared at one another for a long moment. The guard was a few inches shorter than Vic but built like a fire hydrant. He had a very thick neck, muscular arms, and a barrel-shaped torso. He was almost comically belligerent.

"You've got one hell of a weird way of welcoming people to your restaurant, buddy," Vic said. "I bet you don't get many repeat customers."

"You have reservation?" the man asked.

"I have an appointment with your boss," Vic said.

"I do not think so," the guy replied, not budging an inch. "I know you, *Detective*." He made the word sound like it had four letters.

"And I'm hungry," Vic added. "I hear Matrushka's has the best veal *kotleki* around."

"You heard wrong," the guard said. "The food here is for shit."

"I guess that's why you're not in the tourist guides," Vic said. "And there I thought it was the shitty customer service. Or the lousy ambience. Or maybe the little *suka* they have watching the door, yapping at people who go by."

"You leave now," the guard said. Then he made a serious mistake and shoved Vic.

It was what he'd been waiting and hoping for. Cops weren't supposed to throw the first punch. But if a perp, particularly a repeat offender like this guy obviously was, initiated contact, that made it assault on an officer. That gave Vic a whole menu of options, as extensive as Matrushka's dinner selections. The tamer ones included slapping handcuffs on the guy or putting him in a painful but harmless joint lock.

Vic was in no mood to play nice. He took a half-step back, causing his opponent to lean farther forward. The movement brought the other man off balance, which made the follow-up that much easier. As the thug shifted footing, Vic used his longer reach to grab the back of the man's head with both hands. He pulled forward and down, bringing up his knee as he did so.

The head came down and the knee came up. Cartilage crunched against Vic's kneecap. The gangster's cry of surprise cut off in a wet grunt of pain and shock. Vic's own nose had been broken twice, so he knew firsthand what the other guy was feeling. It was a lot of pain to process. Vic thrust his leg to one side, the Russian goon sliding off it to land on his knees, cradling his own face. Blood streamed through his fingers.

Vic leaned in and said in a low voice, "I'm the NYPD, asshole, and this is your lucky day. I could bust you, but I hate paperwork and I'm busy. If you're still out here when I'm done inside, I'll arrest you for being stupid. But if you scram, I'll forget about you. Beat it."

He left the man to put his nose back together as well as he could and went inside. He remembered the layout of the restaurant, including the cloakroom to the right of the door, so he wasn't surprised to find two more thugs waiting there. They reacted much better than the idiot outside. These two moved like combat veterans, quickly stepping apart to widen the angle on him. Both men whipped out handguns and drew a bead on Vic, who held perfectly still.

"Who are you?" one of them demanded.

"Detective Neshenko, NYPD," Vic replied, slowly turning so they could see the gold shield on its chain around his neck. "You guys got permits for those?"

"What do you want?" the other guard asked, ignoring Vic's question.

"Between you guys plus that loser outside, I'd guess Gennady's in back," Vic said. "I want to talk to him."

The guards glanced at one another. One said, in Russian, *"I'll ask the boss."*

"Do that," Vic said in the same language, which earned him startled looks from both men. The one who'd spoken retreated into the restaurant, leaving his buddy to keep an eye on Vic. That guard lowered his gun but didn't holster it. Vic was careful not to make any move that might be interpreted as hostile.

A few tense moments later, the first guard returned. "You come in," he said. "But leave guns."

"Buddy," Vic said, "if you think I'm handing any weapons over, you're dumber than you look, and then you wouldn't even know how to breathe. Forget about it. If I was here for a gunfight, you'd have a tactical team so far up your ass you'd be sneezing bullets. This is a social visit."

Without waiting for an answer, he stalked past the guards. It was forty percent confidence, sixty percent bravado. Vic was feeling a crawly feeling at the back of his neck. The punk outside had given him a false sense of security. He didn't like the look of the inside crew one bit. They moved and looked like professionals; men with training and experience. If these guys decided they were better off with him dead, he wasn't going to leave this restaurant alive. He just had to hope they were cowed enough by the implicit threat of the NYPD to leave him alone. He was increasingly glad Zofia wasn't here.

Yet another goon was standing outside a curtained alcove. This one was wearing a pretty nice suit, but Vic wasn't fooled. If this man wasn't former Russian military, Vic would field-strip his Delta Elite and eat it one piece at a time. Everything from the short haircut to the poised, lethal posture screamed danger. Vic gave him a nod that wasn't exactly polite, but was a little respectful. The man pulled the curtain open, revealing a dimly lit table with a man and woman sitting at it.

The woman was obviously one of the *bratva's* whores. She was young, blonde, heavily made up, and wearing a black dress that showed an awful lot of skin. She was also prettier than average, which Vic took to be one of rank's privileges. He hardly glanced at her, focusing on the man.

He'd seen Gennady Vlasov's mugshot, but the man was much scarier in person. Vlasov was about average height and older than Vic. His NYPD file claimed he was fifty-two. His hair was iron-gray, cut in a military buzz. He didn't have an ounce of extra flesh on his frame; he looked like he was made of leather and steel cables. One eye was dark and penetrating, nearly black. Vic remembered Quint's famous monologue from *Jaws* and how he talked about sharks having black eyes, like a doll's. The other eye was pure white, clouded completely over. It was nestled in a puckered field of scar tissue which blanketed half of Gennady's face.

The mobster's lips twisted into an approximation of a smile. It was one of the scariest expressions Vic had ever seen.

"Detective Neshenko," he said in slightly accented English. "Welcome. Sit down. I understand you want to talk to me."

Vic slid into the seat opposite Vlasov without taking his eyes from him. He edged slightly sideways so nobody could get behind him.

"I hope you did not hurt Mikhail too badly," Vlasov said. "I apologize for any disrespect he offered you."

"He'll live," Vic said. "You know why I'm here?"

Vlasov extended a hand to indicate the restaurant. "Whatever you want, if I can provide it, is yours. Anything on the menu, it is... how you would say, on the house."

"Thanks, but I already ate," Vic said.

"Something to drink, then? I have Stoli, Grey Goose, Belvedere, Smirnoff, and Absolut of course. You like vodka, yes?"

Vic wouldn't have said he liked vodka. That would be like saying he liked oxygen. "I'm not supposed to drink on the clock," he said, not without regret.

"A warmer refreshment, then?" Vlasov winked with his good eye. "Marta here, maybe? She has a room upstairs, very nice. She can give you something you don't get at home?"

The girl turned to Vic and gave him a slow smile. She opened her mouth and slowly ran her tongue along her upper lip. She couldn't be older than nineteen, Vic thought. He felt a shock of contact under the table and nearly jumped out of his shoes. She'd laid her hand on his leg just above the knee and was moving it upward.

He took hold of her fingers and firmly shifted them away. For a second he wasn't sure he'd be able to form words through the rage swelling in his throat. The girl's other hand was resting on the tabletop and he could see the needle tracks inside the elbow. He also saw faint bruises on her forearm and around her throat.

"I don't think so," he managed to say.

"Are you sure?" Vlasov asked. "From what I hear, you had quite the time with a young lady of this sort, not so long ago.

What happened to her? I have been meaning to look her up. I forget her name, but I know I will remember it."

"I want Richard O'Malley," Vic growled.

Vlasov raised his undamaged eyebrow. "Really? Instead of Marta's pretty face? I suppose there is no accounting for taste. He may not be in the mood. It may be difficult to arrange, but I will see what I can do."

Vic didn't take the bait. He knew Vlasov was just screwing with him, and in a contest of rudeness, Vic Neshenko always liked his chances. "Speaking of pretty faces," he said. "What happened to yours?"

"Oh, this?" Vlasov touched his cheek in a deliberately casual, offhand way. "Hand grenade. Chechnya. 1995. Some of the scars come from the grenade itself, some from my comrade. He was standing closer to it than I and was blown to pieces. One of his teeth took my eye."

"Looks good on you," Vic said. "Let's cut out the bullshit. I know Richard O'Malley works for you in the drug trade."

"You are mistaken, Detective. I am in the restaurant business."

"I don't give a shit about the drugs," Vic went on. "What I want to know is who killed Richard's wife and kid and put one in him."

"The word is, one of yours did it," Vlasov said. "You know her quite well. Detective O'Reilly, yes? A good friend of yours, and maybe something more than a friend? Maybe that is why you don't want Marta. I think maybe you like to climb on the back of your loyal *suka* when you feel lonely."

"You're right," Vic said, keeping his tone level with some difficulty. "Erin O'Reilly is more than my friend; she's my partner. And if you say one more thing about her, I'm going to reach under this table, tear your balls off, and shove them down your throat."

"You are a very angry man, Detective Neshenko," Vlasov said, unflinching.

"That's the only thing you've got right so far," Vic replied. "And you don't want me angry at you. I know your guy, Barsov, tried to knife Kyle Finnegan up at Riker's Island. That set up the frame job on O'Reilly. So I know your people were involved. I also know you have plenty of girls on your goddamn chemical leash. Finding one who looks like Erin shouldn't be too hard. I'm gonna ask you once more, politely, what the *bratva* had to do with the O'Malley hit. If you don't give me a straight answer, I'm gonna bring so much shit down on you that you'll drown in it."

"Once more you are mistaken, Detective," Vlasov said. "More than once, in truth. I have no girls who look like Erin O'Reilly. That is too bad. She is an attractive woman. I am not insulting her. It was meant as a compliment. But all the girls I know are too young, and I know of none I would trust with a pistol. Besides, if I have a problem to take care of, I would not use a girl to solve it. You see the men in here with me. They are quite capable, as am I.

"As for Barsov, he did not stab the mad Irishman."

"Bullshit," Vic said. "It's on the record. It's on the friggin' cameras at Riker's!"

Vlasov shook his head. "That is a lie," he said. "Kyle Finnegan is in prison. What would we gain from his death? And if Barsov wished him dead, he would be dead. Barsov once killed a man, in Russian prison, with only a rat bone."

"I don't know about that," Vic said. "I personally saw Finnegan take out three guys with a bottle of hot sauce and his teeth. I'd be surprised anybody'd be able to nail him up close without taking some serious damage."

"I agree," Vlasov said. "So it is curious that Barsov suffered no injury, do you not think?"

"He didn't?" Vic was startled enough to let it show.

"None," Vlasov said. "Have you seen the video of the incident?"

Vic hadn't, but wasn't about to say so to this punk. "Every asshole says he didn't do it," he said. "But most of them did."

Vlasov leaned forward, narrowing his good eye. "Detective, I had nothing to do with the attack on Mr. O'Malley. I had nothing to do with Detective O'Reilly's misfortunes. It was foolish of you to come here alone, thinking I was your enemy."

"Who says I'm alone?" Vic retorted.

"What policeman would walk into a place like this without his partner?" Vlasov countered. "Because do not mistake me, Detective. I *am* your enemy. You hurt my cousin. You came into my place of business and insulted my hospitality. You are a *nekulturny* swine, rude and unpleasant. You will leave alive for only two reasons. Although you are alone and I have many men who would be glad to kill you, it is possible you told another policeman where you were going. If you were to disappear in my restaurant it would be inconvenient for me. Oh yes, Tatiana!"

"What?" Vic was startled.

"That was her name. The little *suka* you were so sweet on. Tatiana Fedorova. I will look her up. I hope she is doing well."

"And the second reason?" Vic asked, refusing to take the bait.

Vlasov's smile became genuine for the first time in the conversation. "Because in spite of everything I said, I like you, Detective Neshenko. You have balls. You may be a policeman, but you are also a Russian."

"How sweet," Vic said. He stood up. "The feeling isn't mutual. And the only reason you're going to walk out of here alive is that I'm not a goddamn bit like you."

"That is where you are wrong," Vlasov said. "We are very much the same. You and I do not roll over like little dogs when we are attacked. We bite."

Chapter 15

ERIN O'REILLY

The black rubber Kong ricocheted off the wall and took a sideways hop when it hit the floor. It was the shape of a lumpy cone, as if three rubber rings had been glued together, making it bounce unpredictably.

Rolf wasn't fooled. He tracked the bounce and snagged the toy on the fly. He was already turning when he came down, his claws scrabbling on the wooden floor. He skidded a little, but found purchase and came barreling back down the hallway, jaws working the rubber around in his mouth. He slowed to a trot and dropped the Kong, slightly slimy, into Erin's hands.

She looked down at the dog. Rolf pranced back and forth, dropping into a playful crouch. He wagged his tail, eyes bright, tongue hanging out, eager for more.

Erin sighed and threw the Kong again. Rolf was in motion before it even left her hand. This time he caught it before it struck the ground.

At least someone was having a good time. Erin was quietly fuming. Other members of her team were out there making things happen while she was stuck at home, ordered to sit still, afraid to move.

That was the worst of it; she was scared. Erin was used to a certain amount of fear. It came with the Job. When she had to walk down a dark alley in a bad neighborhood, or when a punk pulled a knife, or when bullets started flying, there was that old familiar feeling of cold fingers tying her guts into knots. But this was different.

This time she was afraid that whatever she did would be playing right into the hands of the bad guys. How many more bodies would drop, with pieces of evidence conveniently tying them to her? Chaney had been murdered because he'd been a loose end. He probably knew who'd paid him to switch Erin's guns. What possible motive would she have had to kill him, though?

No doubt there'd be something. Maybe IAB would spin it as a half-assed attempt to cover her tracks. The real killers knew she'd figure out when her gun had been swapped, so they had to assume she'd go after Chaney. She might even have left additional evidence tying herself to the crime scene when she'd gone there. It was sheer dumb luck she'd gotten there when she had, after the murderer had slashed Chaney's throat but before the NYPD arrived.

Erin absentmindedly took the Kong from Rolf and flung it again, sending the K-9 on another happy chase. Maybe she was supposed to be paralyzed by fear. Maybe by hanging around the Barley Corner she was doing exactly what the bad guys wanted.

She wanted to call Vic or Zofia to find out what was going on, but what if IAB was listening? She'd never get her shield back, and she'd get her friends in trouble. Come to that, how did she know her apartment wasn't bugged? McDowell might be listening to her play fetch with her K-9 this very moment.

Paranoia, she decided, was one hell of a thing, and she didn't have to listen to it. Her apartment wasn't bugged. Carlyle had the best home security of anyone who wasn't a high-ranking politician or billionaire. But she was getting awfully sick of playing it safe.

"If something doesn't happen soon," she told Rolf, "I'm going to go nuts."

Rolf dropped the Kong at her feet and shuffled away from it, staring at it intently and wagging. Something *was* happening. The only things that would be better were food or chasing down bad guys.

The door at the bottom of the stairs clicked open. Erin recognized Carlyle's familiar footsteps on the stairs. He came into the living room, wearing his usual charcoal gray suit. He'd opted for a dark green tie and pocket square. Erin marveled at how put-together he looked. The man would greet Armageddon in a nice Burberry, sipping Scotch.

"If you're at loose ends, Erin, Corky would like a word with you," he said.

"Sure thing," she said a little too eagerly. "Is he downstairs?"

She was already halfway down the hall, setting the Kong aside, to Rolf's disappointment.

"He's elsewhere," Carlyle said, producing a slip of paper with an address on it. "It's an old warehouse, not far from here."

Erin took the paper and glanced at it. "That's on the docks," she said. "Are you sure this is on the up-and-up?"

"Corky and I have code words," Carlyle said. "If he was under duress, he'd have said so. Are you quite all right, darling?"

"Just jumpy," she said. "Okay, I'll go."

"I'll come with you," he said.

She hesitated. "I think maybe I should go alone. With Rolf, of course."

"It's sweet that you'd prefer not to place me in danger," he said. "But need I remind you I spent two decades as a gangster, and another in the Irish Republican Army?"

"Okay, fine," she said. It was actually comforting to have a person she trusted with her. She just hoped they weren't about to trip over another corpse.

*   *   *

"This isn't creepy at all," was Erin's verdict on seeing the warehouse.

"I think it's what they call a fixer-upper," Carlyle said. "Perhaps if one were to replace the windows and doors, bring the wiring and pipes up to code, and do something with the roof, it might be almost respectable."

Erin fought the urge to keep looking over her shoulder. "Corky calls you to have me meet him at a broken-down, deserted building," she said. "Does he do this sort of thing very often?"

"More often than you'd think," Carlyle said. "The last time he did it, he'd come across a few cases of particularly rare distilled spirits."

"So this is a smuggling cache?"

He nodded.

"How come it wasn't seized along with the rest of the O'Malley properties when we took Evan down?"

"Because it's not an O'Malley property," he replied.

"Who does it belong to?"

"That's a complicated question I'm not prepared to answer."

She gave him a look.

"In other words, I don't know," he said. "My understanding is, this and a few other sites around New York are owned by a *sub rosa* consortium of private interests."

"So... a smuggling ring."

"That's an accurate description, aye."

"Better and better." Erin crouched and pulled her .38 from its ankle clip. "I trust Corky, but what if we meet a trigger-happy gunrunner in here?"

"That won't happen," Carlyle said with more certainty than Erin thought was warranted. "These lads keep out of one another's way."

"There you are!"

Corky came jauntily out of the nearest door. He was grinning broadly, though he looked somewhat dirty and disheveled. "Why is it you're standing about, jawing on the doorstep? Come in! I've refreshments inside."

"We came straight from my pub," Carlyle reminded him. "We didn't drive all this way for a drink."

"But you've found one nevertheless," Corky said, leading them into the broken-down, filthy building. Rolf sniffed at a pile of refuse, disturbing a pair of rats. They scampered away, squeaking indignantly.

"Nice," Erin said. "Corky, what are we doing here?"

"I've a surprise for you in the cellar," he said, opening a metal door to reveal a flight of concrete steps leading down. Erin, Carlyle, and Rolf followed him into a dank basement smelling strongly of mold, rust, and dirty water.

They found themselves in a room lit by a bare incandescent bulb. A card table sat near the stairs, surrounded by folding chairs. On the table were half a dozen bottles of Guinness. But that wasn't what caught Erin's attention. She was looking at the man in the chair facing the door.

She couldn't make out his features, on account of the black bag that had been pulled over his head. He was dressed in what looked like a janitor's uniform, dirty and spattered with apparent bloodstains. His wrists were secured to the chair's supports by two pairs of handcuffs.

Erin turned to Corky, grabbing him by the shirtfront and dragging him back into the stairwell. "What the hell is this?" she demanded in a low, dangerous voice.

"That," he said, "is Lyman Fenwick, professional smuggler."

"Jesus Christ! You *kidnapped* him?!"

"I persuaded him it was in his best interests to accompany me," Corky said. "You did say you needed to talk with him. I thought you'd be pleased."

"Pleased?! You put a *bag* on his *head!*"

"That's for his own peace of mind."

Erin blinked. "What?"

"If he doesn't see where he's been taken and doesn't see the faces of those who're talking to him, it gives him hope," Corky explained. "If we were planning on killing him, we needn't blindfold him."

"The lad's right," Carlyle said. "This poor blighter might be even more frightened if he could see us right now."

Erin leaned against the wall and ran a hand over her face. "I don't believe this," she muttered. "I tamper with evidence, compromise a murder scene, wreck a squad car, and now I'm complicit in kidnapping. That's not even a state crime. That's Federal! The goddamn FBI are going to get involved next. Do you *want* us all to end up in prison?"

"Would you prefer to arrest him?" Corky asked. "Haul him down to the courthouse in handcuffs?"

"You know damn well I'm suspended," she said. "And I'm not supposed to be investigating this case. I can't arrest him."

"And you think he'd tell us all he knows freely, out of his well-developed sense of civic duty?"

"No," she admitted.

"It's not like I've got his bollocks wired to a car battery," he said. "Though now we mention it, you did drive here. I'm certain Cars has a set of alligator clips in his boot. I'm joking!" he hastily added.

Erin was ninety percent sure it had indeed been a joke. Corky wasn't the sort to casually torture someone. Though he did have a surprisingly ruthless streak hiding under his cheerful façade.

"Okay," she sighed. "I'll talk to him. But I'm not going to hurt him, and we're letting him go after this. You understand?"

"Of course," Corky said. "I'll be the one to hurt him if it needs doing. No need to soil your hands. That's how good cop/bad cop works, aye?"

Erin gave him a dirty look. "No jumper cables. No brass knuckles. No knives. Why is there blood all over him?"

"Oh, that? During our wee scuffle, he fell and struck his nose on the floor. It looks worse than it is. You didn't think I'd stab him, surely."

"I didn't think you'd kidnap him either," she shot back. "But here we are."

Corky, for once, didn't have a witty comeback. He had the decency to look a little sheepish.

"You'd better wait outside," she told Carlyle. "I don't want you getting involved if this goes sideways."

"I'm already involved," he said. "I'll follow wherever you lead."

"If they throw me in women's prison, they won't let you follow me there," she said dryly. "Just don't let him see your face, okay?"

"If that's how you'd like to play this."

Erin walked into the basement again. Carlyle crossed the room and stood behind Fenwick's chair. Erin sat down opposite the handcuffed man. Corky stood next to Fenwick, arms crossed. Rolf pulled in his haunches and sat beside Erin's chair.

She nodded to Carlyle, who yanked the bag off the prisoner's head. Her first sight of Lyman Fenwick didn't impress her. He was hollow-cheeked and had small, beady eyes that darted nervously from side to side. His eyes, his long nose, and his scraggly beard reminded her of a gerbil that had belonged to one of her friends when she'd been a girl. Dried blood crusted his nostrils. He blinked rapidly and licked his lips.

"I didn't see nothing," he said, speaking rapidly in a high-pitched whine. "I won't say nothing, neither. I don't know who none of you are, I never heard nothing, and—oh my God, it's you!"

"Good afternoon, Mr. Fenwick," Erin said. "I'm sorry things happened this way. It wasn't how I wanted it to go at all. I hope we can clear up this little misunderstanding without any further unpleasantness."

"You're Erin O'Reilly," Fenwick said, relief and fear playing tug-of-war with his face. "I've seen you on the news."

"That's right," she said. "I just have a few questions for you, and then you can be on your way."

"Lawyer," he said at once. "I'm not saying nothing without my lawyer!"

Corky actually laughed out loud. Even Carlyle smiled thinly. Fenwick darted a look at Corky, wondering what was so funny.

"I'm sorry," Erin said. "That's my fault for not explaining the situation. If you were here in an official capacity, you're right; you'd have the right to a lawyer. But you're not under arrest, Mr. Fenwick. That means no lawyers."

Fenwick licked his lips again and said nothing. Corky reached into a hip pocket, pulled out a folding knife, and began casually trimming one of his own fingernails. The blade was wickedly sharp.

"Corky," Fenwick said. "We've been friends for years. Don't do this to me!"

"I'm doing nothing," Corky said. "Whatever happens in here you'll be bringing on yourself. I told you one of my mates needed some information on the late, unlamented Desmond Chaney. It's you who took it amiss and tried to run off. Some lads might think that was a sign of a guilty conscience."

"I heard what she did to Chaney!" Fenwick said. "I didn't want nothing to do with that! Please! Don't cut me!"

"Put the knife away, Corky," Erin said. She cracked open one of the beer bottles. "Are you thirsty, Lyman?"

He nodded warily, not taking his eyes from Corky.

"Uncuff his left hand, please," Erin said.

Corky did so. Fenwick flexed his arm experimentally, then reached out and took the bottle from Erin. He swallowed a big gulp of Guinness.

"Thanks, ma'am," he said.

"Why do you think I killed Chaney?" she asked.

Fenwick swallowed again, though without the benefit of beer this time. "Did I say that? I didn't mean it!"

"Why did you say it?" she asked patiently.

"Because... well, because he set you up," Fenwick said. "And you think I helped him."

"Did you help him?" she asked.

He shook his head violently. "No! No! I swear I didn't! Please!"

"How did you know he set me up?"

"Because he... and you... and..." Fenwick faltered. Erin could see him trying to work out the right thing to say. That was the problem with interrogating a guy who was scared out of his wits. He'd say whatever he thought you wanted to hear, and whatever he thought would get him out of the room, whether it was true or not. Torture only made it worse, which was why torture, in addition to being evil, just plain didn't work.

"The truth, Lyman," she said. "That's what I want. I promise, if you tell me the truth, I won't hurt you. And neither will he."

"Chaney had it coming," Fenwick said. "He was a bad guy, I swear. All I ever did was small shit. Smokes and tittie mags. What's the harm in that? But Chaney wanted a gun. A dirty gun."

"Dirty how?"

"One that'd been used in a crime," he said. "To shoot someone. You have any idea how hard it is to get your hands on one of those?"

Erin nodded. Plenty of crooks wanted to get rid of a hot weapon after using it, but nobody would want to advertise the fact. "A Glock nine-mil?" she asked.

"Yeah," Fenwick said. "Jesus, Corky, I was trying to help you when you asked!"

"You were eager to help because I offered you two grand for the tip," Corky said. "You're not exactly likely to be canonized for that."

"Who wanted him to get the gun?" Erin demanded.

"I don't know," Fenwick said.

"Who? Tell me!"

He shrank back, holding up the half-empty beer bottle in a pathetic gesture of self-defense. "I don't know! Why would he tell me? I'm a businessman! He wanted a dirty Glock, I got him one!"

"From where?"

"A guy I know who deals guns."

"Which guy?"

"Satchel!"

"That's not a name," Erin said.

"Uh... I think his name's Stan. Stan the Satchel, yeah. He works out of the Bronx."

"Does Stan have a last name?"

"No fear, love," Corky said. "I know the lad."

Of course you do, Erin thought. If you knocked on the gates of Hell, Corky probably knew the doorman. And if you went to Heaven, he knew Saint Peter, too. "Okay, forget about that," she said. "Who told you I killed Chaney?"

"It's all over Riker's," Fenwick said. "Everybody's talking about it. They're just rumors. Nobody knows where they come from. Word gets around, you know, and then everybody knows it. I'm sorry! I don't really know nothing! I'm just doing my job!"

"And it's nothing personal," Erin said wryly.

"Yeah!" he agreed, nodding vigorously. "Exactly!"

"It never is," she muttered. "Okay, I believe you. Corky, give us ten minutes' head start, then cut him loose."

"Don't cut me!" Fenwick begged, his eyes filling with tears. "Please!"

"I said, cut him *loose*," she said. "Let him go. Without making him bleed any more. Sorry it came to this, Mr. Fenwick. You be good from here on out, got it?"

Without listening to his babble insisting he was a born-again good citizen who'd never put so much as a toe wrong, Erin turned away and got out of that awful basement, back into the light and clean air.

Chapter 16

"I'd no idea he was planning that," Carlyle said, once they were back in his car.

"I know," Erin said grimly. "You're not crazy enough to pull a stunt like that." She put the Mercedes in gear with a savage jerk of her wrist. The tires squealed in protest as she accelerated away from the warehouse.

They drove for a few minutes in silence, joining the throng of downtown drivers. For once the gridlock didn't bother Erin. It wasn't like she was in a hurry. She'd just wanted to get away from the warehouse.

"If it's any consolation, that lad strikes me as unlikely to press charges," Carlyle said at length.

"You think that's what's bothering me?" she retorted. "I know that, too. Fenwick wants this to come out even less than we do. He'd lose his job, he might go to jail, and if any of his pals find out he talked to us, they'll kill him. He's going to lie low and pray nobody ever hears about this whole mess."

"Then there's no harm done," Carlyle said.

"No harm?" she echoed. "I just aided and abetted a kidnapping! I'm committing crimes! Actual, for-real felonies! I should've had Corky arrested and I didn't!"

"Are you saying you shouldn't have been loyal to your friend?" Carlyle asked quietly. "A lad who was doing you a favor?"

"I don't know!" To Erin's surprise she felt angry tears filling her eyes. She blinked them furiously away. "This isn't me! I can't do this!"

"You aided and abetted more than once in the course of your undercover work," he said.

"That was different!"

"How?"

"I had permission. It was part of the Job."

"This is part of your job."

"No, damn it! This is me being a vigilante!"

"This is you trying to stay out of prison!" Carlyle snapped. "Erin, this is your life at stake!"

"You think I don't know that?"

"You're the target of a carefully planned conspiracy," he continued more calmly. "The bastards who did this know you. They're predicting your moves. Perhaps some unorthodox actions are precisely what we need."

"Yeah," she said heavily. "But I can't win this way. Either I go down for crimes I didn't commit, or I go down for crimes I *did* do."

"We've already established Mr. Fenwick won't be testifying against you."

"It doesn't matter. When this is over, if I'm still alive, not in jail, and still a cop by some miracle, I'm turning in my shield."

Erin hadn't thought anything she could ever say would completely silence Carlyle, but that did the trick. He didn't make a sound. She glanced at him out of the corner of her eye.

He was staring at her, mouth slightly open. The word Corky would probably use for what he was, she thought wryly, was "gobsmacked."

"I mean it," she said, as if there could be any doubt.

Carlyle found his voice. "Aye," he said. "That's obvious. But it's a large decision. Perhaps you'd best think on it a while."

"There's nothing else I can do," she said. "I can't even imagine looking my dad in the eye after this. He wore a shield half his life and he never did anything like this... I mean, he never dishonored it. Oh, Jesus. What am I going to tell him?"

"He's your da," Carlyle said. "He'll understand."

The tears were threatening to get out of control. "He was always so proud of me," she said, hating the way it sounded. She was being a pathetic little girl, desperate for Daddy's approval. God, what had they done to her?

"Talk to him," Carlyle suggested.

"And say what?"

"Everything."

"You are such a Catholic," she said, smiling through her tears. "You think confession is the solution to everything."

"It's kept me sane these past years," he said. "And clinging to hope, in the face of worse sins than yours. Perhaps you ought to talk to your priest instead."

Erin made a face. "Later," she said. "Let's talk business right now. If Corky's going to pull shit like that, let's try to at least make it worth something. Stan the Satchel."

"Why do we need him?" Carlyle asked.

"Because the Glock they took off me when I got suspended was used in another shooting," she said. "When that comes back on me, and it will, I need to be able to trace the weapon."

"Mr. Fenwick won't testify," Carlyle said. "You've said so yourself. Without him, there's no way to pin it on the Satchel.

You saying he was the source of the weapon may only incriminate you further."

"If I tell IAB," she said. "But I'm going to tell Vic. He'll get results."

"Corky knows the lad," Carlyle said. "I'm sure he'd be willing to—"

"No more Corky!" Erin interrupted. "The last thing we need is some other schmuck locked in a basement."

That was the end of the conversation. They drove the rest of the way back to the Corner without incident. Erin unloaded Rolf and the three of them crossed the street to the pub. They were met just inside by Ken Mason, Carlyle's top security man.

"Sir," he said. "Couple NYPD were just here, looking for Ms. O'Reilly."

"Did they identify themselves?" Erin asked.

"Yes, ma'am. A Lieutenant McDowell and A Detective Schumacher."

"What did you tell them?" Carlyle asked.

"The truth, sir," Mason said. "Told them she went out driving with you, didn't know where or when you'd be back."

Rolf barked sharply. Erin spun on her heel, already having a good idea what she was going to see.

"Detective O'Reilly," McDowell said. She was standing in the doorway, one of the IAB detectives flanking her.

"Lieutenant," Erin said.

"I apologize for bothering you at home," McDowell said. "But I'm requesting you accompany us to the station."

"Voluntarily?"

Erin couldn't help it. The word just popped out. It had been a long day.

"I was under the impression you'd offered full cooperation with our investigation," McDowell said. "That would include responding promptly to requests for interviews from my division."

"Of course," Erin said. "Anything I can do to help."

"I'm further requesting you leave your K-9 here," McDowell added.

Erin's mouth went dry. She told herself not to panic. If she was in really serious trouble, they'd want Rolf somewhere they could keep an eye on him, not cooling his heels in a private residence. Maybe everything was okay.

"Can you take him upstairs?" she asked Carlyle.

He nodded. "Anything else you're needing?" he asked.

"I'll let you know," she said.

*   *   *

Riding in the back seat of Detective Schumacher's black Lincoln, Erin kept telling herself not to worry. This was just a follow-up interview. Cops liked to conduct multiple interviews to see whether the subject changed their story. Erin had the advantage of telling the truth; about Richard O'Malley, at any rate. She'd better make up her mind in advance as to what she'd say if they asked her about Des Chaney. She could truthfully say she hadn't killed him, but what if they asked whether she'd been to his apartment? Maybe Carlyle's Mercedes had been identified at the scene. Maybe someone had seen her going in, or worse, coming out through the hole in Chaney's wall.

It was always best to tell as much of the truth as possible. She'd learned from Carlyle never to lie when a misleading truth would serve the same purpose. But why was she even trying to think how to hoodwink other cops?

She'd been right. Resigning might be the only honorable thing she could do. She'd lose her pension, sure, but Carlyle had plenty of money. She'd also lose her reputation, but so what? Reputations only mattered if you let them.

They'd take Rolf away.

The thought was like being stabbed in the guts with a sharp icicle. Rolf wasn't a pet; he was a working K-9, Department-issued. The NYPD would take him back, just like they'd take her gun and her precious gold shield. They might reissue him to a new handler, but Rolf was getting a little old to start over. He had a lot of miles on him. They might—oh, Jesus—just decide to put him down and save the hassle.

Erin felt trapped, cornered. Her thoughts were racing in circles. Was this how you felt on Death Row, right before they strapped you into the chair and you rode the lightning? New York didn't use the death penalty anymore. At least that was one thing she didn't need to worry about.

The ride to the station was mercifully short. Erin expected to go up to the third floor again, to the IAB conference room. Instead, McDowell pointed her to a more familiar room. It was concrete, its only decoration a set of horizontal lines measuring height increments. The opposite wall was one-way glass, throwing back her reflection.

"This won't take long," McDowell said. "You know how it's done. I appreciate your cooperation."

Five other women were already present, and had apparently been waiting a while. They were all about Erin's height, dark-haired, and of similar build. One smiled nervously at her. The others ignored her.

"I'm in a lineup?" Erin asked McDowell. "Really?"

"As I said, you know how it's done," McDowell said. "You're number four. When your number is called, just step forward. You don't need to say or do anything else."

So this was it; she really was a murder suspect. She didn't exactly feel frightened. It was more of a hollow sensation, like a pumpkin that had been scooped out before being carved into a jack-o'-lantern. She'd looked through the other side of the glass plenty of times, wondering what was going through the suspects' heads. Now she knew.

A uniformed officer had the six women line up against the wall. Each was given a card with a big black number on it. Then they waited, but not for long. McDowell's voice came through the intercom.

"Number one, step forward."

It was a fair lineup. All the women bore at least a superficial resemblance to Erin. She wondered how many black-haired, blue-eyed women there were in New York that were about five-foot-six and athletic. Hundreds, probably. How many of those were criminals?

"Number two, step forward."

Who was looking through the glass? Richard O'Malley? Linda the squirrel lady? Both? Neither? All Erin saw was her own face staring back in reflection. She didn't look so good. Her eyes had dark smudges under them and a hunted, haunted quality.

"Number three, step forward."

The woman to Erin's right took two steps toward the glass. She was dressed shabbily. The cuffs of her jeans were worn through, as were the elbows of her denim jacket. But she was clean and well-groomed. Blue-collar, down on her luck, but still keeping a little personal pride. Erin wondered about the woman who'd actually shot Richard's family. Did she have dirt under her fingernails? Was she a professional assassin? Those were vanishingly rare; the chances of finding one who could be mistaken for Erin were basically zero.

"Number four, step forward."

Erin blinked. It was her turn. She numbly moved out of line, stood still for a few moments, then returned to her place, still thinking. The trifecta for crime, she'd been taught, was motive, means, and opportunity. What made this case tough was the collision of motives: was the killer more concerned with taking Richard's family out, or with making Erin take the fall for it? Were they looking for an enemy of Richard, of Erin, or both?

"Number five, step forward."

Opportunity was easy. All they had to do was watch Erin and wait. She'd been stalking Richard for weeks, but as long as she'd been with Vic, the plan wouldn't work. They'd waited for her to be alone.

"Number six, step forward."

The means was how they'd catch the killer, assuming they ever did. A lookalike assassin, using Erin's service sidearm, was definitely a rarity. Chaney had supplied the gun; that was obvious now. But he'd been a loose end which had been neatly snipped off. That left the real killer. Find the woman and the whole thing would unravel.

But just how the hell was Major Crimes supposed to do that?

"Thank you," McDowell said. "Please exit the room the same way you came in."

The six women obediently trooped out. McDowell and two of her detectives had beaten them to the door and were waiting just outside.

"Detective O'Reilly?" McDowell said. "Don't go anywhere just yet."

"You guys are my ride," Erin said.

"I believe you carry a concealed handgun," McDowell said. "I need to ask you to please turn it over, slowly and carefully."

The other two IAB guys had drifted off to either side and their hands were hovering with false nonchalance near the guns in their shoulder holsters.

"What is this?" Erin asked. The hollow feeling was back now.

"This is a complicated situation," McDowell said. "Let me be completely candid with you."

"That'd be nice."

"Does the name Desmond Chaney mean anything to you?"

Tell all the truth you can, Erin thought. "He's a guard at Riker's," she said. "I ran into him when I visited Kyle Finnegan."

"Have you seen him since then?"

"I've had no communication with him," Erin said, which was absolutely true. She would have needed a medium to run a séance if she'd wanted to talk to Chaney.

"Mr. Chaney was murdered this morning," McDowell said. "We're still working out what happened. The scene was compromised by a second unknown party before the first responders arrived. Our Medical Examiner believes that second party took evidence from the scene which could have implicated them."

That wasn't a question, so Erin felt no need to volunteer information.

McDowell's face was completely unreadable. "Were you at Mr. Chaney's apartment today, Detective?" she asked.

"I did not break into his apartment," Erin said. That was also true; the door had been ajar. Technically, she'd broken *out*.

"I'm trying to help you, Detective," McDowell said.

"By putting me in a lineup?" Erin retorted.

"You won't believe this," McDowell said. "But I was actually hoping the witness wouldn't identify you. Unfortunately, that is not the case. Erin O'Reilly, you're under arrest for the murders of Kimberley O'Malley and Richard O'Malley Junior. I've asked you once to surrender your firearm. Do it now."

"You're making a mistake, Lieutenant," Erin said. She knelt, making slow, obvious movements, and pulled up her pants leg to reveal her snub-nosed .38. The other two detectives now had their guns drawn, though they had enough manners not to be pointing them directly at her.

"I'm doing what I have to," McDowell said. "I'm well aware of the unusual circumstances of the case. Don't worry; you won't be going into genpop at Riker's. You'll be held here until being charged, if you're charged, and I can promise you protective custody."

Erin unfastened the ankle clip and slid the revolver, still in its holster, across the floor toward McDowell. She stood up. "I didn't kill them," she said, looking McDowell straight in the eye. "Do you believe me?"

"I don't have enough information to believe anyone at present," McDowell said. "With this evidence I would arrest anybody, up to any including the Commissioner himself. I'm trying to protect you, Detective."

"By putting me in a cage, unarmed," Erin said. "What's going to happen to my dog?"

"Nothing at present," McDowell said. "You haven't yet been charged. You're still a sworn police officer. For what it's worth, I'm sorry."

Erin stared at her. McDowell actually sounded like she meant it. She hadn't thought the Cast-Iron Bitch was capable of being sorry for *anything.* "Thanks," she said dully.

"Do you need anything before we take you downstairs?" McDowell asked.

Erin licked her lips. Her throat felt like it was lined with rough-grit sandpaper. "I'd like exercise my right to a phone call," she said.

Chapter 17

VIC NESHENKO

Vic almost forgot to call Zofia. He still wasn't used to needing to let people know he was okay. But it occurred to him, as he drove out of Brighton Beach, that his girlfriend might worry if she didn't hear from him after his meeting with an admittedly scary Russian mobster.

Zofia answered so fast she must have been waiting. "Vic?" she said. The little hitch in her voice made him feel bad about what he'd been doing.

"I'm fine," he said. "Seriously. I just talked with the guy, that's all."

"So you didn't get in a fight?"

"Of course not! I mean... not really. You couldn't call it a real fight."

"Vic..."

He knew the look she'd have in her eyes. If he'd been standing in front of her, she'd have her arms crossed.

"Okay," he admitted. "I did break a guy's nose."

"God damn it, Vic!" she hissed, keeping her tone low, probably so as not to attract Webb's attention. "I told you—"

"I know, I know," he said. "It was just a punk who tried to block me out of the restaurant. He wasn't really dangerous."

"Everybody's dangerous," she said. "Whatever. Forget about it. Did you meet the guy?"

"Yeah."

"And?"

"He's a real son of a bitch. The old country was glad to get rid of him."

"I'll bet," she said. "I just got done skimming the Interpol file on him. Jesus Christ. It'd take days to read the whole thing. Did you know he's a war criminal?"

"He told me he got blown up by a grenade in Chechnya."

"That's not all he did there," she said grimly. "He was part of a death squad. He and his buddies specialized in kidnapping Chechen commanders' families and torturing them to death. He did this thing with piano wire... never mind. You don't want to know. I didn't want to know, but it's in my head now, so I'm stuck with it."

"I'm guessing he wasn't tuning pianos," Vic said.

"I thought he was going to start tuning you," she said. "Vic, don't ever go after one of those guys alone again!"

He bit back a sarcastic remark. She was only saying it because she loved him, he reminded himself. "Can we turn him in to the Hague?" he asked instead. "Is there some sort of reward?"

"Nothing outstanding," Zofia said. "Insufficient evidence. What'd he give you?"

"Not much. But get this: he says Barsov didn't stab Finnegan."

"No way! Weren't there witnesses?"

"Yeah. And video."

"Why would he say that?"

"I don't know, but I'm gonna find out."

"How?"

"I'm on my way to Riker's," he said. "I'm south of the River anyway. I figured I'd drop in and brace Barsov, and maybe take a look at their security footage."

"*More* Russians?"

"Babe, in case you didn't notice, I'm Russian, too."

"I'm aware of that," she said. "And I'm Polish."

"Yeah, I know."

"That means I don't trust Russians, as a rule."

"You don't trust me?"

"That's different. Vic, I hope you know what you're doing."

"As much as I ever do. Don't worry, I'll be home before you clock out. Hey, you want me to pick up something for supper?"

"Sure. How about heroes from that deli down the way?"

"Copy that. You want your usual?"

"Italian on ciabatta," she confirmed. "And a side salad. Call me again when you're on your way home."

*   *   *

Vic had been assigned Dante's *Inferno* in high school. He hadn't been able to make head or tails of it; maybe it was better in the original Italian. But he remembered some of the images. One that had really stuck with him was a couple of old Italian guys frozen in ice, one gnawing the other's head. He'd had nightmares about that. Imagine being told you'd spend eternity like that. He didn't even know which was worse: being the guy doing the chewing, or the one getting chewed on.

Riker's Island was a shitty place to spend time. It was nothing but hard surfaces and hardened criminals, top to bottom. But like the circles of Hell, it had layers, and the further in you went, the worse it got. Solitary confinement might be safer than genpop, but given the choice, Vic would take his chances getting shivved in the showers over being crammed in one of the dark, concrete solitary-confinement cells. Down there you had nobody to chew on but yourself.

Barsov had only been there a couple of days, but he already looked like warmed-over crap when the guard opened his cell. His chin was stubbly, his hair uncombed, his eyes bloodshot and wild. Vic had seen eyes like that in a documentary on rabies. Maybe the *Inferno* wasn't such a bad guide. Vic resolved to keep an eye on the man's teeth, just in case. *Killed a man with a rat bone,* he thought.

"This is your lucky day, Inmate," the guard said. "You got a visitor."

Barsov blinked in the unaccustomed light streaming through the door. He raised a hand to shield his face and Vic saw the distinctive Russian prison ink on his forearm and knuckles. The man's lips curled in a sardonic smile.

"Hello, *dorogoy,*" Barsov said. "You come to keep me company?"

"I'm not your sweetheart, *suka,*" Vic said. "But I want to talk to you. Give me something good and I can put in a word for you with the Warden, maybe get you out of this shithole early."

Barsov's smile widened. "You speak Russian," he said. "What is your name, Policeman?"

"Vic Neshenko. You've heard of me."

"I have," Barsov said. "You are a real tough guy. Almost as tough as Russian police, but not so corrupt."

"Go easy on the sweet talk, you'll make me blush." Vic glanced at the guard. "You can take ten, buddy. I got this."

"If you say so," the guard said doubtfully. "Watch it. These guys are animals."

"So am I," Vic said.

The guard shrugged and moved off down the corridor, leaving Vic and Barsov staring at one another.

"What do you want?" Barsov asked. "I have no money for payoffs, and I haven't been in here so long that your ass looks good to me. I will not tell you anything about my friends, so don't bother asking."

"I don't want you to," Vic said, gratified to see the look of surprise in the man's eyes. "I don't give a crap about your asshole friends. In fact, I just talked to some of them. Gennady Vlasov says hi, by the way."

Barsov was wary now, considering him carefully. Vic kept his guard up. You never knew what these guys might do. Barsov wouldn't have a weapon; the Rikers guards might be schmucks, but even they knew to search a guy before shoving him into Solitary. But that didn't matter; Barsov *was* a weapon. Vic saw the scars on his arms and face. This guy had been in fights, plenty of them.

"I do not know this name," Barsov said after a moment.

"Of course you don't," Vic said. "How about Kyle Finnegan? You know him?"

"We write poetry to one another," Barsov said. "Russians and Irish are good poets."

"Why did you stab him?"

"A lover's quarrel."

"That's funny," Vic said. "Because word has it you didn't actually stab him."

"Then why ask why I did?" Barsov replied.

"To establish a baseline."

"What is this baseline?" Vic had used an English word Barsov didn't know.

"I wanted to hear you tell a dumbass lie," Vic explained. "So I could tell when you were bullshitting me. What happened in that cafeteria?"

"Why ask me?" Barsov answered. "You will not believe it."

"Why do you say that?"

"Because the other police did not believe me."

"Try me."

"Why?"

"So you can get out of here."

Barsov spread his hands. His fingertips brushed the walls on either side. Vic had been in suburban bathrooms that had more room. "Maybe I like it here."

Vic knew what was happening. Barsov was testing his bargaining position, seeing if he could angle for something more. It was time to call the prisoner's bluff. He stepped back and took hold of the door.

"Have it your way, buddy," he said. "Enjoy your stay in *chez* shithole."

"I will tell you," Barsov said quickly. "It is not much to tell. I was sitting in the cafeteria, minding my own business. The mad Irishman, he walks over to my table. I am watching him carefully, I know what sort of man he is. You have met him?"

"Yeah," Vic said. "I saw him eat a guy's face once. With hot sauce."

Barsov nodded. "I heard that story too," he said.

"It's no story," Vic said. "I was there."

The prisoner nodded. "So I pick up my fork. It is cheap plastic, but better than nothing. I think if he goes for me, I take one of his eyes."

"Go on," Vic said.

"He pulls a shiv," Barsov said. "So here it is; he has a quarrel with me, or maybe he is just crazy. The guards will not get to me in time, so I know I must fight. I throw my tray at him to put him off balance and I come in close. But before I can strike, he stabs himself in the throat."

"Hold it," Vic said. "He stabbed *himself?* In the *neck?!* Why the hell would he do that?"

"I do not know," Barsov said. "I am not a mad Irishman. I am a violent man, Vic Neshenko, but I am not crazy. It surprises me. He falls to the floor. I should probably finish him off, but why? He did not attack me. I hesitate. The guards come running. I try to tell them, but they do not even let me speak."

It was Vic's turn to nod. Prison guards who thought they'd just seen an inmate stab another one in the throat wouldn't give a damn what he had to say for himself. They'd lock him down immediately.

"Can you prove you didn't do it?" Vic asked.

"If I could, would I still be here?" Barsov shot back.

"I thought you liked it here."

"It reminds me of Russia, only not so cold."

"Just like home, huh?"

"I hate Russia. Why do you think I came here?"

"I thought all Russians loved Russia," Vic said.

"Do you?" Barsov asked.

"That's different," Vic said. "I was born in America. What happened then?"

"They dragged me away and locked me in here," Barsov said. "I did not even get to finish eating. And we had ice cream cups that night."

"It's a tough world," Vic said.

*   *   *

Vic had a lot on his mind, but he remembered to swing by the deli and pick up the sandwiches on the way home. He got Zofia's order right. He even grabbed a six-pack of Heineken; Zofia liked it and he was learning to. He was still trying to figure out what the hell was going on, but he was used to not knowing. People lied to cops at least as often as they told the truth, and what they told you was never more than half the story. But he didn't think Barsov was lying, especially after watching the camera footage.

The only hard thing to believe was that even a guy as crazy as Finnegan would actually stab himself in the neck. Was it a bizarre suicide attempt, trying to frame the Russians? That made no damn sense, but sense had gone out the window when a guy had shanked himself in the windpipe.

On the plus side, Vic could set the whole rotten business aside for the night. He was home. In just a minute he'd be looking into his daughter's eyes, making funny faces at her and listening to her adorable giggles. He and Zofia would share a nice meal in their brownstone, and who knows? Maybe once Mina was asleep, they'd shut the bedroom door and debrief one another, nice and slow.

Vic's pleasant daydream lasted until he opened the door and saw the look on Zofia's face. Her eyes were puffy and she had wet tracks down her cheeks. His brain shifted gears so fast, if it'd been a car the transmission would've fallen out onto the road. Being a veteran police officer, he naturally jumped to the worst possible conclusion.

"Is Mina okay?" he asked. "What happened?"

Zofia crossed the room at a near-run. Her fists were clenched. She banged them against Vic's chest three or four times.

"Whoa," he said, dropping the bags containing the sandwiches and the six-pack and grabbing her shoulders. "Take it easy."

It was the wrong thing to say. She shook him off, wound up, and slapped him across the face. It stung, but didn't really *hurt*. The blow confused him. Zofia wasn't a slapper; if she was going to hit you, she'd use a fist and you'd feel it all week. Before he could think of anything else to say, she wrapped her arms around him and held on tight, burying her face against his chest.

"Why didn't you call?" she demanded in muffled tones. "You said you would!"

"Oh, shit," he said, remembering. "I'm sorry. Jesus, you're right. I should've. There was just one thing after another and it slipped my mind."

"It slipped your mind?" she repeated, drawing back. He braced himself in case she hit him again, but she didn't. "Do you have any idea what's been going on?"

"I didn't mean to make you worry," he said. "Sheesh, I was seeing a guy in Solitary. I know I got in a scuffle that other time at Riker's, but nothing happened this time. Seriously. And I got some good info. Maybe it's time to bring Webb in on it. And we definitely need to call Erin. But I figured we'd all be tired, so we'd eat first and then—"

Zofia was shaking her head. "Erin can't help us," she said.

"Why not?" Vic asked.

"She's been arrested."

It didn't connect. "Huh?" he said. "What do you mean?"

"I mean what I said," Zofia said. She was starting to cry again. "Arrested. For Murder One, double homicide. O'Malley's wife and kid. It was all over the precinct."

"Why didn't you call me?" Vic asked.

That was when Zofia hit him again, on the shoulder this time. "Because I was waiting for you to call me, you idiot! I wasn't going to interrupt you in the middle of interrogating a suspect! I was trying to be a goddamn professional! And I trusted you to do what you said you were going to do!"

"I'm sorry," he said again. "Look, I'm okay, and I'll try real hard not to do it again. I didn't realize it was gonna be so important."

"You matter to me!" she shouted in his face. "I love you, you głupi moron! And one of our partners is in jail right now!"

"Jesus, she's at Riker's?" Vic said. "And I was right there?"

"No. She's in Holding at the Eightball. That bitch isn't dumping her in with all the perps, since it won't look good if she gets murdered. Webb says maybe Erin won't get charged. He says it looks bad, but since she's a decorated officer, maybe we have some time before anything happens."

"Why'd they arrest her?"

"There was a lineup. The squirrel lady from the park put the finger on her. Webb says McDowell didn't have a choice and not to be mad at her."

"Damn it," Vic said. "I'll be pissed at whoever I want."

"I hate her too," Zofia said. She sniffled and wiped her nose with the back of her hand. "Even if she did get you promoted."

"I don't give a crap about that," he said. "Listen, Barsov insists he didn't stab Finnegan. I looked at the tape and you can't see anything. Finnegan's body is in the way."

"So?" Zofia said. "What does it matter whether it was him or some other jerk?"

"According to Barsov, Finnegan stabbed himself."

"What?"

"And pinned it on Barsov."

"Why would he do that?"

"Because he's out of his friggin' mind, that's why. But the point is, if Barsov's telling the truth, the Russians didn't set this whole thing up. For all we know, they're targets, too."

"For Finnegan?" Zofia's brow wrinkled. Vic always thought she looked cute when she was confused, but he knew better than to say so in the moment.

"Maybe," he said. "But think about it. The only reason Erin went to see Finnegan was because she thought the Russians were trying to kill him and she wanted to hear what he had to say. And Erin thinks that crooked guard at Riker's switched her guns when she was there."

"Which means Finnegan is probably connected to the guard," Zofia said. "But Finnegan couldn't have killed him."

"Killed who?" Vic asked.

"Chaney. The guard."

"He's dead?"

"Yeah. Had his throat cut this morning. McDowell's looking into it. For all we know, she'll try to pin that on Erin, too."

"Jesus zombified Christ," Vic muttered. "Where'd it happen?"

"At Chaney's apartment in Queens."

"And IAB has taken over from the Homicide dicks?"

"Looks that way."

"That means Erin's a suspect for that one, too."

"Probably."

"And she's locked up right now."

"Yeah. Did you just call Jesus a zombie?"

"It would explain some stuff."

"You're going to Hell, Vic."

"I know, but I've got some stuff to do here first."

"Like what?" she asked. "What on Earth do we do now?"

"Me, I'm planning to see my kid," he said. "And eat supper, assuming our heroes didn't get squashed when you jumped me a minute ago. Then I'm going to a bar."

Zofia's eyebrows came together in a way that wasn't nearly as cute as her confusion. "You're going to get drunk? That's your big plan? Buddy, if you think you're going to be tossing back screwdrivers at some dive while your partner's in jail—"

"What? No! I'm going to the Barley Corner. It's time to compare notes with Erin's fiancé. The cops aren't on our side, so let's see what the crooks can do for us."

Chapter 18

VIC NESHENKO

"You know, I get into fights half the times I come here," Vic commented.

"Only half?" Zofia said. "I hope this is the other half."

"Obviously," Vic said. "I'm not putting our kid in the middle of a bar fight."

"I'm glad to hear it." Zofia adjusted her chest harness. Baby Mina gurgled happily and twined her fingers in her mother's hair.

Vic scanned the pub's main room. "I don't see him," he said. "Usually he's pretty easy to spot."

A perky waitress popped up, seemingly out of nowhere. "Welcome to the Barley Corner!" she chirped. "I'm Caitlin. Do you have a reservation?"

"No," Vic said. "Where's your boss?"

"I'm sorry?" Caitlin said.

"Your boss," Vic repeated. "Morton Carlyle, AKA Cars. Former IRA, used to be a gangster, runs the place?"

Caitlin did a double-take. "Oh!" she said. "You're that friend of Erin's. Detective Something-or-Other. Sorry, I didn't recognize you with your family."

"Detectives Piekarski and Neshenko," Zofia said, holding up her shield. Mina made a grab for the shiny gold trinket and latched on. "And future detective Piekarski," she added.

"Is this official?" Caitlin asked. "Do you have a warrant?"

"We brought our kid," Vic said. "Does this look official to you? Now would you tell us where he is, please?"

"Mr. Carlyle's in a meeting," Caitlin said. "Important personal business."

"What a coincidence," Vic said. "We're here on important personal business too. Let's join the meeting. Is he upstairs?"

Caitlin bit her lip. "He really doesn't want to be disturbed," she said.

"Just tell him it's us, okay?" Zofia said. "We'll wait."

Caitlin went to the bar and exchanged a few words with the bartender, who picked up a phone from behind the counter and started talking. Vic and Zofia drifted to one side of the room and waited. They looked over the clientele.

"This joint used to be full of thugs," Vic said. "Now look at it. Families with little kids. What a crazy world."

"Yeah," Zofia said. "And look at us. We're a family with a little kid *and* a thug."

"Two thugs," Vic said. "You just don't look like one."

"My sweet exterior lulls the bad guys into a false sense of security," she said with a saccharine smile.

Mina had a loose strand of Zofia's hair in her mouth. She chewed happily on it.

The door swung open again. Both cops reflexively glanced at it. On the street it always paid to know who was walking into a room. They blinked in surprise at the trench-coated, fedora-wearing figure in the doorway.

"Lieutenant!" Zofia exclaimed.

Webb didn't seem nearly as startled. "Detectives," he said.

"What're you doing here?" Vic asked.

"What kind of question is that?" Webb retorted.

"Sorry," Vic said. "What're you doing here, *sir?*"

"That's better," Webb said. "I'm looking after the interests of my best detective."

"I appreciate that, sir," Vic said. "But I'm fine. You don't need to worry."

Nobody laughed.

"I think maybe you shouldn't be here, sir," Zofia said.

"I'm over twenty-one," Webb said. "I don't even get carded anymore."

"I meant that you shouldn't get directly involved."

"Neither should you," Webb replied. "What is she doing here, Neshenko?"

Vic shrugged helplessly. It was pretty hard to stop Zofia doing anything she was determined to do. After his experience in Brighton Beach, she'd flatly refused to let him wander off alone again. He'd tried to point out that if they both lost their pensions they'd be truly screwed, but that hadn't had any effect. So now here they were.

"What about your daughters?" he asked, instead of answering the question.

"They're out seeing the sights," Webb said. "I gave them my credit card and a Manhattan travel guide."

"That's awfully trusting of you, sir," Zofia said. "Trusting them and New York."

"They're good kids," Webb said. "Responsible. They wanted to come with me, but I told them I was working and it'd be dull. Anyway, they're from LA for crying out loud, and violent crime is way down in the Five Boroughs lately."

"Thanks to us," Vic said.

"Danielle and Erica seem nice," Zofia said.

"They are nice," Webb said.

"Really?" Vic said.

"Don't sound so surprised," Webb said sourly.

They were interrupted by James Corcoran, who slipped through the crowd like a redheaded weasel. "How's about you, coppers?" he said. "If you'll follow me?"

"God," Vic growled. "*You're* the guy he's meeting?"

"I could say the same about you," Corcoran said. "But I'm on my best behavior. Who's a lovely wee lass?"

He chucked Mina under the chin. To Vic's disgust, she waved her little arms at Corcoran and giggled.

The Irishman led them through Carlyle's steel door and upstairs to his office. They found Carlyle sitting at his desk, Rolf lying on the carpet beside him. The Shepherd sprang up when they came in, trotting over to Vic.

"Hey, buddy," Vic said, patting the dog's head.

Rolf flattened his ears and whined softly. His tail swept back and forth.

"Sorry," Vic said. "I don't have Erin with me."

Rolf retreated to a corner and sulked.

"Come in," Carlyle said, standing. "Miss Piekarski, Lieutenant, Mr. Neshenko. Thank you for calling. I'm sorry I wasn't downstairs to greet you. I confess I'm a bit distracted at present. May I offer you something to drink?"

"We're on duty," Vic said.

"Whiskey sounds good," Webb said at practically the same time. Vic stared at him in astonishment.

Carlyle had a bottle on a side table. He poured shots for everyone except Rolf and Mina.

"I assume we're all here on the same business," he said.

"You heard about Erin," Vic said.

"I'm her fiancé," Carlyle said. "When they arrested her, I'm the one she called."

Of course she did, you bastard, Vic thought. He'd never liked Carlyle, never trusted him. The ex-terrorist was a little too smooth, a little too put-together. Never trust a man whose hair was always combed and who shaved every day, especially if he wore a slick suit.

"I assume you've provided her the necessary legal representation?" Webb said.

"She's being represented by Mr. Walsh," Carlyle said.

"That son of a bitch?" Vic burst out.

"Something the matter?" Carlyle asked.

"He's a goddamn Mob lawyer!" Vic snapped. "He defends criminals!"

"Which is what your bloody department thinks she is, I'll remind you," Corcoran interjected. "Walsh is a cold fish, I'm the first to agree, but he's a fine lad to get you off if you're ever called to account for your sins."

"Erin's innocent!" Vic said angrily. "She doesn't need a guy like that!"

"She's of much the same opinion," Carlyle said. "And as it happens, I agree with you. Erin would never kill a pair of innocents. But Mr. Walsh knows the legal system inside and out. I've full confidence in the man."

"Oh, good," Vic said, rolling his eyes. "I feel so much better knowing he's got your confidence."

"I'm neither asking nor expecting you to like me, Mr. Neshenko," Carlyle said. "But we're on the same side here. You came to me, I assume in the expectation of pooling our resources. I'm doing my best to assist Erin."

"We know," Webb said. "The first thing we need is Stan the Satchel."

"We were just discussing the very lad," Corcoran said. "His full name's Stanley Shapiro. He's a weapons dealer in the Bronx. I can put you in touch with him. I'd have provided him in the flesh, but I'm told that qualifies as kidnapping in this town."

"Knowing where Erin's replacement firearm came from won't save her," Carlyle said. "Mr. Walsh hasn't fully acquainted himself with the case as yet, but he tells me she's likely to be charged sometime tomorrow."

"That doesn't give us much time," Webb said.

"Hang on," Zofia said. "Even if she does get charged, she can still beat the rap. Hell, we have months before it'd come to trial."

"In which time her career and reputation will be utterly destroyed," Carlyle said. "Even assuming we can prove her innocence."

"It's already started," Corcoran said. "I know a lass in the Commissioner's office who says he's going to be making an announcement in time for the ten o'clock news. What do you think he's going to say?"

"I can guess," Vic said. "That goddamn politician is gonna want to announce they've made an arrest. He's always jumping the gun."

"That's less than four hours from now," Zofia said.

"What bail's likely to be set?" Webb asked.

"That's a complicated question," Carlyle said. "She'll spend the night in jail. Nobody can do anything about that. Normally the District Attorney would demand an accused double murderer be held without bail, but Erin's hardly a typical defendant."

"It depends which judge she draws," Corcoran said. "Unfortunately, it's likely to be either Hennessey or Ferris, and neither lad's buyable."

"I'm going to pretend we weren't discussing the possibility of bribing a New York judge," Webb said dryly.

"Ferris is her friend," Zofia said. "She saved his life, probably more than once."

"He's also as straight as they come," Webb said. "Because of their personal connection, he'll be extra careful to play by the rules."

"Bloody stuck-up, self-righteous do-gooders," Corcoran said. "It almost makes me wish I was still playing for the other side."

"Try it," Vic said. "See how far you get."

"What I want to know," Webb said, "is who benefits from this?"

"It's not the Russians," Vic said. "The O'Malley brat is one of their guys. Maybe he's a total screwup, but if they want to get rid of him they'll just do it. This mistaken-identity crap isn't their style."

"Piano wire," Zofia said. "That's more their thing."

"A competitor, perhaps?" Carlyle suggested.

"There's plenty of drug rings to choose from," Webb said. "But like Neshenko said, this is a little complex for them. The Colombian cartels might go after O'Malley's family, but these aren't guys who disguise themselves. The whole point of sending a message is that the recipient knows who it's from."

"Perhaps the message wasn't meant for Richard," Carlyle said.

"Then who?" Vic replied.

"Who's the other victim?" Carlyle asked.

"Erin, obviously," Vic said.

"She's certainly not short on enemies," Corcoran said. "Evan O'Malley's the obvious one, excepting an inconvenient fact."

"That it's his grandson who got whacked?" Vic said. "Not to mention his daughter-in-law. Plus his kid took a round. O'Malley would need to be a serious psycho to pull a stunt like that."

"I'd thought of Evan O'Malley," Webb said. "Especially with Finnegan's involvement. Is he still loyal to Evan?"

"I've no idea," Carlyle said. "Nor can I claim to understand what goes on in Finnegan's head. He's a cunning lad, though. Perhaps someone ought to see what he has to say."

"Easier said than done," Webb said. "None of us are officially investigating. If one of my team goes to the prison, there'll be a record and there'll be questions from IAB."

"We needn't drag the information out of him," Corcoran said. "All we need do is find the gunwoman."

"And you think that'll be easy?" Vic retorted. "Do you have any idea how many people are in this city?"

"Some idea, aye," Corcoran said with his charming, infuriating grin. Vic wondered if he knew how punchable his face could be, and decided the Irishman probably knew and didn't care.

"We're on a clock," Webb said. "It'd be best if we could find her before ten o'clock tonight, but it's essential we do it before O'Reilly is charged."

"What do you know about her?" Carlyle asked.

"She looks like Erin," Zofia said.

"She knows her way around handguns," Vic said.

"She's connected with Kyle Finnegan," Webb said.

"You think so, sir?" Zofia asked.

"Definitely," Vic answered for Webb. "Finnegan's in this up to his friggin' neck."

"That's a good guess," Webb said. "But we need more than guesswork. I'll go back to the Eightball and start looking at Finnegan's known associates; those few who aren't dead or in prison, that is. Piekarski, you check Desmond Chaney's financials. Discreetly."

"Why am I always the one following money trails?" Zofia asked.

"Because Neshenko's bad at math, O'Reilly's in jail, and Jones got murdered," Webb said.

"Shit, I miss Kira," Vic said. "Not just for the numbers, either. We could sure use someone in IAB right now to let us know what they're up to."

"Neshenko, you go with Corcoran," Webb said. "I want Stanley Shapiro, and I want him in a condition to give admissible evidence."

Vic looked at Corcoran with distaste. "Can't I go alone?" he asked.

"And just how were you planning on finding him?" Corcoran asked, and actually winked at him.

"Erin asked Corky not to be involved," Carlyle said.

"And Erin's not bloody well here, is she?" Corcoran retorted. "Let me help. You'll not regret it."

"Says you," Vic said.

"Shut up," Webb said. "You're taking him with you. I think you might need one another. End of discussion."

Vic glared at Corcoran, who winked.

"Mr. Carlyle," Webb finished. "I know you don't have many street contacts anymore."

"Hardly any to speak of," Carlyle said. "I never thought I'd miss them until now. But all the resources I have are at your disposal."

"Can you think hard about Finnegan?" Webb asked. "Try to figure any connection he might have with killers for hire, especially women. I seem to recall you have some experience with that sort of person."

Carlyle winced slightly. Vic knew he was thinking of Siobhan Finneran, his semi-adopted daughter. The Finneran chick had been smoking hot, absolutely lethal, and out of her goddamn mind. She'd left Carlyle with a hole in his guts and nearly killed Erin into the bargain. She'd flirted with Vic once upon a time, and he was willing to bet sex with the gorgeous redhead would've been fantastic. It might almost have been worth the morning after, when she probably would've killed him.

"I'll see what I can come up with," Carlyle said with impressive calmness. "Shall I ring you with updates?"

"Do that," Webb said. "We'll regroup here just before ten, assuming nothing else happens in the meantime. Let's move, people. This is important."

No shit, Vic thought. "Copy that, sir," he said. He turned to Corcoran. "I guess you're riding with me, punk."

"Not a chance, lad," Corcoran said. "Your car says 'copper.' I'll be driving you in mine."

"I need the Taurus anyway," Zofia said. "You boys play nice, okay?"

"I always do," Corcoran said and winked again. "Unless they like it rough, of course."

Vic rolled his eyes. He could already see how this was going to go.

Chapter 19

VIC NESHENKO

"No," Vic said. "Absolutely not."

"What's wrong with it?" Corcoran asked.

Vic didn't even know where to start. The BMW convertible was yellow, for one thing. Not khaki, not dust-colored, but bright, in-your-face yellow. The seats were custom-fitted, the kind of upholstery that'd commit sexual harassment by grabbing your ass when you sat down. It even had a pair of emerald-green fuzzy dice hanging from the rearview mirror.

"You said *my* car was too conspicuous?!" he settled for saying.

"I said it was obviously a copper's car," Corcoran answered. "Whereas this one isn't."

"You can say that again," Vic said. "It looks like a pimp-mobile."

"I resent the implication," Corcoran said, leaping nimbly over the driver's-side door without bothering to open it. "I've never paid for a lass in my life. Hop in, lad."

Vic climbed into the passenger seat in a more conventional manner, wondering if he'd fit. It was a bit of a squeeze, but he managed it. The seat was even more comfortable than it'd looked.

"I can tell you don't much like me," Corcoran said, putting the BMW in gear and goosing the accelerator. The engine gave a deep, throaty roar and the car rolled smoothly down the garage ramp and out onto the street.

"Really?" Vic said. "Figured that out all by yourself, did you? Maybe you oughta be the detective."

"What I can't figure is why," Corcoran said. "I've been nothing but pleasant toward you. I've even sided with you in a brawl or two. I helped rescue Erin's sister-in-law, if you recall. What, precisely, is it you're needing me to do to prove myself?"

"You're a professional criminal," Vic reminded him. "How'd you pay for this sweet ride of yours?"

"Ill-gotten gains," Corcoran said cheerfully. "But I've paid my debt to society."

"You're an asshole," Vic said. "You don't take anything seriously, you screw everything with tits and a pulse, and you steal everything that isn't nailed down. Oh, and why, exactly, did Michelle need rescuing? Those are just a few of the reasons I don't like you."

"You're an arsehole yourself," Corcoran shot back. "You're rude, insulting, you pick fights with every other lad you meet, just like you're trying to pick one with me now, and you're ugly. But I don't let those wee personal defects bother me. I confess I rather like you in spite of them."

"Really? I'll have to work harder on being an asshole, then," Vic said. "I don't want you to like me."

"Why not?"

"Because I'm not your goddamn friend!"

"You really can't get on with other folk, can you? Christ, but it's a bleak life you're living. Is it because you're Russian?"

"Maybe. I don't give a damn. Where are we going?"

"The Bronx," Corcoran said. "I know where Stan hangs out. He knows me, but with luck he'll not know you on sight. You'll be Ivan Ivanov, Russian arms dealer."

"Ivan Ivanov?" Vic repeated. "You know that's just the Russian version of John Johnson, right?"

"Oh, he'll know it's a false name," Corcoran said. "He'd be suspicious if you gave him a real one. Would you rather be buying or selling guns?"

"Buying," Vic said. "That'll explain why I don't have merchandise with me."

"Best think what you're looking for," Corcoran said. "So you'll be convincing. I don't know much about firearms, myself. Never much cared for the things."

"I know my guns," Vic said. "What's the point of this?"

"To get you and I into a room with him," Corcoran said. "Where we can find out what he knows."

"We can't beat the information out of him," Vic said. "Not if we want to build a case."

"We'll have to use charm and finesse," Corcoran agreed. "Two traits in which I fear you're somewhat lacking, but I'll supply the deficit. Best let me do most of the talking."

"You know how to run good cop/bad cop?" Vic asked.

"I've been in interrogation rooms more than once, if that's what you're asking."

Vic sighed. "Right. You get to be good cop. Just tell me where we're going."

"Do you have cash?"

"Some," Vic said warily.

"In what denomination?"

"A twenty and a couple fives, I think."

"That won't do at all, lad. We'll need small bills and plenty of them. No fear, I'll cover you."

*   *   *

When he'd been young, horny, and stupid, Vic had spent too much time and money in strip clubs. The Internet was just getting started, there were only so many *Baywatch* reruns on TV, and sexy women weren't so easy to come by. There was definitely a thrill to having a topless girl pretend to be interested in you.

But after a while it wore pretty goddamn thin. Even as make-believe it was just sad. Sitting around a dark bar, staring at bored, tired women dancing to cheesy music, pretending not to notice all the other schmucks, made him feel like an absolute loser. Slipping singles into a chick's G-string didn't just make the girl seem cheap; it made Vic feel cheap, too.

He was a little surprised a place like the Cat Scratch Lounge still existed in the 21st Century. It beat the hell out of Vic why anyone would want to go there when you could enjoy the privacy of a broadband modem and a sleazy website of your choice at home. Maybe there was something about real live women that appealed, but he couldn't see it. The whole thing was fake anyway.

It figured Corcoran would know the joint. It seemed like exactly the sort of club he'd hang out in. The punk knew the bouncer by name, for God's sake.

"Evening, Alex," Corcoran said to the gorilla in the too-tight black T-shirt.

"Who's your buddy?" Alex asked, giving Vic a once-over.

Vic returned the stare. Alex was about his height, maybe an inch taller, and a lot heavier, but Vic figured he could take him in a pinch. The bouncer held himself more like a football player than a street fighter. He'd be faster than he looked, but he was favoring his left leg, probably because of an old sports injury. The knees were the first thing to go.

"This is Ivan," Corcoran said. "How's the leg?"

"Not too bad," Alex said. "Hurts when it rains."

"And the wife?"

Alex smiled, showing a gold grille across his front teeth. "She's good, thanks. When you gonna get a girl and settle down?"

"Who says I haven't?" Corcoran replied.

"You're here, ain't you?" Alex fired back.

"So's yourself, big man," Corcoran said.

"That's different. I work here."

"I'm working tonight, too," Corcoran said. "But out of curiosity, who's on stage?"

"BB," Alex said. "And Mindy."

"Grand," Corcoran said. "Are they performing solo, or is it a joint act?"

"One at a time," the bouncer said, laughing. "You couldn't handle the two of them together."

Corcoran pulled a roll of bills from his pocket, peeled off a couple, and handed them to Alex, who stood aside and waved him and Vic in.

"No trouble, buddy," he said in a low voice to Vic. "You touch the girls, I gotta break fingers. Nothing personal. You feel me?"

I'd like to see you try, Vic thought. "I feel you, buddy," he said.

The club was exactly like he'd expected. He wondered whether owners bought a do-it-yourself kit with stripper poles, purple-and-red lighting, and bad dance music. A young woman was on stage, moving her hips in a way he'd have found sexy when he was seventeen.

"You sure our guy's here?" he asked Corcoran, leaning in close so the other guy could hear him over the music. "I can't see a damn thing."

"My lad said he was here an hour ago," Corcoran said.

"Oh yeah? And who's your lad?"

"Lass, really," Corcoran said. "She's a special favorite of his."

"Oh Jesus," Vic said, sorry he'd asked.

"Stanley stays here most evenings, doing business in one of the rooms in back," Corcoran explained. "Follow me."

Following the Irishman wasn't the best idea Vic had ever had, but he didn't have a better one at the moment, so he trailed the other man past the stage. Without breaking stride, Corcoran whipped a dollar bill off his roll and neatly inserted it into the waistband of the dancer, giving her a cheerful nod as he went by. She rewarded him with a smile and a thrust of her hips in his direction.

Vic thought of Zofia and suddenly wanted very badly to get the hell out of this place. He hadn't touched anything and still felt like he needed a shower. Corcoran was making for a back hallway which had three unmarked doors along it. He angled for the first one.

"Hold it," a burly guy said, stepping in front of them. He was wearing a sport coat which flapped momentarily open, showing the grip of a pistol in a shoulder holster.

Too big for a nine-millimeter, Vic thought. *Probably a Ruger .45. And twenty bucks says you don't have a permit, buddy.*

"Darryl?" Corcoran said.

"Corks? That you?" Darryl's scowl turned into a broad grin. He shook hands with Corcoran, doing one of those fancy soul-brother things with fist bumps and finger waggles.

"The very same," Corcoran said. "I presume you're still carrying your spear for the satchel man?"

"That's right," Darryl said.

"Grand. I've a lad here who's wanting to speak with him."

Darryl's grin turned suggestive. "He's a little busy at the moment," he said.

"Traci?" Corcoran guessed.

Darryl nodded.

"Let's surprise him," Corcoran said.

"I dunno," Darryl said. "He don't like being disturbed. You better have a damn good reason."

"I've a few good reasons," Corcoran said, holding up his roll. "And my mate here has a few thousand more. He's interested in buying."

"Gotcha," Darryl said. He knocked on the door. "Hey, boss!"

After a brief pause, a muffled voice from the other side of the door said, "Yeah?"

"Corky Corcoran's here with a buyer."

"Which one?"

"Ivan Ivanov," Corcoran said with a straight face. "From St. Petersburg."

"Russian guy," Darryl said. He gave Corcoran a look. "You vouch for him?"

"Oh, he's one of the most dangerous lads I know," Corcoran said breezily. "But he's solid as they come. Says what he means and does what he says."

"Okay," the man inside said. He sounded grumpy. "This better be worth it."

"Oh, this is a one-of-a-kind opportunity," Corcoran said.

Darryl turned the knob and pushed the door open.

"Not locked?" Vic wondered aloud.

"No locks on these doors," Corcoran explained. "It keeps the lasses safer. The bouncer can get in if a lad gets out of hand."

The room was small and stuffy, smelling of body odor, cheap perfume, and too much air freshener. The only furniture was a two-seat couch and an end table. The table held a half-empty bottle of Jameson, a couple of shot glasses, a box of tissues, a burner cell phone, and a small mirror with obvious cocaine residue on the glass. The couch held a lingerie-clad young woman and a skinny guy wearing cargo pants, an open Hawaiian shirt, and a gold necklace with a rifle bullet for a pendant.

"Evening, Traci," Corcoran said, smiling at the girl.

"Corky," she said, giving him a coy smile. "Haven't seen you in a while. You used to come here all the time."

"How's your wee bairn?" he asked. "He must be what, four?"

"Five," she said. "He just started kindergarten."

"Grand! Where does the time go?"

Jesus, Vic thought. *Does this guy know everybody in New York?*

"Who's your big friend?" Traci asked, giving Vic an appreciative once-over.

"This is Ivan," Corcoran said.

She licked her lips. "You work out, don't you, big boy?" she said, standing up and facing him. "Like what you see?"

Vic would have had to be either gay or dead not to like what she was showing him, but he wasn't tempted. "Some other time," he said, laying on a bit of a Russian accent and pointing at the guy on the couch. "This is the man I've come to see."

The guy in the Hawaiian shirt got to his feet. His movements were quick and jittery, his eyes a little wild. He had a dusting of white powder on his nostrils. "Hey, Ivan," he said. "I hear you want to do business."

"Correct," Vic said. "I hear you are the best man in this town to help me with what I need."

"Hey, you heard right," the guy said. "Stan the Satchel has got you covered, my friend. Traci, why don't you go get yourself a drink."

"Sure thing, honey." Traci blew him a kiss and swayed out of the room on stiletto heels. Vic had always wondered how women could walk in those things. He'd sprain an ankle for sure, if they even made them in his size.

"You want a drink, friend?" Stan asked once the girl had gone.

That was the first test. It was an easy one. A Russian arms dealer wasn't about to turn down free alcohol.

"I like vodka," Vic said. "But American whiskey is also good."

Stan poured him a shot, which Vic took down in one gulp. Jameson wasn't half bad.

"How about a snort?" Stan asked, producing a baggie of powder from one of his pockets.

Vic shook his head. "I had a bad experience once," he explained.

"You sure? This is the good stuff." Stan shook the bag enticingly.

"That is not my thing," Vic said.

"What is your thing, my friend?"

"These." Vic reached behind his back and hauled out his Delta Elite. He set the massive .45 down on the table next to the whiskey bottle.

"Jesus," Stan said. He'd jumped back when Vic drew the gun, but recovered quickly. "Nice piece. Colt, am I right? That's a heavy gun."

Vic thought of Boris the Blade in the movie *Snatch*, the sketchy Russian smuggler. "It is heavy, but heavy is good," he said. "Heavy is reliable."

"I'm all about reliable," Stan said. "What're you looking for?"

"Pistols," Vic said, scooping up his Delta Elite and sliding it back into its holster. He was glad he'd brought it; the Colt was the sort of gun a criminal would carry, not a cop. "Semi-automatic, nine-millimeter."

"Hey, those are all over the place," Stan said. "No problem. How many you want?"

"That depends," Vic said. "I want clean guns. No serial numbers, no history."

"Of course." Stan looked wounded. "What sort of operation do you think I'm running here? My merch is clean."

"Really?" Vic said. "Because I hear on the street, you sold a dirty gun not long ago."

He was looking for Stan's reaction, and even though it was subtle, it was there. The gun dealer was surprised and a little worried. As most crooks tended to do, when he was worried he lashed out, just like Vic had hoped.

"That's a whole different thing," Stan said. "That chick *wanted* a dirty piece of iron! She specifically asked for it."

Bingo, Vic thought. He tried not to show the excitement he was feeling. Instead, he scowled. Vic was a champion scowler. Zofia told him he looked just like one of the Wild Things in the old kids' book when he did it; the blue furry one with the horns. He chose to take that as a compliment. *We'll eat you up, we love you so*, he thought.

"That sounds like bullshit," he said. "I think maybe you are covering your ass."

"I'm not bullshitting you, man!" Stan said angrily. "Look, who told you that?"

"I have good sources," Vic said, nodding toward Corcoran.

"Was it the babe?" Stan demanded. "Because I thought she was more of a pro than that. Jesus! One of your own guys vouched for her, Corky!"

"That's interesting," Corcoran said. "Because *I* knew nothing about it. Which one of my people told you she was a stand-up lass?"

"Why don't you ask him yourself?" Stan retorted. "I thought Fenwick was a friend of yours. But I'm not in charge of the

O'Malleys. From what I hear, nobody is these days. You're practically the only one left on the outside."

"Then I suppose I'm in charge," Corcoran said cheerfully. He was smiling, but Vic was an experienced street cop and he didn't particularly like the gleam in the Irishman's eye or the way he was balanced, light on the balls of his feet. Trouble was brewing in this room.

"Then get your house in order," Stan said.

"I'll be glad to," Corcoran said. "Just give me the lass's name and I'll talk to her myself."

"I don't know her name," Stan said. "Just like I don't know his. Yeah, I know it's not Ivan Ivanov or whatever."

"Pretty girl?" Vic suggested. "Black hair, shoulder length? Blue eyes?"

Now Stan looked puzzled. "No," he said. "Blonde. Pixie cut. Blue eyes, sure, but..."

He paused. His eyes narrowed. "Wait a second," he said. "If you don't know what she looked like, why'd you say you talked to her? What's your game? Are you wearing a wire? Are you even Russian?"

"I'm not wearing a goddamn wire," Vic growled, knowing he was probably blown and not caring anymore. "And I'm Russian. That's all true. You're right, my name isn't Ivan. It's Vic. Vic Neshenko. Maybe you heard of me."

Stan's eyes went wide again and just kept getting wider. Apparently he had heard of Vic, and what he'd heard wasn't comforting. "You brought a goddamn *cop* in here?!" he shouted at Corcoran.

"This needn't get nasty, lad," Corcoran said. "He's not here for you. The lass is all he's after. Just tell us what you know about her and—"

But nobody was listening to him. Stan's hand went behind his back and Vic knew he wasn't pulling out a cell phone or a wallet. Vic was only a couple steps away, so he didn't bother going for one of his own guns. He stepped forward instead.

Stan's hand came back into view, holding a cute little automatic. *Walther PPK*, Vic mentally catalogued it. *James Bond's gun.* A handy little pocket-pistol, ideal for self-defense in close quarters, but not when you were less than two feet from a big Russian. Vic delivered a sideways chop with his left hand, catching Stan on the inside of the right forearm. The Walther went spinning out of the guy's hand and into a corner.

Vic took one more step and slammed his right hand into Stan's face. He didn't make a fist; when you were fighting bare-knuckled, it was risky to punch a man in the head. If you hit the forehead hard, you could easily break your fingers. Vic knew what a boxer's fracture felt like; it was when you broke your pinky, and it was no fun at all. So he delivered an open-hand strike, aiming for the nose.

Mike Tyson once said everyone had a plan until they got punched in the face. He might not be the nicest guy in the world, but he did know a thing or two about boxing. Stan's plan, whatever it was, didn't survive Vic's hard right jab. Vic felt the man's nose crunch under the heel of his hand. Once you'd broken a few noses, you got to recognize the way it felt, and it was a pretty much guaranteed fight ender. Satisfying, too. Most of the time when you hit a guy, you didn't get to feel part of him break on impact. It had worked on Mikhail and it worked on the Satchel.

Stan reeled back, blood squirting out of both nostrils, grabbing at his face with his left hand. His right was a little sluggish from Vic's karate chop. He gave a bubbly scream, caught the couch across the back of his knees, and went down onto his ass.

"Okay," Vic said. He wasn't even breathing hard. "Now let's talk."

The door flew open and Darryl, Stan's bodyguard, rushed in. Vic saw him out of the corner of his eye. More to the point, he saw the gun in Darryl's hands. Way too big for a pistol, too small for a rifle. *Submachine-gun,* his inner gun enthusiast said. *Heckler and Koch MP5K. German export; damn good gun. Where the hell was he keeping that?*

It didn't matter. Vic was on the wrong side of the room, suddenly wishing he'd drawn his sidearm, knowing it wouldn't matter if he had. Darryl had the drop on him and it didn't make a bit of difference if he was a good shot or not. That gun held thirty rounds in its magazine and could spit fifteen of them out per second. That meant two seconds after Darryl started squeezing the trigger, Vic would be Swiss cheese.

Vic turned to face him, beginning to reach for the Sig-Sauer on his hip, knowing he was too slow. Darryl's finger was already inside the submachine-gun's trigger guard and he'd seen what Vic had just done to his boss.

There was a blur of motion and suddenly the gun was falling out of Darryl's hands. Corcoran was standing next to the bodyguard, close enough to kiss him, the edge of a very sharp knife pressed against his throat. The knife's blade was red. Blood was running down Darryl's hand and dripping into the carpet.

Holy shit, Vic thought stupidly. He hadn't even seen Corcoran move. He'd forgotten how fast that bastard was.

"Sorry, lad," Corcoran said. "I didn't mean to take the fingers, but you put me in a bit of a rush. Best scoop them up and keep them cool, so the hospital boffins can stitch them back on. It's a clean cut, no fear. It's not so bad as it looks. I'm sure they've a bucket of ice at the bar."

Darryl was going very pale from shock. He clutched his right hand in his left. It really was bleeding a lot now.

"Careful, lad," Corcoran said, kicking the fallen gun away from the pair of severed digits on the floor. "Nice and slow. You don't want to be fainting."

Vic heard more footsteps running toward the room. He whipped out his Sig and drew a bead on the doorway. "Move," he ordered. Darryl stumbled out of the way, then sank to his knees and threw up. Pain hit some guys that way. It had never happened to Vic, but he'd seen it plenty of times.

The bouncer, Alex, came in hot. He had one of those little eighteen-inch baseball bats ready for action. He pulled up short when he saw Vic, Vic's gun, and the bloody wreckage around him.

"Take it easy, buddy," Vic said, reaching into his hip pocket with his left hand and taking out his gold shield. "NYPD Major Crimes. Everything's under control. I need you to pick up those fingers off the floor and put them on ice. Then I need you to call an ambulance for this guy."

"What about me?" Stan mumbled through his broken face. "I need an ambulance too."

"Not yet, you don't," Vic said. "I haven't forgotten about you. Before you go anywhere, we're gonna have a little conversation about a blonde with a short haircut who likes guns."

Chapter 20

ERIN O'REILLY

Erin could close her eyes to block out the sights, but she couldn't get away from the smells. Everything in the holding cell was washable. Most of it was concrete or stainless steel. Even the mattress was some sort of synthetic vinyl, so they could just hose it off without bothering to remove it. But no matter how much water was piped through, the underlying odors remained: sweat, vomit, cheap booze, disinfectant, and blood. It smelled hopeless.

She had the cell all to herself. Nobody was going to chance throwing her in with another suspect. It wasn't a question of gender segregation; a couple of hookers were in the next cell over. If they tossed a cop and another perp in together, and one of them killed or injured the other, there'd be lawsuits as soon as the sun came up.

That didn't mean she had peace and quiet. Lockup in a New York precinct was a busy place at night. Cops kept coming through, bringing in suspects or taking them out again. The officers pretended Erin wasn't there. They just averted their eyes and concentrated really hard on what they were doing. Erin got the feeling they were embarrassed and didn't want to humiliate her.

The other residents of Holding had no such compunctions. The men gave her catcalls and wolf whistles if they were sober enough to recognize her as female. The women sneered at her and made snide remarks. She ignored all of it.

This must be how Rolf felt in a kennel. Caged up with a bunch of other members of his species in a smelly, hard-floored prison, treated like a criminal, scared and alone. Erin promised herself, if she ever got out of here, that she'd never ever put him in a place like that.

She tried lying to herself, claiming she wasn't scared. But that was such obvious bullshit that it didn't even pass the time. She was terrified. The trap that had been drawing in around her had finally snapped shut. Who was she kidding? She wasn't going to be taking care of Rolf. He'd most likely be put down. It wouldn't be worth it to retrain a new handler on an old, broken-down K-9. There'd be no wedding or promotion for her, no quiet retirement for Rolf. She'd be rotting in prison and her dog would be dead.

It didn't help that she was exactly where she was intended to be. This was it; this was the endgame. The whole convoluted plot had been meant to land her in this cell. Knowing it only made it worse.

Carlyle would be making calls, lining up her legal defense. Vic, Webb, and Zofia would be doing their best to clear her, even though they'd been ordered not to. Everyone was running around being useful, except her. And Rolf. He was probably lying around the apartment, waiting for her to come get him with that trusting patience only animals knew.

Erin didn't even have the energy to swear. She lay back on the smooth, pungent mattress and put an arm over her face. She tried to blot out the sound of a drunk throwing up two cells down, and let her thoughts wander. She had plenty of time for thinking.

What she thought of was Phil Stachowski, her former mentor and undercover handler. Phil was wheelchair-bound, permanently crippled. In a way, he was as much a prisoner as she was. But in spite of his injuries and limitations, he retained an optimistic, cheerful outlook. How the hell did he do it?

When she'd been feeling the pressure of her undercover role, he'd talked to her about the importance of faith. Not as a Catholic, necessarily; as a human being in need of a higher power. And if any human needed a higher power just then, it was Erin O'Reilly.

She didn't pray loudly. That would've just attracted attention and derision from her fellow inmates. She did it almost silently. "Please, God," she whispered. "Help get me out of this. Point me the right way. Give me *something*. I don't ask for much, and I'm not as good as I should be, but could you throw me a bone?"

The weird thing was, after she said it, she felt a little bit better. Then, since she'd done the last thing she could think of, she fell asleep.

*   *   *

"O'Reilly?"

The voice was familiar, but in her groggy state, she didn't recognize it. She blinked and sat up, rubbing the crud out of her eyes. There was an awful taste in her mouth. That, combined with her headache and the smell of vomit, momentarily convinced her she was having the mother of all hangovers. Maybe all the shit she remembered from the last couple of days had been a drunken nightmare.

"O'Reilly."

She focused on the mustached face on the other side of the bars. Captain Holliday was standing there, flanked by a uniformed officer. The Captain didn't look happy, but that wasn't a surprise. If he'd been smiling, she would've been suspicious.

"We need to talk," the Captain said.

The uniform stepped forward, dangling a pair of handcuffs. Erin stared at them, then turned her eyes to her commander.

"I'm sorry, but it's protocol," he said. "You know the drill."

She felt her jaw tighten, but she obediently thrust her hands through the slot in the bars. The steel bracelets felt remarkably heavy on her wrists. That was one thing she didn't think she'd ever get used to.

Erin expected to be marched to an interrogation room, but to her surprise, Holliday and the uniform led her to the elevator. The Captain punched the button for the third floor. Neither he nor the other cop said a word on the ride up. The car came to a stop and the doors opened. Holliday got out and motioned Erin to follow. The other officer started to come along, but the Captain held up a hand.

"Thank you, Zelinsky," Holliday said to the uniform. "I'll take it from here."

"But Captain—" Zelinsky began.

"This is a police station," Holliday reminded him. "I'll have backup if I need it. Go back to your normal duty."

"Yes, sir," Zelinsky said as the doors closed between him and the other two.

"Sir," Erin said. "You can't ask me anything without my lawyer."

"Nobody's going to ask you anything," Holliday said. His face was as grim as she'd ever seen it. "Come with me, please."

"This is pretty damned irregular, sir," she said.

"We agree on that," Holliday said.

Internal Affairs was dark and deserted. A few lights blinked fitfully on sleeping computer monitors. The clock over the stairwell read 10:15. Holliday directed her to the conference room, where a faint glow emanated under the door.

Erin wasn't surprised to see Lieutenant McDowell, still in uniform in spite of the hour. The IAB commander's hat sat on the table next to her. McDowell's expression was stony.

"Thank you for coming, O'Reilly," McDowell said. "Please sit down."

Like I had a choice, Erin thought. She took a seat opposite the other woman. Holliday sat at the end of the table nearest the door.

"You don't have to say a single word," McDowell said. "Though it doesn't much matter what you say. You're here without the benefit of legal counsel, after invoking your right to an attorney, so anything you do say would be inadmissible in court. This conversation is entirely off the record and is not being recorded. Right now I'd just like you to listen."

In other news, I have a bridge in Brooklyn I'd like to sell you, Erin thought. She didn't trust McDowell an inch. It wasn't that she thought the Lieutenant was dirty; it was much worse than that. McDowell was so clean, so convinced of her own righteousness, that she'd stop at absolutely nothing to do her duty.

"You've been out of the loop for the past few hours," McDowell continued. "There have been some developments of which you're likely unaware."

Erin said nothing.

"Earlier this evening, a little after eight o'clock, an altercation occurred at the Cat Scratch Lounge in the Bronx," McDowell said. "Are you familiar with it?"

Erin wasn't, but she didn't say so.

"It's what is euphemistically known as a gentleman's club," McDowell said. "You'd probably call it a titty bar. A man named Darryl Lincoln had the first two fingers on his right hand sliced off. He's at the hospital as we speak, a surgeon attempting to reattach them."

Erin wondered whether her confusion showed on her face, and whether it would help or hurt her case if it did. She'd never heard the man's name before, and didn't have the slightest idea what a brawl at a strip club had to do with her.

"Officers on scene recovered a submachine-gun with his fingerprints on it," McDowell went on. "Unfired. They also recovered a Walther semi-automatic pistol, likewise unfired, with the fingerprints of one Stanley Shapiro, AKA Stan the Satchel. Mr. Shapiro was not present when the officers arrived, though it's likely blood samples at the scene could be matched to him. Mr. Shapiro, according to witness statements by the bouncer and one of the topless dancers, had been partaking of the club's amenities when he was accosted by a pair of gentlemen."

If McDowell wanted Erin to contribute anything, she was disappointed.

"Words were exchanged," McDowell said. "An argument escalated into physical violence. Mr. Lincoln, acting as bodyguard for Mr. Shapiro, tried to intervene and was cut by a knife wielded by one of the two unidentified gentlemen. One of these men subsequently identified himself with a gold NYPD shield and requested the bouncer call an ambulance for Mr. Lincoln. Mr. Shapiro, bleeding from the face, left the club by the back door in the company of the two men immediately prior to NYPD Patrol's arrival on scene."

At the mention of the gold shield, Erin started to feel uneasy. She tried to give nothing away, continuing her stare-down with McDowell.

"We don't have the names of the two men," McDowell said. "The club's owner claims not to have security camera footage of them either. The bouncer says he doesn't recognize either man, but is probably lying. The dancer, Miss Beatrice Toole, AKA Traci, described them as a big blond with a short haircut and a broken nose, and a small, red-haired man with green eyes and, I quote, 'a killer smile.'"

Erin managed not to wince. *Corky and Vic?* she thought in disbelief. *Working together?!*

McDowell sighed, a surprisingly human sound. "You can knock off the poker-face routine, O'Reilly," she said. "We both know Viktor Neshenko was one of the men in that club, and he's trying to trace the history of the gun we took off you."

"That gun was used in a homicide about six weeks ago," Holliday added. "A drug dealer in the Bronx took two in the chest. Unsolved. Ballistics were a perfect match."

"Stanley Shapiro is a black-market gun dealer," McDowell said. "He has a lengthy record. It's obvious that Detective Neshenko thinks Shapiro provided the weapon. However, he isn't following proper procedure."

Because you ordered him not to, Bitch, Erin thought. That retort was probably showing in her eyes, and she didn't give a damn.

"Neshenko isn't stupid," McDowell said. "He wants people to think he is, but he's not. What's interesting is that he's working with James Corcoran outside correct channels."

"We're sure it's Corcoran," Holliday said quietly. "The description fits, as does the MO."

"I've spoken with Lieutenant Webb," McDowell said. "He claims no knowledge of this extralegal endeavor. I believe him. Neshenko would be smart enough to wall off his activities from his superior. He's trying to help you, O'Reilly. And he and Corcoran may have committed at least one serious crime in doing so."

"Why am I here, Lieutenant?" Erin asked, suddenly sick of the whole thing. "I'm obviously not going to comment on any of this speculation. And as you pointed out, even if I did, you couldn't use it in court, whatever I said."

"The dirty pistol doesn't make sense," McDowell said. "Does it, Captain?"

"No," Holliday said at once. "If Detective O'Reilly was in possession of an illegal firearm, that's the one she would have used to attack the O'Malleys. She wouldn't have used her service weapon. The mere fact of its existence suggests she was set up, and reinforces her statement that her sidearm was switched without her knowledge and used by the actual killer."

"I agree," McDowell said.

"Then why am I wearing these?" Erin demanded, rattling the handcuffs.

"Your arrest was necessary for more than one reason," McDowell said calmly. "Firstly, the evidence against you was damning. It was more than sufficient to take you into custody. If you had possessed half as much linking one of your suspects to a multiple homicide, you would have done the same in my place. Secondly, if you were being implicated in additional crimes, such as the murder of Desmond Chaney, placing you in police custody would provide you with an airtight alibi in the event of further homicides and shield you against legal jeopardy. I am now convinced of your innocence."

"Then you can take the bracelets off and let me go home," Erin said.

"The situation is complicated," Holliday said.

"I don't see how," Erin said angrily. "From where I'm sitting it's starting to look a lot like wrongful imprisonment."

"The Commissioner gave a statement to the press a few minutes before I asked you to be brought up," McDowell said. She picked up a remote control from a slot under the table and pointed it at the TV screen on the wall. The PC's big, soft-cheeked face filled the screen. McDowell pressed the PLAY button.

"Detective Erin O'Reilly has been arrested for the double murder of a woman and child in Brooklyn," he said. "Detective O'Reilly has been previously investigated for excessive force, insubordination, and misconduct, and has been involved in numerous fatal shootings. She was placed on suspension, and upon her arrest, her employment with the NYPD has been terminated."

McDowell pressed another button and the screen went black.

Erin felt like the button had killed the power in her heart at the same time. She sat unmoving, unable to speak, unable to think.

"I owe you an apology, O'Reilly," McDowell said, and Erin realized why the other woman hadn't addressed her as "Detective O'Reilly" at any point.

"I think we've gone a little beyond apologies, Lieutenant," Holliday said. His voice was tight and clipped. Erin's scattered thoughts whispered that she'd seen Holliday angry before, but never like this. The Captain's anger was pure, cold fury; the sort of anger that led to lethal violence on the street.

"I know," McDowell said. "I also know Detective Neshenko is trying to clear your name, O'Reilly. It's quite possible he will succeed. I hope so. While it doesn't excuse his bad behavior, it explains it. However, this has become a political matter. If I release you now, without charging you, it will be interpreted as a deliberate attack on the Commissioner."

Who gives a shit? Erin thought. "I can see how it'd be taken that way," she managed to say. Her lips felt cold. She wasn't a cop anymore. Twelve years gone, just like that. She'd lost everything she'd ever worked for, everything she'd tried to be.

And she'd lost Rolf. Maybe other officers were already on their way to the Barley Corner to grab him. She might never see him again.

"Fortunately, I am not a politician," McDowell said. "I will be preparing a full report for the Commissioner, which I will forward to him first thing in the morning, along with my letter of resignation. Captain?"

Holliday stood up and walked over to Erin. He took a cuff key out of his pocket. Erin wordlessly offered her wrists. He unlocked the cuffs and pocketed them.

"So what do I do now?" she asked.

"The first order of business is your K-9," McDowell said. "He's Departmental property, as you know. Someone will attempt to take possession of him, which is the correct legal action to take. I don't know what will be done with him. Officially, you're required to turn him over. If he is located, any NYPD officer is obligated to take him in."

"I know," Erin said numbly. "God damn it, I'm innocent!"

"That is currently beside the point," McDowell said.

"You aren't listening, Detective," Holliday said.

"Neither are you, sir!" Erin snapped. "Stop calling me that!"

"No!" Holliday said sharply. "You're still one of mine, and I'm going to see that you're fully reinstated. In the meantime, I'm going to protect another of my officers. As Lieutenant McDowell said, *if* K-9 Rolf is located, we're obligated to take custody. *If*, however, he were to go missing, what would be the result, Lieutenant?"

"A missing property report would need to be filed," McDowell said blandly. "Through proper channels. It would be a very low Departmental priority and would probably takes weeks, if not months, to be fully investigated."

Erin understood through the fog in her brain. "Thank you, sir," she said quietly.

"I don't expect Lieutenant McDowell's resignation to be accepted," Holliday said. "The optics are very bad. It will put pressure on the Commissioner and his office, and hopefully they'll back off and go into damage-control mode. That may buy us some time."

"Time for what, sir?" Erin asked.

"For you and your misguided colleagues to sort things out, obviously," Holliday said, clearly irritated she'd forced him to articulate it.

"The Major Crimes squad is under strict orders not to participate in the investigation of the O'Malley homicides," McDowell said. "Those orders do not, however, extend to civilians who are outside the NYPD's chain of command."

"Which is what you seem to be," Holliday added. "For the moment."

"Just so we're clear," Erin said. "Am I free to go?"

"Yes," Holliday said. "But I would advise you to be very careful with your movements. You were supposed to be implicated in the Chaney murder as well. I don't know what further attacks on you are planned. It's safe to assume the person who's targeted you has a great deal of potential ammunition, which he or she may not have fully expended."

Erin stood up. She looked at Holliday and McDowell, feeling like she was truly seeing them for the first time. "You're both on my side," she said quietly.

"I'm on the side of the law," McDowell said. "And the truth. That hasn't changed."

"I have your back," Holliday said. "That hasn't changed either. You can't use Departmental transportation, unfortunately. Can I offer you a ride home in my personal vehicle?"

"You'd better not, sir," Erin said. "We wouldn't want any cops stumbling over a K-9 by accident. I'll call a cab."

Chapter 21

"Here you are, ma'am," the cabbie said, pulling over to the curb. "The Barley Corner pub. You know the history of this place? It used to be a speakeasy during Prohibition."

"Yeah," Erin said dully. "I know."

"And more recently, it was a Mob bar," the driver went on. "The owner was allegedly a crime boss, but he cut some kind of deal. Then one of his associates blew the place up and they had to rebuild it."

"Is that so," Erin said. She pushed a twenty toward him, glad that at least they'd given her wallet and phone back when she'd been released. The Department had kept her .38, though Holliday had promised they'd get it back to her ASAP. "Keep the change," she added.

"Hey, thanks, lady," the cabbie said. "You have a good night."

"It's too late for that," she muttered, climbing out onto the curb. The warm light shining from the pub's windows onto the sidewalk failed to cheer her up. Even the thought of alcohol held no comfort. All it promised was numbness, but for the moment that would have to do. She wanted to hammer herself down and just stop thinking and feeling. She'd thought being arrested was the worst thing that could happen to her, but she was starting to find out just how deep that rabbit hole went.

Erin almost went around to the back door for a more surreptitious entry, but decided the hell with it and walked straight in. The pub was loud and crowded, which was a blessing. None of the patrons noticed her. Only Caitlin, the waitress, spotted her.

"Miss O'Reilly!" she chirped, popping up in front of her. "I'm so glad to see you! The news said—"

Erin held up a hand. "I know," she said. "Where's Carlyle?"

"Right this way," Caitlin said, turning with a swirl of her almost-too-short skirt. "We've all been really worried about you. Danny and Matt and Marian and me. I thought you were locked up!"

Erin didn't bother explaining. Caitlin would get the skinny from someone at the Corner soon enough. She followed the younger woman across the room and into the back hallway, where Caitlin knocked on the door to the private meeting room.

The door opened a crack. "Oh, it's you, love," Corky said when he saw Caitlin. "We're not needing more drinks just now."

"Like hell we're not," Erin growled, stepping past Caitlin.

Corky's eyes lit up with surprised delight. "Now here's something I wasn't expecting!" he said. "Come in!"

The room was dimly lit, dominated by a card table covered with green baize. Carlyle was sitting at the table. When he saw her, his jaw fell open. For once in his long and smooth-talking life, Morton Carlyle was at a complete loss for words.

"Erin!" a man exclaimed. Before she could react, Erin was seized in a crushing embrace, lifted clean off the floor. Her nose was mashed into a big guy's shirtfront. She smelled sweat and cheap cologne.

"Vic," she said in muffled tones. "Put me down."

"Holy shit!" Vic said, not letting go. "Goddamn, son of a bitching Christ on a tricycle! What are you *doing* here?"

"I live here," she said, pushing on his chest. It was completely ineffective. "I said, put me down."

"Lad, best set her down," Carlyle said.

Vic gave her a final squeeze and let go. Erin swayed for balance and caught herself with one hand on the table. Something cold and wet poked her other hand. She looked down and saw Rolf staring up at her, wagging his tail and pouring all the love and devotion he possessed into his stare.

Erin sagged to her knees, put her arms around the dog, and burst into tears.

Vic cleared his throat awkwardly. "Geez," he said. "It's okay. I didn't mean for us to get all emotional."

She shook her head and buried her face in Rolf's fur. Even the K-9 was a little uncomfortable. He looked over her shoulder at Vic with a quizzical expression. He was a working K-9, not a therapy dog. He wasn't sure what to do with a weeping partner.

"I think we'll be wanting another bottle, Miss Tierney," Carlyle said quietly. "Glen D, if you please, and another glass. And close the door. Thank you, darling."

Vic laid a clumsy hand on Erin's shoulder. "This is crazy," he muttered, his voice hoarse. "I didn't think we'd be seeing you tonight. How'd you get out? They said on the news you'd been shit-canned. I'm damn sorry. We tried, we really did. There just wasn't enough time."

"I know," Erin said. She pulled back a little from Rolf, sniffled, and swiped the back of her hand across her nose. "McDowell showed me the PC at the press conference."

"That bitch!" Vic said. "It wasn't enough to throw you in Lockup? She had to rub your nose in it? I oughta go over there and kick her ass!"

"You don't get it," Erin said. "She's as mad as you are."

"I doubt it," Vic growled.

"She's resigning tomorrow morning."

"Bullshit."

"No, she's going to do it," Erin said. "I saw the look on her face. She's *pissed* at the PC. She wasn't sure I was the shooter. The arrest was mostly to get me off the street while her team tried to figure what really happened. It wasn't supposed to go public yet."

"I'm sure all these political games are quite intriguing," Carlyle said. He'd come over to stand next to Erin and Vic. "But they're rather beside the point at present. I understand your employment with New York City is at an end."

"Yeah," Erin said bitterly.

"Where does that leave us at present?"

"We need to stash Rolf somewhere," she said. "The NYPD wants him back."

"They can kiss my ass!" Vic exploded. "Goddamn dognappers!"

"Detective Neshenko's admirable sentiments aside," Carlyle said dryly, "I'm certain we can find a safe place for your dog. We've a number of options. Corky's rather skilled at hiding both things and people, and your da's on his way if you'd rather the family take care of Rolf."

"Dad?" Erin said, surprised. "How do you know?"

"He telephoned me the moment he saw the ten o'clock news," Carlyle said. "He and your mum got straight in their car. They'll be here by morning, earlier if they don't stop to sleep on the way."

Erin put a hand over her face. "Great," she muttered. "He's going to kill me."

"He wants to kill a number of people," Carlyle said. "But I don't think you're among them. He's coming to provide support and assistance as he's able. Now, what's your legal status?"

"I'm a civilian," she spat. "I'm not under arrest anymore, I'm not being charged. I'm not really anything, I guess. Not even a pet owner."

"You're Erin O'Reilly," Carlyle said. "And the Erin I know wouldn't let a wee thing like being sacked stand in her way."

"I can look into things on the side," she said. "Holliday and McDowell hinted at it. You're in some trouble, Vic, by the way."

"Me?" Vic said, startled. "Why?"

"You beat the crap out of a suspect and Corky cut some punk's fingers off."

"Oh, that bullshit," Vic said. "That wasn't anything."

"Tell me you at least got some useful intel off Shapiro," she said.

"We're looking for a blonde chick," he said. "About your height and build, blue eyes. Pretty, but hard-faced. 'Ice queen' were the Satchel's words. Her face looks a hell of a lot like yours. No name. I leaned on him pretty hard, but I didn't get anything else. No DNA samples, no fingerprints, no fibers, nada."

"I don't know the lass," Corky added. "And I thought I knew all the big female operators in this town. She may be outside talent."

"But she knew Shapiro," Erin said. "That means she has underworld connections. What'd you do with him when you were done talking to him?"

Vic shrugged. "I gave him a lecture about being a good citizen and ditched him. Then we came back here to figure our next move. We haven't been here much longer than you."

"What condition was he in when you got rid of him?"

"He was more or less okay. I kinda broke his nose a little. And maybe wiggled it around while I was talking to him. He'll get over it."

"Why'd you break his nose?"

"He pulled a gun on me. It was that or shoot him."

Erin turned to Corky. "And the fingers?"

"The other lad was about to shoot my mate here," Corky said. "His finger was on the trigger, so I sliced it off. I didn't mean to take the second one. I'm a bit rusty and I was in a rush."

"I'm not your damn mate," Vic said.

"We've shed blood and drunk whiskey together," Corky said cheerfully. "That's good enough for me, lad."

"Call me 'lad' one more time," Vic said. "You won't believe what happens next. But I could use another whiskey."

Caitlin arrived almost exactly on cue, bringing a bottle of Glen Docherty-Kinlochewe. Carlyle opened it and poured a round for everyone but Rolf.

"Come now," Corky said. "We work well together. There's no more shame in you associating with me than there is with me rubbing elbows with a copper. I'll admit it goes against our natures, but we're united in common cause."

"Yeah, whatever," Vic said. "Zofia's been looking through the NYPD database, trying to find this chick. But so far we've got nothing. And Corcoran and Carlyle say there's nobody connected with the O'Malleys that fits the description. If she's from somewhere else, with no name and nothing to ID her, I don't know how we can possibly track her down."

"So she's a dead end," Erin said. "But I'm pretty sure she also killed Desmond Chaney."

"I don't doubt it," Carlyle said. "If she had dealings with him, she'd have wanted to remove him from the picture. Does that help us?"

"I doubt it," Erin said gloomily. "The only evidence I found there was planted. Some of my hair, I think."

"Is she gonna go after anyone else?" Vic wondered. "If so, we could set up a stakeout. Maybe she'll make another play for the O'Malley brat?"

"Unlikely," Carlyle said. "If I'm reading the situation rightly, Richard was meant to survive the attack."

"Why?" Vic asked. "I mean, what possible use is that little punk to anybody? He's not some big, powerful criminal mastermind. Hell, two of the guys in this room are bigger, better gangsters than he'll ever be."

"That's the nicest thing you've ever said to me," Corky said. "You're too kind by half."

"And that's the first time anyone's described me that way," Vic retorted.

"She wanted a witness who could identify her as me," Erin said.

"So you're certain this blonde lass is our shooter?" Carlyle asked.

"It makes sense," she said. "If she has a short haircut, she could hide it under a wig. The rest of the description is close enough."

"I showed Shapiro a pic of Erin," Vic confirmed. "He said the blonde could've been her with longer, darker hair."

"I guess we have our shooter," Erin said. "Except that we don't have a name or any identifying info."

"Which means we don't have her," Vic sighed. He grabbed the bottle and poured another shot. "Jesus, I'm tired."

"Kyle Finnegan is the key," Erin said. "He's in this up to his neck. It wouldn't surprise me if he's behind it."

"How do we prove it?" Carlyle asked.

"I have no idea," Erin said. "He's too smart."

"Smart?" Vic echoed. "He's a friggin' lunatic!"

"That doesn't make him stupid," Carlyle said. "Does this strike you as the sort of plan a sane man would concoct?"

A knock at the door stopped whatever Vic was about to say. Corky opened it to reveal an apologetically-smiling Caitlin.

"Sorry," she said. "There's someone here asking for you, Mr. Carlyle."

"Who?" Carlyle asked.

"A Dr. Levine."

"What?" Erin and Vic exclaimed in unison.

"You'd best show her in," Carlyle said.

A moment later, Sarah Levine came in. She was wearing her scrubs and lab coat. A pair of noise-canceling headphones was slung around her neck. And in her hand was a serrated knife.

"Whoa there," Vic said, holding up a hand.

Corky, with better reflexes and fewer inhibitions, had already dropped his Scarab tactical knife out of its wrist clip and flicked it open, just in case. The blade shone wickedly in the dim light. He held it lightly, expertly, balanced for a sudden stab.

"Doc?" Erin said. "Please put the knife down."

"Why?" Levine asked. "I didn't expect to see you here, Detective. I wanted to talk to Morton Carlyle."

"Knives make cops nervous," Vic said. "Especially when they're pointed at us. Jesus, you gave me a start."

"Oh." Levine glanced down at the knife. "I just needed it for comparison purposes. I didn't intend to intimidate anyone. It's a steak knife from your restaurant, Mr. Carlyle."

"I can see that, aye," Carlyle said. "Comparison with what, Doctor?"

"The murder weapon recovered from Desmond Chaney's apartment," Levine said. "The Crime Scene Unit delivered it to the morgue for me to compare with kerf marks on Chaney's body. It was a formality. Chaney's blood was all over the knife, but I requested the knife in any case."

"Why?" Erin asked.

"The crime scene had been compromised by a third party," Levine explained. "That third party had removed fibers from

Chaney's hand. It was possible that person had also planted a false weapon at the scene. I was being thorough."

"And?" Erin asked.

"And what?" Levine replied blankly.

"Was it a match?"

"Yes."

"Then why are you holding one of Carlyle's steak knives?"

"I came to ask his permission to borrow it to compare with the murder weapon. I believe they are the same model from the same manufacturer."

"You're saying one of my knives was used to kill Desmond Chaney?" Carlyle asked.

"It's possible the murderer may have obtained the weapon from another source," Levine said. "However, it is a well-used knife that has been repeatedly sharpened. The handle is chipped and worn and the blade has several imperfections, so it is not newly purchased. Other restaurants in the area may, however, have similar blades. I have not yet made a thorough canvass of nearby eating establishments."

"It's one of yours," Erin told Carlyle in tones of absolute certainty.

"I don't doubt it," he said. "But I'm curious how Dr. Levine concluded my cutlery was a likely match."

"When I attended the engagement party here, earlier this year, I noticed the pattern of the silverware," Levine said. "The murder weapon strongly resembled the knife I used to eat my meal here."

Everyone was staring at her, momentarily dumbfounded. Corky recovered first.

"Are you saying you remember every knife or fork you've ever used?" he asked.

"Of course not," Levine said. "My memory of childhood utensils is very unreliable. However, most people only have one set of silverware for home use, so I really only need to notice utensils when eating away from home, which I don't do often."

"But you do eat," Vic said. "Food, I mean."

"Caloric intake is necessary to maintain vital functions," Levine said. "Of course I eat."

"I guess she's not a vampire after all," Vic whispered in Erin's ear.

Erin didn't particularly care whether Levine was one of Dracula's daughters at that moment. "The knife was meant to tie the killing to the Barley Corner," she said.

"That's rather tenuous," Carlyle said doubtfully.

Erin shook her head. "No, the hairs were meant to ID me. The knife was just a little bonus. She used my gun, remember. Damn it, I should've taken the knife too."

"I had hypothesized you were the third party at the scene," Levine said. "I would appreciate it if you would refrain from tampering with my crime scenes in the future. It makes my job more difficult and is also illegal."

"Sorry, Doc," Erin said. "It was necessary."

"I don't see how," Levine said.

"This is good," Erin said.

"How?" Vic demanded. "It's just more fabricated evidence."

"No," she said. "It means the killer was here! At the Barley Corner! That's where she stole the knife!"

"So?" Vic replied.

"We have cameras," Carlyle said, springing to his feet. "And the tapes are in the security office, so they won't have been stolen or tampered with."

"Which means we might be able to put a face on our killer," Erin said.

"We already know she looks just like you," Vic said.

"We can run the image through facial recognition," Erin said. She hesitated. "You can, I mean. I'm not allowed into Major Crimes anymore."

"Screw that," Vic said. "We'll get you back in there, you'll see. We'll make the PC eat every one of his goddamn words, if I have to shove them down his throat myself. Where's this security office of yours?"

"The next door down," Carlyle said. "If you'll follow me, ladies and gentlemen?"

*   *   *

"Figures," Vic muttered, much later. "Even off the clock, I'm still stuck looking at friggin' security footage."

"Would you care for another wee nip?" Carlyle asked.

"No more booze," Vic said. "I've already got a headache. Got any Mountain Dew?"

"Aye," Carlyle said. "This is a family establishment these days. We've all manner of non-alcoholic beverages for the wee ones and their teetotaling parents. Corky, would you be a good lad?"

"Gladly," Corky said, hurrying out of the room.

Erin didn't blame him for leaving. The tiny security office was comfortable enough for a single man at the desk. The four of them, plus Rolf, were making it pretty stuffy. Carlyle had sent Ken Mason, his chief of security, out just to free up some room. Now Vic was seated in front of the computer monitor, fast-forwarding through the footage from the past week.

"I'm gonna be here all night," he gloomily predicted. "Maybe all week. Do you have any idea how many people come through this place every night?"

"I do, aye," Carlyle said. "I flatter myself it's a successful business."

"We've been here three goddamn hours," Vic said. "My eyeballs are falling out."

"I can take over if you're used up," Erin said.

"Who says I'm used up?" Vic snapped. "I'm just bitching. I can go all night and still have plenty left over."

"So can I," Corky said, popping back in, accompanied by Caitlin. "Stamina's important to a lad."

Caitlin smiled flirtatiously at Corky, obviously recalling a previous encounter. "He's not kidding," she said, setting a pitcher of Mountain Dew down on the desk. "What're you guys looking for?"

"A silverware thief," Erin said. Vic picked up the pitcher and drank a big gulp straight out of it.

"Seriously?" Caitlin said. "We lose forks and spoons all the time. I think half of them get thrown out by mistake when the dishes are getting washed, but sometimes people take them. Souvenirs, I guess. It's not a big deal."

"This was a deliberate theft," Carlyle said. "A woman took one of my knives."

"And you're hoping to catch her by looking at that?" Caitlin wrinkled her nose. "Fat chance, boss. You can't even see into half of the booths on that camera, and there's dozens of people in here at a time. It's hard for us to keep track of them all, even while we're open."

"Tell me about it," Vic said. "But unless you've got a better idea, this is what we're stuck with."

"You could ask Danny," the waitress suggested.

"Danny Sullivan?" Erin asked. "The bartender?"

"Yeah," Caitlin said. "He sees everybody who comes in, and he's got a great memory for faces. You could come in here once, and a month later he'd remember what you ordered. He says it's a bartender thing."

"Worth a try," Erin said. "Is he out there now?"

"Of course. We're closing up at two, and he usually stays half an hour after to tidy up the bar."

Carlyle glanced at the clock, which read 1:47. "Things ought to be winding down," he said. "Erin, come with me and we'll have a chat with Danny."

"You keep checking the camera feed," Erin told Vic. "Just in case."

"Hold on a sec," Vic said. "You're not a detective anymore. Hell, you're not even a beat cop. You can't give me orders!"

She glared at him.

"Okay, fine," he said. "I'll do it. But only because I feel like it."

The Barley Corner crowd had indeed thinned out considerably. The big-screen TV on the wall was dark and silent. A few patrons were hanging around the bar. One of Caitlin's fellow waitresses had started wiping down the tables. Danny was behind the counter, serving up beer and whiskey to the hardcore drinkers.

"Excuse me, lad," Carlyle said, sliding into his customary seat at the bar. Erin took the stool next to him. Rolf, unaware of his fugitive status, stuck close to Erin. She didn't see any cops in the pub, so she figured it was okay. Then she realized she was looking out for cops the way a criminal would, and wanted to crawl into a dark hole with a bottle of whiskey and never come out.

"Get you something, boss?" Danny asked.

"I'd like a word with you," Carlyle said. "When it's convenient."

"Sure thing," Danny said. He raised his voice. "Hey guys, we're closing soon. Last round. Let me know what you want, and if you need a cab I'll call you one."

After he'd filled the patrons' last orders, he came back to Erin and Carlyle. "What's up?" he asked, leaning his forearms on the bar.

"Caitlin says you're good at faces," Erin said.

"That's right," Danny said. "After you do this job a while, you pick it up. People love it if they come in and you ask if they want their usual, even if it's just a Guinness. I pay attention to people; that's the key. You have to really look at them, but without staring. It mostly takes time and practice."

"Did you notice a woman in here sometime over the past week or two?" Erin asked. "She'd be about my height and build. As a matter of fact, she looks a lot like me, except her hair would probably be short and blonde. But she might've had a wig."

Danny gave Erin a careful, considering look, marking the details in her face. Erin felt self-conscious. She knew she wasn't looking her best. A sleepless night following a very rough couple of days had left her a little ragged around the edges. Her eyes had dark smudges under them, her hair was oily and scraggly, and she could really use a shower.

"Yeah," Danny said slowly. "Take away the black hair and... wow. She could be your sister."

"Who?" Erin asked in sudden excitement. "When?"

"This would've been about a week ago," he said. "No, exactly a week. She came in alone. Good-looking lady, but dressed down, like she didn't want to attract attention. Blue jeans, hoodie. Dark blue hoodie. She sat in that booth over there."

He pointed to the corner booth next to the dartboard.

"That's amazing," Erin said. "What else did you notice about her?"

"She ordered the New York Strip Steak," Danny said. "Baked potato, I think. And a pint of Guinness."

"So you'd bring her a steak knife with her meal," Erin said, nodding to Carlyle. "Do you remember how she paid?"

"Cash," Danny said. "Crisp twenties."

Erin's face fell. A credit card would have been traceable.

"She got a whiskey at the bar afterward," he said. "When she paid. She ordered the Glen D. Good taste."

"So you got a good close look at her?" Erin asked.

Danny nodded. "She reminded me of you," he said. "I chatted with her a little. She was nice enough. Asked some questions about the place, and about Mr. Carlyle."

"I'll bet she did," Erin said grimly. "What'd you tell her?"

"Nothing much." Danny shrugged. "I don't talk about your personal life, boss. I like working here."

"Good lad," Carlyle said. "I don't suppose she gave you a name?"

"Yeah," Danny said. "But I don't have as good a knack for names as faces. It was something unusual. Started with an O. Olivia? No. Opal? No, that's not it. Crud, I'm sorry. I'm better with faces and drinks than names."

"Ophelia?" Carlyle suggested.

Danny snapped his fingers. "That's it!" he said. "How'd you guess? You know her?"

"I don't," Carlyle said. "I was thinking about our mutual acquaintance Kyle Finnegan and his fondness for Shakespeare. Ophelia is Hamlet's love interest in the play."

"An alias," Erin sighed. "Damn. I guess it's something to go on."

"Thanks, Danny," Carlyle said.

"Don't mention it," the bartender said. Then, turning to the other customers, "Okay, guys, drink up! Closing time! Like the song says, you don't have to go home but you can't stay here."

Chapter 22

"Ladies and gentlemen, we have a winner," Vic said. Armed with Danny's information, he'd been able to zero in on the woman in the hooded sweatshirt.

"She does look a bit like you," Corky said. "Though it's hard to tell from this angle."

"It's not enough for facial recognition," Erin said. "Not with the hood up."

"Which she doubtless knew," Carlyle said. "This is a very canny lass we're dealing with."

"A first name," Vic said. "Which is probably fake. No last name. Still no physical evidence. This might be enough for reasonable doubt, if we still need to get Erin off the hook, but it's not enough to nail this Ophelia chick."

"Ophelia," Erin said softly. "Ophelia. What do we know about Ophelia?"

"Not a goddamn thing," Vic said. "As I was just saying."

"Not her," Erin said. "The character in the play."

"She's in love with Hamlet," Carlyle said. "Then Hamlet kills her father by mistake. Ophelia goes mad and drowns herself, either by accident or on purpose. Her brother and Hamlet kill one another in a duel at the end of the play."

"Yeesh," Vic said. "Talk about a screwup."

"That's why it's a tragedy," Carlyle said. "Misunderstandings culminate in lethal consequences."

"Just like on the street," Vic said. "I guess we're back where we started."

"Only if it's a fake name," Erin said.

"There's no lass called Ophelia in the Irish Mob," Corky said. "I'd know."

"Because you would've screwed her," Vic said.

Corky gave a half-shrug and a sheepish smile. "That's as may be. The point stands."

"She's connected to Finnegan," Erin said. "She's probably been to see him in prison."

"I can check the visitor logs first thing in the morning," Vic said. "But if that Chaney punk was dirty, he might've fudged the records."

"Did you drive your Taurus here?" Erin asked.

"Yeah," Vic said. "Why?"

"Let's look at Finnegan's prison record," she said.

"What're we looking for?"

"Next of kin."

"Finnegan has no relations I know of," Carlyle said. "He's always been a loner."

"Then it'll be interesting to see who he listed," Erin said.

*   *   *

All four of them trooped out to Vic's car, minus Rolf. To the K-9's disgust, he was put back upstairs until Erin could figure a better hiding place.

"They won't be able to go up there without a warrant," she said. "That ought to protect him for a while."

While Erin, Corky, and Carlyle waited curbside, Vic logged into the Taurus's onboard computer and started scanning records. The car was parked in the police space next to the Barley Corner. Manhattan never went completely to sleep, but it was after two in the morning and the sidewalk was sparsely populated. Erin thrust her hands into her jacket pockets and shivered.

"It'll all come right, darling," Carlyle said, standing behind her and wrapping his arms around her.

"I'm not a cop anymore," she said, leaning against him. "They took it away from me."

"Then we'll get it back," he said.

"It doesn't work that way," she said. "Even if we eventually clear my name, it could take weeks to get reinstated. And all that time, they'll be running headlines about Junkyard O'Reilly, Mafia Cop. Forget about my job; I won't even be able to live in New York anymore! I guess I'd better take your name. Then we can move somewhere else, Chicago or LA, and you can open a new pub. Then maybe people won't recognize me and I can have a normal life."

"That sounds rather like witness protection," he said.

"I guess so," she said.

"This is your home, darling," he said. "I know what it's like to leave home. We'll fight for yours, to the last."

"Last what?" she asked, twisting her head around to look at him.

"Last drop of blood," he said. "Last bit of strength. Last round of ammunition."

"That shouldn't be too hard," she said with a dry laugh. "I don't even *have* any ammunition. They took all my guns away!"

"Your partner's well enough armed for a small army," Carlyle said, nodding toward Vic.

The big Russian, as if he'd been called, shoved his key into his car's ignition and twisted it. The Taurus rumbled to life. He rolled down his window.

"Hop in, Erin!" he called.

"What?" she said, disentangling herself from Carlyle's embrace. "Where the hell are we going?"

"Brooklyn," he said.

"Again? What for?"

He waved impatiently toward the passenger side. "Get in! I'll explain on the way!"

Erin glanced at Carlyle. "I guess we have a lead," she said.

"Don't run yourself into the ground, darling," he said gently. "This race isn't over yet."

"I'll be fine," she said, kissing him on the cheek. "You should get some rest."

"Call me," he said. "No matter the hour. I'll not sleep a wink till I know you're well."

Vic tapped the horn irritably.

"Okay, okay," Erin said, jogging around the car and climbing in. "Keep your shirt on."

Vic accelerated away from the curb, leaving Corky and Carlyle in the rearview. Corky waved cheerfully and blew a kiss.

"Was that aimed at you, or me?" Vic asked sourly.

"Both," Erin said. "So what've we got?"

"You guessed it," he said. "Finnegan's next of kin. Ophelia Flaherty, age twenty-two."

"Wife?" Erin guessed.

Vic made a face. "Finnegan's forty-six. That'd be creepy. She's his daughter."

"Finnegan has a *daughter*?!"

"If he had a kid, it's a fifty-fifty chance," Vic said.

"I didn't know he had a kid. Or a wife."

"I have a kid. I don't have a wife."

"I didn't mean it that way," she said. "But this is nuts. Carlyle didn't have any idea. I don't think anybody in the O'Malleys knew."

"Maybe he's one of those guys who likes to keep his work and life separate," Vic said. "He doesn't want his daughter to know he eats other guys' faces."

"If she stole that knife, and got that Glock from Stan Shapiro, she's probably murdered three people," Erin said. "I don't think a little face-munching would bother her."

"She doesn't have a criminal record," Vic said. "I looked. In fact, she doesn't have any footprint in the system at all. Hell, for all we know, she might not be his real daughter."

"Different last name," she said. "The mother's, I suppose."

"Could be. Is the mom important?"

"I don't know," Erin said.

"You *do* have an evil twin!" Vic exclaimed triumphantly. "And she's the daughter of your worst enemy. This is awesome!"

"I'm glad somebody thinks so," she said. "But it doesn't make sense. What are the chances Finnegan would have a kid who looks just like me?"

"Pretty damn good at the moment, I'd say. What're we gonna do when we find her?"

"How the hell am I supposed to know that?" Erin snapped. "You're the one who's driving us to Brooklyn in the middle of the night! I don't suppose you have a search warrant?"

"Of course not," Vic said. "I'm not even supposed to be on this case, remember? And you're a damn civilian! We're breaking all kinds of rules tonight. I'm playing it by ear."

"You're going to get fired too, you know that?"

"If I do, at least I'll get the chance to tell the PC exactly what I think of him," Vic said. "That fat-assed politician can kiss my pucker-hole, and I'll say so on national TV. I'll do all the late-night talk shows. That's a promise. I can't believe he threw you under the bus like that! If we go down, I guarantee he's going down with us. I'm talking scorched earth, everybody loses."

"Vic?"

"Yeah?"

"It's sweet you're that angry on my account, but try not to overdo it. I think we're in plenty of trouble as it is. Which AOS is Ophelia in?"

"The Six-Oh. My old stomping grounds."

"Do you have anyone who owes you a favor? Anybody who's still wearing a shield, I mean, and might be awake?"

"There's Mira," he said.

"Anyone other than your ex-girlfriend?"

"Sheesh. Can you really afford to be picky? Mira's solid."

"You're right," Erin said. "I can't be choosy. Fine. Give her a call."

Vic pulled out his phone and dialed one-handed while steering the Taurus south. He held it to his ear.

"Yeah, Mira, it's me," he said. "No, this isn't a booty call. Sorry to disappoint you. No, I'm not drunk, either. As a matter of fact, I'm heading your way with Erin O'Reilly. Remember her? Yeah, okay, I saw the news too."

He turned to Erin. "Mira sends her condolences," he said. "She says the PC is, and I quote, 'A fat, useless prick who needs to go eat a whole bucket of shit one bite at a time.'"

"No argument here," Erin said.

"Yeah, Mira," Vic said. "We need your help. We're going after the chick we think really did those murders. Okay, awesome. No, we'd better not come to the station. I'll text you the address. Hey, thanks. I really appreciate this. No, not quite that much, but a lot. We'll be there in twenty."

He hung up. "Just so you know, I turned down a hot offer of no-strings sex," he said. "I don't think she was joking, either."

"You're a credit to your gender," Erin said.

"She'll be there," he said. "Now we just need a plan."

"I'm working on it," Erin said.

*　　*　　*

"Ah, shit," Vic said.

"What?" Erin asked.

"Remember that restaurant?" Vic replied.

"The one where that human-trafficking bastard hung out? Peter Vlasov?"

"That's the one," he said. "The same one where I ran into his cousin Gennady. And here we are, with our babe Ophelia right across the friggin' street."

"Better pull around the block," she advised.

"You think?" he retorted. "And there I was thinking I'd just park out front, maybe go in and order some caviar."

Vic drove past Matrushka's without slowing down. Erin spotted a couple of Russian thugs hanging around under the nearest streetlight. In its glow, she could see that both of them were heavily tattooed and obviously armed.

"Looks like they changed lookouts," Vic said, steering around the corner.

"How do you know?" Erin asked.

"Because the last guy would have two black eyes and a broken nose, courtesy of yours truly."

"You're such a people person, Vic," Erin said. Fortunately, the darkness kept the goons from being able to see through the Taurus's windshield.

Vic found a parking space near the end of the next block. He pulled in and popped the trunk. He dismounted, got his Kevlar vest out, and strapped it on, pulling his coat on over it.

"If you conceal that, how am I supposed to tell you're a cop?" a woman's voice asked from a nearby shadow.

Erin nearly jumped out of her shoes. Mira Ivanova emerged onto the sidewalk, a sardonic smile on her face. That face would have been remarkably pretty if not for the scar that ran down one cheek, giving her a slightly lopsided, sneering expression.

"In this neighborhood, a police vest just makes you a better target," Vic said. "Did you bring anyone else?"

"Nah," Mira said. "I figured why share the fun?"

"We ought to have ESU for this," Erin said.

"Really?" Mira asked sharply. "Who's our target?"

"We don't need ESU," Vic said. "We're just after some friggin' chick. She thinks she's hot shit because she's a mob boss's kid, but we can take her."

"She's killed three people," Erin reminded him. "That we know of. She's a good shot, she knows how to use a knife, and we can assume she's armed and dangerous."

"Which is why I'm wearing my vest," Vic said.

"How come we don't have ESU?" Mira asked.

"It's kind of semi-official," Vic said.

"I figured," Mira said. "On account of the newly-minted civilian you've got following you around."

"Hey!" Erin growled.

"Which reminds me," Vic said. "Here."

He drew his Sig-Sauer, reversed the weapon, and held it out to Erin.

"Thanks," she said, taking the gun and doing a press-check to make sure a round was chambered.

Vic nodded and pulled his Delta Elite from its holster in the small of his back. "Our girl's in apartment 401," he said.

"The front door's in view of Matrushka's," Erin said.

"And Matrushka's has a couple *bratva* bastards killing time out front," Mira said. "I clocked them on the way in. Are they involved?"

"Maybe," Erin said.

"Jesus," Mira said. "If we're gonna start shooting it out with the Russian Mob, we really do need backup. Those guys have access to military firepower. I'm talking assault rifles, maybe grenades or goddamn rocket launchers."

"Forget about them," Vic said. "They're not on the same team."

"Finnegan set them up the same way he set me up," Erin said. "He faked Barsov stabbing him. He wants us to go after them."

"Then why is the girl right here?" Mira asked.

"Let's ask her," Vic said. He pointed. "There's a side door. I bet we can pop the lock."

"That's not exactly kosher," Mira said doubtfully.

"Listen," Vic said. "Erin's my partner. She's being set up. These bastards are trying to destroy her. And I'm not gonna let that happen. No matter what. You don't want in on this, go on home. Sorry I got you involved."

"Don't you pull that crap on me," Mira said. "I'll go anywhere you do, even if you gave me up for that cute blonde trick."

"You ever call Zofia that again, I'll kick your ass," Vic snapped. He walked to the door and tried the handle. It didn't turn.

"Here," Mira said. She took a credit card out of her pocket and very efficiently shimmed the latch. "That's the sort of crap you pick up when you're working burglaries," she explained.

The building was battered and grimy. Erin felt grit crunching under her shoes. The overhead lights were a sickly fluorescent greenish-white, several flickering and buzzing. Graffiti decorated the hallway walls.

"What a shithole," Vic said. "Do we want to try the elevator?"

Erin shook her head. "Stairs," she said. "We don't know what's up there."

"And the elevator might not even work," Mira added. She'd pulled her own sidearm, a Sig-Sauer just like Vic's.

Four flights was an annoying climb, but they made it up without incident. Vic led the way to unit 401. The door had a peephole in it and a high-quality custom lock under the knob.

"What if she doesn't let us in?" Mira murmured as they approached.

"She will," Erin said. She couldn't shake the feeling that, in spite of everything, she was still dancing to her enemy's tune. "I don't know if this is such a good idea."

"We'll find out in a minute," Vic said. He stood against the wall, keeping out of the line of fire in case the apartment's resident decided to fire a few rounds through the door. Then he knocked loudly. "Ophelia Flaherty! Open up! This is the NYPD!"

Erin wondered what they'd do if nobody answered. Maybe Ophelia wasn't even home. It was a little before 3AM, but some people were night owls. For all they knew, Ophelia had a boyfriend and was sleeping over. Or maybe she didn't even live there, and this was yet another complicated trap.

"Who is it?"

The voice was that of a young woman, high-pitched and a little nervous. She sounded almost scared, which didn't fit Erin's image of a cold-blooded assassin at all.

"I told you," Vic said. "It's the NYPD."

"What's your name, Officer? And your badge number?"

"Detective Neshenko. Major Crimes. Here's my shield." Vic held it up in front of the peephole, being careful to keep his body to the side.

"What do you want?"

"Are you Ophelia Flaherty?"

"Yes."

"We want to talk to you. We just have a few questions. Open the door."

"Who do you mean by 'we?' How many of you are there?"

"Two detectives," Vic said, winking at Erin, who scowled.

"Who's the other detective?" Ophelia asked.

"What does that matter?" Vic replied.

"I won't open the door until I know who's out there," Ophelia insisted.

"Ludmira Ivanova," Mira said. "Burglary, out of the Six-Oh. Does that answer your question?"

There was a short pause. Vic curled his hand into a fist and poised it to knock again. But before he could, the lock clicked open. The door opened about six inches to show part of an oddly familiar female face.

"Wow," Vic said, blinking. "Lady, you look just like somebody else I know."

"I don't think that's an appropriate thing to say," Ophelia said. Most people, when faced with Vic, tended to keep an eye on him. He was big, male, and dangerous-looking. But Ophelia's gaze wandered past him and fixed on Erin's face. When they made eye contact, Ophelia's expression changed. She'd looked confused and a little worried, but the concern had cleared. Now she was confident. Erin didn't like that one bit.

"No offense," Vic said. "Besides, I think you already know who I'm talking about."

"You can come in," Ophelia said, stepping back and pulling the door the rest of the way open. The three entered cautiously, ready for trouble. Mira and Erin fanned out to either side, checking the corners of the room.

The apartment was sparsely furnished. It didn't really look like a young woman lived there. The furniture was tattered and generic. The walls were bare of decoration. The living room didn't even have a TV.

It was spooky to be looking at her double up close and in person. Ophelia Flaherty wasn't an exact copy of Erin. For one thing, her hair was very different. Ophelia was a blonde with a pixie cut. She was a lot younger than Erin, though it was hard to gauge by looking at her face. It was like someone had tried to mimic Erin's face but had made it a little too regular, a little too smooth.

"You're very pretty, Miss O'Reilly," Ophelia said. "I've been looking forward to meeting you."

"I've been looking forward to meeting you, too," Erin said.

"Jesus Christ," Mira said, staring at the two of them. "Are you seeing this, Vic?"

"He said you'd probably come," Ophelia said. "I didn't think you'd find me, but he said you're really smart. He was pretty sure you'd figure almost all of it out."

"Almost?" Erin said.

"You'll know the whole thing in the end," Ophelia said. "But it'll be too late by then."

"What's it like?" Erin asked. "Being Kyle Finnegan's daughter?"

Ophelia's eyes shone. They were wide, clear, and blue, and if Erin didn't know better she'd think they were innocent. "He's amazing," she said. "He's a genius, you know."

"He's out of his damn mind," Vic muttered.

"People said Mozart was insane," Ophelia said. "And Bobby Fischer. Daddy plays chess, you know. Without even looking at the board. And he sees twenty moves ahead. I'm not bad, but he can checkmate me before we even start playing."

"I guess it comes down to knowing what the game is," Erin said quietly. She was studying the other woman and she'd finally spotted some telltales. "You had plastic surgery done."

"Obviously," Ophelia said, smiling pleasantly. "I had almost the right bone structure to begin with. That was what suggested the idea. It hurt, but it was worth it. I had to train awfully hard, too. You're in great shape, you know that? You run a lot."

"That's right," Erin said, thinking that this was the weirdest conversation of her entire life, and that was really saying something.

"Oh, I know," Ophelia said. "I've been watching you for a while now."

"I'll bet," Erin said. "So you can learn how I move, how I talk, so you can fake being me."

"You could take it as a compliment," Ophelia said. "Imitation is the sincerest form of flattery."

"You've been studying me," Erin said. "Why don't you tell me a little something about you? For starters, who's your mother?"

"I don't really remember her," Ophelia said. "She and Daddy couldn't be together, on account of his work. She would have been in danger. So they lived apart, but she died when I was little. Daddy paid a family to take care of me. I always used their last name, so nobody would know Daddy and I were related."

"Flaherty?"

"That's right. They were all right, I guess. Daddy came to see me when he could, but he couldn't do it too often."

"If it was such a big secret, why did he list you as his next of kin?" Erin asked.

"Once he was in prison, what did it matter?" Ophelia replied. "It meant I could visit him with family privileges. But we shouldn't have done it. That's how you found me, isn't it?"

"You gave the bartender at the Barley Corner your real name," Erin said.

Ophelia blinked. "But that was *days* ago! And I didn't do anything when I was there! That's incredible!"

"Danny's good at his job," Erin said. "So is our Medical Examiner. She's the one who matched the knife you used to cut Desmond Chaney's throat."

"You cut Desmond Chaney's throat," Ophelia replied. "That's what the evidence says. You didn't want him telling people you were lying about your gun, after you used it to kill Richard O'Malley's family. There were witnesses."

"Once we put you in a lineup, they won't be so sure of their ID," Erin said grimly.

"They already did a lineup," Ophelia said. "And that round is over. You lost."

"It's not over yet," Erin said.

"Yes, it is," Ophelia said. "You lost your job. Your reputation is gone. You know what Daddy says about reputation? It can't be repaired. Once it cracks, you can't glue it back together. The head of your Department disowned you on national TV."

"I don't see a TV in here," Erin observed.

"I don't live here," Ophelia countered. "This is just an observation post. It's under my name, but that was just so you'd know to find me here. I watched the news from my real home. Then I came here to wait. I thought you'd come. Didn't you wonder why I was wide awake and dressed? I've been expecting you."

"Well, here's something that wasn't on the news," Erin said. "I've been released, all charges dropped."

"And you think that makes any difference? You think they'll just give your job back like nothing happened? You're compromised, Miss O'Reilly. And that calls into question all the cases you've closed."

"That's why Finnegan's doing this," Erin said. She'd suddenly gotten it. "He could've just tried to have me killed, but he wants his case thrown out. If there's questions about my integrity—"

"—then your undercover work is suspect," Ophelia finished for her. She was smiling a bright, happy, girlish smile that made Erin want to toss her out the window. "Daddy was right; you're smart. Do you play chess?"

"I don't play games," Erin said.

"Everybody plays games," Ophelia answered. "That's all anyone ever does."

"Let me see if I've got this straight," Erin said. "When Finnegan got locked up, he planned to get back at me and screw up his case at the same time. He decided to use you, because you resembled me. He got you to have plastic surgery so you were pretty much a dead ringer. You started stalking me, so through you he knew Richard O'Malley was out to get me. I was investigating him, so that was your entry point.

"Finnegan knew the best way to get a cop's gun away is to have a qualified person ask for it. So he pretended to have something important to tell me. When I didn't bite, he staged an attack on himself to make it look like his information was valuable enough to kill for, and that was enough to get me to Riker's Island. He knew a crooked guard at Riker's, and you'd gotten a dirty gun through Stan Shapiro for him to switch with my service piece. Then you snagged my Glock from him and waited for the right moment.

"You didn't have to wait long. I went down to Brooklyn alone. You were in that car I thought was following me, weren't you?"

"I don't know what you thought," Ophelia said.

"It was you," Erin said. "You must've had someone keeping tabs on Richard O'Malley at the same time. You left me twiddling my thumbs just down the street while you killed Richard's wife and kid. You hit Richard, too, but only because he got in the way. You needed him alive so he could identify me; you couldn't count on the squirrel lady. Then you dropped my gun where you knew CSU would find it and you got out of there. And I showed up, like a chump."

"Don't be too hard on yourself," Ophelia said. "You've been distracted and under a lot of pressure."

"I got suspended," Erin continued, ignoring her. "Which made sense, since I was the prime suspect in a double homicide. Lieutenant McDowell didn't have a choice. She's completely by-the-book, which makes her predictable. But Finnegan knew I'd figure out when my gun had been swapped out, and Chaney knew what you looked like, so you had to take care of Chaney before he talked. You went to his place. He was expecting you; he'd made coffee. I reckon he thought he was your partner in crime, and maybe in something else. Did you offer him any inducement besides money?"

"Men are pretty easy to manipulate," Ophelia said. "Easier than women. We only have one head we think with."

"Hey!" Vic snapped. Everyone ignored him.

"You had some of my hair," Erin said. "I don't know from where, but there's ways."

"Back in the Middle Ages, people thought their hair could be used to work spells on them," Ophelia said pleasantly. "They'd burn their hair trimmings, or throw them in a river. A lot of folks in the present would think that's just a silly superstition, but you know better, don't you? Any sufficiently advanced technology is indistinguishable from magic, after all, and forensic science is extremely advanced these days."

"Fortunately for me, I got there before CSU," Erin said. "I got rid of the hair fibers, but I missed the knife. I should've guessed you'd use a weapon that could trace back to me, even if it was a long shot."

"Professional gamblers know better than to leave anything to chance," Ophelia said.

"You're Finnegan's kid all right," Erin said. "Do you actually understand what he says?"

"Usually," Ophelia said. "He likes riddles. He always tells you the answers, if you have the right questions."

"After Chaney was dead, all you had to do was wait," Erin said. "The legal system already had its wheels turning. The evidence was overwhelming. I was looking at two, maybe three murders. It was a good plan. A little convoluted, but that's Finnegan for you. I'm sure he's the one who came up with it. This bullshit has his style. But he got a couple things wrong."

"Oh?"

"Lieutenant McDowell saw some discrepancies. Her weakness is also her strength. She is absolutely devoted to the truth. As of tonight, she's convinced I'm innocent, so she'll move Heaven and Earth to prove it. There'll be a showdown with the Commissioner in the morning and he won't even know what hit him. Dr. Levine and Danny traced the knife not only to the Barley Corner but to you personally. And Vic, Zofia, and Lieutenant Webb never stopped believing in me. Neither did my friends on the street. Once we all started working together, you didn't have a chance."

Ophelia was still smiling. "You really think you've won, don't you," she said. She giggled.

"Nobody wins a street fight," Erin said. "We all got hurt, but you're the one who's going to get hit hardest. You're going to die in prison, don't you realize that?"

"And you'll die long before I do," Ophelia said, unperturbed. "You're already dead, because you can't see the whole picture. We've beaten you and you don't know it."

"Jesus Christ," Vic said. "Get over yourself, lady. I think I've heard enough. Erin's not a cop at the moment, technically, but Mira and I are, which means we can bust your crazy ass. You may think you've covered your trail, but I guarantee our CSU guys will find something. You wouldn't believe how good they are."

"Oh, we're counting on it," Ophelia said. "Leave no stone unturned. Be sure to check the bedroom."

"Ophelia Flaherty, you're under arrest," Vic said. "For murder. I'm gonna read you your rights, so listen up. Mira, can you secure this site until we get some uniforms here?"

"Sure thing," Mira said.

Ophelia was still looking at Erin, still smiling. Erin suppressed a shiver. If the woman wasn't utterly unhinged, she was doing a great job faking it. Was insanity hereditary? Ophelia didn't blink, even as Vic snapped the handcuffs on her wrists and Mira patted her down for concealed weapons. Vic walked Ophelia out, leaving Mira on guard.

"Hey," he said to Erin as they started downstairs. "You can relax a little. It's just about over."

"This round is," Ophelia said. "The next one's already started. Your move."

Chapter 23

"Where are we going?" Erin asked.

"Eightball," Vic said, pointing the Taurus north.

"Holliday and McDowell won't still be there. They'll be home and asleep."

"I don't care," he said. "We're taking care of this bitch on our own turf. I want her in our house, with people we trust."

"It's not Erin's house anymore," Ophelia said from the backseat.

"Shut up," Vic said. "Didn't you listen when I said you had the goddamn right to remain silent?"

Ophelia began humming a tune to herself. For someone in cuffs, on her way to be charged with multiple serious crimes, she was amazingly cheerful.

"Should we wake Webb up?" Erin asked.

"Let the old bastard sleep a little longer," Vic said. "This chick isn't going anywhere once we get her in Holding. Now that we mention it, I could use some sleep myself. What the hell time is it?"

"Either too late or too early," Erin said. She handed the Sig-Sauer back to him. "Take your pick. You'd better take this, too.

I'll get my guns back soon, and we wouldn't want you getting in trouble for handing yours out."

"No trouble," Vic said, sliding the Sig back into its holster. "Remember in grade school when you had chewing gum and the teacher would only let you chew it if you brought enough for everyone? I'm like that with guns. Plenty for everybody."

When Vic pulled into his space in the basement parking garage, Erin hesitated. "Maybe I shouldn't come in," she said.

"You have a police escort," Vic said. "You're not under arrest, or even under suspicion anymore. I'll just say I'm offering you a tour of the station if anybody asks."

"At three in the morning," she said.

He grinned. "That's the best time to see what things are really like. Just hang out in the lobby while I get our prisoner processed. Then I'll come get you."

Erin used the short break to call Carlyle. "I'm fine," she said. "Things are a little strange, but nothing too dangerous happened. We got our girl. She came quietly."

"Grand," Carlyle said. "Who is she?"

"Finnegan's daughter," Erin said. "And this girl has some serious issues."

"I'd expect nothing less," he said dryly. "Are you certain?"

"I'm sure there'll be a psych evaluation," Erin said. "Especially if her lawyer goes for an insanity defense, but—"

"That's not what I meant," he said. "Are you certain she's his flesh and blood?"

"There isn't any facial resemblance," she said. "But there wouldn't be, after the plastic surgery. She certainly thinks he's her dad, and he's acted like it, in his own messed-up way. Why?"

"The whole thing seems just a trifle too convenient," Carlyle said. "But I don't suppose it matters much. Has she confessed?"

"More or less. But it's weird. She was expecting us... expecting me in particular. Finnegan predicted all of this, which means he was ready to sacrifice her. And if he thought I'd get this far, what was the point of it all? Why bother with all the intricate setup, if he expected it to fall apart?"

"Layers within layers, darling," Carlyle said. "His primary plan was to see you put away for murder. When that didn't work, his backup plan was to see you dismissed from the Department. I'd wager there's a third layer as well."

"That's the problem," Erin said. "I don't know what it is. I'm waiting for the other shoe to drop."

"Half a moment," Carlyle said suddenly. "Someone's at the door. I think it's your da. What do you want me to tell him?"

"Tell him I'm fine," she said. "Give Rolf to him, and tell him to stay at Junior's house. That should keep Rolf safe until this whole thing blows over."

"Will you be coming home soon?"

"Not for a while yet. Don't worry about me. You should sleep."

"I'll be thinking of you, darling."

"Right back at you," she said. "You know, I think maybe everything's going to turn out okay."

"Grand," he said again. "I love you, darling."

She hung up and watched the traffic through the lobby, feeling an unexpected pang of regret at the familiar sights of Patrol officers bringing in perps, citizens lodging complaints, and desk officers running errands. She felt like an outsider and didn't like it. She'd been a cop so long, she didn't know how to be anything else, and while she kept telling herself things would work out, she couldn't quite believe it.

God, but she was tired. Her head kept nodding.

Vic finally came out from Holding and started across the room toward her. Erin jumped up and hurried to meet him, then stopped short at the look on his face.

"What's wrong?" she asked.

"You're not gonna believe this," he said. "I just got a call from Mira."

"What is it?" she asked, feeling cold worms beginning to wriggle around in her guts.

"CSU is checking Flaherty's apartment," he said. "Mira says there isn't a lot to find. It's mostly just old furniture."

"That's what Ophelia told us," Erin said. "She doesn't actually live there."

"But there's one weird thing," Vic said. "The bedroom has a freezer chest in it."

"That is a little strange," she agreed.

"A nice, big one," Vic said. "Big enough to stash a body in it."

"You don't mean—"

"Yeah. There's a dead guy in it, frozen solid."

"Who is it?"

"They haven't ID'd him yet," Vic said. "But Mira got a good look at him. He's a young guy, probably early twenties, with a beard, and he's Russian Mafia. Plus, he's got a busted nose."

Erin blinked. "The guy you ran into outside Matrushka's?"

"I'd bet on it," he said. "Mikhail something-or-other."

"What's he doing in Ophelia's fridge?"

"Being dead, mostly. He's naked, and doesn't have a thing on him except an icepick in his eye."

"Jesus," Erin said.

"CSU also found a phone," Vic added as an afterthought. "They're working on decrypting it."

"Sounds like she may have enticed him into the bedroom," Erin said. "She got him vulnerable, then killed him. What I don't understand is why. Did they find his clothes?"

"Yeah, under the bed. He had a gun, but it was there with his belt and pants. I wouldn't want to try this chick's definition of safe sex."

"There'll be something tying me to him," Erin predicted. "DNA evidence, hairs, something."

"Probably," he said. "But Mira and I can alibi you this time."

"Not completely," she said. "It's hard to fix time of death with a frozen corpse. For all anyone knows, I went down there and stabbed him yesterday."

"Damn," Vic said. "But don't worry, there's no way this sticks to you. Once we pin the other murders on Flaherty, the pattern's gonna be clear. And it happened in her apartment, for God's sake! It's an obvious frame job!"

"You're right," Erin said with as much conviction as she could muster.

"Besides, the little turd won't be missed," Vic said. "Even Gennady Vlasov thought he was a loser. He sure as shit wasn't one of their varsity squad. If you ask me, I think she did him just for fun. That girl's a whack-job."

"You got that right," Erin said. "But it's understandable. Finnegan groomed her from when she was a kid. It's like she was in a cult or something."

"That's exactly what it is," Vic said. "I thought Finnegan was Hannibal Lecter, but I guess maybe he's more like Charles Manson. Why are all cult leaders total whack-a-doodles?"

"Because sane people don't start cults," Erin said. "But you're right. Finnegan programmed that girl. He made her into his damn puppet. She changed her *face* because he told her to! That isn't normal."

"It's pretty screwed up," he agreed. "You think she'll get off on an insanity plea?"

"I don't know. Did she lawyer up?"

"Yeah. She asked for her phone call, too."

"Who'd she call?"

"It was weird. She called her lawyer, but she was only on the phone about thirty seconds. I guess she had some instructions already in place. It wouldn't surprise me. Sheesh, if I knew I was about to get arrested, I'd go to Venezuela or something."

"Who's her lawyer? Is it Walsh?"

"Nah, it's some shyster I never heard of."

"I would've expected Walsh. He's representing Finnegan."

Vic shrugged. "Who cares? Lawyers are like condoms."

Erin made a face. "I want you to explain that, but I don't want you to, either."

"They're disposable and they're all pretty much the same. You don't want to use them, but they're a necessary protection in bad situations. After you use them, you feel kind of slimy. And the moment they come into play, you know somebody's about to get fucked."

"Thanks for that deep and penetrating observation," she said.

Vic snorted. "Word choice, O'Reilly."

Erin smacked him.

"That's assaulting a police officer," he said. "I should arrest you."

She didn't even bother replying to that. "Why'd Ophelia kill a low-level Russian mobster?" she wondered. "What was the possible point?"

"He was a convenient target," Vic said. "I beat that punk up myself, and let me tell you, he was a pushover. I'm not surprised she could take him. I'm telling you, she did it for shits and giggles."

Erin nodded, but wasn't convinced. She didn't think any of this was based on convenience or luck. She remembered Ophelia's words about the next round having already started. And she really wanted the whole thing to be over and done.

"You'll charge her first thing in the morning, right?" she said.

"I'll brief Webb first," Vic said. "And the Cast-Iron Bitch. You think McDowell will be mad at me?"

"She wanted you to do it," Erin said. "But you may have to wait to talk to her. She's going to One PP to tear the PC a new one, remember?"

"Oh, right. I'll try to catch her before she leaves. She ought to be here first, don't you think?"

"Yeah. I'd like to talk to her, too."

"In that case, why don't you grab the couch in the Major Crimes break room and sack out for a couple hours? That way you'll be on site on short notice."

"I'm not supposed to be there," Erin said.

"Then I won't tell anyone," Vic said. "Besides, like I said, you're a citizen in good standing. You'll be fine."

"Thanks, Vic," she said. "You're right. I'm pretty tired. I just wish I had a toothbrush."

"Do what I do when I don't have one."

"What's that?"

"Rinse your mouth out with vodka when you wake up."

"So I can talk to Internal Affairs with booze on my breath? Great plan, Vic."

He grinned. "There's a bottle in the left-hand drawer of my desk. Tastes better than mouthwash. Pleasant dreams."

* * *

Fresh snow lay on Central Park in an unbroken white blanket, like icing on a wedding cake. Anna O'Reilly plunged into the drifts, laughing happily. Lucy, Anna's Newfoundland, galumphed through the snow with her. Michelle O'Reilly watched them and smiled. Erin hadn't seen her sister-in-law so happy in months. Erin's brother, Sean Junior, held his wife's hand, looking at his daughter and dog.

Erin didn't hear the gunshot. She saw the blood explode out of Anna's back. Fluffy bits of Anna's jacket flew on the air. The girl spun around under the impact of the bullet, no pain on her face, just wide-eyed surprise. Anna fell, curling into a tiny broken heap. The snow turned crimson around her.

Michelle's mouth opened in a soundless wail. Erin tried to place where the shot had come from, but her head turned too slowly. Everything was moving in slow motion. She reached for her gun, but her belt was empty. Where had she put her Glock?

Two more bullets slammed into Michelle's midsection. Shelley crumpled. Junior had his arms around her, sobbing, crying something Erin couldn't hear.

Another bullet took off the top of his head. He dropped instantly, the light flicking out in his eyes as if a switch had been turned off.

Erin stood rooted to the spot, unable to move, unable to speak, unable even to think. Everywhere she looked she saw blood-soaked snow and bodies that had been her family.

"This round is over," Ophelia Flaherty said. She was suddenly standing beside Erin, her too-innocent blue eyes shining with childish glee. "It's the last one. Game over." And she giggled.

*   *   *

Erin jolted awake with that giggle still in her ears. She lurched up off the disreputable couch in the break room, groping frantically for a gun that wasn't there. Groggy, expecting the layout of Carlyle's bedroom at the Barley Corner, she banged her shin against the table that held the espresso machine. The pain brought her fully awake and aware. She cursed loudly.

Heavy footsteps ran toward the room. The door flew open, spilling light into her face. Erin blinked and held up a hand to shield her eyes.

"You okay?" Vic asked. "Jesus, you look like something your dog shit out."

"Thanks." She ran a hand through her hair. Her fingers got caught in the tangles. "You wouldn't have a comb, would you?"

"Are you joking?" Vic pointed to his own head. His hair was buzzed close to the scalp. "I got a lousy half-inch here. What would I need a comb for?"

"What time is it?"

"Quarter to eight. I was gonna come check on you at eight, make sure you were still breathing. But I guess you're not dead."

"Not quite." Erin turned on the coffee machine. "This ought to jump-start me."

"I've got Mountain Dew if you want it. And a box of Pop-Tarts."

Erin shuddered. "You're making death sound pretty good," she said. "Any sign of McDowell or the Captain?"

"Not yet. I did talk to Webb. He's on his way in, should be here any minute."

"Any news from our girl?"

"Little Miss Crazy-Pants is still down in Holding. Don't worry, I took her belt and checked her for sharp objects. I looked in on her half an hour ago. She was sitting on the floor of her cell, singing 'Ring Around the Rosie,' if you believe it."

"I do," Erin said. "As soon as the coffee's ready, I'll take you up on a couple of Pop-Tarts, but only if they're toasted. I can't understand why you eat them cold."

"Saves time," Vic said. "You don't think I eat them because I like the taste, do you? They taste like cardboard, but they're portable and convenient."

"Vic?"

"Yeah?"

"Thanks. For all your help."

He looked embarrassed. "Forget about it," he said. "It's no big deal."

"I'm serious," she said. "We wouldn't have gotten Ophelia without you."

"Just doing my job, ma'am."

"That doesn't sound like even you believe it."

"What do you want me to say?" he growled. "That I'd do anything for you, with hearts and flowers and unicorns and crap? Sheesh. You'd do the same for me and you know it. Why are we talking about this?"

"Because I'm grateful," Erin said. "When you're on top of the world, everybody's your friend. When you're down, you find out who your friends really are. You're a good guy, Vic."

"No," he said. "I'm not." But he was smiling.

Erin fortified herself with a cup of fresh coffee and a couple of toasted Pop-Tarts which claimed to be raspberry flavored. She felt marginally better. Her mood improved a little more when her phone showed a text from her dad.

"What is it?" Vic asked. "You look like you've got a little something in your eye."

Erin blinked the tears away before they could overflow. She showed him the text.

"'At Junior's with our friend,'" Vic read aloud. "'All well. You'll always be my daughter the detective. Proud of you, kiddo.' Aww, that's sweet. You're lucky to have a dad like that."

Erin nodded. She didn't trust her voice to say anything just then, but didn't have to. She texted a quick "Thanks. Love you." She might have sent more, but was interrupted by the arrival of five people into Major Crimes: Captain Holliday, Lieutenant McDowell, Lieutenant Webb, Danielle, and Erica. All three cops were wearing their dress uniforms. The last time Erin had seen

Webb in his dress blues had been at Kira Jones's funeral, where he'd been one of the pallbearers. He looked uncomfortable in it, like an overage Halloween trick-or-treater.

"Well, this is a surprise," Holliday said, giving Erin a once-over. "I assume there's an explanation for your presence here, O'Reilly?"

"That was me, sir," Vic interjected.

"As I was saying, sir," Webb said, stepping between Holliday and Vic. "Detective Neshenko captured the culprit in the O'Malley shooting."

"It wasn't just me," Vic said. "I liaised with Detective Ivanova from the Six-Oh. And O'Reilly was along as a civilian consultant."

"Civilian consultants need to be cleared through official channels, and to sign a waiver before being present at arrests of dangerous suspects," McDowell said dryly.

"Fortunately, Miss O'Reilly has been cleared by me," Holliday said quickly. "I seem to have overlooked the waiver. I understand that creates a liability issue for the Department, but I'm pretty sure I have the form in my office. I apologize for the oversight."

"Nobody was hurt, sir," Erin said. "No shots fired."

"But we did find a dead guy in her fridge," Vic added. "He was dead when we got there. Really dead. Frozen."

"Yes, I was just on the phone with Dr. Levine on my drive in," Webb said. "He's been identified as Mikhail Vlasov."

"Vlasov?" Erin repeated. "Oh, no."

"I believe you're acquainted with the family," Webb said. "You're the one who put his father in a prison hospital with a hole in his stomach."

"So Gennady Vlasov would be, what, his second cousin?" Vic said.

"First cousin, once removed," Webb corrected.

"Shit," Vic said. "I can never keep that stuff straight."

"Why is everyone dressed up?" Erin asked.

"Because we're on our way to One PP," Holliday said.

"All of you, sir?"

The Captain nodded. "We're going to present a united front on behalf of the Eightball. I have a strongly-worded letter to deliver to the Commissioner on your behalf, O'Reilly."

"As do I," McDowell said.

"I did some legal work late last night," Erica said. "I think you have a good case for suing the Department, Ms. O'Reilly."

"Nobody's suing the NYPD," Erin said.

"People sue us all the time," Vic said.

"Nobody in this room is suing the NYPD," Erin clarified. "I just want my job back and to get back to business. A public apology would be nice, too."

"Maybe you'd better come along," Webb said.

"I'll come too," Vic said.

"You'll stay right where you are, Neshenko," Webb said.

"But—" Vic began.

"Have you finished all your paperwork regarding the arrest of your perp?" Webb asked.

"Well, not exactly. But—"

"Are you ready to follow up regarding the additional homicide in Brooklyn?"

"More or less. But—"

"Do you think O'Reilly's Lieutenant, Captain, and IAB Lieutenant are capable of safeguarding her interests?"

"I guess so. But—"

"Then you have work to do," Webb finished. "And so do we. As you were, Neshenko. O'Reilly, you're with us. You can ride with me."

"Can you give me a couple minutes?" she asked. "I need to clean up a little."

"I have some makeup," Danielle said, shifting her purse forward. "And a hairbrush. Nail polish, too, if you want."

"Makeover time," Vic said, grinning nastily.

"Thanks," Erin said to Danielle, ignoring Vic. "I'd appreciate it."

Chapter 24

"Why are you girls riding along today?" Erin asked. She was in the shotgun seat of Webb's battered station wagon. Erica and Danielle were in back.

"We came out here to see Dad," Danielle said. "And we're only out here for a few days. He doesn't get to hide out at work for our whole visit. He gets fifty weeks of that already."

"I am not hiding out," Webb said. "This is important life-or-death stuff. I told you that."

"It's always life or death," Dani said, pouting. "He was like that in LA, too. That's why Mom left."

"No, it isn't," Webb said through a tight jaw. "We had irreconcilable differences."

"She wanted you to come home at night, you wanted to stay at work," Dani said. "I used to wonder if you were having an affair."

"I wasn't," Webb said.

"What about that other woman?" Dani pressed.

"Cathy wasn't even in the picture when your mom and I split up," Webb said. "I met her after."

"Yeah," Danielle said. "When you hired your divorce lawyer."

"I worked with another lawyer in Cathy's office," Webb said. "Not Cathy. That would've been unprofessional of her and unethical of me for us to date otherwise."

"But you met her then."

"Well, yes," Webb allowed. "But that's not the point. The thing about divorce is that you're allowed to meet other people. I never meant it to come back on you or Erica. I'm sorry if you feel like it did."

"I didn't know your dad when he was in LA," Erin said, grabbing at any chance of changing the subject. "Tell me something about him."

"He always seemed tired," Erica said. "And a little sad. I used to try to cheer him up when he came home, but it never seemed to work."

"It worked better than you knew," Webb said quietly. "I miss you."

"You have a funny way of showing it," Danielle said.

Webb almost managed to suppress the flinch, but Erin was used to interrogations, and she was good at spotting subtle body language.

"I can see he's glad you're here now," Erin said, embarrassed on Webb's behalf. "And I suppose I should be glad, too. I didn't expect to need a defense lawyer."

"I'm not a lawyer yet," Erica said. "And I'd need to pass the New York Bar if I wanted to practice here, even once I get my degree. You should probably be getting your legal advice from a real attorney. I'm mostly hoping to learn some things. I've never met a Police Commissioner before."

"I think it'll be educational for all of us," Webb said. "But you won't be meeting him today."

"Dad!"

"I mean it," Webb said. "You can come inside with us, but the meeting is going to be private.

"But Dad..." Danielle said in a tone of voice Erin remembered using on her own father, back when she'd been the girl's age.

"It's likely to get unpleasant," Webb said. "And you're not directly involved. His secretary won't even let you in."

"Will they let any of us in?" Erin asked. "Is this scheduled?"

"The PC is slated to meet with Lieutenant McDowell," Webb said. "He thinks he's getting a progress report on the O'Malley shooting."

"So this is an ambush," Erin said.

"You could call it that," Webb agreed.

"And you expect us to sit it out?" Erica demanded.

"It's either that, or I'll drop you somewhere else until this is over," Webb said.

Erica crossed her arms and stared out the window. "Fine," she huffed.

Erin could feel her paranoia crawling up inside her again, urging her to be on the lookout for threats. Her nightmare was still lingering. She glanced around uneasily, but any or none of the cars on the busy street might be following her. Ophelia was locked up, she reminded herself. The woman was a brainwashed cultist, but she couldn't do a thing from inside a jail cell.

Oh, yeah? a sardonic inner voice replied. *Like Finnegan couldn't do anything from jail?*

"The game's not over," she murmured.

"What's that, O'Reilly?" Webb asked.

"Nothing, sir," she said. "I'm just twitchy."

"Get it under control," he said. "This is no time to fly off the handle. You need to behave with dignity and discipline. Do you copy?"

"Copy that, sir." She forced herself to sit still and face forward. How would Ian Thompson handle this? Whether he was a firefighter or a Marine, he'd never change. He'd keep a poker face, stay outwardly calm no matter what, and say "sir" a lot. She could do that. Hell, she was *good* at it.

*   *   *

Erin had been to Number One PP several times. She'd even stopped neo-Nazi terrorists from blowing it up once. She'd been a guest in the Commissioner's office when he'd offered her a promotion and a desk job. Since that job would've entailed handing Rolf off to someone else, she'd told the PC where he could stick it—as politely as possible. He'd been upset about that.

"It's kind of an ugly building," Erica commented, staring up at the inverted pyramid of masonry.

"It's a good example of brutalist architecture," Webb said. "You can see the exposed concrete support beams. Back in the day, architects thought it looked modern and functional."

"Brutalist is a good word for it," Erica said. "It makes me think of police brutality."

"Which my office investigates to the fullest extent of the law," McDowell said.

To get in, they walked across the plaza past a security checkpoint. No public vehicles could drive up to the front door; that was a post-9/11 precaution to prevent a car bomb. McDowell, Holliday, and Webb presented their NYPD credentials and were allowed to retain their sidearms. Erin, Erica, and Danielle had to show their IDs and walk through a metal detector at yet another checkpoint. It was like going to the airport, except that they were allowed to keep their shoes on.

Once they'd jumped through the necessary hoops, they walked across the lobby, leaving Erica and Danielle behind to sulk, and rode the elevator up to the PC's floor. Erin tried not to fidget. McDowell and Holliday appeared completely calm. Webb looked tired, but then, he always did.

"What am I expected to say, sir?" she asked Holliday.

"You don't have to say much," he replied. "Just do your best not to make the situation worse. Try not to talk unless spoken to."

"I find 'yes, sir' works well in most situations," Webb added. "And the rest of the time, 'no sir' is probably the right answer."

"Yes, sir," Erin said.

Webb smiled thinly. "Just like that," he said. "You'll do fine."

The PC's secretary was a hard-faced woman who reminded Erin of her junior high assistant principal. The woman gave them a cool, level stare.

"Lieutenant Fiona McDowell," McDowell said. "Precinct Eight Internal Affairs. Here for a nine-thirty with the Commissioner."

"And the rest of you?" the secretary asked.

"They're here at my invitation," McDowell said. "They have information and insights pertinent to the topic of the meeting."

"Names?" the secretary asked. If she recognized any of them, she gave no sign of it.

"Captain Fenton Holliday," Holliday said. "Commanding officer, Precinct Eight."

"Lieutenant Harold Webb," Webb said. "Precinct Eight Major Crimes."

"Erin O'Reilly," Erin said, nearly stumbling over her own name. She'd come very close to putting "Detective" in front of it.

At that name, the secretary's eyebrows shot up, but her mouth didn't so much as twitch. "One moment," she said. "Please wait here."

She stood up and went into the inner office, leaving the others outside. The chairs looked comfortable, but nobody sat.

Holliday raised a hand and slowly smoothed his mustache. Nobody else moved.

After a few moments, the secretary returned. "Go on in," she said to McDowell. "Your associates can wait here."

McDowell didn't budge. "Their presence is necessary," she said.

"They're not on the agenda," the secretary replied.

"They *are* the agenda," McDowell shot back.

Fifteen seconds of silent stare-down ensued. Erin didn't envy the secretary, or anybody else who had to meet McDowell's eye for that long at a stretch. The IAB Lieutenant's gaze could freeze a hot cup of coffee.

"All right," the secretary said. "But remember where you are."

"Always," McDowell said.

The Commissioner was waiting in his office, surrounded by dark wood and expensive leather-upholstered furniture. He stood in front of his desk with his big hands, big belly, and big smile. The smile flickered slightly when Erin walked in, but the PC had a good public face and recovered quickly.

"Fiona," he said, extending a hand. "Thank you for coming."

"Thank you for seeing me, sir," McDowell said, giving his hand two quick, businesslike shakes.

"Fenton," the PC went on, turning to Holliday. "It's been too long. How's the golf game?"

"I haven't gotten out on the green much, sir," Holliday said. "I expect you'd still beat me by five or six strokes."

"And Harry," the PC continued. "We're coming up on another New York winter. How do your Angelino bones handle it?"

"I manage, sir," Webb said.

"Miss O'Reilly," the Commissioner finished. He didn't offer to shake hands with her.

"Sir," she said stiffly. She'd been around enough Mafia guys to know the look in his eyes. It was a combination of wariness and hatred. Evan O'Malley had looked at her that way the last time she'd seen him, and if he'd had a gun in his hand he would've shot her on the spot.

"I wasn't expecting such a large crowd," the PC said. "Fortunately, I have plenty of chairs. Have a seat, everyone. Can I offer you anything to drink?"

Nobody moved an inch.

"I'd like this to be a little more informal," he said. "Please, sit down."

"I'd prefer to stand, sir," McDowell said.

"Oh come now, Fiona," he said, laughing. "What do your friends call you?"

"My friends already know what to call me, sir," McDowell said coldly.

The Commissioner stopped laughing. "All right," he said. "I suppose you'd better say what you've come here to say, then. You can start by telling me what that woman is doing here."

"Ms. O'Reilly is here at our request," McDowell said.

"She isn't a police officer anymore," the PC said.

"She isn't a prisoner, either," McDowell replied. "She has been released without charges and is a citizen of New York in good standing with the law."

"You're the one who arrested her," the PC said. "You're the one who said she killed a woman and a child!"

"She was arrested, but not charged," McDowell corrected him. "It was a tactical maneuver, intended to protect Ms. O'Reilly and the public. I also hoped to gain time to further develop the case, while she was temporarily removed from the picture. However, events moved quickly thereafter. Once her arrest was publicly announced, I felt it necessary to immediately release her to prevent further unwarranted damage to her reputation and career."

The PC's face was a darker color than it had been a moment before, as blood rushed to his cheeks. "Are you telling me how to do my job, *Lieutenant?*" he asked with venomous emphasis.

"As an officer in Internal Affairs, it is my job to evaluate the performance of all members of the New York Police Department in their duties," McDowell said. "You are not, technically, a member of the Department, and therefore any professional misconduct of yours falls outside my purview."

"What, exactly, are you accusing me of?" the PC demanded.

"I am leveling no accusation," McDowell said. "I am merely stating that Ms. O'Reilly's job prospects and reputation have been severely damaged by a public announcement of her termination, made on national television."

"She murdered two people!" the PC snapped. "Maybe three!"

"That is incorrect, sir," McDowell said. "The actual murderer is now in custody."

The Commissioner gaped at her, for once lost for a reply.

"Lieutenant Webb will explain," McDowell said. "His squad made the collar."

Webb, looking like he would rather not, stepped forward and quickly laid out the circumstances of Ophelia Flaherty's apprehension.

"A fourth body was discovered in her apartment," he finished. "That body was identified as a low-level member of a Russian organized-crime syndicate. That investigation is ongoing, but early evidence suggests another attempt to frame Ms. O'Reilly."

"This is preposterous," the PC said. "You seriously expect me to believe a woman underwent plastic surgery just so she could pose as O'Reilly to destroy her reputation?"

"I can't force you to believe anything, sir," Webb said. "Her motive, in addition to ruining Erin O'Reilly's life, was to taint O'Reilly's case, and the city's, against her father, Kyle Finnegan. I don't personally find it far-fetched that a woman would do something like that for her father, or a father for his daughter for that matter."

"The fact remains, O'Reilly brought the Department into disrepute," the Commissioner said.

"How so, sir?" McDowell asked. Her voice cracked like a whip on her final word.

The PC didn't answer right away.

"Erin O'Reilly has performed her duties correctly," McDowell said. "She has assisted in clearing her own name. I am not a lawyer, but I believe if you consult one, you will be told she has a very strong case for wrongful termination, and another one for defamation of character, if she chooses to take civil action against the Department and potentially against you personally."

"Are you blaming me for this?" the PC retorted. "You think your hands are clean?"

"Of course not," McDowell said. She reached into her jacket and removed an envelope, which she placed on his desk. "Here is my letter of resignation. It is the only thing I can do while maintaining my professional and personal integrity. I fully accept responsibility for my part in smearing Ms. O'Reilly's reputation."

For the second time, the Commissioner was unable to form an answer. He spluttered a little.

Captain Holliday broke the awkward silence. "I am here in support of one of my officers," he said. "It is my duty to state, for the record, that I believe Ms. O'Reilly completely innocent of any wrongdoing in this matter, and further to recommend, in the strongest possible language, that she be immediately reinstated and a full formal apology be issued by your office forthwith."

"Is that so?" the Commissioner said, recovering a little. "In the strongest possible language? You, a Captain, are dictating terms? You work for me!"

"I work for New York City, sir," Holliday said.

"But you answer to me," the PC said. "If I want your shield to hang on my wall next to McDowell's, I can have it."

"That's correct, sir," Holliday said, unmoved. "You have the power to dismiss me, whatever the political fallout may be."

"I am not an elected official," the PC retorted. "I don't answer to the voters or to opinion polls. I serve—"

"At the pleasure of the Mayor," Holliday interjected, and Erin was gratified to see the PC's jaw twitch at the Captain's interruption. "Yes, sir. The Mayor, however, is a politician, and does answer to those same voters. It is up to you and he to decide, of course, how much weight to give to public opinion."

"What about you?" the Commissioner asked, dripping with sarcasm as he turned on Webb. "Are you going to threaten to resign, too?"

"Me, sir?" Webb asked, giving a convincing imitation of surprise. "No, sir. I'm close to retirement. I'm just here to provide factual information and to voice my support for one of my detectives."

The PC dismissed Webb with a flick of his eyes, turning his attention back to Holliday. "You've been an officer over twenty years," he said. "Isn't that worth anything to you? You'd throw all of it away over something this petty? The career of one detective?"

"I was at the World Trade Center, sir," Holliday said, and his voice suddenly radiated a cold fury that made Erin reflexively take a half step away from him. "I was on perimeter duty when the Towers came down. I shifted rubble for two days straight, looking for men and women from my station. I went to eight funerals that month. Don't you dare lecture me, sir, about valuing my career over one of my people. I would have traded my life for any one of those men or women. You talk to me, sir, about valuing my job? This *is* the Job, and any Captain who would do anything different doesn't deserve the bars on his shoulder."

There were a few seconds of dead silence. Everyone looked at one another. Holliday and the Commissioner had locked eyes. Erin was afraid to stare directly at Holliday. She was in awe of him in that moment, and knew her attention would only embarrass him.

"So that's how it is?" the PC said at last.

"Yes, sir," McDowell said.

"Can I ask that you reconsider your decision?"

"As long as this situation exists, my decision is made."

"And if the situation is altered?"

"I would need to examine the new circumstances, sir," McDowell said. "However, my culpability remains."

"You're as stiff as a starched collar, Lieutenant," the PC said, trying a smile once more. It looked weak and fake.

"So I've been told, sir," McDowell said.

"What about you, O'Reilly?" he asked, turning suddenly to her.

"Me, sir?" Erin said, startled.

"What do you want?"

Absurdly, the words "I'm fine, sir," flashed through her mind. She'd told the lie so many times, it was the first thing she usually thought of. But it wasn't the truth, and it wasn't the right thing to say, not here and now.

"I want what I've always wanted, sir," she said. "My whole life. To serve New York as a good cop, just like my dad was before me. I'd like to be reinstated in my previous position."

The Commissioner nodded. He seemed smaller somehow, deflated. "You'll hear from my office," he said. "That will be all. Thank you for coming."

He shook hands with them, one by one. This time he offered his hand to Erin.

She'd shaken hands with plenty of worse men, who'd done worse things. She took his hand for the shortest time she thought she could get away with. Then she and the others got out of that damned office.

*   *   *

"Did we win?" Erin couldn't resist asking, the moment the elevator doors closed and the car started its trip down to the lobby.

"Nobody won," Holliday said. "This was a knife fight. You know what they say about those."

"The loser dies at the scene," Erin said. "The winner dies in the ambulance."

"I'm glad you came along, sir," Webb said to Holliday. "We needed a politician in our corner."

Holliday's mustache twitched. "I know you meant that as a compliment," he said. "And I'll choose to take it as one."

"I appreciate you having my back, Lieutenant," Erin said to McDowell. "It means a lot."

"It was one hell of a bluff," Webb added.

"I don't bluff," McDowell said. "And I didn't do it for you, Ms. O'Reilly."

"I did," Holliday said quietly.

"Thank you, sir," Erin said. "I won't forget it. You either, Lieutenant."

The elevator reached the ground floor. The doors slid open, and Erin felt the residual paranoia Ian Thompson had instilled in her. There was just an instant of fear, before she could clear the ready-made killbox. Then she saw Erica and Danielle loitering in the lobby, surrounded by armed officers, and told herself again to stop being so damn twitchy.

"How'd it go, Dad?" Danielle asked as the two young women attached themselves to the group.

"As well as it could, I think," Webb said.

"Are you suing the Department, Erin?" Erica asked.

"I don't want to," Erin said. "And I don't think I'll have to."

"You won't," Holliday predicted. "The Commissioner definitely won't want to can all of us. Firing a precinct captain is a big deal by itself, and would require gross misconduct to justify. He'll want to keep this quiet, to do damage control."

They left the building and started across the plaza toward the parking garage, disturbing a flock of pigeons that irritably fluttered a short distance away, then forgot about them and resumed pecking at the concrete.

"I meant what I said about the Mayor," Holliday continued. "You're a decorated hero, O'Reilly. Now that we've got the real culprit, as soon as they put a picture of her next to one of you on the evening news, you'll be home free. It'll look like the Commissioner jumped the gun, which he did. If he doubles down on the termination, the Union lawyers will chew him up like a pack of junkyard dogs."

"That's my Mob nickname, you know, sir," Erin said. "Junkyard O'Reilly."

"So I've heard," Holliday said. Erin thought he was smiling, but the mustache made it hard to tell. "The PC will try to shape the narrative. He'll focus on the diabolical cunning of the plot, and applaud the intelligence and skill of the NYPD. He'll deflect what he can away from himself, but I don't think he'll accept Lieutenant McDowell's resignation. He can't, because if the reasons for it come out, people will want to know why he hasn't resigned too."

They walked into the parking garage. It was a five-story structure, and since they'd arrived during a business day, parking had been at a premium. Both cars had parked on the fourth level. Webb, middle-aged and overweight, pushed the call button for the elevator.

"Would the Mayor really fire the PC over this?" Erin asked.

"That depends on what the opinion polls say," Webb said. "If he thinks it would get him re-elected, he'd pimp out his own mother in Times Square."

"Dad!" Erica said in reproving tones.

"Sorry," he said. "I forgot you were there for a second."

They piled into the elevator car and started up. It was a somewhat rickety contraption, shaking as it strained to lift the six people.

"I'll get a call later today," Holliday predicted. "It'll say you've been reinstated, fully retroactive. Then I'll pass the word to you and we can put this whole thing behind us."

"What about Kyle Finnegan?" Erin asked.

"It's not like we can throw him even more in jail," Holliday said. "But if we can prove he masterminded this, we can certainly add it to the massive array of charges against him. Once his trial is over and he's convicted, we'll ship him somewhere very far from New York, and with luck, you'll never hear from him again."

"Proving it will be tricky," Webb said. "Our best bet is his daughter. If we can get her to flip..."

The elevator rattled to a stop. Its doors slid open. Erin took a step through the doorway.

Half a dozen men clad in dark clothes were standing around the door. They had ski masks on their faces and guns in their hands. The guns were pointed directly at her.

Erin's hand dropped to her belt, where her Glock should have been. She was unarmed, unarmored, and totally helpless. *Damn it,* she thought. *Ian was right. Goddamn elevators!* The thought flicked through her head in a terrible, hopeless instant. Then she saw the muzzle flash of the shotgun in the middle guy's hands and felt the impact just under her ribcage.

All the air was driven out of her body in a single brutal blow. She doubled over and fell, sobbing for breath, unable to inflate her lungs. The pain was instant and immense. All she could do was clutch at herself and gasp.

Dimly, through the pain, she heard more gunfire and people shouting. She heard the rattle of a couple of automatic weapons and the pop of what might have been Holliday or Webb's .38. She tried to crawl to one side, but scrabbled ineffectually at the concrete floor. A woman screamed, high-pitched and terrible.

Get up! Erin's brain screamed, but her body wasn't listening. All it could think about was air, and it couldn't find any. She retched, coughing up bile. She couldn't feel any blood on her hands, but that was no consolation. Her perceptions were shattered and fragmented.

A man shouted something unintelligible. Strong hands grabbed Erin under the shoulders, hoisting her upright. She had a dizzying impression of a masked face just inches from her own. Then a cloth bag was jammed over her head. She tried to struggle, but she was too weak from pain. Her arms were wrenched back, her hands forced behind her. A plastic zip-tie was yanked tight around her wrists, so tight it dug into her flesh. She was carried, her toes scraping the ground, further into the garage.

A pistol fired several times in rapid succession. A man grunted just to Erin's right and she was abruptly dropped. Unable to break her fall with her hands, she landed hard on her shoulder. There was another rattle of automatic fire, very close by, and another pistol shot in response.

"Go! Go!" a man yelled. Erin was grabbed again, lifted bodily, and tossed like a sack of flour. She landed on rough carpet, like you'd find on the floor of a van. A metal door slid shut. An engine sputtered to life and the unseen vehicle started rolling.

Erin knew she didn't have much time. At all costs she had to get out of the van, slow them down, do *something*. A man had a hand on her shoulder, not really holding her down, just keeping tabs on her. Erin's lungs were working now, though her abdominal muscles were on fire. She sucked in a slow, deep breath, knowing she'd only get one shot at this.

She rolled abruptly away from her captor, planted her knees on the floor, and lunged forward. A man cried out in alarm. The guy next to her made a grab at her and got a handful of her shirt. Fabric ripped. The arm of a car seat jabbed her in the gut, bringing a wave of fresh pain.

Someone seized her ankle. Erin coiled her free leg and kicked, feeling the heel of her shoe slam into something hard, round, and solid; probably a skull. The hand abruptly let go of her.

"Get that *suka!*" a man snarled.

Erin curled her legs in as far as she could. The toes of her shoes barely scraped through the gap between her arms. Then she was up, her hands still tied together but in front of her now. She whipped the bag off her head and caught a confused glimpse of the interior of a van. There was a driver up front, and another guy in the other seat. A third man, behind her, was standing up and groping for a shotgun. The van was spiraling down the parking garage ramp toward the exit.

The guy in the passenger seat pointed a pistol at her. The barrel was probably only nine millimeters, but it looked as wide as the Lincoln Tunnel from where she was.

"Sit down!" he snapped.

They'd shot her with a beanbag round. That meant they wanted her alive. So her best bet was to hope they wouldn't dare shoot with real bullets.

Erin looped her arms over the back of the driver's seat and yanked back as hard as she could.

The driver gave a stifled yelp of surprise as she got him by the throat. The steering wheel slewed hard to the side. Metal shrieked as the van scraped the wall of the ramp. Erin lost her balance and went over sideways, still choking the driver. A concrete support column loomed through the windshield, terrifyingly close and solid.

She felt no sense of impact, no sense of anything; there was only instant, complete darkness.

Chapter 25

IAN THOMPSON

Firefighters spent almost none of their time fighting fires. Even when they went out on calls, most of the time it was for car crashes, construction accidents, building collapses, or other incidents. When not protecting New Yorkers from the consequences of their own carelessness, FDNY trained or hung around the station, killing time. They cleaned and checked equipment, scrubbed floors, cooked if they knew how, ate vending-machine food if they didn't.

It was a lot like being in the Corps. Ian felt right at home. He never minded the downtime. Scout Snipers didn't get bored easily. Sometimes the rest of his engine crew thought he was asleep, but usually he was cultivating stillness. He liked the rush of action; needed it, if he was honest. But he'd had enough of it to appreciate the lulls.

It had been a quiet shift, right up until the call: multi-vehicle accident, intersection of Park Row and Spruce. Outside the L-20's normal area of service, but the locals were engaged at a minor fire a couple blocks south. L-20 hadn't been doing anything, so they'd been brought in to assist.

Pretty basic incident response. Assess situation, make sure nothing was burning, access casualties. Pop car doors with Halligan tool if jammed, break windows if necessary. Triage casualties. Ian was just a Probie, so he did what he was told. Lieutenant Rawlins was in command of L-20 and the incident.

Lieutenant Rawlins was one of the better COs Ian had served under. Calm, competent, didn't pile chickenshit on top of the daily crap. Tough and fair. Would've made a half-decent Marine platoon commander. Rest of the engine crew were solid, too. Tight bunch, but they were starting to warm up to Ian. He'd expected that; didn't bother him. Veterans were always cool toward replacements until the FNGs—Fucking New Guys—proved themselves.

Crew got the situation under control quickly. No fatalities, only two serious casualties: one broken collarbone, one probable skull fracture. Got the ambulance cases loaded on the bus and off to Bellevue, rendered the scene safe. Then it was time to stow equipment and head back. Let the maintenance folks deal with the wreckage. That'd take time, but wasn't an emergency. Would screw up traffic for an hour or so.

Some guys took their time packing up, figuring there wasn't any rush now they'd dealt with the situation. Not Ian. Same principle as reloading. Keep your mag full, because you never knew when you'd need to return fire. Keep the truck loaded, because the next call might already be coming in. Plenty of time to goof off once you were prepped.

Paid off this time. Just finished packing up, was climbing onto the truck when Dispatch got on the horn.

"Nearest available units, respond. We have a 10-13S at a parking garage, Park Row and Pearl. Multiple officers down, active shooters. All available Patrol units and ESU, respond."

Like any good sniper, Ian had studied the terrain. Pretty much memorized Manhattan's road network. Pearl was about a click away. They could be there in no time.

Lieutenant Rawlins grabbed the handset. "This is FDNY engine L-20," he said. "Show us responding, ETA two minutes."

Truck got moving, lights and sirens engaged. Ian grabbed the handle nearest him and started getting psyched. Went over what they could expect. 10-13S meant an NYPD officer in a firefight. Multiple officers down was bad. Probably meant multiple shooters. Serious GSWs. Fatalities.

Ian didn't carry these days. Even if FDNY permitted it, which they didn't, Cassie didn't like him being armed. Thought it was bad for him, made his PTSD worse. Knew she was right, but at the moment, would've felt a hell of a lot better with a Beretta nine-mil and an extra mag or two.

"Okay, boys," Lieutenant Rawlins said. "You know the drill. When there's an active shooter, we don't go in until NYPD clears us. Not even if you see casualties. I'm not calling your wives and sweethearts to tell them you got killed trying to be goddamn heroes. We wait till the lead stops flying, *then* we go in. Copy?"

The crew murmured variations on "yes, sir." Ian added his voice to the others, but his inner voice, the one he heard when the shit went down, had a different opinion. Hadn't heard that voice in a while. But it was still there.

Too bad you don't have your rifle, Marine. Clear field of fire, you could knock out the shooters just fine all by your lonesome.

He wasn't a Marine anymore. Couldn't think like that.

Just keep telling yourself that. You'll never stop being a Marine.

Parking garage just ahead. Patrol units already out front; two cars. Cops weren't in sight; they'd gone inside. Plenty more inbound; they were in sight of police headquarters. Probably five dozen cops on foot already on the way.

Ian felt the old thrill of going into combat. Nothing like it. Sort of like when a girl asked you back to her place. Nothing happening yet, but you knew it was about to get hot and heavy. Adrenaline pumping. Colors got brighter, outlines sharper. Never felt more alive than when people were about to get killed.

God help him, but he loved the feeling. Almost made it worth the price he had to pay.

Truck pulled over to the curb, idled. Nothing to do just yet. Ian leaned out the side of the engine, getting a sense for the ground. Couldn't hear any gunfire; that was probably good. Saw everything. Cars passing, slowing down; drivers rubbernecking. Wondering what all the lights and emergency vehicles were about. Pedestrians standing back, taking pics on their phones. Smells on the air: engine exhaust, metal, oil. Sky overcast; might be rain later.

Hypervigilance was a mixed bag. Ian saw every threat, whether it was there or not. Got jumpy over things that weren't dangerous. It was exhausting, just going outside. Wished he could turn it down, except those times it paid off.

Rapid gunfire, just ahead. Ian's combat-trained ear placed it inside the garage, not fooled by echoes off surrounding buildings. Automatic rifle; Kalashnikov. Know that sound anywhere.

NYPD doesn't use AKs, Marine. That's the bad guys.

Ian was out of the truck without thinking about it, ducking back, crouching behind it. Better to be mobile when rounds were incoming. Didn't want to get pinned down. Wished for a weapon again.

"Everybody get down!" Lieutenant Rawlins was shouting. "Keep your heads down!"

Kept his own head up. Had to maintain situational awareness. Saw three tangos exiting the garage. Two of them carrying someone else; female, struggling. Third guy had an AK in his hands. Moved like soldiers; former military for sure. Piled into one of the squad cars, tossing her in the back seat with one of the bad guys. Car peeled out, heading straight for the L-20 engine.

Those bastards just stole a police car, Marine. These are some bad-ass operators, they're desperate, and they have a hostage. Watch out you don't get killed.

Car rolled by right across the divider from the fire truck. Ian watched it go, saw the hostage in the window, woman trying to get upright. She got wrestled down by the guy in back with her, but Ian saw her face, just for a second, less than ten feet from him. Strangely clear.

Christ. That's Erin O'Reilly!

Ian didn't know what was going on. Didn't have a plan. Didn't matter. Mr. Carlyle was like a father to him, and Erin was going to marry Mr. Carlyle. Made her family.

"Probie! Thompson! Get back here!"

Couldn't waste time explaining. Couldn't even tell Lieutenant Rawlins where he was going. Couldn't spare the breath. Needed it.

Ian ran.

Didn't have a prayer of catching up to the car, even in Manhattan traffic. Car was doing twenty, twenty-five, thanks to the other cars getting in the way. Ian couldn't run better than fifteen and couldn't keep that up for long. But couldn't let them out of sight, so he gave it everything he had.

Running a marathon was one thing; sprinting was something else. Ian was in great shape, but try running flat-out more than four or five minutes and you'd really feel it, no matter how much cardio you did. Losing ground every second. But the bad guys were headed back the way L-20 had come, down Park Row, and Ian knew something they didn't.

The crash at the Spruce Street intersection wouldn't be cleared yet. Traffic jam would stop them, or at least slow them way the hell down.

Ian ran on the sidewalk, arms swinging, legs eating up the concrete. Kept taking deep breaths, found his rhythm. Car drawing away, already half a block ahead. Didn't care, didn't slow down. Lungs hurting. Ignored the pain.

What're you going to do if you catch these guys, Marine? They've got friggin' assault rifles. You didn't even grab a Halligan. You planning on deploying some harsh language, maybe? A few strong verbs?

Figure it out when he got there. Didn't pay to think too hard in combat. Made you hesitate. Got you killed.

Passed other police cars, going the other way. Couldn't flag them down; no way to communicate fast enough. Cell phone in his pocket; if he slowed down to make a call, he'd lose the bad guys. Losing them anyway. Car pulling farther away, around the curve under the Brooklyn Bridge Promenade. Really starting to feel the burn now in calves and thighs. Embraced the pain. Sped up.

Not much sidewalk at the curve, just a few inches of curb by a retaining wall. Ian went into the street. Brake lights ahead; excellent. That'd be the backed-up traffic from the accident. Saw the squad car again, stopped near the intersection.

Lots of horns honking, as if noise would clear the road faster. There'd be cops here, on foot, directing traffic. Ian could warn them, get some armed backup. Maybe end this, whatever it was, right here.

He'd gotten within about thirty yards when the getaway driver got impatient. Park Row was divided at the intersection, a little wrought-iron fence separating the lanes. Driver just rammed straight through the fence, took it out and blasted across, threading oncoming traffic. Undercarriage scraped the curb, throwing sparks. Left the muffler right there, torn clean off the car. Traffic cop yelled, dove out of the way. Car squeezed through on the sidewalk, made a tight left onto Spruce, southbound in the open lane leading away from the crash site.

Ian cut the corner, leaped the fence. Gained a few yards diagonally, lost them again as the car picked up speed. Ran straight past the traffic cop, who was just picking himself up off the pavement.

"Kidnapping!" Ian gasped at him as he went by. Hoped it'd be enough. The way the bad guys were driving, ought to at least show they weren't cops, no matter what their car looked like.

Squad car wasn't moving great. They'd screwed up something when they'd gone over the fence. Car had a shimmy. Even as he noticed it, Ian saw the left front tire go. Hubcap went spinning away, rolling along the street next to the car.

Driver knew his stuff. Didn't lose control, didn't spin out. But driving on a flat was never easy. Wheel rim hit the road, showering sparks. Bled off a lot of speed. Ian hoped it made them too busy to check their rearview or they'd see him, running after them like Forrest goddamn Gump.

Another block and Ian really started feeling the burn. Getting harder to breathe. Cramp starting in left calf muscle. Got pissed. Body letting him down. Used the anger, poured it right back into himself. Dug deep, found more. Why'd they want Erin? Was she just a hostage? Or something else going on?

He'd seen the news last night, knew she'd been fired. Knew she'd been set up. Erin would never kill a little kid. She was better than Ian was. This had to be connected.

Decided it didn't matter how. Figure it out later. Mission right now was to maintain contact. Good Scout Sniper objective.

Three more blocks, Spruce Street onto Gold, and knew he didn't have much left. Eased up just a little, let the car get more lead. No choice. Car turned south on Fulton, which let Ian cut the corner through DeLury Square. As he came out the other side of the square, a bicycle messenger swung into view going the other way.

No chance of avoiding it. Ian hit him broadside, sent the poor guy flying over the handlebars. Thank God for helmets. Kid tucked and rolled, actually landed pretty well. Probably not the first time he'd taken a header on the street. Ian came off worse, scraped a knee and banged his arm on the bike.

But he ended up next to the bicycle.

Didn't have enough spare breath to apologize. Just nodded to the guy and took his bike.

It was a little better. A change was as good as a rest; that's what they told you in boot camp. Pedaling a bike used different muscles than running. Feeling it in his quads instead of his calves now.

You'll be hurting all over by the time this is done, Marine. Just try not to catch any bullets.

The half-disabled car swung onto Water Street a block ahead of him. Attracting all kinds of attention, but nobody trying to stop it. Why would they? It was an NYPD squad car. Never mind it was laying a trail of sparks through downtown Manhattan. Ian pedaled harder, trying to close.

They didn't seem to have noticed him, which made sense. Even if they'd spotted him running, their search image was a guy on foot. Now he was riding a bike, so couldn't be the same guy. People in combat situations tended to think in straight lines. Complications confused them.

Car shot straight down John Street, trying to speed up on the more sparsely-traveled side street. But it couldn't go too fast. The damaged wheel wobbling dangerously, the car all over the road. Ian was only fifty or sixty meters back when the car cleared the final stoplight at South Street, went under FDR

Drive, and fetched up at the Greenway by the East River. Finally rolled to a stop.

Now what, assholes? You planning on swimming the river? Or did you really think nobody would notice a flaming police car screaming across town? NYPD is going to be all over your ass in about five minutes.

They obviously knew that, unless they were complete morons. Which was why it didn't make sense they hadn't gotten out of the car and started running yet. Which in turn meant they had a plan Ian didn't know about.

He turned the borrowed bicycle and coasted nice and easy to the right, pretending not to be interested in the car. Avoided eye contact with the vehicle. Looked for any real police. Didn't see any. Figured.

Don't mind me. I'm just your typical New Yorker out for a little mid-morning ride. Might be a good time to call the cavalry.

Reached for his phone, caught movement. The three guys getting out of the car. Not wearing their masks anymore. Figuring it was better to blend in. Had Erin with them, struggling. One smacked her in the face. She sagged down, would have fallen if they hadn't caught and half-carried her. Took all Ian's training not to rush over and start kicking asses. Reminded himself they had guns and knew how to use them.

They took her out onto the pier. Somebody called to them. Typical concerned bystander, wondering if everything was okay. One of the tangos waved pleasantly in reply. Smart of him.

A boat coming down the river. Little pleasure craft, the sort of thing a yuppie might call his yacht. Everything made sense now. They'd been headed for a rendezvous, but the accident on Park Row had made them switch pickup points.

A boat. Damn it all. Bad guys hustling. No baggage to load. They'd just jump on board and sail merrily off to God only knew where.

Ian only saw one thing to do. Another pier in front of him. Steered his bike out onto it. Pedaled harder. Knew he had to get enough of a lead. Stood up on the pedals. Pedestrians jumped out of his way, cursing at him. Didn't care.

Ran out of pier. Jumped off the bike, let it skid away. Hoped maybe the bike messenger would get it back somehow. No boats tied up here; some rich jerk had turned a ferryboat into some sort of waterfront restaurant. Saw a motorboat on the river about twenty meters out, puttering along. An old guy sitting at the back, rocking a gray beard, baseball cap, and flannel shirt. He'd have to do.

A row of benches sat at the edge of the pier, just short of the guardrail. Ian sprang onto a bench at a run and jumped the rail. Hoped the water wasn't as cold as it looked.

It was a whole lot colder. Temperature change shocked him, made his whole body try to curl in on itself. Weight of clothes and shoes dragged him down. Fought his way to the surface, started swimming.

Veterans loved to bitch about stupid military decisions. Put half a dozen Marines in a room and you'd get five dozen stories about inefficiency, unnecessary risks, and lowball defense contracts. But give credit where it was due; when they made you a Marine, an amphibious warfare specialist, they taught you how to swim. And they taught you to do it fully clad, in combat boots, carrying eighty pounds of crap, in lousy weather. Sometimes they just chucked you into the pool and let you figure it out. Good practice.

Ian covered the distance to the motorboat in a matter of a few seconds, choosing his angle right so he intercepted it. The old guy saw him in the last couple of meters, blinked, and gave him a curious look.

Ian reached up and grabbed the gunwale with one hand. The old man leaned forward and offered his own hand. Ian pulled himself up, grabbed the hand with his other one, and hauled himself into the boat.

"Thanks, sir," he gasped.

"You all right, son?" the man asked.

"I'm good, sir." Mostly true. Didn't think he'd taken too much damage from the bike collision. But he was shivering, dripping wet, every muscle sore. Now he wasn't moving, realized he was running on fumes. How far had he gone? Three kilometers? Four? At a dead run? Not counting the bike and the quick swim at the end.

"Son," the old man said slowly. "What in the hell are you doing?"

Ian dropped to the bottom of the boat and lay as flat as he could. He'd spotted the yacht coming. It churned by at a pretty good clip, wake making the motorboat pitch.

"Damn fancy boys and their toy boats," the old man grumbled. "Think they own everything, even the river."

"Need your help, sir," Ian said urgently, speaking in short, breathless bursts. "Follow that boat. Keep some distance. Don't let them know."

"Who are you, kid?" the man asked. "What's going on?" But he put a hand on the tiller and guided his boat into the spreading wake of the yacht.

Ian tried to get his breath back. Wasn't easy. "Bad guys," he said. "Kidnappers. Got a woman."

"Well, damn," the old man said quietly. "You a cop, son?"

Ian shook his head. "No, sir. FDNY."

"Then we'd better get to shore and fetch us some cops."

"No time. We'd lose them. Have to keep on the trail, see where they go. Call 911 from here, get air support."

"Well, son," the man said. "Here's the thing. I never really took to those gadgets. My daughter gave me a cell phone for my birthday, but I don't have it with me. When I'm on the water, I like being alone."

Ian reached into his pocket, pulled out his phone. Lot of water came with it. Screen black. Dead.

Of course your phone is dead, Marine. You got rocks for brains? You just went swimming with it, idiot. Maybe you should ask if he's got a bag of rice, as long as you're being stupid.

"You have a gun, sir?" Ian asked.

"A couple," the man said. "Hunting rifle and a shotgun. But they're at home, locked up. I can't exactly go cruising around Manhattan with a bunch of shooting irons. You sure you're all right?"

"Still in the fight, sir."

The man gave him a sharper look. "Were you in the service, kid?"

"Marine Corps."

He nodded. "Thought so. Where'd you serve?"

"One tour in the Sandbox, one in the 'Stan."

The old man kept steering the boat with his left hand. He held out his right. "Glad to know you. Larry Cole. Coast Guard, Chief Petty Officer. Retired, obviously. Ferried some of you boys around the Mekong back in '69."

"Ian Thompson," Ian said, shaking hands. "Scout Sniper, Sergeant." Saw the guy's baseball cap up close: dark blue, crossed-anchor insignia, yellow letters spelling out US COAST GUARD.

"Semper fi, Marine," Cole said. His weathered face cracked into a smile. "Who're these guys we're chasing?"

"Don't know, sir. They shot some cops downtown, grabbed Ms. O'Reilly. Don't know where they're going. Chased them from One Police Plaza."

"Well," Cole said. "They're in one hell of a hurry. Anyone else know they're out here?"

"No, sir. Not as far as I know."

"These boys armed?"

"Yes, sir. At least one AK, probably more guns."

"What I wouldn't give for a Swift boat," Cole said thoughtfully. "Like we had in 'Nam. Pair of fifty-cals in the bow. That'd get their attention. Turn that fancy yacht into a colander. I've got beers in the cooler. Help yourself. You look like you could use a drink."

Ian wasn't much of a beer drinker, but needed to hydrate. Had sweated a lot on that run, in spite of the cool weather. "Thank you, sir," he said. Got a Coors out of the cooler, popped the tab, drank. Not bad.

"We're headed west," Cole commented. "Going to Jersey, you think?"

"Could be, sir."

"We've got a little time in front of us," Cole said. "So why don't you tell me exactly how you got here?"

Chapter 26

VIC NESHENKO

If he ended up in Hell after he died, Vic decided, they'd make him fill out a DD-5 in the waiting room outside the Infernal gates. It would set the right tone for the skull-chewing that'd come later. He'd been up all night. The adrenaline from the Flaherty arrest had worn off hours ago. Lieutenant Webb and Erin had gone off to yell at the Commissioner and he'd been left in Major Crimes to do friggin' paperwork.

Mountain Dew helped a little. Caffeine could only boost you so much, but it was a hell of a lot better than straight sleep deprivation. When Zofia turned up a little after nine, that was even better. She'd dropped Mina at her mom's, so it was just the two of them in the office.

Zofia was, predictably, irritated to have missed the Flaherty takedown. "A genuine, honest-to-God corpse-sicle in a freezer?" she said. "And I missed it?"

"I get where you're coming from," Vic said. "Right now I'm missing a once-in-a-lifetime opportunity to tear the PC a new one, with my CO backing me up. It's happening this minute!"

"Poor baby," Zofia said, trailing her fingertips along the back of his neck. "It must be so hard on you."

"I'm almost done," he said. "Maybe once I get this last report filed, you and I can take a little break time."

"I wonder if the Captain left his office locked," Zofia said with a mischievous gleam in her eye.

Vic blinked. "You want to get it on in Holliday's office?"

"Right on his desk," she said. "Why not?"

"Because we'd both get fired!" But it was strangely tempting. "You're a real piece of work, you know that?"

"And you love me for it," she said, winking. "Now there's some incentive to finish your work."

"I'll get right on it," he promised.

The phone on Webb's desk rang.

"Damn," Vic said. He stood up and walked quickly to the Lieutenant's desk. When the boss was out of the office, the ranking detective had to mind the phones. When you called the cops, you expected someone to answer.

He scooped up the receiver. "Major Crimes," he said. "Detective Neshenko."

"This is Dispatch," came the answer. "There's been an incident."

The voice sounded wrong. Dispatchers were known for their ability to keep calm, delivering the worst possible news in the steadiest voice. But Vic caught something just a little off.

"Talk to me," he said. Zofia, catching the change in Vic's tone, was suddenly all business, poised for action.

"We have a 10-13S at a parking garage," Dispatch said. "Park Row and Pearl. Five officers down, one civilian missing."

"*Five?!*" Vic exclaimed, losing his own professionalism for a second. "Wait a sec. Park Row and Pearl? That's right next to One PP. Shouldn't the main Major Crimes unit have this? They're a block away!"

"They're on scene," Dispatch said.

"What do you need from us?" Vic asked, confused. A shootout outside Headquarters with five police casualties was a big deal, but shouldn't have anything to do with the Eightball. Unless...

The bottom dropped out of Vic's guts.

"Who are the casualties?" he asked.

"Two Patrolmen; Brinkley and Myers. Lieutenant McDowell, Lieutenant Webb, and Captain Holliday. All three are from your AOS."

Only the numbness of shock kept Vic talking. "What about Erin O'Reilly?" he asked. "She'd have been with them. And Webb's daughters. Are they okay?"

"According to initial reports, O'Reilly was last seen being dragged into a black van by three masked gunmen. Her current status is unknown. The other civilians are on their way to Bellevue to be checked out."

"How bad were they hit?" Vic asked. "Our people, I mean."

Zofia was standing in front of him now, her big blue eyes wide with worry. She mouthed the word "who?" He shook his head and held up a hand, silently telling her to wait a moment.

"Officer Brinkley is dead," Dispatch said. "The other four are either at Bellevue or en route."

"Who has incident command?" Vic asked. Somehow his brain was still functioning. He didn't know how. The world felt like it was tilting sideways and he was about to slide right off the surface.

"Captain Stoneman, Major Crimes."

"Any orders for my squad?"

"Not at this time. We have a BOLO out for Erin O'Reilly, and a group of men dressed in black, wearing ski masks and armed with shotguns, pistols, and assault rifles. Your squad is to await instructions."

Like hell I'm gonna sit on my ass waiting for instructions, Vic thought. "Copy that," he said and hung up.

"What happened?" Zofia whispered.

"The bad guys hit our people," Vic said dully. "Webb and the Captain got shot. McDowell, too."

"Are they okay?"

"Beats the hell out of me. People who get shot usually aren't."

"Erin?"

"They took her."

"Took her where?"

"Took her! Kidnapped her!"

"Jesus," Zofia murmured. "What do we do?"

"We find her. Fast."

"How?"

Vic's mind was racing. He pretended to be dumb a lot of the time, because if people thought you were an idiot, they underestimated you. Plus, he didn't like thinking hard. It made him tired and irritable. That was why, though he'd never admit it, he liked having a commanding officer calling the shots. But right now he *was* the commanding officer. The Eightball had been neatly decapitated. With the Captain and Webb out of commission, and Erin off the table, that left Vic as the ranking Major Crimes officer. Hell, at that moment, he and Zofia were all that was left of the Eightball's Major Crimes squad.

It really was all up to him. If he made the wrong call now, it might mean Erin's life.

He didn't have enough information to make decisions. That made his first decision easy, in fact: get more information. And line up some resources so when they knew where to go, they could move quickly.

Vic started talking very fast.

"Zofia, you know where Erin's brother lives? The doctor? Good. Get over there right now and get Rolf. Her dad's gonna want to come help. Don't let him. He's too old for this shit and he'll get in the way. They'll have something Erin's worn or handled. Get it, too, and put it in a bag. Call me when you've got the dog and I'll tell you where to meet me. Copy?"

"Copy," Zofia said.

"Go."

Zofia ran for the stairs. Vic was right behind her. Bellevue Hospital would be his first stop. He prayed at least one of their guys was awake and able to talk. Thank God he and Zofia had their own cars.

Vic left the lights and sirens on and drove like a maniac, but the Taurus seemed to move in slow-mo. Anger and fear were fogging his brain. How could they have been so goddamn stupid? Waltzing around assuming they'd won. No wonder Ophelia had been so friggin' smug. She'd had this planned the whole time.

Think, he ordered himself. Ophelia had made a phone call. She'd set this in motion. But why? It wouldn't get her out of jail, wouldn't help her dad. This was a revenge play, pure and simple. Who had she called? A lawyer? This sounded like a paramilitary hit. Finnegan didn't have that kind of muscle. Not many organizations did, and those that did wouldn't be keen to take on the NYPD. This was a bold strike, one that needed dangerous men who didn't respect the police.

"The Russians," Vic growled aloud. "Gennady Vlasov. Mikhail was his cousin. That's why he kept the loser around. The rest of his guys are ex-military hardasses, but Mikhail was family. Flaherty killed him. Jesus Christ. She didn't want to set Erin up with the Department for killing Mikhail. She wanted to set him up with the goddamn *bratva* so they'd kill her!"

That had to be it. Ophelia's phone call had been the signal to leak something about Mikhail to Gennady. If he was convinced Erin had murdered his cousin, he'd go batshit nuts.

Vic got on the radio to Dispatch and asked them to patch him through to Captain Stoneman.

"Stoneman here," the Captain said briskly. Vic heard a lot of noise in the background.

"Cap, this is Detective Neshenko at the Eight."

"Did they tell you about your CO?"

"Yes, sir," Vic said.

"Good. I'm really busy right now, so I don't have time to do medical follow-up. Go to Bellevue. They'll help you."

"I'm on my way now," Vic said. "But that's not why I'm calling."

"Make it quick, Neshenko."

"Sir, I think you're looking for Gennady Vlasov and his guys. This whole thing was a plan to snatch Erin O'Reilly. I think you're after a team of Russian ex-military. They hang out at Matrushka's Restaurant in Brooklyn. They might be headed there now."

"How good is this info?" Stoneman asked.

"I don't have proof," Vic admitted. "But I ran into them a couple days ago. They're in this up to their necks, and Vlasov thinks O'Reilly whacked his cousin last night."

"I'll look into it," Stoneman promised. "And I'll keep you posted."

"Thank you, sir."

Vic hung up and felt better for a few seconds. Then he realized Vlasov wasn't a moron, and would never take Erin back to his own restaurant. He'd have a safe house somewhere else.

He'd always known New York was big, but at the moment it felt absolutely huge. Rolf would help, if they could get him close enough, but not if the bad guys were in a car.

Vic couldn't think of anything else to do for the moment, so he cursed the rest of the way to the hospital, monotonously and continuously. The situation was best described by four-letter words, and it was better than thinking about Webb lying on a stretcher or cooling in the morgue, and Erin on her way to be tortured or—

He derailed that train of thought with another string of profanity. Thinking, he was discovering, wasn't the real problem. He could think all day. What he couldn't afford to do right now was feel, because if he let himself do that he'd fall apart, and he couldn't afford to fall apart. Today, Vic Neshenko needed to keep his shit together. There'd be plenty of time to go to pieces after they'd rescued Erin and taken those bastards the hell down.

*   *   *

The first thing Vic saw in the ER waiting room was Webb's daughters. Erica was sitting with her back straight, no expression at all on her face. She had her arms around Danielle, whose head was buried against her sister's shoulder. Vic saw blood spattered on them, but they looked more or less intact.

He hated this sort of thing, but this was no time to get awkward. He walked straight up to them and cleared his throat. Erica blinked once and gave him a look that seemed to come from about ten miles away. Danielle didn't move. Her shoulders were trembling.

"Hey, ladies," Vic said. "I don't know if you remember me. Detective Neshenko, but call me Vic. I work with your dad."

"I remember you," Erica said in a soft monotone.

"Are either of you hurt?" he asked. "Physically, I mean."

"No," Erica said quietly. "We didn't get hit."

Vic swallowed, but there was no getting around the next question. He went for it.

"How's your dad doing?"

"He's in surgery," Erica said, her voice still holding zero inflection. She was in deep emotional shock, Vic realized. He'd seen it before. The girl was running on autopilot, but at least her brain was working. It was probably just as well. These young women looked like they'd been shoved straight into the shit.

"Did the doc talk to you yet?" Vic asked.

"No," Erica said.

"How long has he been in there?"

"I don't know. We just got here."

"Did the medics say anything about him? His condition?"

"He got shot," Erica said. "In the stomach. The liver, the paramedic said. He used a word I didn't know. I think it was *laparotomy*. Emergency laparotomy. I don't know what that means."

Vic knew more than a normal person should about gunshot wounds and emergency first aid. "It means they need to open up his abdomen," he said. "So they can go in and fix him up. Was he just hit the once?"

"No," Erica said. "Three times. In the stomach. Once in the shoulder."

"Jesus," Vic murmured. Then, remembering he needed to keep up a front for Webb's kids, "They got him here alive. That's a good thing. These docs know their business. Do you know who's operating?"

"I didn't hear his name," Erica said. "He was a little shorter than you. Dark hair. Blue eyes."

"Sounds like Sean O'Reilly," Vic said. "I thought so. Listen, Erica. He's one of the best damn surgeons around. Your dad's in the best possible hands, okay?"

"Okay," Erica echoed, but her eyes stayed flat and lifeless.

"What do you know about the others who were brought in with you?" Vic asked.

Erica shook her head. "I don't know," she said.

"What do you remember about what happened?"

It was a hell of a thing to ask, but he had to know, and he didn't have time to wait for her to feel better. Vic felt like an asshole, but he was used to feeling that way and it didn't bother him too much.

"We didn't see a lot," Erica said. "The elevator doors opened and I heard a gunshot. Erin fell down and I saw a bunch of men with guns. Then Dad yelled 'Get down!' and stepped in front of Dani and me. And everybody started shooting. It was really loud. Not like in the movies. It hurt my ears. Dad made this sound, like he'd been punched in the stomach. I grabbed Dani and lay down, and Dad fell on top of us. People were still shooting and I heard a man say, 'Get the sucker,' I think. Then there were some more shots and the same man said, 'Go! Go! Go!' A car drove away. Then, a minute later, I heard a crash."

"What kind of crash?" Vic asked.

"A car crash," Erica said. "It was a couple of levels down from us. Then there was some more shooting, downstairs. Then, a few minutes later I guess, some police officers came running. They tried to help."

"What did you do?"

"Dad was groaning," Erica said. "We had to get out from under him, but he was heavy and I didn't want to hurt him. It took a while. And there was so much blood."

Vic nodded. "I'll bet."

"I wanted to help him," Erica said, and for the first time Vic heard the pain in her voice. "But I didn't know what to do. And Dani was screaming, and I thought she'd been hurt too. I didn't know what to do. I didn't know."

"You did fine," Vic said. "You and your sister got through it okay. You're gonna be fine."

Danielle raised her head from her sister's shoulder. Her eyes were puffy, her nose was running, and tears were streaming down her face. She said something completely unintelligible.

"Sorry?" Vic said.

"I told Dad he didn't care about us," she sniffled. "I said he had a funny way of showing it. I just meant... I wanted to say we missed him. And that was... was almost the last... the last thing... And then he... he... he stepped in front of us!"

Danielle lost it again and started sobbing. Vic didn't even have a handkerchief to offer. He used disposable tissues, and at the moment he didn't have any. He looked away, feeling impatient and awkward.

"He stepped in the way of the bullets," Erica said quietly. "Between us and the bad guys. He got shot because of us. We would have both been shot."

All of a sudden the only thing Vic could think about was Mina, and what he'd do to keep his own daughter from getting hurt. Stopping bullets with his own body was the absolute minimum. Now he wanted to cry, damn it.

"Another detective's gonna be here soon," he said gruffly. "They'll take your statement. Thanks."

Then he went to the ER reception desk, leaving Webb's kids to do the best they could. They needed more help than he could give them. Hell, they'd need years of therapy to start with, and that was if Webb didn't die.

Damn it, Webb had better not die. It'd be just like the weary old bastard to kick off like this, without any warning. Vic would be seriously pissed if Webb didn't pull through.

The reception nurse wasn't very helpful, but Vic was stubborn and eventually got past her. He ended up face to face with Dr. Nussbaum, a guy he knew from previous visits. Nussbaum had treated some of Erin's many injuries.

"Talk to me, Doc," Vic said. "I need to know if any of the cops in here are awake."

"I don't have time for this, Officer," Nussbaum said. "I have a couple of urgent surgical cases. Dr. O'Reilly is already engaged. We don't have enough hands."

"This is important," Vic said.

"So is this," Nussbaum said, gesturing around himself. "If I don't scrub in soon, an officer is going to die."

"If I don't talk to someone who was there, another cop is gonna die," Vic said grimly.

"I have an unconscious officer with an obstructed airway in there," Nussbaum said, cocking his head toward the operating room. "The only reason the woman with the shattered leg isn't already in surgery is that she's not going to die in the next couple of hours. Good day, Officer."

"It's 'Detective,'" Vic said under his breath, watching Nussbaum hurry away. He was momentarily frustrated, but then he thought about what the doctor had said. He flagged down a busy-looking nurse.

"Whaddaya want?" she demanded in a thick Brooklyn accent that took Vic right back to his childhood.

"I gotta follow up with the cop with the busted leg," he said, laying his own accent on even thicker than usual. "Where is she?"

"Second door on the left," the nurse said over her shoulder.

Vic pushed through the door and found a stretcher. On it lay Lieutenant McDowell. The IAB cop's dress blues were a mess. Her uniform was torn, disheveled, and bloody. The EMTs had cut away the right leg of her trousers, exposing a thigh that in other circumstances might have been sexy. At the moment it was wrapped in a blood-soaked bandage, which wasn't attractive at all. McDowell was pale-complected to begin with. Now she was ashy white. An IV bag hung from a hook above the stretcher, dripping God only knew what into her arm. Her eyes were closed and her face was clenched tight.

Looking at her, Vic felt something he never would have thought he'd feel toward any Internal Affairs officer, let alone McDowell: pity. The pain she was feeling was so intense he could actually feel it radiating off her in waves. It put him on edge and made him want to run out of the room.

"Lieutenant?" he said.

She didn't answer. She probably didn't even hear him.

"Lieutenant McDowell?" he tried again, reaching out and touching her hand.

Her fingers curled around his with startling speed and strength. Her eyes snapped open and focused on his face. The pupils were contracted. She was on some pretty good drugs, probably morphine. If she was still in this much pain with the benefit of the happy juice, Vic didn't want to think about how bad it would be without.

"How're you feeling, Lieutenant?" he asked, knowing it was a dumbass question even as he asked it.

"Detective Neshenko," she said in a tight, strained voice. "What's the situation?"

"I thought you could tell me," he said. "I only just got here. What happened?"

"It was an ambush," McDowell said, speaking slowly, enunciating carefully. "They must have followed us to the hospital and waited in the garage. I saw six shooters. Caucasian, but wearing ski masks and dark clothes. Black van getaway vehicle. We put three of them down. All our people got hit. Lieutenant Webb has stomach wounds. Captain Holliday took three in the chest, maybe more. O'Reilly caught a shotgun blast in the stomach."

"A shotgun?" Vic repeated, feeling like he'd taken a slug in his own gut.

"Beanbag round, I think," McDowell said. "There wasn't any blood and she was still moving. The other shooters waited until she went down. Then they opened up on us. I think their mission was to take her, alive."

"I was afraid of that," Vic said.

"It was the only thing that gave us a chance," McDowell said. "It bought us a second to recover. The Captain cleared his gun and dropped one of them. Then I drew and started firing at the same time the shooters did. That's when I got hit. I think I hit one, but he didn't fall. The Captain shot another, then he got hit. I was half-hidden behind the doorway, lying down. Two of them grabbed O'Reilly and started carrying her away, so I fired at them and got one in the back of the head. He fell and the other dropped O'Reilly on the ground. I exchanged fire with the others until they put O'Reilly in the van and drove away. By then my Glock was empty and I didn't have any spare magazines. I called it in on my cell and reported what happened. Then I think I passed out. The next thing I remember is being in the ambulance."

Vic stared at her with newfound respect. "You ever been in a shootout before, Lieutenant?" he asked.

"No," McDowell said. "I never fired in the line of duty before today."

"You did good."

"That's a little consolation," McDowell said grimly.

"You're sure Erin was alive? When they put her in the van?"

"She was moving and struggling. They'd put a bag over her head and secured her hands."

"Did they say anything?"

"I didn't hear," McDowell said. "The shooting was too loud. It echoed in the elevator."

"And you don't know where they went?"

"They were on their way out of the garage. I couldn't see where they went after that."

Vic rubbed his face. "Shit," he said. "Do you know if Holliday or Webb are gonna pull through?"

"That's not your problem right now," McDowell said.

Vic flinched as if she'd slapped him. *What a bitch*, he thought. "The hell it's not," he said.

"It isn't," she said coldly. "Remember chain of command. Your Captain and Lieutenant are incapacitated. Your senior detective was fired and is now abducted. That leaves you in command of your Major Crimes unit."

"What unit?" he retorted. "It's me and Zofia. Some friggin' squad!"

McDowell's fingers tightened on his hand. "Captain Holliday is probably dead," she said. "He got hit trying to protect his people. If you want that to matter, stop pouting, get out there, and *do your job*."

A dozen angry replies ricocheted around Vic's head. "Anything you can tell me that might help me find these guys?" he asked instead.

"There'll be camera footage from the garage," McDowell said. "But the kidnappers won't keep the van. They'll change cars as soon as they can."

Vic nodded. "Captain Stoneman is in charge of the main investigation," he said.

"What are your orders?" McDowell asked.

"To stand by and wait," he admitted. "I'm not even supposed to be here."

"But you are."

"Yeah," Vic said. "I'm disobeying orders, Lieutenant. You got a problem with that?"

And McDowell, to his astonishment, smiled. Her jaw was still tight, and it looked more like a grimace, but it was genuine. "Not today, Detective," she said. "Stoneman is good. He'll catch these guys, but not in time to save O'Reilly. That's going to be up to you."

Chapter 27

Coming out of unconsciousness wasn't like waking up. It was disorienting in the extreme. Erin had no idea where she was, or how long she'd been out. Something wet and sticky was on her forehead. She was lying in the middle of a crumpled tube of steel. She smelled blood, oil, and metal. She couldn't remember how she'd gotten there.

From somewhere very close came an explosion of noise, an earsplitting rattle that some part of her identified as gunfire. She shrank down lower, but no bullets came anywhere near her.

"Take their car!" a man shouted. "Get the girl. Go!"

Erin struggled to sit up. It was difficult. Her hands were stuck together. She became aware of a strip of plastic around her wrists, digging in deep. She looked for something to cut it with. She was in a wrecked van. She dimly remembered being picked up and carried. The people who'd done it were bad guys. Where was everybody else?

A man clambered through the sliding side door, huge and terrifying in a black ski mask. A shotgun was slung over his shoulder. He grabbed her and dragged her out of the van. She kicked, connecting with one of his shins, and he cursed in a foreign language.

Russians, Erin thought. She flailed at him with her bound hands, achieving basically nothing.

He backhanded her across the face, so hard it snapped her head back. She saw stars and lost all sense of balance. Dimly, she was aware of being hoisted up and bodily carried. Then she was hurled into the back seat of a car. Her captor slid in beside her. Two more guys got into the front seat, separated from her by a screen of metal mesh.

Patrol car, Erin thought dazedly. *They're stealing a squad car.*

The car rolled out into daylight, made a hard left turn, and accelerated. All three men started talking at once.

"What was that back there? What a balls-up!"

"Did you see what happened to Artur and Daniil?"

"They got killed, that's what happened to them!"

"Killed? What do you mean?"

"Shot in the head, that's what I mean!"

Erin stretched her neck, trying to see out the window. She caught a glimpse of a fire truck as they drove by, but then the guy next to her grabbed her hair and forced her head back to the seat.

"Stay down, or I'll break your skull!" he snapped.

"What about Abram?" the driver asked.

"I think he's dead, too," the man in the passenger seat said. "He caught one in the throat. That old man was faster than he looked."

"Another thing," the guy in the back seat said. "You could have killed the *suka!* Then where would we be? Gennady would be very angry. Alive, he said. And not hurt. Look at her! She has blood all over her!"

"Don't look!" the guy in front snapped. "Watch the road, idiot!"

"Someone is following us!" the driver said.

The man in the back seat looked out the rear windshield. "Just a fireman," he said dismissively. "On foot. He won't catch us, and if he does we will kill him."

As he spoke, he pumped his shotgun, ejecting shells. The shell casings were green instead of the usual red. Erin recognized them as beanbag rounds. When she saw them, she remembered the muzzle flash and the feeling of being power-kicked in the stomach. Her abdominal muscles ached. Having reloaded, he thrust a hand under Erin's hip, but he wasn't trying to grab her ass. He came up with her phone, which he handed forward.

"Damned New York traffic," the driver grumbled. "Remember the old days, in Leningrad? The traffic was never this bad."

"That's because nobody could afford automobiles," the passenger replied, opening the window enough to shove Erin's phone out. "I don't miss communism."

"We're stopping!" the driver said in disbelief. "Look! There's some sort of accident!"

"Forget it! Go around! Turn left!"

"There's no room!"

"Take the fence!"

The car lurched, its undercarriage making a horrible scraping sound. Something fell off the bottom with a clang. Erin's stomach heaved, but she managed not to throw up. She was trying to think. The back doors of a police car didn't open from inside. She'd have to wait for them to stop. Then she could make a move. She'd have to be quick and violent. They might shoot her, but she'd heard the name Gennady and didn't think her chances would be any better where they were taking her.

Better to go down fighting. If she was less confused and in pain, she'd be utterly terrified.

A short while later, a buzzing became audible. It was coming from the left front wheel. Just as Erin was wondering where she'd heard a sound like that before, the tire blew out. All three Russians swore. The car fishtailed wildly, but the driver knew his shit and kept them moving the same direction.

The man in the passenger seat had a phone in his hand. He was talking rapidly, giving instructions to someone on the other end of the line. Then he hung up.

"Masks off," he told the others, pulling off his ski mask to reveal a heavy-featured face with a scar running across the left eyebrow. His comrades obeyed. Erin didn't recognize any of them, but they all had the same look: hard-faced ex-military types.

She was distinctly aware what it meant that they didn't care if she saw their faces. Now she was starting to be genuinely scared in spite of her disorientation.

"When we go, you come with us," the shotgun man said to her. "If you try to call for help, I will gut you and leave you bleeding, and we will kill everyone who sees us. You understand?"

He drew a fearsome-looking survival knife from his belt for emphasis. Erin gave him the toughest stare she could muster, but she knew it wasn't convincing.

The car came to a stop. Then they waited, but only for a minute or two. Erin heard sirens, somewhere behind them. Maybe the first responders would get to them in time. There'd be a shootout, but the NYPD had lots of people and lots of guns.

"Go!" the leader ordered. He and the driver got out of the car, the driver opening Erin's door. The shotgunner was still holding the knife. The driver hauled Erin out, helping her stand on wobbly legs. She saw a river in front of her and recognized

Brooklyn on the other side. The Brooklyn Bridge was away to her left.

They marched her out onto a pier. The water was very close. Acting on sudden impulse, she let her legs buckle in a fake fall. Her plan was to go straight into the river. It would be hard to swim with her hands bound, but if she could get a fair distance away under the surface, they might have trouble hitting her and might be reluctant to shoot for fear of attracting attention.

But the driver was on the ball. He caught her by her torn shirtfront, holding her upright with one well-muscled arm. He shook her and snarled, "Don't even think it, bitch!"

A New Yorker called, "You okay, ma'am?" He was about thirty yards away, looking at the little group with an expression of concerned curiosity.

The leader waved pleasantly to him. "All good!" he replied.

Erin felt the point of the knife digging into her side. She had no choice but to keep quiet and keep moving, waiting for another opportunity. If she tried to signal the bystander, she'd be putting him at risk.

A boat pulled alongside the dock. It was being piloted by another tough-looking eastern European type. Erin was lugged on board and hustled down to the cabin belowdecks. She was shoved down onto a bench. A man was sitting there, cutting an apple with a nasty-looking curved knife. He smiled at her in a way she didn't like one bit.

"Erin O'Reilly," he said. "You know who I am?"

She'd seen his mugshot. "Gennady Vlasov," she said quietly.

"Correct," he said. "I confess, I am looking forward to this."

"To what?" she asked. "Kidnapping a New York police officer?"

He shook his head. "You are no police officer. You were fired. I saw it on the news."

"I'm being reinstated," she said. "That's why I was at Police Headquarters."

"Ah yes," Vlasov said. "With your friends. Such good friends, standing by you. Drago!"

The leader of the snatch team poked his head through the hatch. *"Da?"*

"Where are Miss O'Reilly's very good friends right now?"

"They shot at us," Drago said. "They killed Artur, Daniil, and Abram. So we killed them all."

The words echoed in Erin's aching head. *Killed them all.* Webb. Holliday. McDowell. Even Webb's children? All of them?

"I got the old man with the gray mustache myself," Drago said. "I put a burst through his chest."

"There," Vlasov said to Erin. "You see? This is what happens when you do things like this. The people around you get hurt. But I think almost enough people have died, don't you?"

"I didn't touch your cousin," she said.

"Ah! You admit you knew him!" Vlasov exclaimed. "But then, I do not see how you could deny it, not with the proof I received. You have no shame. And you killed Mikhail. I know this for a fact. Deny it if you wish, it will only give me more pleasure destroying you."

Erin didn't answer. Nausea welled up in her, riding a tide of sick despair. She was going to die. These men were going to kill her. She was completely sure of it now. She wondered how much it would hurt, and if it could possibly feel worse than she felt right now, thinking of Webb's weary eyes and his fresh-faced, energetic daughters. She remembered Holliday's mustache, the way it seemed to have a life of its own. What in God's name had she done, dragging all of them into this?

She wouldn't let herself cry, not in front of Vlasov. She tried to feel nothing but hatred and anger, to draw strength from it, but she was so tired. All she really wanted to do in that moment was give up, curl into a ball, and scream.

The boat continued cutting through the chop on the East River, headed west. Vlasov smiled coldly at her. "Now you rest," he said. "I think you will need it."

Strong hands seized her from behind. Something sharp jabbed her in the side of the neck. She felt the drug spreading through her flesh, cold and numbing. Her eyes went blurry and her thoughts drifted apart.

Unconsciousness was a blessing.

Chapter 28

VIC NESHENKO

Vic hesitated in the doorway to the waiting room. He knew he needed to move, and move fast, but he didn't know where. What would Erin or Webb do? They always seemed to end up in the right place. He wasn't sure which was worse; people not believing in him, or people believing in him too much. Either way tended to end badly.

"Vic!"

He spun around. Erica was waving to him. Danielle was sitting next to her, no longer bawling, but looking very drained. Erica was more animated than she had been, though she had deep, dark shadows around her eyes.

He hustled across the room. "What's up?" he asked.

Erica held up a cell phone. "This keeps getting texts from an unknown number," she said.

"Whose phone is that?" he asked.

"Dad's. A nurse gave it to me when they took him into surgery."

"I don't suppose you know how to unlock it," Vic sighed.

"I do," Danielle said.

"Really?" Vic was surprised Webb would be so sloppy with his security.

"I mean, I think I do," Danielle said. Her voice was hoarse and scratchy. "Dad likes to use the same number code whenever he needs a four-digit number. It's one-six-two-nine."

"Oh, right," Erica said. "Our birthdays. Mine is August Sixteenth, Dani's is December Twenty-Ninth."

"Might as well try," Vic said. "Do you mind?"

Erica handed over the phone. Vic punched in the numbers at the unlocking screen. To his astonishment, the phone unlocked. Webb's wallpaper, he noted, was a portrait of Cathy Simmons, his second wife. He decided not to mention that to the girls.

The phone informed him that Webb had seventeen unread texts, all from the same number. The most recent one, in all caps, said ANSWER YOUR BLOODY PHONE. Vic scanned the preceding messages, which started calmly enough, asking if Webb had seen Erin, because she wasn't answering her phone. Then they grew more agitated and closer together. The third message said HAVE IMPORTANT INFO RE RUSSIANS. That got Vic's attention.

He called the number. It hadn't even finished the first ring when it was picked up.

"Where the bloody hell have you been?" a familiar Irish voice demanded.

"I should've guessed," Vic said. "Corcoran."

"Oh, it's you, lad," Corcoran said without missing a beat. "Grand. I've been trying to get hold of your lot for the past half hour, but didn't know your number. Where's Erin?"

"I thought maybe you'd know," Vic said. "I need whatever you've got on Gennady Vlasov and I need it now."

"That's what I was wanting to tell her about," Corcoran said. "But she won't answer her phone. Is she all right?"

"Let me worry about that," Vic growled. "Russians. Now."

"Two things," Corcoran said. "First off, I have it on good authority our dear friend Gennady just recruited some particularly hard lads from the old country. Your government might call them private contractors, but mercenaries is a better term. They're also Russians, led by a lad called Nogti."

"I've heard of him," Vic said. "His name means 'Fingernails,' because he tore out some poor bastard's eyes with his fingers. What about them?"

"They're expensive and they're vicious," Corcoran said. "Gennady wouldn't have hired them if he wasn't planning something. I heard someone shot up some coppers not long ago, and I'm thinking it might be them."

"Me too," Vic said. "Any idea where they'd go afterward? If they had a hostage, maybe?"

"That's the other thing," Corcoran said. "I've just heard from Wayne McClernand. He's been asking some difficult questions of the Russians at Riker's Island and he's found out a bit about Gennady's smuggling operation."

"Keep talking," Vic said.

"Gennady's lot work out of Brooklyn, but that's not the half of it. Most of their product comes in through the Jersey side, out of Hoboken. He knows your lads are watching him, so the Brooklyn operations are mainly a front. His main hub is across the bay."

"McClernand found that out just by asking?" Vic asked doubtfully. "That doesn't sound like the sort of stuff people would just be spilling in the Riker's cafeteria."

"As I understand it, he asked in rather a forceful manner," Corcoran said. "Are you needing to know the particulars of his methods?"

"Christ, no," Vic said. "Forget about it. Where in Hoboken?"

"Somewhere on the docks, near the Transit Terminal. I'm sorry I can't do better than that. Wayne said his contact was finding it hard to speak clearly by the end of their conversation. I'm asking my lads in Jersey to see if they can nail it down further."

"Anything else?" Vic asked.

"Not at the moment. Now will you kindly tell me what's happened to my best mate's woman?"

"Vlasov's people have her," Vic said grimly. "So if you hear anything, let me know the second you do. I'll have this phone on me."

"Sweet Jesus," Corcoran said softly. "I'll tell Cars. And anything you're needing, you've only to say and it's yours. I'll put the word out on the street."

"Do that," Vic said. "But don't go starting World War Three, okay? The last thing we need is the cops tripping over more bodies."

His own phone chose that moment to start buzzing. He fumbled it out of his pocket and saw Zofia's name on the screen.

"I gotta go," he said. "Thanks."

He hung up before Corcoran could answer, stuffed Webb's phone in his opposite hip pocket, and brought his phone to his ear. Erica and Danielle watched him anxiously.

"Hey," he said, without waiting for Zofia to say anything. "Listen, Webb's in surgery. Multiple abdominal GSW. Erin's brother is working on him as we speak. McDowell's leg is busted pretty bad, but she oughta pull through. It doesn't look good for Holliday. What've you got?"

"I'm in my car," Zofia said. "Rolf's in the backseat. Vic, all hell's breaking loose. Have you been listening to the police radio?"

"No, I've been talking to people at the hospital. I'm still there. What's up?"

"Get in your car and get moving south. I'll tell you on the way."

Vic waved to Webb's daughters and gave them what he hoped was an encouraging smile. Then he jogged to his car and got the Taurus moving.

"Okay," he said. "I'm getting on the FDR, southbound. Where am I going?"

"Pier Fifteen," she said. "East River, just west of the Bridge. The bad guys hijacked one of the Patrol units at the garage after they shot our officers. They took off, ran through a crash, and blew out a tire. They drove it on the rim down to the pier and ditched it. Nobody's clear on what happened after that."

"Did they have Erin with them?"

"I don't know. Units are on scene now, but nobody seems to know what the hell is going on. FDNY is missing one of their guys, too."

"Missing? How do you mean?"

"The engine crew that responded to the garage reported their probie ran off in the middle of the incident."

"Some kid got spooked," Vic said. "It happens."

"That's what I thought," Zofia said. "But then Dispatch reported a hit-and-run. A bike messenger ran into a guy in an FDNY uniform. The messenger said the guy knocked him off his bike, stole it, and rode off in one heck of a hurry. And this is right on the route the stolen car took. The messenger said he was looking over his shoulder at the squad car, and that's why he didn't see the runner coming."

"So you think this probie's involved?"

"Maybe. Does it matter? Anyway, the car's a hot lead, right?"

"Absolutely." Vic held the phone between his ear and his shoulder and brought up a map of Manhattan on his onboard computer. He was just begging to rear-end someone, driving with so many distractions, but that was far from his top priority at the moment. He zoomed in on the southeastern part of the island.

"The bad guys crashed their getaway car," Zofia said. "So I figure they're improvising. That means they might be making mistakes."

"These guys are ex-soldiers," Vic said. "They know how to improvise. And I don't think they panic. Three of them got killed at the garage, right?"

"That's what they're saying on the net," Zofia said. "Our people figure three got away with Erin."

"And an FDNY probie chased them," Vic said thoughtfully. He swerved around a car and threaded between two others, drawing honks.

"So?"

"Thompson," he growled.

"That made sense to you," she said. "I know it did. But I have no idea what you're talking about."

"Remember Carlyle's bodyguard? Ian Thompson? The friggin' vigilante?"

"Yeah, I guess so," Zofia said, sounding bewildered. "What's he got to do with anything?"

"He's a firefighter now," Vic said.

"You don't think...?"

"That's exactly what I think. He's just crazy enough to try to run down a bunch of armed nutjobs on his own. Shit, I don't know how to contact him. There'll be cops all over the scene by now, right?"

"For sure. Stoneman's team is already there. That's how I heard."

Vic made a command decision. It was surprisingly easy, which made him wonder if it was the right one. "Forget the pier," he said. "Turn around. Get to the Holland Tunnel."

"Vic, you're not making any sense. That's the opposite direction!"

"I know. We're going to Jersey. You'll get there ahead of me. Get off 78 once you hit the Jersey side of the tunnel. There's a bank off Washington Boulevard. Chase. You know it?"

"I can find it."

"I'll meet you there."

"Vic, what're we doing? Erin's in South Manhattan, not Jersey!"

"No, she's not," Vic said. "Think, Zofia. These guys drive on a flat all the way to a pier, *then* get rid of the car? Why would they do that?"

"They had a boat waiting," Zofia said. "Oh, no. They could be going anywhere!"

"They're either going to Brooklyn or Jersey," Vic said. "Those are the places Vlasov's crew works out of. Stoneman knows about Matrushka's Restaurant. He'll have people on their way to Little Odessa. If the bad guys go that way, they're toast. We need to cover the Jersey side."

"Copy that," Zofia said. "What backup do we have? New Jersey State Patrol?"

"Hold off on them," Vic said. "This is just a hunch, and we aren't officially on this. If we start diverting resources, it'll cause confusion and make things harder for everyone. Besides, I don't know exactly where we're going yet, and it's not like we have any authority here."

"Seriously? We're going to Jersey on a hunch, and you don't know where in the whole state these guys might be going?"

"It'll be near the Hoboken docks," he said. "I'm hoping we can get a better fix soon. If we do, I want to be close by, so we can move fast. I'm doing the best I can, Zofia. What do you want me to say?"

"I want you to say you know exactly where Erin is, that we have a plan in place, and ESU is on its way."

"I thought you didn't like it when I lie to you," he said.

"See you in Jersey," she said.

Vic had been driving like a maniac. Now he started *really* moving.

Chapter 29

IAN THOMPSON

"That's quite a story, son," Cole said.

Ian didn't think he'd told it well. Had only given him the short version. Left out most of the details.

"Let's suppose, just for a moment, you find out where these boys are going," Cole said. "What, exactly, were you planning on doing about it?"

"Find a way to get Ms. O'Reilly back, sir," Ian said.

"Alone? Unarmed?"

"A Marine's never unarmed, sir."

Cole chuckled. "I don't doubt it," he said. "I've known plenty of Marines."

"Hope I can tell local law," Ian said. "Get some backup. But can't risk losing them. These guys are pros. They have an exfil plan. Once they touch dirt, they're gone in thirty seconds, maybe a minute. Won't be time for cops to get there."

"Tell you what," Cole said. "Why don't I drop you off, once we see where these bad boys are going, and then I'll find a

Harbor Patrol boat. I'll flag them down and tell them what you told me. They'll see word gets to the right people."

"Appreciate that, sir," Ian said. "You're already going to a lot of trouble. Don't have the right to ask for more."

"Well hell, son," Cole said, smiling. "You've got my blood pumping again, like it hasn't done since '69. It's my pleasure. I just wish I could do more."

"Ms. O'Reilly's fiancé has money," Ian said. "I guarantee he'll compensate you for your time."

"I'm retired," Cole replied, no longer smiling. "I've got nothing but time these days. But don't you dare offer me money again, son."

"I apologize, sir. No excuse."

Cole's lips curled up again. "You're a Marine, all right. I don't think those blockheads have the slightest idea we're on their tail, do you?"

"Negative, sir." Ian was keeping low in the bow of Cole's boat, watching the yacht. It was chugging up the Hudson after leaving the East River, innocent as anything. If he hadn't seen Erin get loaded on board, wouldn't have thought anything was weird about it. Range about two hundred meters. Wished for a rifle again. They'd taken Erin below, but two bad guys were topside. Not carrying their guns openly. Could've popped both of them before they knew what was happening.

Reminded himself to wait. Scout Snipers had to be patient.

"Who is this lady to you?" Cole asked. "I would've guessed girlfriend, but you're talking about her fiancé."

"Hard to explain, sir," Ian said. "She's a friend. And she'll be sort of like my stepmom."

"Family's important," Cole said. "I buried my wife last year. Cancer. My son died in a car crash ten years ago. So now it's just me. You're lucky, son."

Lucky. Ian had never thought so. Wasn't lucky surviving when so many buddies didn't. Sometimes worse being the one left. Thought about it, about all the people he'd met, what they meant to him: Mr. Carlyle, Erin, Cassie, Ben. All the love he carried with him.

"Yes, sir," he said, knowing it was true. "I'm lucky."

"Looks like your pals are making for shore," Cole observed. "That there is Sinatra Park. Named for the singer, of course. You know Sinatra?"

"I'm a Springsteen fan, sir. Sinatra's before my time."

"They say he was in with the Mafia. You believe that?"

"Yes, sir." Considered telling Cole he knew more about the Mob than the Coast Guardsman ever would. Probably more than Sinatra did, too. Decided not to. "You know the shoreline pretty well?"

"Like the backs of my own two hands," Cole said. "I'm a sailor, son. I'd be a pretty poor one if I didn't know the coastline."

"Why do you think they're stopping here?"

"It's a low-traffic area," Cole said. "They're sailing a pleasure craft. If they docked at a freight pier it'd attract attention. Sinatra Pier's for fishing, and there won't be many people there in the middle of a weekday. It might even be deserted, and you can't say that about much of the Jersey waterfront. One good thing, though."

"What's that, sir?"

"Your sort-of stepmother's still alive."

Ian hadn't wanted to consider the alternative, but his heart jumped when Cole said it. "How do you figure, sir?" he asked.

"If they'd done her in, they'd have dumped the body while they were still in the East River," Cole explained. "Our divers have found plenty of bodies there over the years. Just wrap it in chicken wire, weight it down with a cinder block, and toss it over the side. They wouldn't want to risk getting caught with a fresh corpse on board. They must want your old lady alive for something."

Ian nodded. Tried to feel good about it. Almost succeeded. "Put me off there," he said, pointing to a tiny island about two hundred meters short of Sinatra Pier. Another pier jutted out into the river there and a causeway connected the island to the mainland.

"You sure?" Cole asked.

The other boat was definitely moving toward Sinatra. "Absolutely, sir."

Cole steered the motorboat alongside. The island was a park. A playground, surrounded by walking trails. Weirdly peaceful.

"Here you are," Cole said. "Good luck, son. I'll find the first cops I can. Don't go taking stupid chances."

"I'm a Marine, sir," Ian reminded him, planting a foot on the gunwale. "That's what we do."

Didn't wait for the boat to come all the way in. Jumped with about a meter left to go. Made it easily, landed already running. Shoes wet. Socks squelched in them. He'd have blisters. Not a problem. Cold from the river water, but running would help.

This was the risky part. Might be out of sight of the boat for a little while, repositioning. Had to get on the landward side, and fast. They'd have a car waiting. If he wasn't in position to spot the car, might as well give up.

He'd had the chance to rest and get his breath back, which was good. Muscles had stiffened up, which wasn't. Risking cramps, maybe pulled hamstrings. Didn't care. Laid on the speed. Ran past a couple moms with strollers, gave them a scare. Cleared the causeway to the mainland in a few seconds. Glanced right, saw the yacht at the pier. One guy at the bow, tossing a line to another guy on the dock.

Path ran along the shore, through Sinatra Park. Decent sight line to the pier. Ian closed the distance, reminded himself to blend in. Didn't know if they'd spotted him back in Manhattan, or if they'd recognize him here.

That'd blow their minds, wouldn't it, Marine? They'd think they were going nuts, seeing crazy firemen everywhere.

Café up ahead, called Blue Eyes. Wasn't that Sinatra's nickname? Didn't matter. Put it out of his mind, hooked to the right around it. Came to a soccer field, ringed by a fence, too tall to climb in a hurry. Saw the bad guys on the far end, coming off the dock. Had to speed up, find a shortcut. Angled left around the field. Legs already hurting again, not a good sign.

Came out onto Frank Sinatra Drive. Not much traffic. Stopped a moment, took his bearings.

Damn, Hoboken really loves Sinatra. Must be the only famous guy from around here. Everything's named after him.

Red minivan, pulled over by the park entrance. Four guys, hustling a woman with them. Range about sixty meters. Positive ID: Erin in the middle, head lolling. Either wounded or drugged. Didn't blame them. Erin could put up one hell of a fight, even outnumbered and unarmed. Wouldn't have risked taking her alive if it'd been his job to snatch her. Van was pointed his way.

Ian crossed the street, taking advantage of their distraction while they loaded Erin into the van. Found himself next to a concrete wall, painted with a cute neighborhood mural; lots of primary colors, bright and cheerful. Not what he thought of when he thought of Jersey. Jogged around the nearest bend. Waited there, screened by the wall.

This is a good spot, Marine. Bad guys have to come this way; the other two roads are one-way. But when they do, you can't ambush them with no guns and you won't be able to follow them, not far. What's your plan?

Didn't have one. Had to hope for the best. And hope wasn't a plan. What he needed was transportation. Millions of cars in America. Had to be one he could get his hands on. No cops in sight. No unattended vehicles. No time.

Ian got ready to run again.

Chapter 30

Zofia was waiting in the Chase Bank parking lot. She had Rolf on leash on a narrow patch of grass. The dog was sniffing at a shrub, deciding whether it was worth watering. When Vic pulled into the lot, Rolf gave up on the bush and trotted toward him, Zofia close behind.

As Vic got out of the Taurus, he saw the tears on Zofia's cheeks. The look in her eyes nearly made him start crying, too. She swallowed hard and he saw the muscles clenching in her jaw. She was right on the edge of losing control.

"What is it?" he asked, afraid of the answer.

"The Captain," she said. "They called it on the radio a few minutes ago. He..."

"Yeah," Vic said. "I figured. Jesus, what a mess." He felt like throwing up.

"Both Patrolmen, too," she went on. "He... Captain Holliday... he was just trying to help."

"I know," Vic said. "He was a damn good man. Best captain I ever had."

It was a shitty epitaph, but he couldn't think of anything else to say. He pulled Zofia in and put his arms around her. Just for a moment, long enough for her to know he cared, not so long that she came loose.

She must have felt the same way, because she drew back right as he was about to let go. She wiped her eyes on her coat sleeve and sniffled. "Okay," she said. "Here we are, on account of your crazy damn hunch. Now what do we do?"

"I got Thompson's number from Corcoran on the way," he said. "But he's not answering. It just rolls straight to voicemail, so he's got it turned off. I left a message for him to tell me where he is, but I'm not holding my breath.For now, we put on our vests. We tune in to the police band and we wait. We'll hear something, either from our people or from Corcoran. He's got guys on the waterfront. Longshoremen, probably. He knows people here, remember? When we nailed that crooked lawyer?"

"Right," she said. She popped her trunk and strapped on her Kevlar over her jacket, so the white POLICE letters were obvious. Vic did the same with his own armor. Then Zofia got her shotgun off the rack in her car and checked the loads.

"You shouldn't use that thing," Vic said, unlimbering his M4 and giving it a quick once-over. The rifle was in perfect condition. He cleaned and oiled it religiously and zeroed the sights at least once a week on the range.

"Why not?" she asked. "You're not going to say it's too big for me, are you?"

"Hell no. But a rifle gives you a lot more capacity, better rate of fire, and better penetration."

"Men are all the same," Zofia snorted. "Always thinking penetration is the main thing."

Vic smiled. He was glad to see she still had high enough spirits to make a joke, even one at his expense.

"That's the problem with rifles," she went on. "They overpenetrate. I'm used to doing takedowns in crappy apartments with thin walls. If I fire a high-powered round in a tenement, I might kill some schmuck two units away. Besides, I'm a crappy shot with a long gun and you only need to get close with a twelve-gauge."

Rolf gave the two of them a dubious look. He'd gotten excited when he'd seen Vic, thinking Erin might be with him, but now he was confused and worried. He kept looking around, like his human might suddenly pop up from anywhere.

"I raided Erin's locker on the way out of the Eightball," Zofia added, producing a paper bag. "Here's a spare pair of Erin's socks. They're clean, but they should still smell like her, right?"

"Yeah," Vic said. "I'll take them." He stowed the bag of socks in one of the extra ammo pouches on his vest.

Then they got into Vic's Taurus, turned on the radio, and started listening. The police band had a lot of chatter on it. Most of it was about the parking garage shootout. A citywide manhunt was on. Dozens of sightings were being reported. Most were well-meaning citizens who were genuinely trying to help. The rest, Vic figured, were jerks trying to feel important or genuine assholes trying to screw up the search.

ESU was getting set to raid Matrushka's Restaurant in Brooklyn. They had a helicopter overhead and a full tactical team at the ready. A whole lot of hell was about to rain down on little Odessa.

"You were right to play it quiet," Zofia said.

"You think we'd just get lost in the noise?" Vic asked.

"I think the bad guys probably have a police radio," she replied.

"Shit," Vic said. "You're right. I should've thought of that."

"You didn't plan for it?" she asked.

"I'm not planning anything," he admitted. "I never expected everybody who outranks me in the Eightball to get taken out of the chain of command at once. I'm playing this by ear."

"Attention, all units," a man said over the radio. "This is Dettweiler, Harbor Patrol."

"Hey," Vic said, sitting up. "I know that guy."

"I've got a report from a civilian who claims a boat with three gunmen and a female hostage, who he identified as Erin O'Reilly, was seen heading north up the Hudson. It docked at Sinatra Pier in Hoboken a few minutes ago."

"Oh my God," Zofia murmured.

Vic was already on his phone. Zofia had reignited his residual paranoia, so he didn't want to talk over the radio when the bad guys might be listening. He called Dispatch and rattled off his shield number.

"Can you patch me through to Harbor Patrol?" he asked. "Officer Dettweiler? Phone, not radio."

In a moment, the call went through. "Dettweiler," the harbor cop said. Vic could picture him in his mind's eye: an eager kid, young but with all the right instincts. He'd been a big help taking down a Mob lawyer who'd been trying to flee the country, and had nearly gotten himself killed saving another gangster from drowning. Good police, Vic thought.

"Gus Dettweiler?" Vic said.

"That's me," the kid said. "Do I know you?"

"This is Detective Neshenko, Major Crimes. Officer, how good is the tip you just got?"

"The guy who flagged us down seemed pretty solid," Dettweiler said. "Former Coast Guardsman, totally calm. He didn't see O'Reilly himself. But get this. He says he followed the boat on account of this FDNY guy who jumped in the East River and swam out to his boat! Some former Marine who tracked the bad guys all the way from the shooting. Sounded pretty wild to me, but the guy was dead serious."

Vic felt a crazy urge to laugh. "This fireman wouldn't be named Thompson, would he?" he asked.

"How the heck did you know that?" Dettweiler asked, his mind totally blown.

"Never mind," Vic said, starting the car and putting it in gear. "Your info is good. Here's what I need you to do. Get on the horn to Hoboken PD, but keep it off the net. We're gonna need HRT on alert as soon as they can swing it. I'm talking tac teams, negotiators, air support, the whole nine yards. But it's gotta be set up quiet, you copy? We have to assume they're listening to our comms."

"Copy that," Dettweiler said. "Where's the target?"

"I don't know yet. But it'll be somewhere close to where they landed. In the neighborhood of the freight docks."

"I copy," Dettweiler said. "But it'll take some time to line them up. What sort of window do we have?"

"Not enough of one," Vic said grimly. "Do what you can. Neshenko out."

"Go north on Washington Boulevard," Zofia said, looking at the map on her computer. "We're fifteen minutes away."

"I'll make it in twelve," Vic promised, accelerating. "If any cops try to pull me over, they can follow me there. They'll be good backup."

"What do we do once we get to the pier?" Zofia asked.

"Ask around, I guess," Vic said. "Someone may have seen where they went."

"There has to be a better way to find them," Zofia said.

"Rolf can find Erin," Vic said. "But he needs to be close and they need to be on foot."

He tried to think. There were better ways to find bad guys than chasing them. The best way was to know where they were going and head them off. But he didn't know their destination, so that put him back to square one.

Except that he wasn't.

He got back on the phone to Dispatch. "Get me Narcotics," he said. "The guy in charge of the Vlasov fentanyl case."

After a maddening wait, which Vic occupied with reckless driving, Dispatch put him through to the Narcos.

"Lieutenant Pemberton," the man said. "Narcotics."

"Neshenko, Major Crimes," Vic said. "Your boys have been keeping tabs on the Vlasov crew, right?"

"That's right," Pemberton said. "But we lost him overnight."

Vic couldn't believe this shit. "Lost him?" he repeated. "How? What happened to your surveillance guys?"

"We have some of the crew," Pemberton clarified. "But Vlasov himself slipped. He got on a boat sometime after midnight, but we can't afford to have a helicopter hovering over him all day."

"For Christ's sake," Vic said. "ESU's about to hit Vlasov's restaurant and you're telling me he isn't even in *Brooklyn?!*"

"Watch your tone, Detective," Pemberton said.

Vic didn't give a shit about his tone. "What about Richard O'Malley?" he asked.

"Who?"

"Richard O'Malley," Vic said again, grinding the syllables out slowly and clearly. "Small-time fentanyl guy? Wife and kid got killed a couple days ago, when your people weren't watching him? Ring a bell?"

"He was wounded," Pemberton said. "Out of action. We were shorthanded on another surveillance detail, so his guys got pulled."

"Pulled," Vic said flatly. "You mean nobody's watching him? He could be anywhere right now?"

"That's right," Pemberton said. "Listen, Detective, you may think we have unlimited resources here, and in a perfect world we'd have plenty of plainclothes guys to send after the little fish, but this is the real world and we have to make allocation decisions."

"You're a real credit to the force," Vic said and hung up. He resisted the urge to squeeze his phone until the screen cracked. "God *damn* it!"

"It was worth a try," Zofia said. "What's plan B?"

"When's the last time you went to church?" he asked.

"Sunday. You know that."

"Then maybe you're in good with God. Better than I am, at any rate. Pray."

Chapter 31

She swam slowly back to the surface of consciousness, groggy and confused. Where was she? Her memory had gaps. Her head ached. Her tongue was dry and swollen, her throat raspy. It reminded her of particularly bad nights of drinking.

She was sitting on a chair, a metal folding one, uncushioned. Her skin shrank from the cold metal. She forced sticky eyelids open and got a blurry impression of a dark room with brick walls and a concrete floor.

Erin tried to stand up, knowing she'd probably fall right back down, and found she couldn't. Her hands were shackled to the chair's back. Her ankles were tied to the legs.

"Ah," a man said from somewhere behind her. "You are awake. Good."

She heard his footsteps approaching and fought down rising panic. She felt horribly vulnerable, completely helpless and exposed. A light clicked on above her, a bare yellow bulb that only half-illuminated the room.

A hand touched her shoulder. She flinched and nearly screamed. The touch was oddly friendly, which didn't make her feel one bit safer.

"I thought perhaps Gennady used a bit too much tranquilizer," the man continued. He walked around the chair, trailing his fingertips across the back of her neck.

Erin lunged suddenly toward him, craning her neck, snapping with her teeth, hoping to get a piece of his arm. But the tensing of her muscles had warned him and he easily yanked his hand away, chuckling softly.

"Get your fucking hands off me!" Erin snarled.

"You are a fiery one," the man said, giving her a comfortable berth and settling into another metal chair a few feet in front of her. "But you should be careful. If a *suka* begins biting her master, she will be beaten. If she persists, she may be put down."

"I'm not your bitch!" Erin retorted.

"You speak Russian?" The man was surprised. He raised a gray eyebrow. He was an older man, probably in his late fifties, with steel-gray hair and a lined, weathered face. In the dim light, his face was a maze of dark shadows. His pupils looked like black marbles. Shark's eyes.

"Just the swear words," Erin said. "Who are you?"

"You have no need to know my name," he said. "My nickname, you would say, is Nogti. You know what it means?"

"Fingernails," she blurted.

He smiled without showing his teeth. "You have heard of me, yes?"

"You got mentioned once," Erin said. She was in no hurry to explain, but he'd been implicated in a power struggle between Russian crime rings. Major Crimes had inadvertently gotten rid of some of his competition.

"Fame is a blade with two edges," Nogti said. He casually studied his fingernails. "But it pleases me you know of me. You know how I got this nickname?"

"I heard the stories," she said, fighting down another surge of panic. The story she kept thinking of was the one in which he'd hooked out another man's eyes with his bare hands. She was having a lot of trouble not staring at his fingers.

"Gennady is very angry with you," Nogti said. "If it were only up to him, we would already be starting."

Starting what? Erin both did and didn't want to ask. "Why is he mad?" she asked instead.

"Because of his cousins, of course," Nogti said. "It was not enough for you to shoot Pyotr and throw him in prison. You had to kill Pyotr's son as well."

"I didn't touch his cousin's kid," Erin said. "That was Ophelia Flaherty. We found his body in Ophelia's apartment."

"What astonishes me is that you made a tape of the deed," Nogti said. "To send it to him, though, that was very foolish."

"I'm telling you, I didn't do it!" Erin insisted.

"I have seen this tape," Nogti said. "The quality is not perfect, I grant. Hidden cameras are not like Hollywood movie cameras. But your face is visible. You seduced the boy, then you killed him."

"You think I'd be stupid enough to do that?" she shot back. "I'm not a murderer!"

"Maybe you truly did not know about the tape," Nogti admitted. "As I said, it was taken from a hidden camera, concealed in a corner of the room. Perhaps it was recorded by one of your enemies. But whoever was watching you, it remains that you killed him."

"It was Ophelia!" Erin said. "She got herself cut to look like me. This is a setup!"

Nogti's smile widened. "You would like me to believe that," he said, standing. "But it will make no difference. I do not care, one way or another. I am being paid, and paid very well, to do only one thing, and that is the only reason I am here."

"If money's all you care about, call Morton Carlyle," Erin said. "He'll offer you double what you're being paid in exchange for me."

Nogti shook his head. "A man in my business cannot change sides to the highest bidder," he said. "Trust is so very important, you see. Once I have agreed to a contract, I always fulfill my side of it. I have my reputation to consider. I will tell Gennady you have woken. I would suggest you rest, while you can. You will need all your strength for what is to come. You can consider what that is likely to be."

He nodded toward a table that lay a couple of yards to Erin's left. Then he walked to a rickety-looking wooden staircase that ran along one side of the room, said something to a stony-faced man at the foot of the stairs, and began to climb. The other man crossed his arms and watched Erin with no expression in his eyes.

Erin's own eyes were drawn to the table. It was a simple folding job, about six feet by eighteen inches. On it lay a pair of pliers, various knives, some things that looked like dental tools, a cordless drill, a coil of piano wire, and a blowtorch.

For a few seconds she didn't process what she was seeing. It just looked like a bunch of tools. Then the truth started to sink in and the fear took hold.

It was more reflex than intention that made her try to break the handcuffs by brute force. She strained against the steel with everything she had. It wasn't enough. She tried again, with no better luck. She gave it up, breathing hard. She felt sweat running down her face and neck in spite of the cold air, and was more frightened than she'd ever been in her life.

Dear God, Erin prayed silently. *Help me. Oh God, please. Don't let me die here. Not like this.*

Chapter 32

VIC NESHENKO

"Take a right on Third Street," Zofia said. "Then a left on River, another right on Fourth, and you're there."

"These bastards are gonna be long gone," Vic muttered. The radio was full of excited chatter. ESU had just gone into Matrushka's. They'd arrested some people but hadn't found Erin, Vlasov, O'Malley, or anyone else of consequence. Nobody had breathed a word of Vic's news. Apparently Dettweiler had been discreet.

"We have to try," Zofia said.

"I friggin' hate Jersey," Vic said. It wasn't that Hoboken was ugly. It was just so... lacking in personality. It was like Brooklyn but without any attitude. He glanced at the generic brick buildings and the cars stacked along both sides of the one-way street. Even the cars were boring. Just one Japanese-made sedan after another after...

He blinked. They'd just crossed Hudson Street. He hadn't seen anything, his conscious brain told him. But his subconscious had caught something familiar.

Vic jammed on the brakes. Zofia gave a startled little squeak as the Taurus came to a sudden halt.

"Vic!" she exclaimed. "What's the matter with you?"

The car behind him thought the same and honked. Without even thinking about it, Vic raised his right hand and showed the other driver his middle finger through the rear windshield. Vic pulled over and stopped the Taurus directly in front of a fire hydrant.

"What is it?" Zofia pressed.

"Back there," Vic said, pointing his thumb in the direction of Hudson. "I saw a car. Red. Volvo."

"So?"

"I have to check something."

Vic couldn't back half a block down a one-way street, so he got out and started jogging. Zofia followed, clutching her shotgun. Rolf trotted eagerly beside them, ears at full attention, head up, sniffing the air. The dog smelled action, just like Vic did. A couple of pedestrians, seeing their long guns and police vests, stared and pointed. Vic ignored them.

"Vic, we don't have time for this!" Zofia called. "You parked in a fire lane! And if these guys came by boat, they didn't bring a car!"

Vic stopped at the intersection and looked. "Yeah," he said. "But that's Richard O'Malley's car."

"How do you know?" Zofia asked

"Because I spent weeks with Erin watching the punk drive around in it," he said. "Come on, follow me."

He headed up the west side of Hudson, keeping close to the front walls of the row houses to minimize the chance of being spotted from a window. The east side had a parking garage, and he wasn't worried about anything over there.

They reached the Volvo. Vic peered through the windows. "It's him all right," he reported.

"You sure?"

"Yeah." Vic pointed to the rearview mirror. "I know those green fuzzy dice. But which building did he go into?"

"Gray brick, two doors down."

Vic's dad had died of a heart attack. The sudden lurch in his chest gave him an inkling of what that might've felt like. He died a little on the inside as he spun, bringing his M4 up to point at the man he hadn't even known was there.

The guy wasn't particularly big or impressive. He was five-ten at most, a hundred sixty or so. Short haircut, lean physique. He was wearing a dirty, wet set of clothes; dark blue shirt and pants. But there was something about the man that radiated danger. The look in the eyes and the way he stood, half-relaxed, half-tense.

"Ian Thompson," Vic said. "How'd you get here?"

"No time," Thompson said. "O'Malley just got here. Went in past the guard."

"Okay," Vic said. "Call it in, Zofia. Forget playing it quiet. We need the cavalry and we need it right the hell now."

"No time," Thompson repeated. "O'Malley wants to kill Erin. He's got nothing to lose. He hears sirens, he'll do it. Best chance is we go in now, let the reinforcements mop up after."

"We?" Vic said doubtfully. He'd never liked Thompson, never trusted him. But there was no denying the punk was tough. And he was a damn good shot. He'd killed something like three dozen people as a Marine sniper, plus at least four more in New York.

Zofia was on the phone, talking to Dispatch, giving them the ultra-quick version. Major Crimes wasn't in hot pursuit. They didn't have any jurisdiction here. Neither Zofia nor Vic could order the Hoboken cops to do a single damn thing. Zofia was just hoping to cut through the red tape and get a bunch of the Jersey boys on site. If Dettweiler had done his job, she just might succeed.

"Five minutes on backup," she reported, hanging up. "Fifteen on the tactical guys."

Five to fifteen minutes. Thompson was right. They couldn't afford to wait.

"How many bad guys?" Vic asked.

"Four tangos with Erin," Thompson said. "Plus O'Malley. Could be more inside."

"I'll take point," Vic said. "Zofia, keep behind me. Thompson, you bring up the rear. You're not wearing body armor, are you?"

"Negative," Thompson said. "Won't matter, though. These guys have AKs. Kevlar won't stop a rifle round unless it hits a plate."

"Thanks for reminding me," Vic said sourly. "What're you carrying?"

"Nothing," Thompson said.

"You're shitting me," Vic said.

"Don't carry anymore," Thompson said. "I'm a firefighter now."

"Jesus Christ," Vic said. Then he did something he could've sworn he'd never do. He handed his M4 to a vigilante killer. He pulled his two spare magazines out of the pouches on his vest and handed them over, too.

Thompson shoved the mags into the side cargo pockets of his pants. He gave the rifle a quick once-over and seemed to like what he saw. He held it like an old familiar friend.

Vic pulled his Delta Elite. "I'll take Rolf," he told Zofia. "I have a hand free."

Zofia handed him the leash. Rolf pranced on his paws, toes tip-tapping with excitement. It was bad-guy-biting time.

"Rules of engagement?" Thompson asked quietly.

Vic spared him and Zofia one more look. "This isn't police work," he said. "This is friggin' combat. These are soldiers, not street punks. They'll kill us if they can, and they know how. Don't hesitate, don't waste time telling them to give up. If they have guns in their hands, you put them down. You copy?"

"Copy that," Zofia said. She looked terrified and excited, all at the same time.

"Roger," Thompson said, cool as the September morning.

Vic didn't hear any sirens yet. He waved a hand to the others to follow and started toward the door of the gray house. His heart was pounding so hard he could swear he felt it against the inside of his ribcage. He thought of all the house-clearing drills he'd done with ESU. Move fast, clear doorways, check your corners. Don't shoot friendlies.

"Slow is smooth," he said under his breath, reciting the old piece of ESU combat advice.

"And smooth is fast," Thompson added, right behind him.

Chapter 33

ERIN O'REILLY

The footsteps on the stairs sounded unnaturally loud. At least two men, maybe more, were coming down.

Erin straightened her back and took a couple of slow, deep breaths. She had to hold down her fear, keep a clear head, and watch for any opportunity. Carlyle had talked his way out of rooms where the inhabitants wanted to kill him, more than once. The least she could do was try, and barring that, stall as long as she could. Fight with everything she had. People would be looking for her. She had no idea where she was, but just maybe someone would find her in time.

Stay strong, darling, Carlyle's voice said quietly in her brain. *Stay alive.*

"You see, my friend?" Nogti said. "As agreed, alive and intact."

"Oh, I've been dreaming about this," Richard O'Malley said.

Richie looked rough. His eyes were bloodshot and wild. His hair was uncombed, his clothes were wrinkled, and as he crossed the room to look down at Erin, she discovered he didn't smell so good either.

"She is not just yours," Gennady Vlasov said. "I must have my turn with her as well."

"Plenty to go round," Richie said. "Look at you. Erin O'Reilly. Hero cop. Not so high and mighty now, are you?"

It was such a cliché thing to say that Erin had to suppress the hysterical urge to laugh in his face. It was like he'd studied how to be a villain by watching old B-movies. But that wasn't the point. She was still tied to a chair in a basement, and no matter how banal these assholes were, she was in extreme danger.

"Richard," she said, speaking as earnestly as she knew how. "Ophelia Flaherty killed your wife and kid. She did it for Kyle Finnegan. I was watching you, but that was because you tried to kill me."

"Shut up!" Richie shouted. Erin saw his hand coming, but there wasn't a lot she could do about it. The slap connected with her cheek and rocked her head to one side.

"I'm sorry about your dad," she went on, ignoring the stinging pain in her cheek. She had nothing to lose by talking. They intended to murder her no matter what. "But that was my job. It was the only thing I did to your family, I swear. I'd never hurt a little kid. You're the one who tried to kill me. Twice."

"Do you believe this bitch?" Richie said to Gennady. "She is such a goddamn liar!"

Gennady shrugged. "That is women for you," he said. "They always lie. My cousin, he knew how to keep them in line. I could demonstrate, if you like."

"I'm telling the truth," Erin said. "You tried to run me over outside the hospital. Don't you dare deny it!"

"Hell yes, I did!" Richie snapped. "Because you ruined my life! You threw my dad in jail and took everything! Our house, our cars, our money, everything!"

"And then you had Black Jack McGraw try to beat my head in," Erin went on.

"Huh?" Richie said. "What're you even talking about?"

"Didn't you?" Erin said, momentarily stunned. She'd been so sure Richie had been behind the hit attempt on her that had sparked her surveillance of him.

"Of course not! I don't even know who that is!"

Erin's mind whirled. "Listen to me, Richie," she said quickly. "This whole thing was a setup from the start. Kyle Finnegan's behind it. Ophelia's his daughter."

"Finnegan doesn't have any kids," Richie said.

"That's what Ophelia thinks, at least," Erin said. "Finnegan pitted us against each other. He wants you to kill me."

"That makes two of us," Richie said.

"He tried to frame me for murder," she went on. "This is his fallback plan, to get back at me for busting him. This is what he does! He finds people who hate each other and gets them to go to war. He does it for fun, Richie! Think, damn it!"

"How long must we listen to this nonsense?" Gennady asked.

Richie slapped her again, harder. "I said, shut up! You'd say anything to get out of the mess you're in, and you'd do anything. You're a goddamn slut, a killer, and an evil bitch. And I'm going to kill you for what you did to me. See this?"

He opened his jacket and yanked a revolver out of the front of his pants. He shoved it in her face. She recoiled, but still felt the hard jab of the muzzle against her red, swelling cheek.

"Open your mouth!" he shouted.

Erin kept her lips shut. She was damned if she'd do any such thing.

"You'll do it," he promised. "My buddy Nails here is going to make sure of it. He'll make you beg to swallow this gun, but I won't do it. I'll wait until you're hurting so bad you'll offer me anything if I'll make it stop. You understand me? You'll be broken and bleeding and screaming, crying and begging me, and that's when I'll shove this right down your throat and you'll thank me for it!"

Tears were spilling out of his eyes as he ranted at her. He waved the pistol barrel around wildly, his hand shaking. Nogti and Gennady kept a wary eye on the gun, making sure it wasn't pointed their way.

Richie swung the revolver. The metal barrel crashed against Erin's skull with a hard, jarring impact. She gritted her teeth and took it, feeling something wet beginning to trickle down her scalp just above her ear.

Stay strong, darling, Carlyle whispered in her ear. *My brave, beautiful darling.*

"Richard, please don't do this," Erin said quietly. "You can still stop. You can honor your family's memory. This isn't the way."

Richie abruptly stopped moving. He stared at her for a long moment. Then he laid the revolver down on the table next to the other implements.

"She's all yours," he said to Nogti. "But don't finish her until I say so."

The gray-haired Russian nodded. "I promise she will not die," he said. "No matter how much she wishes to."

He picked up a knife from the table, one with a long, curved blade. He advanced on Erin, his black marble eyes showing neither compassion nor excitement. It was like trying to stare down a mannequin.

Erin gathered her strength and hurled herself sideways with all the force she could muster. The chair toppled. The concrete floor rushed up at her. She pulled her head up, but her right shoulder and arm hit the floor hard. The chair gave a squeal of protesting metal.

"Still some fight, I see," Nogti said calmly. "Please pick her up and hold her, Mr. Vlasov, and I will show you something remarkable."

Gennady bent over her, reaching down and grabbing her by both shoulders. He hoisted her back upright. Erin started to try to escape again, but stopped herself short.

She'd felt something give in the chair. One of the back supports had sheared off when it had struck the floor. It was loose now. If she tried, she thought she might be able to slip her right-hand cuff free.

But she didn't. Not while Gennady was holding her. If she made her move now, she'd lose her only chance. So she forced herself to hold still, in spite of every instinct urging her to fight for her life. She had, at best, one shot at this.

When you only had one shot, you'd damn well better make it count.

Nogti took hold of her chin in his left hand, holding her face up, keeping her from headbutting him or biting. With the other hand, the knife hand, he deftly began slicing the buttons off her blouse.

"Women are much more interesting to work on than men," he said, in the tone of a classroom lecturer. "There are so many ways you can hurt them."

Richie, in spite of his angry words, had retreated halfway across the room. He wasn't looking directly at Erin, and his face showed a mixture of anguish and disgust.

"Now then," Nogti said. "Let us see what we have to work with. I think—"

Chapter 34

VIC NESHENKO

The single most dangerous moment in an ESU raid was the initial breach. If the bad guys knew you were coming, and were waiting for you, the front door was the place you least wanted to be. Get the door open, get through, keep moving; that was your best chance. Dynamic entry kept the enemy off-balance and surprised. If you gave them the chance to recover and get organized, that was when you took casualties.

The house's exterior door was solid wood, with a sturdy lock and latch. It didn't make a damn bit of difference. Vic's shoe slammed into the wood right next to the doorknob, tearing the brass plate clean out of the wood, stripping the screws, sending the door swinging wide open.

Vic expected a guy to be waiting inside, on guard duty, and wasn't disappointed. A stairway led up to the second floor from the entryway. The sentry was sitting on the steps, an assault rifle across his knees, one hand resting on the gun, the other holding a cigarette to his lips. The cigarette dropped from the guy's mouth and he snatched at the gun as Vic burst in, Rolf panting eagerly at his hip.

Vic fired twice, center mass. The Delta Elite's heavy slugs punched into the man. But he was wearing some sort of body armor. Vic didn't wait to see whether the Russian was out of the fight. He shifted aim slightly and fired a third shot directly into the man's face, just the way they taught you in the Mozambique Drill. The guard flopped back onto the stairs and slid down them to the floor, leaving a smear of blood on the steps.

The noise of the door-kicking and gunshots was incredible in the confined space of the hallway. Vic, ears ringing, hustled inside and hooked left into a living room. Rolf was tense and eager, but stuck close, true to his training. Zofia went straight up the middle, shotgun at the ready. Thompson covered the stairs, M4 snugged in close to his shoulder.

Two more bad guys were in the living room. One was in the process of jumping up from the couch, the other stood in the dining room doorway. Vic reflexively squeezed off two quick shots at the guy on the sofa. One missed. The other caught his target in the shoulder, knocking him back onto the couch. The other man whipped up his AK and returned fire.

Vic dropped to one knee and rolled to the side, plaster dust exploding above and around him. He fired again, blindly, in the gunman's general direction. He let go of Rolf's leash as he hit the carpet and shouted *"Fass!"*

Rolf saw two men. The one closest, on the couch, had a pistol in one hand, but Rolf didn't care. That just told him which arm to aim for. When K-9s trained in bite work, they always, always won. Rolf didn't just think he was invincible; he *knew* it. He didn't hesitate. He just dug his claws into the living room carpet and lunged.

If the wounded mercenary had been just a little bit faster, he might have gotten a shot off. Rolf hit him in midair, the weight and force of his leap tipping the couch clean over. Man and dog went down, Rolf on top, the K-9's jaws closed tight around his victim's right wrist. When the man didn't drop the weapon, and tried to punch him with his other hand, Rolf bit down with all the force of his massive jaw muscles. The bones in the man's wrist shattered. He let go of the pistol and started screaming.

The gunman with the Kalashnikov couldn't fire at Rolf for fear of hitting his buddy. He swept the rifle in an arc across the room, blasting away at Vic. But the AK had a lot of recoil on full auto and the muzzle climbed high enough that the rounds just missed.

Vic, lying flat on the carpet, brought his pistol in line and fired. He rushed the shot and missed, cursing inwardly. He saw the muzzle of the AK coming down as the merc wrestled it under control. Then the gunman's body jerked convulsively as three high-velocity rounds smashed into his chest, went clean through his armor, and sprayed blood across the room. He pitched over and lay very still.

Vic glanced over his shoulder and saw Thompson aiming down the M4's iron sights. The former Marine, having satisfied himself all targets on that side were down, turned his attention back to the stairs. He immediately fired another burst from the rifle. Vic, almost deafened by gunfire, felt more than heard a body fall on the upstairs landing.

"Rolf!" he shouted. *"Pust! Komm!"*

Rolf immediately let go of his newest chew-toy and bounded back to Vic, tail wagging happily. He'd done a great job and expected his rubber Kong ball. The man he left behind was curled into a helpless, whimpering ball, bleeding heavily from wrist and shoulder.

Vic stood up and kicked the downed man's gun away. Then, for good measure, he kicked the wounded guy in the face, to make sure he stayed down. "Clear!" he called, and hauled out the bag containing Erin's socks. He opened the bag and held it in front of Rolf's snout.

"*Such*, buddy," he said. "Go find her."

Rolf's nostrils flared wide. His ears perked and his tail lashed. He knew that smell better than any other in the world, and he'd follow it anywhere. He bounded joyfully back into the entryway, claws scrabbling on the tile floor, and rushed deeper into the house past Zofia. Vic ran after him.

"Cover our ass," he told Thompson on his way.

"Roger," Thompson said.

Chapter 35

ERIN O'REILLY

The basement was well insulated, but the sudden burst of gunfire, shouting, and screams was still remarkably loud. Everyone in the cellar froze, listening.

Gennady recovered first. He let go of Erin and ran, rapping out orders in Russian to the guard at the foot of the stairs. The two men rushed upstairs, leaving Erin with Nogti and Richie.

Erin deliberately let herself slump in the chair, presenting no visible threat whatsoever. Nogti took a step back, still holding the curved knife.

"What the hell is going on?" Richie asked.

"Why don't you go find out?" Nogti replied. "You could be a big hero."

"Screw you," Richie said. "Why don't you go?"

"Because my job is to take care of her," Nogti said.

Carefully, slowly, trying not to shift her shoulders, Erin eased her right handcuff down to the separated piece of the chair. There was plenty of noise to cover the faint clinking of metal on metal. The bracelet caught for a moment, then slid free.

"Screw it," Richie said. "Let's just do her and get out of here."

"I thought you wanted her alive so we could torture her," Nogti pointed out. "If all you wanted was her death, we could have done that with so much less trouble."

"That was then!" Richie exclaimed. "Look, just slit her throat. God damn it, we don't have time—"

The two men were looking at one another, their attention momentarily focused on their words. Nogti had taken a step toward Erin and his knife hand was within reach. It was now or never.

Erin brought her right hand around, one handcuff bracelet still dangling from it, and grabbed Nogti's wrist. She yanked him toward her, across her lap, pulling and twisting. He was caught totally off balance, falling onto her with a startled cry. She felt the edge of the knife dig into her forearm, cutting through her sleeve, drawing blood, but she ignored it. She kept twisting, turning his wrist inward.

He cursed in Russian and let go of the knife, which clattered to the floor. But he moved like a weasel, his body whipping around. His left hand came up, fingers like claws, gouging at her eyes.

Erin closed her eyes just in time, feeling his nails tear her skin. Acting on instinct, knowing there were no rules in this kind of fight, she snapped at him. Her teeth came down on his middle finger. She bit as hard as she could. Her mouth was suddenly full of blood. She felt resistance and kept biting. Something horribly hard and bony came loose. Nogti screamed.

Nausea churning in her belly, Erin spat the awful thing out in the Russian's face, along with his own blood. He wrenched his knife hand free, tumbled to the ground, and scooted away from her, clutching his maimed hand.

Richie was staring at her in disbelief, momentarily rooted to the spot. Then his gaze shifted to one side. He rushed toward the table.

Erin's feet were still tied to the chair. She was some two yards from the table. There was no way she could reach the weapons on it. She rocked the chair away from the table, then flung herself toward it, falling once more to the hard concrete and banging her left knee. She stretched out her right hand, using the extra reach her fallen body provided, and grabbed the nearest table leg. Her leverage was terrible, but adrenaline was one hell of a drug, and her body was operating at a hundred percent fight-or-flight. With a desperate heave, she pulled the table over toward her.

Richie lunged for the revolver, but it was already falling. He caught his shin on the edge of the toppling table, tripped, and fell headlong, face-planting on the ground. Erin clawed at the floor, feeling a tearing pain as one of her nails bent back, dragging herself a foot closer, then another.

Richie rolled over and came up to his hands and knees, crawling frantically back toward her. Nogti was somewhere on the other side of the table, but Erin couldn't see him. She made a final desperate stretch and felt her hand close on the revolver's handle.

Richie snatched up a knife from the jumble of fallen torture implements. He rose up on his knees, blade poised, and Erin shot him twice, point-blank. The bullets hit him just below the sternum, tearing through his lower chest. He sagged back on his haunches, arms falling limply to his sides, an expression of stunned disbelief stamped on his face.

Nogti came over the table, his nine remaining fingers clawing at her. Erin was immobilized, tied to the chair. She rolled awkwardly onto her side and pulled the trigger once, twice, three times. The first bullet missed wide. The second put a hole in the Russian torturer's upper torso. The third went straight through his throat.

He tumbled on top of her, twitched a couple of times, and went still. Blood and smothering weight enveloped Erin. She pushed frantically at the limp deadweight, trying to get free. After far too much effort, she managed to thrust the body aside.

"You shot me," Richie said quietly, still looking like he couldn't quite believe it.

"Yeah," Erin said, trying to get her breath back. "What'd you expect?" That was why you never brought a gun into a jail cell or interrogation room.

Slowly, unceremoniously, Richard O'Malley keeled over sideways and lay still.

Erin trained the revolver toward the staircase, trying to remember how many shots she'd fired. Two for Richie, three for Nogti. That meant, if the gun had been fully loaded, she was down to her last round.

If one bad guy came down the stairs, she'd have one shot at him. If two came for her, she'd have a hard choice to make.

Chapter 36

IAN THOMPSON

Never forgot how to do some things. No matter how much he wanted to. Rifle was part of him, like his hand. Easy as pointing a finger.

Tactical situation unstable. Hostiles upstairs, probably downstairs too. Neshenko and Piekarski were solid. So was Rolf. But such a small fire team was one bad move, one unlucky bullet from disaster.

Rolf was heading toward the back of the house, so that was where Erin was. Ian wanted to be there, make sure she was safe. But Neshenko was right. Someone had to guard the rear, keep the bad guys pinned upstairs.

Grenades would've been best. Toss a couple frags up, take care of them. But Ian didn't have any. Just the M4.

He'd hit two tangos so far; one in the living room, one on the landing. Could see the second guy's hand, dangling over the stairs. Heard more moving around, talking in Russian. Didn't speak Russian, but could guess.

They're making a plan, Marine. Once they do, they're coming down. And they know where you are.

Time to relocate. A good sniper never fired twice from the same spot. Ian sent a three-round burst up the stairs, suppressive fire. Keep them back, keep them guessing. Then he fell back to the living room, got behind the doorframe, covered the stairs from a back angle.

Not a second too soon. Kalashnikov rounds tore up the floor right where he'd been standing. Probably blind-fire from someone upstairs, trying to suppress him. Bad guys knew what they were doing. Professionals.

The problem with being professional, it made you predictable. A gunman came barreling down the stairs right behind the gunfire, hoping to take advantage of Ian being pinned down. Except Ian wasn't pinned and wasn't where they thought.

As the bad guy came downstairs, Ian had a clear view of his legs through the banister. Waited until he saw the lower back. Squeezed the trigger, three rounds. This one had ballistic plates in his vest, might've stopped the incoming rounds, but Ian aimed just below the backplate. The 5.56-millimeter bullets tore through Kevlar like tissue paper.

Ian was already moving before the gut-shot bad guy had time to fall all the way down. Usual thing would be to displace backward, find a new hiding spot. But they'd expect that. Ian went forward, to the foot of the stairs.

Just like he expected, two more bad guys on their way down, behind their buddy. Ian gave the first a burst, aiming low to avoid the armor. Perforated his groin and guts. Shitty way to kill a man, but no time to get squeamish. That one started falling and screaming. Ian shifted targets. Fired again at the same time the third merc opened up.

Bad guy's AK sprayed slugs all over the place. That was full auto for you. Hard to control, impossible to take careful aim. This guy firing from the hip, made his aim even worse. Ian felt a couple bullets come close, little puffs of wind by his neck and ear, hardly noticed. Fired another three-round burst, partially blocked by the falling body of the second guy, hit his target smack in the chest. Bullets hammered into ballistic plate, smashing the ceramic insert. Didn't penetrate, sent the tango stumbling backward.

Ian took a step up, moved around a twitching body without thinking about it. Fired another burst. Saw at least one bullet go through Kevlar and flesh. Bad guy down now, lying on the steps, not dead. Struggling to bring up his rifle.

Ian took his time, lined up his sights, put a single round into the man's left eye.

Moment of quiet. Couldn't assume all the bad guys were dead. Fell back to the living room, got behind the tipped-over couch. Wounded bad guy lying on the floor, moaning. Bloody face, shoulder, hand. Thought about shooting him, just to be safe. Decided not to. Popped the half-empty mag out of the M4, slapped in a full one, chambered a round.

Still wanted to go after Erin.

Do your job, Marine.

No choice but to trust Neshenko and Piekarski. Got settled behind the rifle. Found his stillness. Waited.

Chapter 37

VIC NESHENKO

Rolf rushed down the hallway, head forward, tail whipping the air. He was making eager little whines. Vic was right behind him. Then came Zofia.

Vic knew they had to keep moving. Give the bad guys half a chance and they'd kill Erin. They'd probably kill him, too, and everyone else. At least Thompson had their backs. The guy might be an asshole, but put a gun in his hand and he was a stone-cold killing machine.

Rolf came to a door at the end of the hall. He scratched at it and barked sharply. Vic grabbed the knob, nodded to Zofia, twisted it, and shouldered the door open.

He just had time to see a kitchen, all stainless steel and white-painted cabinets, before his attention was caught by a small, olive-green sphere that flew past his ear in a lazy arc. It bounced off the wall and ricocheted in the hall.

"Grenade!" Vic yelled. The hallway had no cover, so he sprang forward into the kitchen instead.

A Russian mercenary was in the corner, covering the door. He and Vic saw each other at the same time. Vic saw the Kalashnikov's muzzle flash as he emptied his pistol. He felt a massive impact on his chest, just over his heart, and lost his footing. He went down on his ass, feeling another blow on his left bicep. He saw the other man falling, half the guy's face gone, and knew he'd gotten him. But black spots were flaring in front of his eyes and he couldn't draw breath.

He was lying down, not sure how it'd happened. A man was standing over him, pointing a pistol at his face. Vic vaguely recognized Gennady Vlasov, raised his Delta Elite, and pulled the trigger. Nothing happened. The slide was locked back and the gun was empty. Vlasov sneered at him. His finger was on the trigger of his own pistol. *Makarov nine-millimeter*, Vic's internal firearm enthusiast commented. Figured he'd get killed by a Russian gun.

There was a massive roar and Vlasov was tossed sideways. The kitchen counter caught him in the stomach and he folded up. He turned, bent double, somehow still standing, and fired his pistol toward the doorway. Vic saw Zofia there, pumping her shotgun and firing it again.

How many seconds since he'd seen the grenade? Vic had no idea. "Get down!" he tried to shout, but the hit to the chest had knocked the wind out of him and all he managed was a breathless wheeze. Zofia ducked to one side. Then the world exploded.

A storm of wood splinters and plaster dust tore through the doorway, peppering the kitchen. The noise of the grenade blast was deafening. Vic's hearing gave up completely and turned into a dull, obnoxious buzzing sound, like a malfunctioning doorbell. Bigger chunks of the house, pieces of the ceiling, clattered down, but he didn't hear them. He just felt faint vibrations through the linoleum.

He finally managed to suck in a deep breath. Oxygen burned like gasoline fumes in his chest, but it gave him a boost of energy. He sat up, hit the magazine release on the Delta Elite, ejected the empty mag, and groped for a spare in one of his vest pockets. His body armor showed a hole dead center, right over the "I" in the POLICE insignia. Under it, he could feel what was left of his ceramic chest-plate shifting and grating against itself. It had done its job, but he'd need a new one. He probably had cracked ribs.

Vic slid the fresh magazine into the gun and racked the slide. His left arm was bleeding, but he wasn't aware of any pain. His ears were still ringing. The air was full of dust and smoke.

"Zofia!" he shouted. His own voice seemed to come from really far away, like hollering down a subway tunnel. He braced himself with one hand on the floor and got unsteadily to his feet. His inner ear was all out of whack and he nearly fell down again.

Zofia was crouched near the wall, bending over something dark and furry. As Vic watched, Rolf clambered up. The K-9 was only using three legs. His fur was matted with blood. Zofia was touching him, saying something Vic couldn't hear.

"Where's Vlasov?" Vic asked.

Zofia gave him a blank, confused look. Then she pointed wordlessly toward the sink. Vic looked and saw the Russian boss slumped on the floor. At least, he assumed it was Vlasov. There wasn't much head left to speak of. A headshot from a twelve-gauge at less than ten-foot range was a spectacular thing.

Rolf, ignoring his own wounds, limped to a closed door. He scratched and barked. Then he did something Vic had never heard him do. He raised his head and howled. Even with Vic's ears ringing, it was a hell of an eerie sound.

"Are you okay?" Zofia asked Vic. At least, that was what her lips seemed to be asking. He nodded. Then he pointed to the door. He grabbed the knob. Zofia pumped her shotgun again, chambering a fresh shell, and nodded back at him. He tugged the door open.

Chapter 38

It sounded like Armageddon upstairs. A massive explosion rattled the rafters and sent a shower of dust down on Erin from the ceiling. She'd decided to risk putting the gun down long enough to grab one of the knives and cut her legs free. Then she picked up the revolver again. She was still handcuffed to the chair by her left wrist, but that wasn't a big deal, considering. She knelt behind the chair's dubious cover, wrapped her left hand around her right, and drew a bead on the stairs. By the sound of things, the fight was coming to an end. She wondered who'd won, and what it meant for her.

A small, slender figure came down the stairs in a rush. The intruder had a shotgun in hand, ready for action. Erin slipped a finger inside the trigger guard and started squeezing the trigger. Then she saw it was a woman; a woman she knew.

"Erin?" Zofia said.

Erin sagged in relief, letting go of the revolver. All the adrenaline drained out of her at once. She didn't care how cold and hard the basement floor was. It was solid underneath her, and that was plenty. She rolled onto her back and stared up at the bare lightbulb. It suddenly seemed very bright, like looking at the sun. She closed her eyes.

"She's here!" Zofia was shouting. "She's alive! We're clear!"

Something blotted out the light. Erin opened her eyes just in time to see a big pink tongue incoming. She caught a full slurp right in the face. Then she saw a pair of serious, anxious brown eyes looking down at her from a few inches away. She smelled smoke, blood, fur, and dog breath.

"Rolf?" she murmured. "What're you doing here?"

"Saving you, of course," Zofia said. "Oh my God, Erin, you're a mess. Are you okay?"

"I'm fine," Erin said. "You should see the other guys."

"Jesus Christ chugging vodka communion," a man said very loudly. "What is going on here?"

"Hey, Vic," Erin said, struggling to sit up. "Took you long enough."

"Bite me," Vic said. He looked awful. His left sleeve was soaked with blood. He was covered with plaster dust. But he was grinning.

"You don't want me doing that," Erin said. "Trust me." She spat, trying to get the taste of Nogti's blood out of her mouth.

"Speak up!" Vic said in a near-shout. "I'm not hearing so good right now."

Erin paid no attention. She was looking at Rolf. The dog was standing on three legs, trying to pretend he wasn't hurting. But a big chunk of shrapnel was sticking out of his hip and he was bleeding. She didn't try to remove the piece; proper first aid procedure was to leave the foreign object in the wound. The vet would take it out.

"Jesus," Vic exclaimed, still talking way too loud. "That's Richard O'Malley!"

"*Was* Richard O'Malley," Erin corrected wearily.

"Who's this other guy?" Zofia asked.

"Nogti," Erin said. "Russian. Liked to hurt people."

"What's with his hand?" Zofia asked, peering more closely. "He's missing a finger."

"It's over there," Erin said, gesturing.

"Did you bite it off?!" Zofia burst out.

Erin didn't answer.

"Shit," Vic said. "You're so much like your dog, you basically are one, you know that?"

Erin held up a hand to silence him. She thought she heard sirens. A moment later she was sure of it. Men were shouting upstairs, comforting phrases she knew by heart.

"Police!"

"Drop your weapon!"

"Hands up!"

"Can you walk?" Vic asked, extending a hand to her. Zofia had found a handcuff key on Nogti's body and unshackled Erin's left hand from the wreckage of the chair.

She took Vic's hand. He pulled her to her feet. And she walked out of that damned basement, leaving the cold, dark room to the dead.

* * *

"Vic," Zofia said as they climbed into the kitchen. "You've been shot."

"It's fine," Vic said, tapping his chest. "Vest stopped it."

"No," she said. "Your arm."

"It's fine," he insisted.

"Vic," she said. "You have a *hole* in your *arm*."

He looked at his upper arm. His sleeve was crimson. A neat little circular hole had been punched through the fabric and his bicep.

"Oh," he said. "Huh. I didn't notice."

"Freeze!" a Patrolman shouted. Two uniformed cops stood in what was left of the kitchen doorway. One held a pistol in both hands, the other a rifle. Both guns were trained on the detectives.

"NYPD," Zofia said, holding up her gold shield. "We're on your side. We need a bus. Detective Neshenko's been wounded."

"Who's downstairs?" the other cop asked.

"Two dead guys," Erin said dully. She was utterly exhausted. She could feel blood on her face from Nogti's fingernails. Her head ached. She could still taste the man's blood, still feel the way his finger had broken between her teeth. The lingering sensations were the only things convincing her she'd really done that.

"I'll clear the basement," the cop with the rifle said. "You get these three out of here."

The other officer led Erin, Vic, Zofia, and Rolf down the hallway. More uniforms were spilling into the house, spreading out.

"Hey!" Vic shouted suddenly. "What is this crap?"

Three cops surrounded Ian Thompson. He was lying on his stomach, hands cuffed behind him. Two of the cops were pointing their guns at him.

"He's a shooter," one of the Hoboken cops said. "We're taking him into custody."

"Like hell you are," Vic retorted. "Let him go!"

"He's a suspect," the cop said.

"He's one of us!" Vic snapped.

"He had an assault rifle," one of the other officers said.

"That's my gun!" Vic said angrily. "I gave it to him! He's a friggin' combat veteran, he saved my life, and he's on our team! Get those goddamn cuffs off him right now!"

The other cops looked at the sergeant who was apparently the ranking officer, who shrugged.

"Okay," he said. "Let him go. I just hope someone can tell me what the hell is going on. I've got six dead bodies and another guy wounded out here."

"Two more bodies in the kitchen," the detectives' escort said helpfully.

"And two more in the basement," Zofia added.

One of the cops took the handcuffs off Ian, who stood up and nodded politely to him.

"Thanks," Ian said to Vic.

"Forget about it," Vic said. "Don't go thinking I like you or anything."

"Of course not, sir," Ian said.

*　　*　　*

There were miles of red tape to untangle. Vic was the ranking NYPD officer on scene, but he was wounded. Erin and Ian were technically civilians, so it fell to Zofia to sort out the jurisdictional mess with Hoboken PD. She succeeded in convincing the locals to redirect Vic's ambulance to Bellevue. Erin would also need to be checked out, but she flatly refused to go to the hospital until she'd seen to Rolf.

The news that Webb, McDowell, and Webb's daughters had survived was a tremendous relief. But Vic just shook his head when she asked about Holliday.

"He was a tough old bastard," Vic said. "And he took two of those scumbags down with him. McDowell got one of them, too. Never thought that bitch had it in her, but she's a real one."

Erin borrowed a phone from one of the cops to call the Barley Corner. Carlyle had been going out of his mind since Corky had called him. Relieved beyond words, he'd immediately made some calls of his own. One of Corky's associates turned up with a minivan less than ten minutes later to take Erin and Ian wherever they wanted to go: in this case, straight to the emergency vet.

The driver, certainly a smuggler, provided her with another phone, a burner, which she used to call her dad.

"O'Reilly," he said, answering almost immediately. The strain in his voice hurt Erin's heart.

"It's me, Dad," she said. "I'm okay."

There was a short pause. "Thank God," he said after a moment, only barely able to get the words out. "Where are you?"

"Rolf got hurt. I'm getting him some attention. Then I need to go to Bellevue."

"I'll meet you there," he said. "What happened?"

"I'll tell you later," she said. "I don't know all of it myself."

"I'll see you soon, kiddo," Sean said. "You sure you're okay?"

"It's me, dad," she said. "I'm pretty hard to kill."

During the drive, Erin got most of the story from Ian. He told it in his usual way; no drama, no description, hardly any pronouns.

"So you ran, biked, and swam after me?" Erin said when he'd finished. She was in the back seat with Rolf's head on her lap. The Shepherd's ears were laid flat against his skull and he was panting quietly, still trying not to show pain.

"Affirmative," Ian said.

"Congrats," she said. "You're a triathlete now."

"Hadn't thought of that," he said. "Didn't take time to think. Probably get in trouble with Lieutenant Rawlins. Left my post without permission."

"If you need a reference, you know where to find me," Erin said. "I'll send him a note. You saved my life."

"Just doing my job," he said.

"That's bullshit and we both know it," she said. "So you and Vic are friends now?"

"Negative," he said. "Not friends. But he'd have made a pretty good Marine."

That was one of the highest compliments Ian could pay anyone.

*   *   *

"Rolf's a very lucky boy," the vet said, an hour later.

Erin let out a breath she hadn't known she'd been holding. "He'll be okay?" she said.

"He's in no danger," the vet said. "And he should keep the use of his leg. But the hip joint's been injured. The bone is badly chipped."

"He's a tough dog," she said.

"He is that," the vet said. "And I think he'll recover reasonably well. But he won't be able to put as much weight on the limb, and he won't be able to run as fast as before."

The bottom dropped out of Erin's stomach. "What do you mean?" she asked.

He smiled sadly. "Between this and all the other wear and tear, and considering his age, I think his police days are over."

"You don't mean that," Erin said.

"He was already pretty worn down," he said. "He's broken his ribs and a leg before. He's been concussed, shot a couple of times, Tased, and lit on fire. I think your boy's earned a quiet retirement."

Rolf, lying sullenly but obediently on the examining table, gave Erin a soulful look.

"It'd break his heart," she said.

"It'll break his body if he tries to keep going," the vet said. "You need to think what's right for him."

"He'd kill himself to keep riding with me," Erin insisted.

"Yes," the vet said simply. "He would."

"Isn't there something you can do? Some surgery?"

"Ms. O'Reilly, can I give you some advice? As a medical professional?"

She braced herself. "Go ahead."

"Don't *ever* ask a doctor if there's anything more they can do. Because the answer will always be 'yes.' And too often the kindest thing to do is actually nothing."

Erin kept looking at Rolf's face. The Shepherd's tail thumped on the table three times. She laid a hand on his neck and tried not to cry. It was getting harder every minute.

"We'll operate to remove the bone splinters," the vet said. "And we'll need to keep him overnight. But he should be good to go home in the morning. We'll call you with any news."

"Thanks," she said numbly. "But I don't have my phone right now. Call Morton Carlyle if there's an emergency. Here's his number."

*   *   *

The waiting room at Bellevue was packed with cops. Word had gone out and it seemed like every off-duty officer from the Eightball was holding vigil. Erin had to push through a crowd of uniforms just to get into an examining room. Dr. Nussbaum came in a few minutes later to shine a light in her eyes, ask her questions to test her memory, and check her various bumps and bruises.

"There's blood on your mouth," he said. "I should check you for internal injuries."

"Oh, that?" Erin said. "It's not mine."

He blinked. "Is this where you tell me some silly vampire joke?"

"Nope. I bit a guy's finger off."

He gave her a long look. "You're serious."

"Yeah."

"Why?"

She indicated the fingernail marks on her cheek. "He was trying to pry out an eyeball," she explained. "So I did what I had to."

He sighed. "Most of your injuries are superficial. But it looks like you've suffered a concussion. I should say, *another* concussion. Frankly, I'm astonished you're able to stand up, let alone form a coherent sentence. I'm going to recommend you remain here for observation, at least overnight."

"I can't do that!" Erin snapped. "I have—"

"Work to do?" he interrupted gently. "It'll keep until tomorrow. Anyway, as I understand it, you're currently unemployed."

"Does everyone in New York know?" she asked bitterly.

"I think everyone on the eastern seaboard knows," he said. "But if it's any consolation, you have company."

"What do you mean?" she asked.

"I've been busy in here," Nussbaum said. "Picking up the pieces of all the madness on the street. But rumor among the nursing staff has it that you're looking for a new boss."

"Oh, that," she said. "Yeah. I heard about Captain Holliday. It's a damn shame."

"That isn't what I meant. The Mayor fired the Commissioner of Police about half an hour ago. It seems some questions arose about his recent conduct."

Erin tried to feel anything about the news and couldn't. She was too tired and heartsick to care. "That's nice," she mumbled.

"Now, we're a bit crowded," Nussbaum said. "I hope you don't object to sharing a room. We can't give private rooms to every patient."

"As long as my roommate isn't a total jerk," she said.

Nussbaum smiled. "You'll have two," he said. "One of my patients and one of your brother's. I think you'll get along just fine."

Chapter 39

"Nice of you to join us," Lieutenant Webb said quietly.

"Sir, I've never been so glad to see you," Erin said. Webb was lying in a hospital bed, tubes running an IV drip into one of his arms. He was hooked up to machines that were beeping with monotonous, reassuring, maddening regularity. His color was a little off and he looked very tired.

Beside him, in an identical bed, lay Lieutenant McDowell. The IAB officer appeared to be asleep, probably with pharmaceutical assistance. McDowell was alone, but Webb was surrounded by his daughters and Vic. The big Russian's arm now sported a clean white bandage, standing in stark contrast to his filthy skin and clothing. Danielle had pulled up a chair and was holding her dad's hand.

"We're doing co-ed rooms here now?" Erin asked.

"Captain Stoneman asked for us all to be in the same place," Webb explained. "I think he wants to keep an eye on us."

"I saw the guard in the hallway," Erin said. "How're you feeling, sir?"

"Like I got shot," Webb said. "On the plus side, I've developed a much greater understanding of our nation's opioid fixation. I would absolutely love a hit of morphine right about now."

"Very funny, Dad," Erica said.

"You're not on pain drugs?" Erin asked, appalled. "Why not?"

"I got shot in the liver," Webb said. His skin was pulled tight around his eyes. He was in more pain than he was letting on. "Guess which organ processes narcotics, along with alcohol and all the other things that make life worth living?"

"So what can they give you?"

"Acetaminophen."

"Translation," Vic said. "Friggin' Tylenol. We can't even smuggle him in any booze, unless we want to kill him. Which is tempting, come to think of it."

"I think I've taken about half a bottle of Tylenol," Webb said. "It helps. A little. You know what the doc is telling me? He says I shouldn't drink. He didn't even say anything about moderation. Zero, zip, zilch."

"You'll probably live longer than if you hadn't been shot," Vic said.

"I'm aware of the irony," Webb said. He turned back to Erin. "Neshenko's been telling me what went down. Did he really deputize Ian Thompson? And loan him a gun?"

"I guess so," Erin said. "I didn't see it, but I heard the shooting and I saw the results."

"I thought you hated him," Webb said to Vic.

"He's not that bad," Vic said. "We couldn't have done it without him."

"Ian's a good guy," Erin said.

"I wouldn't go quite that far," Vic said.

"What else did they say about you, sir?" Erin asked.

"I'll live," Webb said. "My liver might even recover eventually. I guess that's something to look forward to. Maybe I can have a celebratory drink in a few years."

"Dad saved our lives," Erica said. "He took bullets for us."

"Your dad's one hell of a cop," Erin said. "And one hell of a man."

Danielle nodded and squeezed Webb's hand. She was crying quietly.

"From what I understand, Richard O'Malley and Gennady Vlasov planned the attack?" Webb asked.

"That's right, sir," Erin said.

"And both of them are dead?"

"I shot Richie," she said.

"And Zofia got Vlasov," Vic said. "Took his head clean off with a shotgun. Boom. Nine dead Russian mercs, plus O'Malley. The Hoboken cops have the only survivor in custody. Looks like a clean sweep."

"Ten dead," Webb said, shaking his head. "I don't know whether to be impressed or horrified. How about you, O'Reilly? What's your condition?"

"I just got banged on the head," she said. "I'll be fine."

"Of course you will," Webb said, rolling his eyes. "And I'm glad O'Malley's been dealt with."

"He was a victim, too," she said.

"Seriously?" Vic said. "Erin, you shot him because he was trying to murder you!"

"He was set up, the same as I was," she said. "Finnegan, not Richie, sent Jack McGraw to kill me. Finnegan made us go after each other."

"Can you prove it?" Webb asked.

Erin shook her head. "Only if we can flip Ophelia Flaherty."

"Good luck with that," Vic said. "Asking a daughter to flip on her dad? Why don't you ask these two if they'd do it?"

"Never," Erica said firmly. "No matter what." Danielle nodded agreement.

The conversation was interrupted by a knock at the door. The cop on guard duty stuck his head in.

"Sorry, folks," he said. "I have a visitor."

"Another one?" Vic said. "It's gonna be Grand Central friggin' Station in here. We have to shoo them out every five minutes or so. The whole Eightball's coming in, one after another."

"Who is it?" Webb asked.

"A guy named O'Reilly," the guard said. "Sean O'Reilly. Says he used to be a cop."

"Let him in!" Erin said at once. A moment later, her dad came in. He looked a little frazzled, which made sense, given that he'd driven down from upstate New York on extremely short notice to help his daughter in her hour of need.

"Excuse me," he said.

"Dad!" Erin exclaimed. A moment later she was in his arms. Neither one was a particularly huggy person, but right then it didn't matter. They held on tight.

"Kiddo, your mom's been so worried," Sean muttered through his mustache. "She's downstairs, but she wants to see you too. What've you been doing with yourself?"

"See, this is another good dad," Vic said. "I bet he wouldn't send his daughter out to whack people for him."

"Of course not," Sean said, raising his head but not letting go of Erin. "There isn't a single damn thing I wouldn't do to protect my girl. I'd never use her as any sort of tool. What's the matter with you?"

"Of course not," Erin echoed. She suddenly sprang back, so quickly she nearly knocked her dad over. "That's it! I know how to get Finnegan!"

"That's great," Webb said dryly. "Too bad you haven't been reinstated, and Major Crimes isn't exactly open for business."

"Come again?" Vic said.

"I mean there *is* no Major Crimes squad as of this moment," Webb said. "Look around, Neshenko. Your Lieutenant's out of action, probably for good. Your Detective First Grade may or may not be coming back. And you yourself aren't looking so hot."

"This?" Vic demanded, flexing his wounded arm and wincing. "This is nothing!"

"As of this moment, Major Crimes has exactly one active member," Webb went on. "Detective Third Grade Piekarski who is, along with you, on modified assignment after a multiple fatal shooting incident. Not to mention the fact that the Eightball is currently without a commanding officer. We're closed down until further notice."

"I can get him," Erin insisted.

"Good," Webb said. "But he's not going anywhere, and for the moment, neither are you. So why don't you get comfortable and let this wounded hero try to get some rest?"

Erin tried. She was tired enough that in spite of her aches, pains, and memories, she fell asleep almost as soon as she sank onto the hospital bed.

The nightmares weren't too bad, considering.

Chapter 40

A week later, the bruises had faded and the cuts had scabbed over. The dreams were still bad. Whiskey helped a little, but Erin was trying not to lean on it. She was sitting on the couch in Carlyle's apartment above the Barley Corner, slowly sipping an after-dinner shot of Glen D. Carlyle sat next to her, an arm around her shoulders, his own drink in hand. Rolf lay on the other side of her, enjoying his sofa privileges. The dog wore a padded cone to keep him from gnawing at the stitches on his hip, but he bore the indignity with quiet grace.

Carlyle's phone vibrated with an incoming text message. "Pardon me, darling," he said, leaning forward and picking it up from the coffee table. He scanned the screen for a moment.

"Anything serious?" Erin asked.

"I don't know," he said. "According to Ken Mason, there is, and I quote, 'a shifty-looking guy' downstairs asking to speak with you."

"Does he look like trouble?" Erin asked.

"I'll ask," Carlyle said, tapping out a response. After another moment, Mason's reply popped up on screen. "He says the lad's the acting Commissioner of Police. I'm afraid I can't tell whether he's trouble or not."

"No kidding," Erin said. "I guess I'd better talk to him."

"He's asking to come up," Carlyle said. "If you're wanting a private meeting, my office is at your disposal."

"I want you there," she said. Rolf raised his head and blinked at her. "Yeah, you, too," she added, reaching into the cone and rubbing his ears.

The Deputy Commissioner, now Acting Commissioner, reminded Erin uncomfortably of the late and unlamented Lieutenant Andrew Keane. He was slick, well-dressed, buttoned-down, and every inch a smooth, cold politician. He was tall, slender, black-haired, and one of the few men to walk into the Corner whose suits probably cost as much as Carlyle's.

"I apologize for intruding on your evening, Ms. O'Reilly," he said. "Thank you for seeing me."

"My pleasure, sir," she lied, shaking hands with him. His fingers were cool and dry, his grip firm.

"You're wondering why I'm here," he said. "Instead of inviting you to meet in my office."

Erin said nothing.

"This is an unofficial visit," he continued after a brief pause. "I trust you'll understand. My predecessor was, shall we say, a bit premature and public in some of his pronouncements. I apologize for his treatment of you."

"A public apology would be both more sincere and appreciated, sir," Carlyle said dryly.

"It will be forthcoming tomorrow morning," the Commissioner said.

"Regardless of the outcome of this meeting?" Carlyle pressed.

"Regardless."

Erin kept watching the man, trying not to give anything away. Her trust was operating at a pretty low level these days.

"Your commanding officer, Lieutenant Webb, speaks very highly of you," the Commissioner said. "As does your most recent fitness report, and a personal memo from Captain Holliday I found in my new office."

Erin flinched. *And I got him killed,* she thought.

"He believed you were suited to a command position," the Commissioner went on. "When the appropriate situation and your personal career path intersected. I believe you were offered a job in my predecessor's office some time ago?"

"That's correct, sir," Erin said, wondering how he knew.

"It is my personal belief, which is very definitely stated off the record, that your refusal of that job offer contributed to the animosity between you and he."

"I wouldn't know anything about that, sir," she said stonily.

"As you are probably already aware, Lieutenant Webb has submitted his request for early medical retirement," the Commissioner said.

"Yes, sir." Webb had told her so himself during her last visit to him in the hospital.

"This leaves the Precinct Eight Major Crimes unit in need of a replacement Lieutenant."

"Yes, sir."

"Is that a job for which you would wish to be considered?"

Erin blinked. "Sir?"

"It is my understanding that your K-9 may also be retired," the Commissioner said, glancing at Rolf, who returned his gaze with cool disdain.

"That depends, sir," she said.

"There is a slight irregularity here," the Commissioner said. "Technically, it is against Department procedures to retire a K-9 with a civilian. I'm confident my office can find a way around that rule, but I don't think that's necessary, do you?"

"Not if I'm a member of the Department, sir," Erin said.

"And would you be more amenable to being promoted to desk duty, now that it does not entail separating you from your dog? Particularly since I understand you have also sustained injuries which may preclude further street work?"

Erin took a deep breath. "Yes, sir," she said. "I would."

"Then allow me to be the first to congratulate you, Detective Lieutenant O'Reilly," he said, offering his hand once more.

Erin hesitated. "Sir," she said. "May I ask why this offer was made privately?"

The Commissioner's smile was as cool and dry as his handshake. "I would think that was obvious," he said.

"You didn't want me turning you down publicly," she said. "And you wanted to make sure I wasn't going to sue the Department. You wanted to sound me out in a deniable way."

"I'm going to have to disagree with one aspect of Lieutenant Webb's evaluation of you," the Commissioner said. "He says you don't have the instincts or mindset of a politician. I believe you have just proven him wrong. What do you say?"

Erin considered her options. The thought of desk work had always been abhorrent to her. But she couldn't run down alleys and kick down doors forever. It was sheer dumb luck she hadn't been killed or crippled a dozen times over. She'd been in too many gunfights, seen too many people die. Her head couldn't handle many more hard knocks. And without Rolf running by her side, the chase had lost some of its thrill.

She looked at Carlyle, asking him a question with her eyes. He smiled gently and spread his hands, indicating the choice was hers. She turned back to the Commissioner.

"Who would be serving under me?" she asked.

"The present Major Crimes roster includes Detective Viktor Neshenko and Detective Zofia Piekarski, I believe," the Commissioner said. "They would remain, unless you have some objection. You would be expected to fill out the remaining positions from the list of qualified candidates. You would have final approval over personnel."

Erin extended her hand. "Then I'd be honored to accept, sir," she said.

"Excellent," he said, giving her hand another brisk, firm shake. "If you have no objection, I'll make the announcement public tomorrow morning. Incidentally, the official investigation of the shootings in Hoboken has concluded, I'm pleased to say, with all officers involved cleared of all culpability. All police shootings were clean."

"And Ian Thompson, sir?" she asked.

"The Hoboken Police Department has determined Mr. Thompson acted entirely within the law, in the best interests of the public. He bears no legal responsibility for the five fatalities he inflicted on the criminals in that house."

"I know, sir," Erin said. "But I'm glad to hear you say it."

"I won't impose on your time any further," the Commissioner said. "Except to offer my congratulations on your upcoming nuptials."

"Thank you, sir," she said automatically.

"And to you as well, of course," he added to Carlyle.

"Thank you," Carlyle said.

After the Commissioner had left, Erin went immediately to the bottle on the side table and poured herself another Glen D. "Jesus," she muttered.

"Congratulations, darling," Carlyle said.

"Thanks," she said wryly. "I don't believe this."

"Why not?" he asked. "You've earned it."

"I never thought I'd want it. I'm a street cop, not a desk jockey."

"Your Captain Holliday was a street copper once upon a time," he reminded her. "And it's a good thing he was."

"He still died," she said.

"As a hero," Carlyle replied. "I seem to recall the Bible saying something about that. Greater love hath no man…"

"Yeah, yeah, I know," Erin said. "But he died because of me."

"He died because of Kyle Finnegan," Carlyle said sharply. "And a number of other evil men. Don't go taking all the weight of the world's sins on your shoulders, Erin. You're not our Lord and Savior."

"You're right," she sighed. "I just feel lousy about it. He's dead. Webb's hurt. McDowell has her leg pinned together. My brother said it was like putting a jigsaw puzzle together; a used one from a garage sale, with no box and a few pieces missing. They wouldn't have been in that elevator if they hadn't been trying to save me."

"That's true," he said. "How many times have you laid your life on the line to protect another human being?"

"More than I can count," she admitted.

"And if you'd perished in one of those encounters, would you have wanted any of them blaming themselves?"

She gave him a small, sad smile. "No. Of course not."

"Then perhaps you'd best extend that same mercy to yourself, darling."

Erin took his hand. "How do you always say just the right thing?" she asked.

"Years of practice talking dangerous lads out of killing me," he said. "But with you it's easy, darling. I simply tell you the truth."

"Your truths are complicated things," she said.

"Not always," he said. "I love you, Erin O'Reilly. That's a plain and simple truth. And I'm very much looking forward to being your husband."

"Just a few more days," she promised. "But it looks like I have something to take care of first."

"Finnegan?" Carlyle guessed.

"Finnegan," she agreed grimly.

*　　*　　*

Major Crimes looked almost the same, but it wasn't. Webb's desk—Erin's desk, she corrected herself—was bare except for the Department-issued computer and an empty file tray. That would fill soon enough, she thought. Holliday's corner office was locked. The acting Captain, some guy named Nathanson, was operating out of the meeting room on the third floor. Holliday's stuff had been boxed up, but nobody had come to take it away yet.

Holliday left a widow and two kids behind. Erin had seen them at the funeral; a thin, graying woman who'd stood stone-faced and stoic as the Chief had handed her a folded flag, and a pair of young men in whose faces she'd caught fleeting glimpses of the Captain, like distant echoes. One of them was in the Army, and had worn his dress uniform. The other was an air-traffic controller. The tradition of public service ran deep in the Holliday family.

Erin blinked away the tears before they could overflow. She cried too easily these days. She walked over to her old desk, bent, and picked up the folded blanket that lay next to it. She carried it to her new desk and carefully laid it out on the floor beside it. Rolf watched her.

"Go on, kiddo," she said. "*Platz.*"

Rolf limped to the blanket and very carefully circled, arranging his injured hip. He made three complete rotations, then settled with a sigh. He was tired. Healing took a lot out of an animal, as Erin knew better than most.

"Uh oh," a man said from the stairwell.

"Glad to see you too, Vic," she said.

"Hide the booze," Vic said, walking in with Zofia a half-step behind him. "Looks like we've got a new boss. Am I supposed to call you sir? Or Ma'am?"

"You'll call me whatever you feel like," Erin said. "I've heard all about you, Neshenko. Your file's chock-full of insubordination rips. But don't think that crap's going to fly with me."

"Well, shit," Vic said to Zofia. "The new Lieutenant's a nut-buster."

"Good thing I don't have any nuts to bust," Zofia said. "Good to have you back, Erin."

"Thanks," Erin said.

"So when are we gonna get a full squad?" Vic asked. "I see two empty desks."

"I've only been your Lieutenant for..." Erin paused and looked at the clock. "...eleven minutes. These things take time. I have a list of applicants."

"Anyone we know?" Vic asked.

"Gus Dettweiler," she said.

"The kid from the Harbor Patrol?"

"The same."

Vic nodded. "He wants to come play with the big boys downtown?"

"Yeah. He's requesting a transfer. I think we'll take him. He's solid. Good instincts."

"And he's got your back when the shit goes down," Vic agreed. "Besides, it'll be nice having a rookie to push around. But

I was kinda hoping we could bring in some of your old friends. You know those two guys you used to work with back in the One-Sixteen?"

"Lyons and Spinelli?" Erin asked, raising an eyebrow.

"Yeah, that's them! The big fat one and the little one who looks like a weasel."

She gave him a flat, hard stare. "No."

Vic smiled nastily. "If I'd thought you'd say yes, I wouldn't have asked. I hate those bastards. How about the other vacancy?"

"I don't know yet," Erin said. "Someone will turn up."

Zofia rummaged in her handbag and produced a copy of the *Times.* "Did you know you made the paper?" she asked.

"Oh, God," Erin said. "Do I even want to know?"

"They say you've made a meteoric rise through the Department's ranks," Zofia said. "What do you think of that?"

"I thought meteors went down," Erin said. "Not up."

Vic snorted. "See, that's why they made you Lieutenant. You're the brains of the operation. So what's today's plan?"

"We're going to jail," she said.

"Am I gonna get stabbed this time?"

"Nobody's going to get stabbed." Erin considered what she'd just said and amended it. "Probably."

*   *   *

"This is the first time I've been to this part of the joint," Vic said.

"It's nice to see how the other half lives, isn't it?" Zofia said.

"The Rose M. Singer wing," Vic said, reading the sign aloud. "It sounds like a hospital, not part of the lousiest damn prison on the East Coast. Know what they call prisons for men? Friggin' Alcatraz, that's what."

"Florence Supermax," Erin said mildly. "Or Sing Sing. There's plenty of violent male offenders in those. Do they really sound macho to you?"

She took out her Glock, a newly-issued one, and paused long enough to double-check the serial number. Then she handed it over to the tough-looking female Corrections Officer behind the mesh screen.

"I bet you always look at your gun from now on," Vic said.

"If I'd done it from the beginning, I wouldn't have been in this mess," Erin said. She turned her attention to the CO. "Okay, I'm ready."

"Name of inmate?" the guard asked.

"Ophelia Flaherty."

"I'll have her brought to Room Three. Take the first right, then second left."

"Thanks," Erin said as the guard buzzed them through the security door.

"Are you sure about this?" Zofia asked quietly. "I really don't think you're going to get a girl to flip on her dad. You or I wouldn't."

"Finnegan's not our dad," Erin said.

"Are you sure about *that*?" Vic chimed in. "Because I saw him eat a guy's face once, and you're working up to it. How about after this we go get some lunch? We could get finger sandwiches. I understand you've got a taste for them now."

Erin made a face. "Just let me do most of the talking," she said. "And follow my lead."

"Sir, yes, sir!" Vic said.

"Detective Neshenko?"

"Yes, sir?"

"Shut up. That's an order."

Vic grinned. "Just like old times," he said. "Shutting up now, sir!"

Erin returned his smile. Then she put on her game face. She hoped she could handle this as well as Webb would have. It was scary being in charge, but it was also liberating; like going skydiving, she supposed.

She opened the door to the interrogation room and went in.

Chapter 41

"That was really something," Vic said, two hours later.

"Yeah," Zofia agreed. "You okay?"

"I'm good," Erin said, and it was true. She was exhausted, wrung out, but she was feeling good.

"Let's get some food," Vic said. "I was joking about the sandwiches, but I could go for a burger."

"Later," Erin said. "Let's finish the job first. Just one more thing."

It was only a short trip to the men's facility on Riker's Island. Erin reflected that this was where the case had started. It all came back to one murderous man with a diseased brain. It wasn't that he was a genius. It was that he didn't have the mental safeguards normal people took for granted. He thought in unusual ways and was willing to go places others wouldn't.

"I'll talk to him alone," she said as a guard led them to the visiting area.

"Bullshit," Vic said. "He might go for you."

"He'll be chained," she said.

"So would a rabid dog," he objected. "But I wouldn't get close to one."

"You can watch," she said. "But stay back. I think he'll talk, but only to me."

Vic shrugged. "You're the boss," he said.

Kyle Finnegan didn't look like much. He'd lost weight from his already scrawny physique. He still wore a bandage on his neck. His gaze was unfocused, wandering vaguely around Erin as she sat down opposite him. His hands were secured to a ring on the table by a short chain and a pair of handcuffs.

"Good morning, Kyle," Erin said.

"Morning without you is a dwindled dawn," Finnegan said.

"Ophelia says hi," she said.

"Nymph, in thy orisons, be all my sins remembered," he replied.

"That'd be quite the list," she said. "But I don't need to know all of them. In fact, I don't need anything from you. This is a courtesy visit."

"Discourtesy is unspeakably ugly to me," Finnegan said, and for just a second his eyes gleamed mischievously.

"Then this might get a little ugly," Erin said. "First off, I want you to know you lost. Completely. I didn't just keep my job; I got promoted, thanks to you. I'm Lieutenant O'Reilly now. I didn't die, but most of the guys who came after me did. All you succeeded in doing was getting three good men, fourteen bad ones, an innocent woman, and a little kid killed. I'm sure you're proud of yourself, so enjoy it while you can."

"We live in a primitive time," he said. "Neither savage nor wise. Half measures are the curse of it. Any rational society would either kill me or give me my books. I wish you a speedy convalescence and hope you won't be very ugly. I think of you often."

"You use other people's words a lot," she said. "I could look them up later. But I won't. When I walk out of here, I'm going to start forgetting you right away."

"We both know that isn't true," he said, and the glint was back in his eye. "And are you so certain you're the one who's won?"

"I didn't say I won," she said. "Not every fight has a winner. I said you lost. And this is the last round of our vicious little game. I didn't even know I was playing against you, not until recently. But I get it now."

"I'm listening," Finnegan said. "I have two ears and only one tongue."

"This is what you do," she said. "You pay attention to people. You figure out who's at odds and you find ways to escalate the conflict. You're like the ancient Romans with their gladiators, watching people fight to the death and betting on the outcome. I guess you mostly do it for fun. I beat you last Christmas, when I threw you in jail. Ever since then you've been planning to get me back. You tried to hit me with Black Jack McGraw, figuring if I survived, I'd assume it was Richard O'Malley who hired him. And I did, until I spoke to Richie. But he didn't know a thing about it. You planned the feud between Richie and me, not caring which of us won. You stabbed yourself to implicate the Russians, and you used Ophelia to set Gennady Vlasov on me.

"You forced me to kill two men," she continued. "And plenty more died in the crossfire. I've finally got you figured, Finnegan. Most bad guys are selfish. They're out for money, or power, or women. But you're just plain evil. All you want to do is hurt people; you enjoy it."

"And therefore, since I cannot prove a lover to entertain these fair well-spoken days, I am determined to prove a villain and hate the idle pleasures of these days," Finnegan said.

"Back to the Shakespeare, I see," Erin said, recognizing the cadence of the lines. "There's one thing I should thank you for.

You reminded me why I wear a shield. I do it to protect the world from people like you."

"You're very welcome," Finnegan said, smiling slightly.

"Of course, I wouldn't be able to prove any of this if I hadn't had a nice long chat with your so-called daughter," Erin said, ignoring his words. "Oh, she thinks you're her dad—or at least she did. Now she's not so sure. See, I know a few fathers of daughters, and not a single one of them would sacrifice their kid. They'd do anything to protect them, in fact. Because that's how love works. I had Vic show Ophelia some of the baby pictures on his phone. She saw the look in his eye when he talked about his daughter, and she believed him when he said he'd die before he'd let any harm come to her.

"You brainwashed her. Maybe she's got your DNA and maybe not, but it doesn't matter. You were never a dad to her and now she knows it. She's not your pawn anymore. She killed for you, four times. She's going behind bars, but she'll get the psychiatric help she needs. But even in prison, she'll be freer than she ever was under your thumb. I've started deprogramming that poor girl, and I'll make sure the psych guys finish the job. She's already started to understand what you did to her. You've lost her, and she's started finding herself. Even if she gets out, I guarantee you'll never see or speak to her again."

"Sometimes people don't understand the promises they're making when they make them," Finnegan said.

"I know exactly what I'm saying," she said. "I also know you were behind the bomb in Mickey Connor's car."

She'd finally succeeded in startling him. Finnegan blinked and his vacant stare focused on her. "What?" he said. "I'm sorry, I didn't catch that."

"You heard me. The bomb that Mickey thought Carlyle planted? You knew he'd think that, and he'd come after Carlyle and me. But he didn't stop there. He came after my family, and you did it for your own amusement, you bastard. I can't prove it, but I don't have to. Here's what I have to say, and you'd better listen closely.

"Thanks to Ophelia's statement, we can tie you to multiple murders, enough so you'll die behind bars. But it gets better. We can also link you to a kidnapping conspiracy to take me to Hoboken. The real beauty of that is, by taking me across state lines, Gennady and his buddies made this a Federal case. That means, as soon as I can get the bureaucracy in motion, given your history of violence and your demonstrated ability to cause harm from inside prison, you're looking at a transfer to Supermax. Do you know what that's going to be like?"

Finnegan, for once, didn't have anything to say. Erin gave him a moment, but he stayed silent. She savored it.

"You'll be in solitary confinement," she said. "Twenty-three hours a day. You'll only come out of your cell to go to the exercise yard, alone. You'll see a few guards but they won't speak to you. That's it. No other human contact. Nobody to swallow your poison. No interpersonal drama to use in your twisted little mind games. They're going to bury you alive, you son of a bitch, and I'm going to be the one who hands them the shovel.

"Oh, and one more thing. I'm submitting a request for you to be put in solitary custody at Riker's until you're transferred. It's for your own protection. Once Evan O'Malley learns what you did to his son and grandson, your life won't be worth a pack of smokes in here. So if you were thinking of doing anything sneaky, firing a last parting shot, you won't have the chance. Your weapons are gone. Do you copy?"

"You have grown wise," Finnegan said quietly. "And cruel."

"*I'm* the cruel one?" Erin retorted. "Was there anything else in this for you? Or was it really all just for fun? All the death and misery?"

"I do love Ophelia," he said. "No matter what you may think."

"I don't think you know what love means," she replied. "Love isn't about control. You know, I thought I'd enjoy it more, seeing you suffer. But you know what makes it worth it? Knowing you can't hurt that girl any more than you already have. I wonder what you'll do with yourself when you don't have your pawns to push around anymore."

"Demand me nothing," Finnegan said, and he smiled, but she could see something else hiding behind the smile: fear. "What you know, you know. From this time forth I never will speak word."

"That's the best news I've heard in a long time," she said. She stood up and turned her back on Kyle Finnegan forever.

*   *   *

"Did you get what you need?" Zofia asked quietly as they walked away.

Erin thought about it. "I hope so," she said. "Because it's all I'm going to get out of him. Mostly I just want to be done with that sack of shit."

"Amen to that," Vic said.

"Now I'm going to do what I promised him," she said. "I'm going to do my best to forget he ever existed."

"Is that smart?" Zofia asked.

"It's the only way to beat him," Erin said. "As long as he's in my head, I'm playing his game. That's the point of all his riddles and quotations."

"Did any of what he was saying make any goddamn sense?" Vic asked.

"Who cares?" Erin replied. And it was true. She really was finally ready to let go.

Epilogue

Erin O'Reilly sighed. After twelve years on the Job, she wasn't used to going without the shield and Glock on her belt. The gold shield marked her as part of a team, gave her authority and purpose. She liked to wear black and dark blue. Now she was clad in white, of all things, wearing a dress; and not a practical one either. She wasn't even sure she felt like a cop. The woman in the mirror looked like a stranger. A dolled-up, fancy stranger.

"I don't know about this, Rolf," she said. "Maybe I should've worn my dress blues."

Rolf panted happily. He'd recently graduated from the cone and was still enjoying his freedom. His hip had a horrible shaved spot, scored by the surgical incision, but for today he was wearing the canine version of a tuxedo and the coattail covered most of it. He even had a cute little bowtie at his throat.

Erin looked closer at her reflection. Some of the scabs and bruises were faintly visible, even under her makeup. Her eyes were serious.

"You're getting married," she told herself. "So smile, damn it."

She tried on a smile. Her hair was distracting her. A smart female cop always wore her hair up on duty, for the same reason cops' neckties were clip-ons: you didn't want to give the bad guys an easy handhold on your neck or head. Michelle had done Erin's hair. She had no idea what was going on above her ears, but the complicated arrangement spilled down one cheek in a ringlet.

"I look like a Disney princess," she muttered.

A knock at the door startled her out of her reflections. "Come in," she said, turning away from the mirror.

Erin's dad looked, if anything, more awkward in his tuxedo than she felt in her dress. He stared at her for a long moment, not saying anything.

"Well?" she finally asked. "How do I look?"

He cleared his throat. "Beautiful," he said hoarsely, and she realized it wasn't awkwardness at all. Sean O'Reilly was trying his very best not to break down in tears.

"You're not really giving me away, you know," she said. "I'll always be your daughter."

"And I'll always be your dad," he said, opening his arms to her.

She hugged him tightly. "I love you, Daddy," she said, the endearment she almost never used.

"I love you," he said and sniffled. "I'm just... I'm so proud of you, kiddo. So damn proud. Your mom and I... both of us are."

"Is it time?" she asked.

"Yeah. Everyone's here."

"Carlyle didn't make a run for it, did he?" she joked.

"He wouldn't have gotten far," Sean said. "This church is full of cops."

"And reformed gangsters," she added.

"Them, too," he muttered gruffly. "All right, are you ready?"

"Let's do this," she said.

He offered his left arm. She looped her hand through it. "*Fuss*," she murmured to Rolf, who took up his place at her hip and walked proudly beside her, limping only a little.

Zofia and Michelle joined them: Shelley tall and elegant, almost impossibly gorgeous; Zofia petite, perky, and pretty. The groomsmen—James Corcoran, Sean Junior, and Ian Thompson—fell in step beside them.

"It's a grand day for drinking and dancing," Corky said, winking at Erin.

"And getting married," Michelle said, frowning.

"Aye, that too," he said cheerfully. He offered an arm to Michelle. "No fear, love. I promise this is the only time I'll walk down the aisle with you."

Sean Junior scowled, but said nothing. He was on his best behavior, but seeing his wife and her almost-lover arm in arm would be hard on any man. Erin gave him a grateful smile and received a nod in reply.

They walked into the sanctuary, hearing the music swell as they entered. Erin caught a momentary glimpse of the altar, Carlyle standing next to the priest. Then the guests rose to their feet and turned toward her, in the time-honored tradition of bridal processions, and she lost sight of him amid the sea of familiar faces.

As her dad had said, many of them were cops, but some were from other walks of life. She recognized Vic Neshenko, actually looking pretty good in a suit and tie; Brendan Malcolm, the Eightball's desk sergeant; Lieutenant Murphy and Officer Paulson from the 116; Paul Logan, Bobby Firelli, and Marek Landa from Zofia's old Street Narcotics squad; Lieutenant Lewis and his ESU team, almost unrecognizable in civilian garb; and many others. She saw Sarah Levine and Levine's fiancé, Jasper Ackermann. There were Cassie and Ben Jordan, Ian's family. Teresa Tommasino was watching Corky and weeping unashamedly. Still seated, unable to stand, were Phil Stachowski with his wife Camilla; and Harry Webb, just out of the hospital, flanked by his daughters who'd extended their stay in New York to care for him.

Erin drifted through friends and family, conscious of the smiles and tears on their faces. The whole thing felt oddly dreamlike, as if it was happening to somebody else. She saw only a few of Carlyle's friends; nearly all the people he'd hung around with in New York were either dead or in prison. Erin came to the front of the sanctuary and saw the family pew, populated by the O'Reillys who weren't wedding attendants: Mary, Michael and his wife Sarah, Erin's kid brother Tommy, and Sean Junior's children Anna and Patrick. They'd thought about making Patrick ringbearer, but Erin had taken pity on the shy little boy and had listened when he said he didn't want to. Rolf had the ring in a box buckled to his collar, a responsibility the Shepherd took as seriously as all his other duties.

Carlyle had no family present at all. He had a brother in Africa and a mother in Belfast, and they'd both been invited, but neither had showed. Erin wondered how he felt about that.

Then Carlyle was standing in front of her, devastatingly handsome in a perfectly-tailored tuxedo, a look on his face of awestruck love, and Erin realized that this was really happening, right now, and she smiled at him and watched his eyes light up with so much joy that she thought both their hearts might melt right there on the spot.

She didn't take her eyes off him for the entire ceremony. When it was time for the rings, she just held out her hand and let him slip the gold band on by feel. The actual marriage, the readings and music and vows, was a blur, in large part because her eyes kept filling with tears, no matter what she did.

Then it was official. Carlyle clasped her hands and leaned in. She tilted up her head and kissed him, the sweetness of the moment salted by tears, but that was okay, too. They both knew life wasn't all sunshine and flowers. They'd come too far, and lost too much, to have any illusions about that.

After the kiss and the applause and the recessional, everyone else decamped for the Barley Corner to get the party started, while Erin and Carlyle stayed to have some pictures taken. The photographer was a serious professional who'd done a lot of celebrity weddings. Corky knew her in some unspecified way, because of course he did, and had somehow prevailed on her to do the event. Erin didn't even want to know how. He'd also arranged the musicians, the food, and all the other details.

"Corky really is good at this best man stuff," she commented to Carlyle.

"Aye," he agreed. "The lad can be quite competent, when he sets his mind to it."

"There weren't any strippers at your bachelor party last night, were there?"

Carlyle smiled. "Nay," he said. "Though we did have a performance by a lovely troupe of Irish step-dancers, and while I'll confess their legs were attractive, their skirts and blouses remained draped over them."

"He's really reformed, then?"

"For the most part. Perhaps we'd best get through the reception before saying for certain. I'm half-expecting a nude woman to burst out of the cake."

* * *

The Barley Corner was full of celebrating wedding guests. Some were already drunk, and just about everyone was getting drunker. The booze bill was going to be astronomical, but Carlyle could afford it. Danny Sullivan was tending the open bar, pouring drinks with impressive efficiency. Caitlin Tierney and a couple of other waitresses threaded through the crowd, refilling drinks and laying out the supper.

"I can definitely see the advantages of marrying a pub owner," Erin said.

"Aye, it does simplify some matters," Carlyle said.

Everyone appeared to be having a good time. Tommy O'Reilly had his guitar out and had joined the live band. Sean Junior and Jasper Ackermann were engaged in a detailed medical conversation. Ben, Anna, and Patrick were playing darts under Ian's careful supervision. Nobody had lost an eye yet.

"I guess this is happily ever after, huh?" Erin said.

"In my experience there's no such thing," Carlyle said.

"Oh God," she said. "I wasn't thinking. I know this is the second time you've done this. I didn't mean—"

"It's all right, darling," he said. "But I'd prefer to think of this as a beginning rather than an ending. We've so much to look forward to, such a life to build."

"Yeah," she said. "I'm a Lieutenant now, and you're just a peaceful, law-abiding publican."

"There's many worse things to be in this world," he said. "And I'll admit I'll sleep better knowing you're not quite on the front lines anymore."

"It's a little weird," she admitted. "I talked to Webb. He promised to impart some of his hard-earned experience to me before he leaves."

"He's going away?"

"Yeah. Back to LA. He wants to be closer to his family."

Carlyle smiled. "That's a grand idea," he said. "I hope he recovers well."

"He's the only guy I know whose quality of life has been improved by getting shot," Erin said. "His kids think the world of him now, and he'll be a lot healthier laying off the booze. He'll probably be more relaxed in retirement, too."

"Speaking of which, how's Rolf taking to office life?"

"He misses chasing bad guys," she said. "And he misses his morning runs, but his leg still bothers him. He still gets to be with me, so he knows I'm not trying to get rid of him. He gets to be involved. But I think he'd like having a job to do."

"I could purchase some sheep for him to guard," Carlyle offered. "It's against zoning ordinances, but perhaps a loophole could be found. Corky knows a lad at City Hall."

"I'll just bet he does," Erin laughed. "I don't think that'll be necessary. Remember how Rolf is with Vic's kid?"

"I do, aye. The dog can't get enough of the wee lass."

"Before too long I think he'll have a babysitting gig," she said.

Carlyle nodded. Then he froze, blinking slowly as what she'd just said hit him.

"Do you mean...?" he said quietly.

Erin nodded.

"And I'm just now hearing this?" he asked.

"I'm not a hundred percent sure," she said. "I haven't taken any tests. But I think so."

She'd thought he couldn't look any happier than he had at the altar, but she was wrong. His face was positively radiant.

"Don't tell anyone yet," she said, laying a hand on his arm. "Not until it's certain."

"Mum's the word," he promised, kissing her cheek. "But I'll be thinking of little else."

The tinkle of a dinner fork against a wineglass interrupted them. Corky was standing up, tapping his glass for attention. The music died away, as did the side conversations.

"Thank you, you grand gaggle of lads and lasses," he said. "I'm sure you all join me in congratulating the second-loveliest couple in New York City on finally making their union official, despite the best efforts of both the underworld and local law enforcement."

A cheer went up, accompanied by some good-natured catcalls from the cops present. Corky waited for it to subside before continuing.

"As you all know, it's customary for the best man to offer up a toast. As most of you also know, I'm hardly shy about opening my mouth, but I promise I'll not keep you long from your excellent dinner and even more excellent liquid refreshments. Cars Carlyle and I go all the way back to boyhood, to Belfast. He's older than I, though I'll not say by just how much, and he's always looked after me, no matter how many scrapes I got into. We've stood by one another through good times and bad, and I'd like to say before all of you, I've never known a finer man."

He paused and, to Erin's astonishment, wiped his eyes with the back of his sleeve.

"Just how much have you had to drink, Corky?" Carlyle asked, drawing a burst of laughter.

"As to that, I've scarcely started," Corky said. "But let me get through this. Cars married young, and lost his wife to the Troubles, as did too many other lads. He went on, but the light had gone out of his life. Until he met Erin O'Reilly. Now Erin, she's something of an extraordinary lass in many ways. I could sing her praises till sunrise, but she'd be the first to shut me up, so I'll just say she put the light back in my best mate's eyes. I think we can best be judged in this life by the company we keep, and if that's so, then the two of them are the very best character references anyone could want.

"So far as that goes, all of you are here with me tonight, so that goes for all of you. But there's some folk who couldn't be here, and I'd like this toast to be drunk in their honor as well. So we'll mix a wee bit of sorrow with the joy, which shouldn't come amiss to the Irish, and I'll pledge to you the memory of

Kira Jones, a grand lass; and Fenton Holliday, a true friend and a good man, despite being coppers, the both of them. Now, if you'll listen, I've a short tune to sing. It's a song that can be sung at weddings or funerals, with joy in our hearts or tears in our eyes."

Corky cleared his throat, very loudly in the silence. Then he began to sing, in his clear, lovely tenor voice, an old Irish tune.

> *"Of all the money that e'er I had,*
> *I spent it in good company.*
> *And all the harm I've ever done,*
> *Alas, it was to none but me.*
> *And all I've done for want of wit,*
> *To memory now I can't recall.*
> *So fill to me the parting glass,*
> *Good night and joy be to you all.*
>
> *"So fill to me the parting glass,*
> *And drink a health whate'er befall.*
> *And gently rise and softly call,*
> *Good night and joy be to you all.*
>
> *"Of all the comrades that e'er I had,*
> *They're sorry for my going away,*
> *And all the sweethearts that e'er I had,*
> *Who begged me one more day to stay.*
>
> *"But since it fell unto my lot*
> *That I should rise and you should not,*
> *I'll gently rise and softly call,*
> *Good night and joy be to you all.*

"So fill to me the parting glass,
And drink a health whate'er befall.
And gently rise and softly call,
Good night and joy be to you all.
Good night and joy be to you all."

Corky fell silent. He raised his glass, the overhead lights shining through the amber whiskey. Tears streamed down his boyish cheeks. He nodded to Carlyle and Erin, tilted the glass, and drank.

Erin hoisted her own glass, saying a silent goodbye to Kira, to Captain Holliday, to the past, and ushering in the future. Was this what victory felt like? She didn't know. She'd made it this far, and she and so many others had paid a terrible price. There'd be other days, other battles. You didn't become a cop thinking your job would ever be done. There were always more crimes to solve, more bad guys to bring down. But here and now, she could feel both the sadness and the joy, as Corky had said, and they amplified one another. Her heart felt very full in her chest as she tasted the hot, fierce burn of the Glen D.

"Good night and joy be to you all," she said, speaking to the living and the dead.

Author's Note

"I promise I won't kill the dog."

I said those exact words to my wife, fairly early in Erin's journey. I knew roughly where this saga would end up from the beginning, but some characters' fates were up in the air. I didn't want Rolf to die, not only because I was afraid of being lynched by a horde of angry dog lovers, but because I'd fallen in love with the furry good boy. But as recently as the start of "Last Round," I thought Lieutenant Webb might not make it to the closing credits. His entire character arc seemed destined for tragedy, to die literally in the arms of his daughters, having given everything to save them. But sometimes things go better than planned. Sometimes the dark forces in the world are held at bay. Sometimes people don't get what they deserve and expect; and sometimes this is called grace.

The Erin O'Reilly Mysteries have their roots in a roleplaying game I ran back in 2014 for my wife and some of our friends. I'd designed a game system to model 20th-Century firearm combat for replaying World War II battles, and after watching way too much of the TV show "Castle," realized it could easily be adapted to the world of crime and police officers. Over the following two years I crafted dozens of cases, some original, some based on existing books, TV, and movies. As time went on, the world became more fleshed out with fascinating characters and a vast, sprawling storyline.

Morton Carlyle was originally designed as an antagonist: a shadowy, clever, polite gangster who would always be one step ahead of the heroes, his competence spurring them to greater efforts to try to bring him down. But then the unexpected happened; Carlyle proved a little too charming. He morphed into first a friend, then a romantic interest for Erin. That relationship, and the bonds of friendship within the Major Crimes squad, provided the framework for the narrative and suggested to me that maybe I ought to write some of this down.

I started writing "Black Velvet" in 2015 as a hobby, with no great hopes of it ever getting published. I'd previously self-published an epic fantasy novel in 2011, "Ember of Dreams," of which I was very proud. I hope the sixty or seventy people who've read it enjoyed it, but the, shall we say, modest sales of that book tempered my expectations.

I still tried to make as good a story as I could. I attended my local police department's Citizens Academy to learn how real-world police officers talk, think, and do their jobs. I learned a lot, the most valuable lesson being that getting Tased hurts—a lot. I'm not sorry for volunteering to ride the lightning; it was an educational experience. But I don't recommend it for anyone else. I also read several police autobiographies, including Edward Conlon's excellent "Blue Blood," Stephen Osborne's "The Job," Richard Greelis's "Cop Book," and others. "Werewolf," by David Alton Hedges, is a particularly good and moving account of a K-9 officer and his dog. John Douglas's "Mindhunter" provided insight into profiling and serial killers.

By more or less dumb luck, while I was working on "Irish Car Bomb," my wife happened to mention on social media that her husband was working on a series of police procedural novels. One of her college friends had started his own small publishing house. He expressed interest, I sent him the manuscript, he loved it, and the partnership was born. With hard work, a few leaps of faith, and a generous additional helping of luck, we were able to get the series enough attention that when my day job disappeared, in the middle of the COVID pandemic, I was able to transition to writing as a full-time vocation.

The drink names I used for the books are a naming convention that I thought was fun and a little clever. Erin, a high-functioning alcoholic, and Carlyle, a pub owner, suggested the idea. It's nice having a thematic link between stories, and the titles I came up with often suggested whole plotlines. A surprising number of cocktails have names that suit themselves disturbingly well to describing violent crime.

The series was originally intended to be between twelve and fifteen books. But as Ian Thompson might say, mission creep set in. I realized as we went that the series was structured much like a modern TV miniseries, with every five books roughly equivalent to a season of television. Every fifth book featured some sort of recurring antagonist who had been previously introduced. The stakes were higher, the drama more intense, before toning things down a little for the next season and building toward a new crescendo.

Now, with thirty volumes (plus five short stories and one spin-off novel), Erin's story is mostly complete. Erin has earned her laurels, and Rolf can enjoy his retirement position of pampered office pet and soon-to-be babysitter. Webb is on his way back to sunny southern California with a rekindled relationship with his family. Vic and Zofia get to keep doing what they love, riding the thrill of the action. Ian can go on healing with his newfound family. Corky and Carlyle, too, have a happier ending than they may have expected or felt they deserve.

That said, I don't intend to say a full goodbye to this fictional world. I plan to write at least one collection of short stories, filling in the edges. I would love, for example, to explore Rolf's adventures in babysitting from the K-9's own unique point of view. I'd sit down to listen to Corky spin a yarn about his wild escapades in Northern Ireland in his youth. And there are so many other tales to tell.

I'm also ready, after ten years serving as Erin's reporter, to embark on a new series of stories, with a new protagonist, in a different time and place. Coventry Adams is a very different heroine from Erin; less physically strong, but at least as clever and a born survivor. I hope some, at least, of my readers will enjoy meeting her as much as I'm enjoying writing her.

For now, we will leave Erin toasting fallen friends and future hopes, celebrating the victory of love, loyalty, and courage in the face of evil. In our real world, all too often the forces of darkness seem insurmountable, and it is all too easy to give in to anxiety and despair. But that's one of the reasons we need our fictional heroes so very much. They light the way, encouraging us with their example.

I'd like to offer an enormous thank-you to everyone who's shared this saga with me: my wife Ingrid, who has never stopped believing in me; Carl and Mary Caroline Henry, my father and mother, who raised me as a reader and provided the sort of stable, loving home that helped ensure I wouldn't embark on a life of crime; the members of my gaming group, who created the personalities of some of the core characters of the series (David Greenfield as Lieutenant Webb, Justin Moor as Vic, Hilary Murphy as Dr. Levine) and those others who were present in more temporary capacity; Ben Faroe, my publisher and editor; and last but definitely not least, my readers. Without all of you, I wouldn't be able to do this. I hope I've brought you some enjoyment.

Raise your glasses, everyone. *Sláinte.*

> *So fill to me the parting glass,*
> *And drink a health whate'er befalls.*
> *And gently rise and softly call,*
> *Good night and joy be to you all.*

Chapter 3

Numbly, Coventry let Finn lead her back upstairs to the gambling hall. Finn guided her with one hand on her cuffs, carrying her suitcase in the other. Whisper had vanished as soon as the fight had started, sliding away like a blob of quicksilver. He was too canny an alley-cat to hang about once fists and feet began to fly.

Slinky McGee stood in the doorway, mouth hanging open. He'd heard the commotion and arrived just in time to witness its end.

"Here now, guv," he said to the Irishman. "What's all this?"

"Detective Finbar Farrell, Metropolitan Police," Finn said. "Doing my civic duty, sir. If you'd be so kind as to lend me the use of your fine establishment for the space of a few minutes, I'd be obliged."

Slinky's face darkened and he gave the inspector an unfriendly look. "How do I know you're a detective?" he demanded.

Finn opened his coat, showing the gleam of a white metal badge and the handle of a stout truncheon. "Here's my authority," he said. "If the badge won't suffice, I'm thinking my shillelagh will."

Slinky held up his hands, palms outward, and retreated indoors. Finn steered Coventry in behind him and sat her down at one of the tables. She offered no resistance. After the reflexive attempt at flight, she had collapsed in on herself. Perhaps she deserved to be caught, she thought bitterly. She had betrayed her last principles. She truly was nothing now, deserving neither mercy nor forgiveness.

"Now then," Finn said, taking out a notebook and a little nub of a pencil. "Let's start with your name, shall we?"

She made no answer.

"Come now, lass," Finn said. "Surely that much will do no harm, aye?" His voice was surprisingly gentle, and he showed no anger, though he now sported a swelling under one eye and blood trickled down his cheek where her nails had raked him.

"What's in a name?" Coventry retorted. "You calls it a rose, but it's still got bloody thorns on it, don't it?"

Finn's smile showed straight, white teeth; a rarity in Whitechapel. "That's not precisely how I've heard it said, but near enough. Round the public houses hereabouts, I've heard the name Coventry. Coventry Adams. Have I heard right?"

"You tell me, you bloody great mutton shunter. You've naught better to do than hassle working girls, so I guess you ought to know."

Finn raised an eyebrow. "You're misinformed, lass," he said. "I've never been on that particular detail. I fear my work's a mite more serious than chasing tarts off street-corners. I'm tasked with investigating the murder of the honorable Bartleby Horrocks."

"Honorable, was he?" Coventry snorted. She was trying to rebuild some semblance of defiance, but she knew it was no use. She could feel her lip quivering, could feel the tears trying to spring up again.

"It's a title, not a character reference," Finn said. "Be that as it may, he was found murdered in his bed in the wee hours. One of the hotel's other guests reported hearing a disturbance in his suite. A young woman clad in red was seen both entering and leaving the hotel. She entered in his company and departed a short while later on her own, disheveled and visibly distressed. The woman in question was described as some eighteen years of age, reddish brown hair, pale skin, unusually pretty."

Coventry bit her lip to still its quivering and stared into Finn's midnight-blue eyes, searching for hope, for some escape from this nightmare.

"Upon speaking with the late Mr. Horrocks's driver, I discovered the neighborhood in which the mysterious woman had been taken up," Finn went on. "This approximately matched the area of Whitechapel in which a cabbie deposited a woman, identical in appearance, later that night. I made discreet inquiries, dropping a few coins in public houses, and learned the lass's name and occupation. She calls herself Coventry Adams and passes as a lady of, shall we say, negotiable affection."

"I'm no bloody tart," Coventry spat. "Not anymore."

"Nay, that's true enough," Finn said. "My understanding is, you make your living posing as a wagtail, but you're really more of a pickpocket, a roller, and a hornswoggler, aye?"

"You're bloody well-informed," she said. "I've no idea what you're talking to me for. Sounds like you've got it all figured, you damned clever-boots."

Finn leaned forward. "I want to know why, Coventry Adams," he said softly. "Why'd you kill him? It looks bad for you, I'll grant, but you're young and just a wee lass. He was a great fat jollocks of a lad who could scarce fit through a doorway. Did he hurt you? Did he misinterpret something you said and try to take advantage? Did he ravish you? What happened?"

"If I was a Papist, I'd confess to my priest," she said. "But you're no clergyman and I'm no bloody Catholic."

"I'm a member of the Catholic Church," Finn said placidly, rattling her portmanteau. "If I open this, might I be finding a red satin dress inside it?"

She said nothing.

"What about a knife?" he pressed. "I'm not surprised a lass would want one for protection. Do you carry a knife, Coventry?"

"I didn't mean to kill him," she blurted out. Something seemed to break within her. She began to weep, despising herself for weakness but unable to stop. Remorse was filling her to overflowing.

Finn nodded understandingly and made a note on his pad. "I'm certain you didn't," he said.

"I just needed him to lie quiet," she said, and now the tears were definitely flowing. "I couldn't have him pawing at me. I just needed a few minutes and to get out."

"It was robbery, then," Finn said. "You were after his money, aye?"

She nodded. "But he wasn't supposed to die. I'd never... never k-k-kill a man. Not... not on..." She tried to bury her head in her hands, but they were still cuffed behind her. She bowed her head and started to sob.

"Here now, lass, no need for that," Finn said. He produced a pocket handkerchief, plain but clean, and gently dabbed at her eyes. "Lads can be beastly to women, Lord knows I've seen it often enough. I've only been a detective these few months, but I walked my beat before that, and I know what men can do. It'll be all right. Now, I'm just needing the knife. Did you keep it?"

"Knife?" Coventry repeated dully.

"Aye, the knife," he said. "The one you stabbed him with."

"I never did," she said, confused. "What are you talking about?"

It was Finn's turn to look confused. "You told me you didn't mean to kill him," he said. "You were there. He stripped off his clothes, and likely tried to disrobe you as well. He came at you and you stabbed him. Four times." He indicated his chest with his index finger, poking it into himself at three points and finishing by jabbing himself under the chin.

Coventry shook her head, slowly at first, then more emphatically. "That's not what happened," she said.

"So now you're telling me you weren't there?" Finn's eyes grew still darker and more intense. The compassion was fading from them, replaced by the stern gaze of the Law.

"No! I was in the room! But I never stabbed him!"

"Where's your knife, Coventry?"

"I didn't... I don't..." she stammered.

Finn hefted her suitcase onto the table and flipped the catches, opening the lid. He began rifling through her belongings with quick, experienced hands.

Coventry's mind was racing. If Mr. Horrocks had been stabbed, then someone else had been in the room after she had left. Someone else had killed him. She was not the person for whom Finn sought. But like a bloody idiot, she had already confessed to having been there. Now the detective would never believe she she'd not done the deed. Once he'd finished with her baggage, he'd search her person. The moment he found the knife up her sleeve, it would be all over for her. She'd have a short future terminating at the gallows.

But the knowledge of her innocence had kindled new determination in Coventry. She sagged back in her chair, tilting her head to point her face toward the ceiling. In the process, she lowered the back of her skull toward her cuffed hands. By flexing her elbows, she was just able to reach her braid where it twined around her head. With her fingertips, she extracted one of her hairpins, then another.

"You made a tidy job of it," Finn observed, smoothing out her red dress and examining it. "I'm not seeing any bloodstains on the satin, though I warrant they'd be hard to spot against this color. Done this before, have you?"

"I never!" she snarled indignantly. Best to keep him talking and looking for clues. Behind her back, working by feel, she eased the first pin into the keyhole at her left wrist.

"Ah, no wonder you're feeling it, then," he said. "They say the first one's the hardest. But you needn't fret, lass. If you can give extenuating circumstances, it's possible the court may decide on transportation instead of the gallows, especially given your tender years. How old are you, lass?"

"Seventeen," she lied, fingers still working furiously. She had the second pin in place now and was trying to turn the tumblers. Handcuffs had simple locks, no real challenge, but when she had to work practically one-handed, behind her own back, all while doing her best not to jangle the chains, it was taking all her skill as a picklock.

He nodded sympathetically. "I'm a mite young for a detective myself," he confided. "Just twenty-five. But we do the work we've a knack for, aye? I think it's likely you'll be for Australia. You can make a new start there, find a good lad in need of a wife. It'll be a clean start of a sort. Now what else have we here?"

He took out the food and laid it on the table. He opened her cosmetic case and looked over the powders and paints. Coventry felt a slight shift in the cuffs. She feigned another sob to cover the click of the lock as it fell open. Her right wrist was still encased in its manacle, but her left hand was now free.

"I didn't kill Mr. Horrocks," she said, meeting Finn's eye. "I'm a thief, I'm a fallen woman, a bloody painted Jezebel, but I'm no damned murderer. Do you believe me?"

"It doesn't much matter what I believe," he said. "You'll have your chance to tell your story at trial. I'm not finding a weapon here, Coventry. I should've searched you first, and done a thorough job of it. I hope you'll forgive me taking liberties with your person. Have you a knife on you, by chance?"

He started to stand up, reaching toward her. It was now or never. Coventry sprang to her feet, grabbed the edge of the table, and tilted it. The table fell with a crash between the two of them, spilling all her worldly possessions across the floor of Slinky's gambling hall. Then she ran, but not for the exit. He'd be expecting that. She made for her old room, running the opposite direction.

Finn was surprisingly quick and nimble. He recovered from his surprise, dodged around the table, and came on fast. She had only the smallest of leads, but it sufficed to get her through the door three strides ahead of him. She slammed it in his face. He skidded past the door, his momentum carrying him too far, but she knew he'd be back in half a moment.

Coventry lunged for her mattress and came up with the key. She and Finn hit the door simultaneously. His greater bulk forced her back a pace and his hand came around the door. She saw his fingers right in front of her face.

With her left hand, she thrust the key into the lock. At the same moment, she swung her right arm against the door. The loose iron manacle, still shackled to her wrist, struck Finn square on the knuckles.

He let go of the door with an oath. Coventry rammed her shoulder against it and the door closed. She twisted the key, engaging the lock. Then she set her back against the wood planks and drew a few quick breaths.

"You've nowhere to run, Coventry," Finn said grimly. "You're only making this worse on yourself."

"I didn't kill him!" she snapped. "If you won't believe me, I'll find someone who bloody well does!"

"You'll have your day in court," he promised. "But the harder you fight, the worse things will go. My patience is wearing a bit thin, lass."

A heavy impact jarred against the door as he kicked it. The wood was flimsy and would not hold for long. Already one of the boards was cracking. The lock was cheap and might give way at any moment.

Coventry reached down and picked up the water-jug. She judged the distance and hurled it, end over end. The heavy pewter vessel went through the window with a splintering crash. Coventry followed it. A shard of broken glass scored her arm as she went through, another tore at her dress on the other side. It was a squeeze to get through the tiny garret window, but she was slender and she managed it.

As she braced herself on the slope of the roof and pulled her legs the rest of the way through, Finn delivered another mighty kick to the door and it gave way. She caught a glimpse of him rushing across the room, but she was already out and the window was too small for him. His shoulders were too broad.

They stared at one another for a moment, the girl just out of the detective's reach. The look in Finn's eyes now was reluctant admiration. He was actually smiling slightly.

"I didn't kill him," Coventry said for what felt like the tenth time.

"Then who did?" Finn asked.

"Damned if I know. I ought to ask you. You're the bloody detective."

"I'll chase you if you run," he said. "And I'll catch you."

She winked at him. "Promises, guv," she said, offering a saucy smile of her own. Then she turned away and started picking her way along the rooftop, holding her skirt free of her feet with one hand and bracing herself with the other.

Finn watched her a moment longer, shaking his head and chuckling softly. Then he left the window and ran out of the room.

*   *   *

Coventry knew she hadn't much time. Finn might not be able to reach her just then, but he knew exactly where she was. It was fortunate he apparently was not carrying a firearm. Most coppers were not issued guns, but enough of them carried the big Beaumont-Adams revolvers for her to be wary of them. Perhaps he did have one and simply had no wish to shoot down a fleeing woman. He did strike her as a chivalrous sort, particularly for a copper.

Her choices were to remain on the rooftops or to get down to street level. Both paths had advantages. As long as she stayed elevated, Finn would have to climb up to her. But true safety, such as it was, required her to descend sooner or later. He could summon more policemen and surround the row of houses. Then she'd be proper buggered. On the street, she might manage to lose herself in the crowds. But Finn was down there, along with God only knew how many more coppers. He might not have come alone.

She made her decision and started along the rooftops, making for the end of the row. The shingles were rotten and slippery and the going treacherous. She set one shoe on a particularly weak shingle and her foot plunged straight through. A startled cry came from the attic below.

"Sorry," Coventry said, jerking at her foot. It was a surprisingly difficult struggle to draw it back into the light. Her departure was hastened by a flood of invective from the inhabitant of the upper floor, who strongly objected to the ventilation of his roof. He'd be cursing her the next time it rained.

She climbed from one roof to the next, clutching the edge of a gable for support. As she went, she looked for a good way down. The distance was too great to chance a jump; if she so much as turned an ankle, her goose was truly cooked. But thus far, the only drainpipes she saw looked rusty and decidedly frail. She considered the edge of the roof. Just maybe, if she hung by her fingertips to shorten the distance, and aimed for a rubbish heap, she might make it without serious injury. Or she could chance breaking in through a gable window and making a run for it through whatever home lay below.

A familiar *meow* brought her up short.

"Whisper?" she said in surprise. There was the cat, perched nimbly on the next gable, staring with his eyes like green lamps.

How had the cat gotten up there? She marveled that she'd never considered it before. After all, in order to use her window, he must have a regular means of getting to the roof. But was it a path she could take?

"Go on, Whisper," she said, making a shooing motion with her hand.

He blinked lazily. Then, as if he had all the time in the world, the cat stretched luxuriously and trotted along the peak of the roof. Coventry watched him as he suddenly angled to his right, hopped easily to the top of another gable, and leapt out into space.

He landed nimbly atop a clothesline that slanted at a downward angle across the alley. With the aplomb of a circus tightrope-walker, he pranced across and dropped to a little metal railing that ringed the window across the way. From there, he sprang down to the angled roof of a rickety shack someone had propped against the far wall. He slid down the roof and made three more quick hops down a pile of rubble to the alley.

"Nothing to it," Coventry muttered. "I just need to walk a blooming tightrope myself."

She wondered whether she was strong enough to go hand-over-hand across the alley and decided she was not. She was quick and agile, but not well-muscled in the arms. Most likely she'd make it halfway, then dangle helplessly until her fingers gave out and she fell, breaking her legs or her neck. She stood there, trying to think what to do. Precious seconds slipped away.

"Coventry Adams!"

"Oh bloody hell," she said under her breath. There was Finn, coming out onto the roof not more than twenty paces behind her. He'd opened a gable window from the inside and was crawling onto the rooftop. He was a quick one, no doubt of it. She backed toward the edge of the roof, keeping her eyes on him.

"You don't want to do that, lass," he said, breathing hard from his sprint and climb. "Just give me your hand and come in with me. We'll call it a day, aye?"

He extended a hand to her. It looked welcoming, but she knew what lay behind that hand: the courts, Newgate Prison, then the gallows at Tyburn or a transportation ship to Australia. She'd heard being transported was little better than being hanged, particularly for a young woman, no matter what Finn said.

"You're bloody persistent, Finn Farrell," she said.

He smiled slightly. "You don't know the half of it," he replied. "I'll not stop till I've got my hands on you."

"You know how many blokes have said the same?" she retorted, risking a quick look over her shoulder. Her heels were just at the very lip of the chasm. "I do seem to have that effect on most lads."

Finn advanced cautiously. He might be a dedicated copper, but he clearly had no wish to drag the both of them over the brink. "Help me and help yourself," he urged.

"One or t'other," she shot back. "Not both. You want me, Finn, you'll have to try a sight harder than that. Best prove your devotion, mate."

He had covered half the distance between them by now. He was still moving slowly, making sure of his footing. There was no rush; she clearly had nowhere to go.

Coventry suddenly crouched low, stooping over the clothesline where it was anchored to the wall. She tossed the empty bracelet of the handcuff over the line and grasped it with her free hand. Then she sucked in a quick breath and pushed off with both feet as hard as she could.

"Don't!" Finn shouted, but it was too late. Coventry felt a terrible jerk on her right wrist, the metal ring digging painfully into the base of her hand. She hung onto the other end of the cuffs for dear life. The chain whistled as she slid toward the opposite wall with increasing speed. She scarcely had time to swing her feet up and cushion herself. Her feet met the bricks with a jarring shock that traveled all the way up to her jaw. Her teeth clicked together hard, nearly snipping off the tip of her tongue.

Pressing herself flat against the wall, she felt down with her feet and found the railing beneath her. She let go of the chain and pulled herself free of the clothesline. As she did so, she looked back and saw Finn jump for the line. He caught it and began to cross after her, hand over hand.

Coventry flexed her wrist. Her concealed knife dropped into her hand. She held it up and nodded to Finn, thinking it only fair to give him a hint of warning. He started to say something, a protest or denial, but she cut off both words and clothesline with the same quick sweep of her hand. The line parted. Finn swung back the way he had come, slamming into the wall on the other side of the alley. A great many men would have lost their grip in such circumstances and taken a nasty tumble, but he managed to hold on. He dangled there helplessly, better than fifteen feet of air between him and a hard landing.

"Sorry about that, guv," she said, tucking the blade back into its hiding place. Then she took another deep breath and jumped for the roof of the shack, praying it would hold her weight.

Fortunately, it was sturdier than it looked. She nearly lost her footing, but caught herself with one hand and stayed more or less upright. The roof held. She skidded down it just as her cat had done, dropped over the edge, caught the lip with both hands, then let go and fell the last few feet to the ground.

There was Whisper, nonchalantly bathing himself and looking decidedly smug. Coventry shook her head at him. Then she left the alley, walking quickly, not running. A running woman attracted attention. Just before she melted into the crowded street, she took one last look over her shoulder. Finn was climbing doggedly back onto the roof, holding the clothesline and walking up the side of the building.

"Bloody persistent," she repeated.

Get a reminder when the new series is out

Join Steven's list at
clickworkspress.com/join/steven

Ready for more?

Join the Clickworks Press email list
for the latest on new releases, upcoming books and
series, behind-the-scenes details, events, and more.

Be the first to know about
new releases from Steven Henry
by signing up at
clickworkspress.com/join/steven

About the Author

Steven Henry learned how to read almost before he learned how to walk. Ever since he began reading stories, he wanted to put his own on the page. He lives a very quiet and ordinary life in Minnesota with his wife and dog.

Also by Steven Henry

Fathers

A Modern Christmas Story

When you strip away everything else, what's left is the truth

Life taught Joe Davidson not to believe in miracles. A blue-collar wood-worker, Joe is trying to build a future. His father drank himself to death and his mother succumbed to cancer, leaving a broken, struggling family. He and his brother and sisters are faced with failed marriages, growing pains, and lingering trauma.

Then a chance meeting at his local diner brings Mary Elizabeth Reynolds 

into his life. Suddenly, Joe finds himself reaching for something more, a dream of happiness. The wood-worker and the poor girl from a trailer park connect and fall in love, and for a little while, everything is right with their world.

But suddenly Joe is confronted with a situation he never imagined. What do you do if your fiancée is expecting a child you know isn't yours? Torn between betrayal and love, trying to do the right thing when nothing seems right anymore, Joe has to strip life down to its truth and learn that, in spite of the pain, love can be the greatest miracle of all.

Learn more at clickworkspress.com/fathers.

Ember of Dreams

The Clarion Chronicles, Book One

When magic awakens a long-forgotten folk, a noble lady, a young apprentice, and a solitary blacksmith band together to prevent war and seek understanding between humans and elves.

Lady Kristyn Tremayne – An otherwise unremarkable young lady's open heart and inquisitive mind reveal a hidden world of magic.

Robert Blackford – A humble harp maker's apprentice dreams of being a hero.

Master Gabriel Zane – A master blacksmith's pursuit of perfection leads him to craft an enchanted sword, drawing him out of his isolation and far from his cozy home.

Lord Luthor Carnarvon – A lonely nobleman with a dark past has won the heart of Kristyn's mother, but at what cost?

Readers love *Ember of Dreams*

"The more I got to know the characters, the more I liked them. The female lead in particular is a treat to accompany on her journey from ordinary to extraordinary."

"The author's deep understanding of his protagonists' motivations and keen eye for psychological detail make Robert and his companions a likable and memorable cast."

Learn more at tinyurl.com/emberofdreams.

More great titles from Clickworks Press

www.clickworkspress.com

The Altered Wake

Megan Morgan

Amid growing unrest, a family secret and an ancient laboratory unleash long-hidden superhuman abilities. Now newly-promoted Sentinel Cameron Kardell must chase down a rogue superhuman who holds the key to the powers' origin: the greatest threat Cotarion has seen in centuries – and Cam's best friend.

"Incredible. Starts out gripping and keeps getting better."

Learn more at clickworkspress.com/sentinel1.

Hubris Towers: The Complete First Season

Ben Y. Faroe & Bill Hoard

Comedy of manners meets comedy of errors in a new series for fans of Fawlty Towers and P. G. Wodehouse.

"So funny and endearing"

"Had me laughing so hard that I had to put it down to catch my breath"

"Astoundingly, outrageously funny!"

Learn more at clickworkspress.com/hts01.

Death's Dream Kingdom
Gabriel Blanchard

A young woman of Victorian London has been transformed into a vampire. Can she survive the world of the immortal dead—or perhaps, escape it?

"The wit and humor are as Victorian as the setting... a winsomely vulnerable and tremendously crafted work of art."

"A dramatic, engaging novel which explores themes of death, love, damnation, and redemption."

Learn more at clickworkspress.com/ddk.

Share the love!

Join our microlending team at
kiva.org/team/clickworkspress.

Keep in touch!

Join the Clickworks Press email list
and get freebies, production updates, special deals,
behind-the-scenes sneak peeks, and more.

Sign up today at clickworkspress.com/join.

www.ingramcontent.com/pod-product-compliance
Lightning Source LLC
Chambersburg PA
CBHW020323010826